STRONG
AS
DEATH

By Sharan Newman from Bella Rosa Books

Catherine LeVendeur Mysteries

STRONG AS DEATH
CURSED IN THE BLOOD
TO WEAR THE WHITE CLOAK
THE DIFFICULT SAINT

STRONG
AS
DEATH

A CATHERINE LeVENDEUR MYSTERY

SHARAN NEWMAN

BellaRosaBooks

STRONG AS DEATH
ISBN 978-1-933523-27-9
2008 Reprint Edition by Bella Rosa Books

Previously Published in the U.S.A. by Tom Doherty Associates, LLC.
First hardback edition: August 1996, ISBN 0-312-86179-6,
First mass market edition: September 1997, ISBN 0-812-53935-4.

Printed in the United States of America on acid-free paper.

Cover illustration by Joyce Wright – www.artbyjoyce.com

BellaRosaBooks and logo are trademarks of Bella Rosa Books

10   9   8   7   6   5   4   3   2   1

For Pauline Cramer, friend, navigator
and fellow pilgrim. With thanks and love.

Acknowledgments

It has been a constant source of delight and amazement to me how many fine scholars are willing to take time from their own work to help me with mine. Those listed here have been of invaluable assistance. I thank them from the bottom of my heart. I also want to assure the reader that any historical inaccuracies are solely due to my own muddled understanding of the data and not in any way the fault of my advisers.

Professor C. Julian Bishko, who sent me references and advice on the probable route of Peter the Venerable, even though it meant having Peter leave the story for a while.

Professor Fredric L. Cheyette, Amherst College, for sending me a draft of his work on the twelfth-century south of France and for being willing to do research in archives all over that inhospitable region.

Dr. Judith Cohen, Toronto, for sharing her knowledge of Spain and the jongloressas and for making their music live in her recordings. Maruxa's voice is hers.

Jeff Davies, who sent me guides to the pilgrim trail and is mad enough to want to do the Compostela route by bicycle.

Dr. E. Roseanne Elder, Cistercian Press, Kalamazoo, Michigan. For graciously permitting me to quote from translations of twelfth-century authors published by the press. The work of Cistercian Press has made it possible for non-Latin readers to learn about medieval scholars from their own writings. As a slow reader of Latin, I appreciate it very much.

Professor Lynn Nelson, University of Kansas, for information on the French in Spain, good advice on where to drape a body in church and for not being too proud to hang out with writers.

Professor Jeffrey B. Russell, University of California at Santa Barbara, for moral support, Latin translations and corrections, editorial comments and champagne.

Professor Richard Unger, University of British Columbia, for boats, beer and sympathy at also having to write a book in summer.

Fr. Chrysogonus Waddell, Gethsemani Abbey, for boundless enthusiasm, liturgical corrections and informing me that Peter the Venerable always rode a white mule.

One

Vézelay, the shrine of Saint Marie Madeleine, March 12, 1142; The Feast of Saint Gregory the Great, pope.

In hiis autem que dicturus sum nichil auctore Deo scribam, nisi quod visu et auditu verum esse cognovero, vel quod probabilium virorum scriptis fuerit et auctoritate subnixum.

In this which I intend to tell, with the aid of God, I will write nothing except that which I have seen and heard and know to be the truth, or that which was written by men of good character and supported by authority.

—John of Salisbury
Historia Pontificalis
Book I, Prologue

*T*hroughout the bone-chilling night, the four men knelt motionless before the altar of Mary Magdalene. The lamplight reflected off three bald heads and glistened on that of Gaucher of Mâcon, whose hair had gone from blond to white at the siege of Antioch, it was said, but was still thick and full, with a streak of gold down the left side. They all wore pilgrim-grey mantles, but underneath, at least one of them still wore the mail shirt he had lived in for forty years. All of them had daggers hidden and even in this holy place, not one of them could have surrendered his weapon and felt secure.

Dawn was drifting down from the high clerestory windows to the nave far below before they finally rose. All of them were stiff from the vigil, and Norbert of Bussières, the eldest of the four, had to be helped to his feet by the others.

The church was beginning to fill with pilgrims as they left. Norbert walked slowly in the rear, cursing his aging knees. At the entrance, he tripped on an uneven stone, fell forward and was caught by a young woman on her way in.

In the grey light, the blue of her eyes startled him almost as much as the fall. Not really pretty, he thought—too dark, her chin and nose too definite. He had always liked his women small and pale, with yielding features. Whoever had charge of this one would need a firm hand, he guessed. All the same, there was something about her that made him wish he were thirty instead of seventy and that they were not in the doorway of a church.

"Are you hurt, my lord?" she asked, all daughterly concern.

He pulled away from her supporting arm. "No, of course

not," he said huffily. "The parvis of this church is very badly
maintained. Some poor, infirm pilgrim could be seriously hurt.
I shall speak to the abbot about it the next time I see him."

She released him at once and backed away in embarrass-
ment, bumping into the man who had come up behind her.

Norbert assumed that the man was with her from the way
he caught the stumbling woman, as if used to doing it. The old
knight grunted the minimal greeting required as he limped
away from them. The woman's companion was as odd-looking
as she, he thought—tall and thin with hair almost as white as
Gaucher's even though the man was obviously still in his twen-
ties. The old knight shivered, pulled his cloak closer and tried
to move quickly enough to catch up with his friends. In another
moment, he had forgotten the couple entirely.

Catherine stood at the church door for a moment, watching
him go. "A very proud old man," she commented to her husband, Edgar. "Look at how straight his back is."

"And how bowed his legs," Edgar answered. "He must
have spent his life on horseback."

"I wonder if he fought in the Holy Land," Catherine said.

Edgar shrugged. Most of the knights of that age claimed to
have followed Godfrey of Boullion and his brothers to
Jerusalem. Now, almost fifty years later, how many were left
to prove them wrong?

Edgar had other things to think about.

"We should be returning to Paris soon, *leoffaest*," he said
as they entered the church. "We've prayed here every day for
a week. Our candles have all burnt down to stubs. Saint Marie
must have heard us by now. We can only wait to see if she is
able to intercede for us in heaven."

Catherine knew he was right. Edgar had been more than patient with her determination to come to Vézelay to ask the help
of Saint Mary Magdalene with their problem. But she had felt
no sense of fulfillment during their visit, no sudden descent of
grace.

Perhaps after all, Mary wasn't the right one to ask this special favor of. The Magdalene had renounced carnal activities

and come to France to be a hermit after the Resurrection of Our Lord. Catherine and Edgar had renounced their plans for the cloister and the priesthood for a life of carnal activity. Not something this saint could be expected to approve of.

Catherine could feel the color rising to her face. What a thing to be thinking of at a holy place! She sighed. No wonder their prayers and offerings had been ignored.

"One more day, Edgar," she begged. "Just one. It's such a little miracle we ask for."

Edgar looked down at her and smiled sadly. He had given up his patrimony in Scotland, his family's plans to make him a bishop, and settled in France to live out of his country and his station—all for this woman. He had done it gladly. Perhaps being allowed Catherine was all that heaven planned to bestow on him. Even a little miracle might be too much more to expect.

Norbert of Bussières reached the inn at the bottom of the hill not long after his companions. They hadn't waited for him, knowing how he hated them condescending to his age. He grunted as he pushed the door open. They weren't all that much younger than he, but recently his years seemed to weigh more heavily. He could feel the icy breath of eternity on the back of his neck tonight, even through the fur lining of his hood.

There wasn't much time left. They must go back to Spain this spring or never. Norbert had convinced the other three of that. But he hadn't yet told all of them his real reason for making the trip.

Rufus of Arcy looked up from his bowl as Norbert entered. He shook his head slightly, then returned to his beer. The old man would never survive the journey, Rufus worried. If Norbert fell ill on the way, one of them would have to stay to care for him, then take his possessions back to his grandchildren. It would be better for them all if Norbert stayed behind.

But Norbert would never trust them to take care of this endeavor on their own. He had known all of them far too long for that.

Rufus was only sixty-one himself, and still felt capable of

hunting all day and occupying himself with a serving maid half the night. Once it would have been all night, but some concessions had to be made to time. He moved over on the bench to allow Norbert to sit.

The fourth man, Hugh of Grignon, poured a bowl of beer for Norbert and another for himself.

"So," Hugh said. "We are resolved to begin our journey at last. We shall place our faith in the Lord and trust to the saints to protect us in our final great adventure."

The other three stared at him in disdain. Hugh's wife had been fond of wandering storytellers—too fond, some said. Over the years, Hugh had picked up their way of saying the obvious as if it were a new directive from Rome.

"I don't know about you, Hugh," said Gaucher, "but I have never trusted anyone but the saints. And even some of them can be duplicitous."

"At this point in life," Rufus added, "even a trip to the outhouse in winter could be my final adventure."

Norbert simply glared.

Hugh ignored them. They had known each other all their lives. So well that sometimes he thought they only bothered to speak to each other to prove they were still breathing. He signaled the boy to bring more bread. It *would* be a great adventure, he told himself, and more than likely, the last for at least one of them.

Catherine stood outside the church, looking out over the fields far below to the dark forest beyond. Clusters of huts huddled together, the tilled land stretching behind, the vines in their tidy rows just beginning to bud. As she watched, she could make out a few pigs snuffling in the brush where the cleared area met the trees. A woman was going out to milk her goat, tethered in a field along with the others of the village. She swung the bucket at her side with a rhythm that made Catherine think she might be singing. Behind her followed a child of three or four. He stopped now and then to examine something that caught his eye, then ran to pull at his mother's skirts. She lifted him to her hip with one arm and kissed him as she walked.

Catherine turned away, her eyes suddenly blurred.

Had she sinned so terribly? Master Abelard and Mother Héloïse said not. Neither she nor Edgar had taken final vows; there had been no canonical impediment to their marriage. There are many roads to heaven. Everyone told them that.

But then why were they given the promise of a child, only to have it taken away? First a stillbirth, then two miscarriages even before the babies quickened. It preyed on her mind. People reminded her that the queen of France, Eleanor, had been married longer than she and not conceived at all. That was little comfort to Catherine. The hope and then the disappointment, not to mention the pain and fear of her own death in childbed, were more than she could bear. Added to the rest was the guilt she felt for having taken Edgar away from his land, his family, his place in life, only for a wife who could give him no living children.

Someone touched her arm. Catherine jumped and nearly went over the edge of the low stone wall.

"Were you pondering the words of Saint Augustine?" the young man laughed. "Didn't you hear me calling you?"

"Astrolabe!" Catherine hugged him in surprise. She had known the son of Abelard and Héloïse since her days in the convent, but hadn't seen him for nearly two years. "I'm sorry. My thoughts were all too secular. I'm glad to be rescued from them. What are you doing in Vézelay?"

"Carrying messages, as usual," Astrolabe explained. "The abbot of Cluny sends greetings to his brother, the abbot of Vézelay, and I am the one chosen to deliver them."

"But I thought you had gone back to Brittany," Catherine said.

Astrolabe nodded, his expression more serious. "The venerable Abbot Peter sent me a message as well, suggesting that I return as soon as possible," he said. "I arrived at Cluny last month."

"Is it your father?" Catherine knew the answer already. Peter Abelard had not been well the last time she had seen him, just after the condemnation of his work at Sens. "Is he . . ."

"Father has been moved to the priory of Saint-Marcellus

at Chalon," Astrolabe answered. "After coming to Cluny and then reconciling with Bernard of Clairvaux, his health seemed to improve, but in the last month he has suddenly become much weaker. Abbot Peter felt that Cluny was too stressful for him. The priory is quiet, and the monks there care for him well."

He took a deep breath, fighting to control his voice. "My father has made his peace with God and Abbot Bernard," he said at last. "Perhaps that was a mistake. He was never one to tolerate peace for long."

Catherine nodded. She took his arm and they started walking down the hill to the guest house where she and Edgar were staying.

"It will be very difficult for your mother," she said.

That was a feeble statement for what Catherine feared Abelard's death would do to Abbess Héloïse. It was only since she had met Edgar that Catherine had begun to understand the passion that Héloïse had felt for her former lover and husband. Twenty years in the convent had not, could not, diminish it.

"It will be," Astrolabe answered. "But her daughters in Christ and her faith will help her."

"And you?" Catherine asked. "What will you do after he is gone?"

"I don't know," he said. "Perhaps I'll become a priest and spend my life saying Masses for his soul. Mother would like that."

There was a trace of bitterness in his voice that Catherine chose to ignore. "Will you dine with us tonight?" she asked.

"Yes," he smiled. "You can tell me all the news from Paris. Is Edgar's friend, John, still studying? When does he intend to stop learning and start teaching?"

"I believe he prefers the role of gadfly," Catherine laughed. "He has said something about trying to get a position that will take him back to England so he can visit his family."

They continued chatting of old friends and recent events. Peter Abelard was not mentioned again, but Catherine felt an emptiness opening inside her at the thought of the world without the opinionated, arrogant, quarrelsome master, who had taught her logic with the patience of a father during her time at the convent he had founded.

After dinner, Catherine decided to return to the church.

"Just one more candle, Edgar," she promised. "One more prayer. Tomorrow we'll go home. You don't need to come with me. I'll walk up with the people from Orléans. Come fetch me when the bells ring for Compline."

She had scarcely left when Edgar turned to Astrolabe. "I'm afraid for her," he said.

Astrolabe nodded. He had seen the change in Catherine himself. She had always been thin, but now she was gaunt, her cheekbones pushing sharply against her skin. She moved too quickly, with random gestures. Astrolabe remembered that Catherine's mother had driven herself mad with worry over sin and punishment. She was in a convent now, not far from the priory where his own father lived, totally unaware of anything but her own misery.

He looked at Edgar. "What about you?" he asked. "Are you regretting having returned to France to marry Catherine?"

Edgar slumped forward on his bench. His pale hair hung limply on his shoulders. His hands were scarred from various attempts at manual labor over the last two years. His clothes were in the somber tones of a penitent, made of thick wool but without design, and grimy from days of travel.

"I don't believe our marriage was a sin," he told Astrolabe. "Nor even a mistake, as some have suggested. I thought Catherine had recovered fairly well after we lost the first child. But when no others came . . . Her brother's wife, Marie, says it's starting them and losing them that's hardest. I know it happened to Marie, before their son was born. Perhaps she behaved like this, too."

He emptied his cup and stared at the dregs. "I don't know what to do to help her," he said. "We can't spend our days wandering from shrine to shrine in the hope of a miracle."

"There are people who do," Astrolabe observed.

Edgar banged the cup on the table. A sleepy serving boy jumped up and refilled it. Edgar drained it in one gulp.

"If I were dying, I might seek the aid of relics," he admitted, "but I don't think so. It seems a waste of the life we've been given to pass it constantly begging for something else. In any case, how can one ever be sure which saint will intercede for him, which relic is genuine?"

Astrolabe, used to conversations with his father, knew the question was rhetorical.

Edgar went on. "Perhaps the fault is mine. My faith isn't strong enough. I would go to the antipodes if I truly believed it would help Catherine."

"And you?" Astrolabe asked. "Don't tell me this hasn't worried you."

Edgar was silent for a long moment. Then he sighed. "I grieve as well," he said. "The first child was a girl, you know, perfectly formed. I never knew they could be that small and still have each finger and toe in place. Burying her was the hardest thing I ever did. How many times can we go through that? And don't tell me that everyone does. I know that. It brings me no comfort. Obviously, the only answer is to be celibate."

"I don't believe that would be an attainable goal for you at the moment," Astrolabe observed.

Edgar smiled ruefully. "*Mea culpa*," he said.

The bells began for Compline and the two men went up to the church to get Catherine. There, Astrolabe bid them good night.

"If you can, come see Father," he told them. "His old students don't seem comfortable visiting him now and he says he doesn't mind, but I think he would like to see you."

On the walk back, Catherine was unusually quiet.

Edgar took her hand. She mustn't continue brooding in this way. "Home," he said. "Tomorrow."

"Yes," Catherine agreed. "We've been gone too long. But first we must go to Saint-Marcellus and say good-bye to our master."

"Yes," Edgar said, "we must."

In spite of his sadness at the reason for the journey, Edgar felt a flicker of hope. This was the first time in weeks that Catherine had taken notice of anything outside her own despair.

They were both so wrapped up in each other that neither one noticed the figure in the black cloak moving silently in the shadows behind them. It followed almost to the door of the guest house, then slipped away noiselessly.

Gaucher of Mâcon got up from the table and said good night to his companions. They didn't notice. Norbert was either dead or meditating. The others had drifted into blurred renditions of tavern songs and parodies of hymns. Rufus was stuck on the *bibits*, muttering *"bibit ille, bibit illa"* over and over in a hoarse croak. He had sunk cross-legged to the floor, resembling nothing so much as an ancient toad pontificating on its lily pad. Gaucher patted his smooth head fondly before heading up to the sleeping loft.

Gaucher and Rufus were exactly the same age, but Gaucher had always felt that keeping his hair made him the younger. His teeth were mostly accounted for as well. Therefore, he not only thought Hugh was being pompous in his declamations about this being their last great adventure, but also premature. Gaucher had a number of plans for the future of which this pilgrimage was only the beginning. And a profitable beginning as well, he believed.

He was humming along with the drone below when he entered the chamber. There were already a few men rolled up on the straw pallets on one side of the room. Gaucher fumbled in the darkness for his blanket and pack, left with the others in the corner. He put his hand into the bag, rummaging for his second-best tunic. Instead, he touched something cold and sticky. He recoiled, dropping the bag.

Resisting the impulse to shake whatever it was out the nearest window, Gaucher carefully picked up his bag and carried it downstairs. He set it next to the fire and slowly pulled on the string to open it.

"Whassa matter, Gaucher?" Rufus peered up from the floor. "Someone steal your jewels?"

Gaucher paid him no mind. Hugh and Norbert stared over their bowls at him with a stupefied lack of interest. Slowly Gaucher inverted the bag. Two bloody gobbets squelched onto the hearth.

Rufus leaned back, wrinkling his nose at the smell. Hugh peered at the lumps in confusion, then suddenly realized what they were. Automatically, he checked between his legs and sighed in relief. At his age, he feared he might not notice they were gone.

"Looks like Gaucher's the one with the jewels," Rufus laughed. "Not yours, I presume? A gift from a friend?"

Gaucher wasn't laughing. With his boot, he scraped the things into the coals, where they sizzled horrifyingly.

"The same fate awaits us all," Hugh intoned, "if we do not repent our sins on this earth."

Norbert blinked and came to life. "What are you talking about?" he asked sharply. "What have you put in the fire, Gaucher, that makes such a stink?"

Gaucher turned on all of them. "Which one of you did it?" he roared. "This is no joke!"

Hugh covered his ears with his hands. "None of us did it," he told Gaucher. "We haven't been apart all the last night and day. You know that."

Gaucher did know, but he was too angry to wait to find someone else to blame. He took the rest of his things from the bag and held up the tunic. "Look at this!" he shouted. "It's ruined!

"Will someone tell me what you're talking about?" Norbert repeated. He sniffed. "Is someone cooking bacon?"

Rufus started laughing, then put his hand over his mouth. He crawled toward the doorway, but got only halfway there before he vomited. In the corner, the serving boy groaned, knowing who would have to mop up after him.

Hugh leaned over to his friend and said in what he thought was a whisper, "Pig's testicles, Norbert. Someone's left a pair with Gaucher. Can't imagine why. He always insists his own still function just fine."

Gaucher saw that he would get no sense or sympathy from

his friends. In a fury, he threw the bloody tunic on the fire as well, then stomped out into the night.

The serving boy waited for a few minutes, then retrieved the tunic, barely scorched. Only a madman would waste good wool.

In their curtained corner of the room above, Catherine and Edgar heard nothing.

The swelling moon shone down on the town and into the tiny window over Catherine's head. She twitched in her sleep and cried out once. Edgar pulled her closer without waking.

Eventually all four of the knights slept, Rufus stretched out under the table, still reeking of vomit.

Catherine woke up shaking.

"Edgar . . ." She nudged him partially awake and curled herself against his body, drawing his warmth to her in the early morning chill. "I've had a dream, Edgar. A dream inside a dream, actually."

Edgar opened one eye, rolled to his side to face her and wrapped his free arm around her. He smiled and brushed an errant black curl back behind her ear. At that moment he had no trouble remembering why he had abandoned home and family for marriage in a foreign land.

"I need to tell you about it." Catherine tilted her head so that she could see his eyes. "It was a true dream, I think, but I don't understand it."

She stopped. His hand cupped her cheek, his little finger vibrating against the rapid pulse in her neck. With the ease of habit, he traced her collarbone and the curve of her breast.

"So tell me," he said, still smiling. "What about it has upset you?"

"I can't tell you if you keep moving your hand like that," she scolded. "This is serious."

"I'm seriously listening," he promised, leaving his hand where it was. "What was your dream?"

"Very well." She took a deep breath. "Please, Edgar, pay attention. It was vague at first, then suddenly very clear, as if I were watching from somewhere far above. I was walking on a narrow road, a cliff on one side and a chasm on the other. The wind was cold and cut through my cloak. The only one with me was our son."

She could feel him go abruptly still, his fingers tightening painfully. "How did you know it was ours?" he asked. There was no trace of teasing in his voice now.

Catherine didn't answer, but continued her story. "The road was steep but not difficult at first. Then we went around a bend and came to a place where there was no more road, only a wooden board stretched between two rocks. It was as narrow as the span of my hands and rattled in the wind. We had to cross it. We couldn't go back."

Edgar put his arms around her, holding her so tightly that she could barely breathe. She pressed against him, wishing that they could merge somehow and be truly one flesh, Eve returned to Adam's side. She turned her face so he could hear her.

"On the other side there was an old man, a holy man," she said. "He was watching us, waiting for us to cross. He wouldn't come to us."

"What was his name?" Edgar asked. "Did you recognize him?"

"No," Catherine answered. "But in the dream, I knew him. I put our child on the bridge before me. I was afraid I couldn't keep my balance if I carried him. I stepped onto the bridge, holding the boy's shoulders to guide him. But halfway across, something went wrong. The wind or our weight—something—made the board shake and bend. The end on the other side slipped away from its mooring and we began to fall."

"No!" Edgar was becoming more unsettled by this dream.

Catherine went on. "I screamed and caught hold of a crevice in the cliff with one hand and reached out for our son with the other, but he fell away from me. As I was about to let go and follow him into the chasm, the old man reached out and caught the boy. I saw him gather the child up and put him on his shoulders.

"So I knew our son was safe on the other side, but I was still hanging onto the side of the cliff. My fingers were slipping.

I could see there was a way to edge over and return to the road I had come up, but between me and the other side there were only tiny fingerholds. I reached out for one and almost grasped it. My hand scraped the rock. I can feel the roughness even now. But I couldn't hold on. I screamed over and over as I fell. I thought I would fall forever. Then I woke up."

She shivered.

Edgar kissed the top of her head. "That *is* frightening. But you're safe now," he said shakily. "It was only a bad dream. Nothing more."

"No, Edgar." Catherine pushed away. "That wasn't the end. That was only the inner dream. I woke up *within* the dream; my arms stretched out and you were there. You were with me," she repeated more softly. "You held me and swore that you would always be there. And I believed you. But I knew that our son was still on the other side of the bridge . . . and I knew we would have to go find him."

She exhaled. "And then I did wake up. But, Edgar, it was a true dream. I believe it. There was a message in it."

"But what does it mean?" Edgar asked. "Why couldn't you reach the other side? Are we doomed never to have a living child? We came all the way here to Vézelay to ask the blessed Marie Madeleine to help us. What else can we do? What more could be expected of us? And have you considered that only part of the dream was a sending? Are you sure the boy with you wasn't created from your own desire?"

"I'm not sure of anything, Edgar," she answered, "but I know we've been told to go somewhere, to do something together. And if we don't, the child I saw will never be born."

Two

The Cluniac Priory of Saint Marcellus, Chalon-sur-Saône, Saturday, March 21, 1142; The Feast of Saint Benedict, abbot.

Tali nobiscum vir simplex et rectus, timens deum, et recedens a malo, tali inquam per aliquantum temporis conversatione, ultimos vitae suae dies consecrans deo, pausandi gratia, nam plus solito, scabie et quibusdam corporis incommoditatibus gravabatur, a me Cabilonem missus est.

Thus he lived among us, a simple and upright man, fearing God and shunning evil, and so he remained for some time, dedicating the final days of his life to God, for the sake of contemplation, for he was suffering more than ordinarily from scabies and other distresses of the flesh until I sent him to Chalons.

—Peter, Abbot of Cluny, to
Héloïse, abbess of the Paraclete,
on the death of Peter Abelard

Catherine had imagined that he would be lying on a cot in the infirmary, attended by watchful monks eager to record any last confession from him or vision of the next life. Instead, the doorkeeper told them that Master Abelard was in the scriptorium, working, and would join them shortly.

"Perhaps his health has improved?" she suggested to Astrolabe.

The philosopher's son smiled sadly. "I doubt it. He's been working there ever since he arrived. He stops only to say the Divine Office, they tell me. He will likely die with his cheek against the page of a book."

It seemed appropriate to Catherine, who had once wished no more for her own last moments. "No one has sent for Mother Héloïse?" she asked.

"It hasn't been suggested," Astrolabe said. "I don't know if either one of them could bear it."

Catherine wondered how Astrolabe's mother would bear it in any case. She remembered Héloïse's great, burning eyes that could not hide the passion she still felt for Peter Abelard. Héloïse was now a woman in her forties, the competent and respected director of a monastic house. Her formidable intelligence was totally focused on its survival. She allowed herself no weakness. She professed herself satisfied with her life. But it had been the desperate grief in those eyes that had convinced Catherine to risk losing her place in heaven for a life in the world with Edgar.

Had she been wrong?

Astrolabe and Edgar were talking quietly as they waited.

Without looking at her, Edgar put his arm around her waist, resting his hand on her hip. He continued talking in the same casual tone, apparently oblivious to her presence. Catherine could feel her heart beating rapidly as the warmth of his hand spread through her.

Isn't it about time you admitted, Catherine, that a hundred years in an anchorage wouldn't make you chaste as far as this man is concerned?

Catherine sighed. Her conscience had the loudest, most annoying voice in Christendom. It always amazed her that no one else could hear it.

The doorkeeper returned to tell them that Abelard was waiting for them in the prior's chamber.

The last time Edgar and Catherine had seen their old master was two years before, at Sens, where his work had been roundly condemned by Bernard of Clairvaux and a group of bishops. Abelard had vowed to take his case to Rome, but Bernard had sent messengers to the pope, and the confirmation of the judgment made at Sens had reached Abelard at Cluny, barely a month after the council. Broken in spirit, the philosopher had decided to take the offer of sanctuary from Abbot Peter and, by all accounts, he had become a model monk.

Catherine blinked as they entered the room. Even with the warning, she wasn't prepared. Next to her, she could feel Edgar start as well.

Her former master's skin was roughened by the scabies, but he had had that before. He was frail, but not much more so than when they had last seen him. No, the change was internal. Something had happened to his spirit. In Paris, it was said that the arrogant Peter Abelard had finally been humbled, and many thought it not soon enough. But Catherine did not see a man defeated by the world; rather, one who had transcended it. She knelt for his blessing.

Abelard put his hand on her head. "*Benedicite*," he said. "*Dominus tecum.*"

She looked up and he smiled. Her eyes filled with tears.

Edgar knelt beside her. "Thank you for granting us an audience, Master," he said. "We are honored to see you again."

Abelard paused, his hand over Edgar's head. "Is this the boy who once told me that he could see no sense to my argument and that he didn't believe there was any?"

Edgar bent his head lower. Catherine stared at him in surprise. "I was much younger then, Master," Edgar mumbled. "I ask your pardon for my arrogance."

Behind them, Astrolabe laughed and Abelard joined him.

"I am delighted to see both of you again." He gestured for them to rise. "And you, renegade daughter of the Paraclete, are you still happy to be living with my old student?"

"Sinfully so," Catherine admitted.

"But there is something wrong, isn't there?" Abelard looked at both of them.

"We would like your advice, Master," Edgar said.

"I have always been happy to give it," Abelard told them. "But why don't you let my son take you to the hospice, where you can wash and be fed first? After None, we can speak again."

He swayed a little as he stood and all three of them leaped forward to help him, but he waved them away. "My faith supports me now," he said. "I need nothing more."

"Can you now understand what I was trying to tell you?" Astrolabe asked them after his father had left. "Do you see how he has changed?"

"Yes," Edgar said. "The difference frightens me, but it awes me as well. I almost felt that I could see light shining through him."

"It's as if he's already looking into the next world," Catherine said. "I don't see how he can remain in this one much longer. If anyone can tell us what my dream meant, it will be the Master."

Edgar agreed. He only hoped the interpretation would be one they could accept.

Peter of Montboissier, abbot of Cluny, at the age of fifty already styled "Venerable" by his contemporaries, not for his years but for his authority, was receiving a guest, Bishop Stephen of Osma. The bishop was being given all respect due

to his office, but to Peter he was really no more than an emissary from Alfonso VII, self-proclaimed emperor of Spain.
Bishop Stephen had been entrusted by the emperor with an invitation to the abbot that Peter found most opportune.

"The emperor would be honored if I would consent to
come to Spain?" Peter said. "And there a meeting would be
arranged for us to discuss . . ."

"Mutual welfare," Bishop Stephen replied. "The elimina-
tion of the Arab heresy from our lands. The reconversion of
those poor souls recently recovered from Saracen territories.
And then there would be the opportunity for you to visit the
third most holy pilgrimage site in the world, Santiago de Compostela. Have you never wished to worship at the shrine of the
Apostle James?"

Peter put his fingertips together and sat for a moment,
opening and closing his hands like a spider on a mirror.

"It has been brought to my attention," he said thoughtfully,
"that the most noble emperor's grandfather, Alfonso the Sixth,
many years ago generously pledged to the abbey of Cluny an
annual donation of two thousand *metcales*. According to my
secretary, this pledge hasn't been paid since the present emperor's election."

The bishop shrugged an apology. "My Lord Alfonso has
needed all his funds in his continuing struggle against the enemies of Christ," he explained. "You could not disapprove of
such a use of his resources. But he has authorized me to say that
his financial situation is better now, although there is still a
threat of invasion from the south, especially from those lands
near Galicia."

"I was not aware that Portugal was made up of infidels,"
Peter observed.

"But their sympathies lie in that direction," Stephen assured him. "And their politics are in turmoil. The people there
could easily be lost to the Faith without proper guidance. The
archbishopric of Santiago is vacant at the moment, you are
aware of that? The emperor feels that Berengarius of Salamanca
would be an excellent candidate for the see."

"I have heard no ill of him," Peter admitted. "Actually, I hear little of him at all. In any case, I certainly can have no influence on the election."

"You are too modest," the bishop said truthfully. "Your approval of Berengarius would carry a great deal of weight with the deciding bishops and with Pope Innocent."

"Even if that were so, I'm afraid I know too little of his capabilities," Peter answered. "I could not in good conscience recommend a man merely on hearsay."

"Another reason for you to come," Stephen said. "To meet him and judge for yourself. You would give us such joy if you would agree. The emperor would get down on his knees and weep with gratitude if only I could tell him you would soon be in his presence. The people of the land would greet you with flowers and prayers."

"It is a most kind offer," said Peter, who had already decided to set out after Easter. "I will consider it."

When the bishop had been shown to his quarters, Peter sent for his secretary. He needed to dictate a few letters. It was true that the restoration of the Spanish tithes would be most welcome to Cluny and its building projects. But Peter had another reason for going, one that was just as close to his heart.

"Pierre," he told his secretary, "send messages to our houses in Spain. Tell them to start looking for men who are proficient in both Latin and Arabic, and for someone who understands the subtleties of the lies of the infidels. I want to hire them for as many months as necessary to translate the books of Mohammad into a Christian tongue."

That afternoon Catherine sat once again at the feet of the master and told him of her dream. Edgar sat at her side, listening quietly.

"It was so clear, Master Abelard," she said. "I don't believe it was merely the result of *ventris plenitudine*."

"Looking at you, Catherine," Abelard replied, "it's clear that you have not been indulging in gluttony. But it may have been the result of fasting."

"Fasting is supposed to release the mind to apprehend true *revelatione*," Catherine objected. "But it was not that, either. I had eaten well enough that night. I don't think it was an illusion or a demonic sending, but a gift. The old man in the dream didn't seem evil to me, but protective of the child."

"Ah, yes." Abelard leaned back. "But that might have been a deliberate deception on the part of Satan to lull you so that he could attack. Tell me again the progress of this dream. You say you were on a steep cliff and the wind howled around you?"

"Yes, and it was so cold." Catherine shivered at the memory.

"And the old man, you said he seemed holy. How did you know?"

Catherine frowned. "I can't remember. He had a beard, I think, like the patriarchs on tympana. But it wasn't by any outward sign. I just knew."

"Very well," Abelard answered. "Now, try to remember. When the board broke and the child fell, what happened?"

Catherine scrunched her eyes tightly, trying to see back into the dream. Edgar took her hand. Slowly the memory was becoming clear. Yes. That was it.

"The board didn't break," she told them. "It shook horribly, perhaps from the wind, or from someone behind me shaking it. I don't know. It flew up and I was pushed against the cliff, but my child was tossed into the air. The old man reached out and caught him."

"How?" Abelard asked. "In his arms? Why didn't the man fall as well?"

"I don't . . . Wait." Catherine stumbled on her breath in the effort to remember. "There was something, something in his hands. It was white and the child landed in it."

"What did it look like?" Edgar asked. "You didn't tell me this before."

"I didn't remember," Catherine said. "It happened so quickly and I was frightened for myself as well as for our son. But now I can see it. The man held out his arms and there was this thing in them."

"Like a basket?" Abelard asked.

"No," Catherine answered, and she seemed puzzled. "It was smooth and white, and there were ripples at the edge. It was hard and shallow; the boy lay on it, not in it."

Abelard asked no more questions. The two waited. Finally, he leaned forward again. He took Catherine's chin in his hand and turned her face up to his.

"I believe I know the meaning of your dream," he said. "I may be mistaken, but I must agree that this was no corporeal illusion brought on by mere sensations of the body. You have had a true sending. The holy man you saw was, I believe, the blessed apostle, Saint James the Greater. He has rescued your son in the scallop shell of his shrine. If your prayers will ever be answered, I believe you must go to Compostela, Catherine."

Edgar jumped to his feet. "Master, that's a month's journey or more over hard roads, among wolves and robbers. Catherine isn't well enough to survive it."

"I think she is, Edgar," Abelard said calmly. "That was the rest of the dream."

"What do you mean?" he asked.

"She dreamt that she woke up and you were there," Abelard said. "She knew then that she was safe. If you go with her, Edgar, if you both take your petition to Saint James, I believe with all my heart that you will return, that *three* of you will return."

Edgar sank back onto the rushes, his mouth open. He had planned to go no farther than Saint-Marcellus, bid farewell to his old master and return to Paris. He remembered that it was while on a mission for Master Abelard at the abbey of Saint-Denis that he had first met Catherine, three years before. At that point his life had been thrown into a box, shaken and tossed out like dice on a table.

He still didn't know which side would come up.

"Very well, Master," he said. "Catherine and I will make arrangements to visit Saint James. When we return, we will tell you if we succeeded."

Abelard sighed. "It won't be necessary, my children. I will know the answer long before that."

That evening in Paris, Catherine's father sat alone by the fire. Hubert LeVendeur, merchant, was achingly tired. He held a bowl of broth in his hands and tried to remember when he hadn't had this sense of total exhaustion and despair.

He couldn't.

He wished Catherine would come home. He missed her. He was even getting used to Edgar. Not quite enough to miss him, but enough to feel content that his daughter had chosen to marry this odd foreigner, who said he was English but came from even farther north. Hubert knew almost nothing about Scotland except that trade was poor there. If Edgar had insisted on taking Catherine back to that horrid land, Hubert would have forbidden the match, no matter what. He was glad it hadn't come to that.

This restless desire for pilgrimage on Catherine's part frightened him more than he dared consider. She thought she was expiating the sin of leaving the convent for marriage. Hubert feared she was in danger of falling into her mother's belief that if she prayed long enough, all consequences of her sins would vanish. But his poor wife, Madeleine, had driven herself into some sad world where no amount of prayer brought forgiveness or comfort. If that happened to Catherine, Hubert thought it would kill him.

But what if the sin were not Catherine's? Hubert feared that the fault was really in him. Perhaps it was punishment for his sin that was being visited on his best-beloved daughter. And what could he do? He knew that there was no forgiveness without true contrition and that he wasn't sorry he had been born a Jew, or that after his forced conversion in childhood, he had found the way secretly back to the faith of his fathers. He sipped and grimaced; while he was brooding; his broth had gone cold. All he tasted was the congealed grease along the rim of the bowl.

Someone was pounding at the door.

Ullo, the serving boy, appeared a moment later, accompanied by a man still muffled in his cloak.

"Is there any soup left for me?" the man asked as he unwound his scarf. "There's nothing so bone-chilling as a Paris spring. I'm half frozen."

"Solomon!" Hubert jumped up to greet his nephew, his mood lightening at the sight of him. No, Hubert could never repent finding his family again.

"What are you doing back so early?" he asked as soon as Solomon had settled himself on the stool opposite him.

"What do you mean, Uncle?" Solomon answered. "I've been gone for four months, over those damned Pyrenees twice in snows up to my waist."

"So long?" Hubert said. Catherine and Edgar had left barely three weeks ago and it seemed much longer. "And was the trip successful?"

Solomon finished his broth and put the bowl on the hearth. He rubbed his forehead, then ran his fingers through his black curls. Hubert knew the gesture.

"What went wrong?" he asked.

"Nothing," Solomon said. "Everything. I have the pearls and spices for Saint-Denis."

"I see," Hubert said. "So, then. What's her name?"

Solomon stared at him, then laughed long and hard. "Aristotle, Uncle," he said finally. "Her name is Aristotle. I've become trapped in the snares of the stars. I only wish it had been a woman's arms instead."

Hubert stared at his nephew in disbelief. "What are you talking about?" he asked. "You don't mean that pagan nonsense that says our lives are decided by the motions of the planets, do you? I thought you had more sense."

Solomon didn't take offense. He knew how odd it sounded. "It's more than that, Uncle," he said slowly. "There are people working in Provence and Spain—Christians, Jews, Moslems, sometimes even together—deciphering and translating books of lost knowledge. The heavens are only a small part of it. Uncle, don't you ever wonder why we are here, why our lives have unfolded in a certain way?"

"I know why," Hubert answered. "It is as the Almighty One decrees."

Solomon exhaled in irritation. "Of course, but don't you want to know the pattern, how our lives fit into the web of the universe?"

Hubert looked at his nephew in bewilderment. Who was this young man? Solomon had never questioned the universe before. Something more had happened to him than he was telling. Despite his protestations, Hubert suspected that there was a woman behind all this.

"Do I look like a rabbi, Solomon?" he asked. "How can I know why? I saw my mother and sisters slaughtered. And yet I was raised with love by those who should have been my enemies. I pass my life suspended between two worlds, waiting for the thread that holds me to be cut, dropping me into the abyss. Why? If I wondered such a thing, I would go as mad as my poor Madeleine. It's not my business to question my Creator, whose mind is as far above mine as mine is above an insect's."

Solomon ladled himself more broth from the pot next to the fire. He inhaled the steam with relish.

"I grant you that we can't understand the mind of the Lord," he said, "but we were given the power to reason and question. There must be a purpose to everything. What if, along with the Oral Law, other clues were left by Him to enable us to piece together the *schema* of His plan for us? Or even merely to approach Him more closely? What if that is what we were meant to do?"

Hubert emptied his cold broth back into the pot. "What if the Archangel Michael were to appear in this room and tell you that you're a blithering fool?" he grunted. "That's the sort of nonsense Catherine used to spout. You've been listening to her and those street philosophers too long."

Solomon only laughed. "Perhaps," he said. "Or perhaps I've been infected with the poetry of the south."

"That, I could believe," Hubert said. "Especially if there were a perfume to it and a feminine voice reciting it."

Solomon sighed. "Only in a perfect world, Uncle, and I have given up ever finding that."

Hubert didn't answer. He had never even tried to hunt for such a thing as a perfect world. Security was the most he ever hoped for.

Solomon finished his broth and yawned. "Can you give me a bed for the night?" he asked. "I would have gone to Aunt Johannah on the Île but I didn't want her to know I'd been traveling on the Sabbath."

"Always wise," Hubert agreed. "If you'll help me, we'll set up a bed here where it's warm. Ullo will give you sheets and quilts."

"Thank you, Uncle," Solomon said. "You are good to your mad relatives."

"I have to be," Hubert sighed. "I seem to have no other kind."

Catherine tried not to cry as she said good-bye to Abelard, but she failed completely. He smiled at her grief, hugged her gently and kissed her forehead.

"We should rejoice that I will soon be going home," he said. "As for you, my child, you will always be a daughter of the Paraclete and so one of mine. Promise me that you will be a friend and sister to my son and that you will do what you are able to comfort Héloïse after my death."

He spoke so calmly. Catherine could only sniff and nod.

Abelard turned to Edgar, who was not sure of his own ability to restrain tears. In the master's eyes there was a flash of the wicked look he had always had before he set about demolishing the one debating him. Edgar braced himself. Abelard grinned at him.

"To you I leave a much harder task," he said. "Into your keeping I give this daughter of the Paraclete. I witnessed your wedding with some trepidation, but now I am sure that this is what God planned for you both. He rarely gives those He loves the easy path. But follow it with her and have faith."

Edgar put his arm around Catherine, who sobbed damply onto his tunic. "Thank you, Master," he said. "I don't think I'm able to do anything else."

Abelard placed his hands on their heads, giving them his

blessing. "And now, I would like to speak with my son alone," he told them.

They left Astrolabe with his father. Edgar sat Catherine down on a bench outside the priory door. "*Carissima*," he said gently, "could you please wipe your nose on your handkerchief instead of my sleeve?"

She sniffled, but complied. "I'm not crying just for myself," she explained, "but for Mother Héloïse and Astrolabe and all the things that went wrong for them."

"We don't know that things went wrong, just because they didn't happen the way we think they should have," Edgar answered. "The master as much as told us that himself. Catherine, can't you believe that, for our sake, too?"

Catherine's noisy tears began to quiet. Edgar said no more, but held her in the cool spring afternoon until she stirred in his arms and looked up into his eyes.

"We will go to see Saint James," she said firmly. "If he cannot give us a living child, then I will accept our fate. Perhaps being given you is as much as I've a right to ask for."

He had no answer for that. She did know how to embarrass him.

"Very well," he said after a pause. "We shall go to Compostela. And before you say it, I already know. We'll start from Lyon, not from Vézelay or Orléans. Heaven forbid we should take the easiest route through gentle, vine-laden country. We can pass by Cluny first. Perhaps someone there is making up a party to go on pilgrimage. My only condition is that we take horses with us to carry our packs and, if necessary, ourselves. Therefore, we'll need your father's help. He'll have to know what we're doing in any case. I want you to survive the journey and it will be much harder without supplies from him. After that, I refuse to worry."

Catherine smiled. "You're right, *carissime*, and practical, as usual. That must be why Saint James told me not to leave you behind."

Gaucher ran his hands through his white hair. Rufus watched sourly, wishing it would all fall out through his old friend's fingers. He reflected grimly that he might get his wish if Gaucher tugged at his curls much more.

"I tell you, it's not a joke," Gaucher said for the third time. "Either one of you is trying to frighten me into giving up the journey, or—"

"Why would we do that, Gaucher?" Norbert interrupted testily. "We've suffered your snoring for forty years. We can endure a bit longer."

"Saint Lucie's limpid eyeballs!" Gaucher roared. "Are you all too far in your dotage to see what's happening here? Someone wants to kill me! Look at this!"

Gaucher held out his drinking cup. He had left it on the table at the hostel where they had stopped the previous night. This morning he had come down to find it filled with dung.

The other three men were not impressed.

"Odd way to commit murder, Gaucher," Hugh observed. "Unless the dung is poisoned."

"And the murderer knows your tastes," Rufus added.

Norbert sniffed. "Smells like pig shit to me," he said. "First the offering in your tunic, now this. Perhaps there's a sow somewhere in love with you."

Rufus laughed. "Any piglet on your property with a gold streak in its tail? We've warned you, Gaucher, that one day you'd go too far with your livestock."

Gaucher threw the cup across the room, where it shattered, splattering the contents against the wall. "I'm going out to buy a new cup," he announced. "When I return, I'm leaving this place. You may come with me or not, as you wish."

He stalked out.

Hugh ignored the stench and reached for a pitcher of beer. He carefully checked inside his wooden cup before he poured.

"Don't bother, Hugh," Rufus said. "You can't tell the difference anymore."

Rufus stretched contentedly on the bench. He was in rare form this morning. He picked up his own mug and took a long swallow. Something cold and furry brushed his lips. He lowered the cup and looked in. He gagged and sprayed beer all over the table.

Floating in the milky dregs was a dead mouse.

Norbert sighed. He had hoped they had left this sort of foolishness behind with the other vices of youth. Of course, Rufus showed no sign of giving up any of his vices. Gaucher probably hadn't even considered it. This wasn't the pilgrimage Norbert had planned. What point was there in traveling a thousand miles to ask for remission of one's sins if the sins came along? Or even worse, if their sins were pursuing them, knowing, perhaps, of the other, less holy reason for their journey?

Norbert made up his mind. When Gaucher came back, he was going to propose that they change their route. This road was too easy, too protected. They would head south and start from Lyon, going across the plateau and the mountains. There were many holy places along that trail. Conques, for one. Norbert had always had a fondness for Saint Foy, the little-girl martyr whose body rested in the church there.

Norbert had always had a fondness for little girls.

Once again the Jews of Paris had managed to survive Easter week. Hubert had not dared to visit Solomon or his own brother, Eliazar, and sister-in-law, Johannah, during that time. It was better not to advertise friendships between Jew and Christian while all were being reminded daily of the Crucifixion. But news had arrived the following week that sent him hurrying from his house on the Right Bank to that of his brother on the Île de la Cité.

"She's insane!" he shouted before the door was barely opened.

He stopped at Johannah's shocked expression.

"A blessing upon all in this place," he said quickly. "I tell you she's gone mad and taken that English boy with her. And they say Peter Abelard suggested it! Everyone knows he's been addled for years. How can we stop them?"

"May you be blessed as well, Brother," Johannah said calmly. "Come and sit down in the solar. Eliazar will be right down. I'll have the maid bring you a basin to wash your hands in, and then some wine and cheese."

"Johannah, I've no time for this," Hubert said. "Catherine

intends to go to Spain! She'll never survive the trip. What am
I to do?"

"You and Eliazar just sent Solomon to Spain in the dead
of winter without a qualm," Johannah answered. "Why are you
so concerned about Catherine making the journey in the
spring?"

She guided him to a chair. "Sit. Eat. Then we'll talk."

Hubert followed her orders mechanically. When Johannah
insisted, one obeyed. By the time he had finished his wine and
cheese, he was somewhat more composed.

Eliazar had been given a quick explanation before he entered. "*Shalom*, Brother," he said, kissing Hubert on both
cheeks. "So what has this troublesome child of yours decided
to do now?"

Hubert repeated as best he could the message Catherine
had sent. "She asks me to send clothes and funds for the journey," he ended. "I would deny her request, but I know her too
well. She would simply start out without them. What am I to
do? They leave from Lyon next week."

Eliazar pursed his lips and tugged on his beard. It seemed
to provoke more intense concentration. "Solomon has just returned from Spain," he said at last.

"So your wife reminded me," Hubert answered.

"For some odd reason, he wants to go back there as soon
as possible," Eliazar said. "He says he wants to study Aristotle, or some such."

"There must be a woman," Hubert answered. "Our
nephew would never commit himself freely to travel for the
sake of philosophy."

"I only know what he tells me," Eliazar said.

He was silent again. Hubert waited. Eliazar was the elder
brother. Sometimes respect must be given.

Eliazar looked up at the ceiling, studying the pattern of the
wood, no doubt. "I was thinking," he said. "It's been many
years since I've visited with our brethren in Spain."

Hubert glanced up sharply. "You would go with her and
watch over her?" he asked, hope dawning.

Eliazar kept his eyes focused upward. "Your Catherine has

always needed more care than I could give," he said. "And I will be occupied in discovering what has so agitated our Solomon that he's been home barely two weeks and is preparing to leave yet again."

Hubert finally realized where this was going. To his surprise, he found himself becoming excited at the prospect. "Eliazar, I haven't been farther than Toulouse in twenty years."

"It would do you good," Eliazar said. "You're getting soft."

"But my other children . . . my grandchildren." Hubert flailed about for an excuse.

"Your other daughter hasn't spoken to you in months and is quite content living with her mother's family," Eliazar said bluntly. "And your son is busy with his own life. He doesn't need you. I don't believe your grandchildren will forget you. Bring them presents on your return. They'll love you all the more."

"There speaks a man with no children," Hubert muttered.

Eliazar ignored him. He waited once more.

Hubert got up and paced the room a few times. "We can't reach Lyon before they go," he said at last.

"We'll meet them at Le Puy, then," Eliazar answered.

Hubert still had one more bolt to his bow. "Johannah is going to kill you if you do this," he told his brother.

Eliazar nodded. "But she'll not do it until my return."

Three

Le Puy, Saturday, April 25, 1142; The Feast of Saint Mark, evangelist.

Quator vie sunt que ad Sanctum Jacobum tendentes, in unum ad Pontem Regine, in horis Yspanie, coadunantur: alia per Sanctum Egidium et Montem Pessulanum et Thosolam et Portus Asperi tendit; alia per Sanctam Mariam Podii et Sanctam Fidem de Conquis et Sanctum Petrum de Moyssaco incedit; . . .

There are four roads leading to Saint James, which become one at Puenta la Reina in the lands of Spain. One goes through Saint-Gilles and Montpellier and Toulouse and the Somport Pass; another through Saint-Marie at Le Puy and Saint-Foi of Conques and Saint-Peter of Moissac. . . .

Codex Calistinus, Book IV
The Pilgrim's Guide to Saint James

$\mathcal{N}$ow that a way had been shown to her and she was in the process of following it, Catherine's mood changed remarkably. She had always loved travel from the time her father had decided she was old enough to accompany him to the fairs at Saint-Denis, Provins and Troyes. Then she had ridden behind him, gripping his belt for dear life and thinking in delight of how far above the ground she was from her perch on the back of his horse. While on the road with Hubert, the rules of deportment were slack and the world a pageant created just for her entertainment. Now Catherine was eager to share it all with Edgar.

She had never been as far as Le Puy before, and the area around the town enchanted her, with the strange volcanic cones rising up above the valley. Le Puy was also much more a pilgrim town than Lyon, and she felt it to be the true beginning to their journey. The first day there, she and Edgar climbed the twisting staircase of the pillar of Saint Michel D'Aiguilhe to the small Carolingian church at the top. It was on the ascent that Catherine began to realize the scope of the adventure she was about to become a part of.

The stairs winding up the side of the pillar had only a low wall to divide the pilgrims from the air and the ground far below. There were so many pilgrims making their way to and from the top that a monk had been stationed at each bend to keep them moving in good order. Those who had vowed to climb on their knees were told bluntly to either get to their feet or come back in the middle of the night, when the congestion was less severe.

Despite the glare from the monk waiting for them at the

top, Catherine paused before entering the church to look out over the edge to the valley below, with the river winding through it. Directly across from them, on another pinnacle, she could see the cathedral, with its own line of pilgrims. She and Edgar would climb the stairs of that next.

She bent over the edge, trying to make out the trail between the two sites. At that point, her arm was pulled roughly and she was spun about to face the angry monk.

"No dawdling!" he said. "No leaning over. We haven't had anyone miraculously saved from falling in over a century, and I for one don't want to waste my prayers on you."

"Yes, Brother," Catherine replied. "I ask your pardon."

She looked around for Edgar, but didn't see him. Odd. It wasn't like him to go on without her.

She found him at last in a curve of the church. The building was small and round, with fading frescoes. The sunlight coming through the many narrow windows turned the room to gold. Usually Edgar would have been busy studying the carvings on the capitals, but now he was on his knees, eyes closed, lips moving silently.

Catherine felt a pang of guilt. She had been enjoying the view and here he was concentrating on the purpose of their pilgrimage. She would have knelt beside him but there was no room, so she laid a hand on his shoulder and added her prayers to his.

The monk stationed at the door was still glaring at them. Gently, Catherine squeezed Edgar's shoulder. He didn't respond. She bent over and whispered in his ear.

"*Carissime*, we must allow others to make their devotions here." His eyes remained tightly shut, his head bent over clasped hands. Catherine tried again. "Edgar, the good brother here is insisting that we go back down. We'll have many more chances for supplication as we continue the journey."

She shook him more roughly. Edgar lifted his head and lowered his hands to his sides. A shudder passed through his body as he rose.

"Edgar?" Catherine felt a tinge of panic. "What's wrong? Are you ill? Why didn't you tell me?"

"No," he said, "I'm fine."

She didn't believe him. He was even more pale than usual. Beneath the glow of the golden sunlight there was a greenish cast to his skin, and his lips were tight, as if holding back nausea.

"Edgar, we're going back to the hostel at once," Catherine told him, taking his arm. The sudden tensing of his muscles frightened her even more. Edgar was never sick. She guided him to the door.

At the threshold he stopped, causing the pilgrim behind him to stumble with a not-quite-muffled curse. Catherine dragged Edgar out onto the narrow walkway leading to the stairs.

"Help me!" she ordered the annoyed man. "Can't you see that my husband has been taken ill?"

Instead of helping, the man gave a gasp of horror and backed as far away as possible, which led to a number of other collisions. All those within hearing range followed his example.

"Catherine!" Edgar growled between clenched teeth. "Stop it. I'm not sick."

"What!" she said. "Then what is it?"

Before he could answer, the monk who had been glaring at them came and took Edgar's other arm.

"Don't worry, young man," he said quietly. "I understand. I struggle with it myself every time I'm sent up here. Just lean on me and look at the ground."

Edgar exhaled in relief and obeyed the monk's command. Catherine followed them, bewildered. As they descended, she continued to peer over the edge whenever the chance came.

"Oh, look!" she exclaimed. "There's our hostel. Gracious, I didn't know we were so close to the river. I wonder how often they get spring floods here. Edgar, look over there. Aren't those four old men down by the hostel the ones we saw at Vézelay? What could they be doing here? Edgar?"

Edgar didn't answer. The monk shot her a poisoned glance over his shoulder. Catherine subsided.

When they reached the field at the bottom, Edgar sat heavily upon the grass. He reached in his pilgrim's scrip and found a coin for the monk.

"A thousand blessings on you and your order," he said. "Thank you."

The monk smiled. "Don't look so ashamed," he said. "You're not the only one. It happens every day, especially to us low-landers. I'm from Picardie. They had to carry me all the way down the first time I went up."

He gave Edgar a sympathetic pat on the shoulder and returned to his duties. Catherine sat down next to her husband.

"Will you please tell me what that was all about?" She tried not to sound annoyed but didn't entirely succeed. "I thought you were dying."

"So did I," he said. "Halfway up, the crowd pushed me close to the wall, so that I was almost pressed over it. I looked down and felt a great black wave wash over me. I couldn't move. I knew I was going to fall and part of me just wanted to step over the edge and be done with it. Horrible."

Catherine put her arm across his shoulders. It took her a few minutes to piece this out, the concept was so new to her. "Edgar," she said at last, "do you mean that you were frightened?"

"That is a singular understatement," he answered. He sighed and Catherine could feel his muscles relax. "I was never fond of high places, but there aren't many in my part of Scotland. I didn't know how bad it was until Master Abelard sent me to work at Saint-Denis while they were building the tower. I went up on the scaffolding to take some measurements for the statues. They almost had to dismantle the thing to get me down."

"And you never said a word to me." Catherine shook her head. "But, Edgar, it's not unreasonable to be afraid on a narrow scaffold. Workmen fall to their death all the time."

"Thank you, Catherine," he said. "That's a great consolation."

She tried to think of a way to extricate herself from that,

but couldn't come up with anything that wouldn't make matters worse.

Edgar got to his feet. "Let's go back to the hostel," he said.

Catherine took his arm again, this time for her own comfort. She didn't understand it. He wasn't afraid of anything. She had seen him in real danger of death and he hadn't flinched. Why should being somewhere high up disturb him so profoundly?

He had been wondering about her as well. "You weren't frightened at all on the pinnacle, were you?" he asked.

"No, of course not," she answered—as usual, without thinking. "It was exciting to see the world from above. I felt like an eagle. It was all I could do to keep from flying away, soaring higher and higher."

This was the first time in their lives together that Edgar had no way to understand Catherine's heart. Her face was glowing with the memory. Then her expression changed to one of deep concern.

"Edgar," she said, "we'll have to go home now. We can't possibly finish the pilgrimage. Do you know how many mountains there are between here and Compostela?"

Edgar nodded. "We will cross them all," he said, and she knew there would be no more discussion. "That is part of my offering to Saint James."

At that moment, Catherine loved him more than she had ever believed possible.

"We'll never find a bed without fleas in it tonight," Hubert grumbled as they approached Le Puy. "What put it into the mind of Peter of Cluny to travel now?"

"I don't think he's taking your bed, Uncle," Solomon observed. "The abbot usually brings his own."

"And generally finds a cleric to give him a corner to set it up in," Eliazar added.

Hubert was not in a mood for literal-mindedness. "Once the abbot announced he was going to Spain, the road became clogged with pilgrims. They all want to travel in his wake."

"And why not?" Eliazar asked. "They not only benefit from the guards he brings, but from the extra notice Saint Peter is sure to take of them."

"Do you think we can also hide under the cloak of the patron saint of Cluny?" Hubert asked scornfully.

Eliazar shrugged. "Saint Peter can take care of his own, if he likes. But I wouldn't mind staying near the guards."

Hubert didn't answer. He was appalled by the traffic along the road. How would he ever find Catherine in all this? And which path was he supposed to walk upon when he did find her? On his earlier journeys, he had started out as a Christian from Paris and managed to join with Jewish traders farther south. He feared that this time he would be forced to choose one or the other and keep to it. The problem was that his soul lay in one camp and his heart in the other.

They were coming to the river.

"As I recall," Solomon said, "the toll at the ferry here is outrageous but there's no ford for miles and no bridge."

"Then they can charge anything they like," Eliazar said.

"And this is only the beginning," Hubert sighed. "I shall be a pauper by the end, I foresee it. How did this happen to me?"

Solomon grinned. "You were born, Uncle, and from then on, your life was not in your control."

"Ah yes, your new philosophy," Hubert said. "It smacks of heresy to me, Nephew. The Almighty sends our joys and sorrows, but how they affect us is our decision."

"Then I suggest you bear this minor discomfort with more fortitude," Solomon said. "Or the Lord may decide to test you as He did Job."

Hubert made a sign with his right hand, warding away evil. "That is not a joking matter," he said.

Eliazar was concentrating on the immediate problem. "There's a line at the ferry," he grumbled. "And as usual, someone seems to be arguing over the fare."

As they drew closer, they saw that the delay was being caused by a woman on horseback, wearing a widow's long purple veil. She was accompanied by two armed men, a maidservant and three pack mules, but it was clear who was in charge.

"Pilgrims are to be allowed free passage on all ferries and toll roads," she stated. "I refuse to give you a sou."

The ferryman did not seem upset. "Pilgrims travel with only the clothes they can carry," he replied. "They bring no money but rely on the charity of those along the route. You are no pilgrim."

"I most certainly am!" Her voice rose. "What I am not is a fool. No woman would take this road without protection and the money to pay for it. Now let me pass."

The ferryman shook his head and motioned for the next party to come aboard. This consisted of three people: a *jongleur* and his wife, both carrying their *vielles* strapped to their backs and small tambours hanging from their belts; waiting near them was another woman, barefoot and swathed in a deeply cowled black cloak despite the warmth of the day. As she passed, the ferryman pointed her out to the woman on horseback.

"That, Lady, is a pilgrim," he said. "She need pay me nothing."

The woman snorted. "That, *Sieur*, is a whore. I imagine you've been paid already."

With that, she turned her party around and led it away from the river.

Solomon looked after her with interest. "Where does she think she's going?" he asked. "If there were another way across, the line here wouldn't be so great."

Hubert shrugged. "With that much arrogance, perhaps she'll have a floating bridge made just for her, or simply walk across on the water. Still, she has a ready tongue. There aren't many who could have had the last word in that encounter."

"Well, I agree with the ferryman," Eliazar said. "We pay our tolls and so should she."

"Uncle, we have letters of remission of the tolls from almost every lord from Paris to Narbonne," Solomon said. "It's only places like this where we pay."

"There are too many places like this," Hubert grumbled.

"You can be sure he'll add what he's lost on that pilgrim woman to our fee."

"Do you think the lady was right about her occupation?" Solomon asked. He couldn't make out much from under the heavy cloak the woman wore. Really, he was surprised that the lady on horseback could tell the pilgrim was female.

Eliazar gave him a sharp glance. "It makes no difference to you whether she was right or not," he warned. "The woman's a Christian, and even if she were a prostitute, it's evident that she's reformed. Stay away from her."

"I was merely speculating, Uncle," Solomon grinned. "Come along. Our turn to risk drowning."

"Just be sure the horses are securely tethered to the rings on the side," Eliazar told him. "All we need is the expense of replacing one in a town that has already doubled the price of everything."

Griselle, widow of Bertran, castellan of Lugny, was perfectly willing to ride fifteen miles farther downriver to a ford rather than give that *avoutre* ferryman a sou. She could well afford the toll for the ferry, but it was a matter of honor. Simply because she had brought along a comb and clean clothing, it did not mean that her dedication to the pilgrimage was less sincere than anyone else's. Like many of the people on the road to Compostela, she did not expect to survive the journey, but she was determined to live at least long enough to arrive at the shrine of Saint James and, as she told the ferryman, she was not fool enough to think she would be safe traveling alone.

As they approached the town, Griselle wrapped the long widow's veil around the lower half of her face. She made sure every bit of her hair was covered. Even with the guards along, it was necessary to attract no untoward attention. A whisper of scandal could destroy everything.

"Goswin," she ordered one of the guards, "find me a bed for the night, in the monastery hostel if possible. Take the packhorses with you. I'm going to the cathedral."

Motioning the maid and the other guard to come with her, Griselle set out to light the first of many candles and make the first of many offerings in the hope of convincing one of the saints to grant her heart's desire.

The *jongleur*, Roberto, and his wife, Maruxa, had no expectations of a real bed in a hostel. They carried their beds with them. For blankets, they had their cloaks, and for pillows, each other's arms. The instruments, their most valuable possessions, slept between them. They fully expected to sing, dance, even juggle, for their meals. The only pilgrimage they were making was home to Astorga, in Spain, but it was good to find such a large and well-protected party to journey with. They had no doubt that they could earn their keep.

The woman on the ferry with them did not appear a likely customer for their music, however. She was swathed in her black cloak, with only her tanned and callused toes peeping out from beneath the hem of her robes. The cowl was pulled well over her face, so that nothing could be seen within. Maruxa shivered every time she looked at it. The *jongleuse* tried to move as far away from her as possible. Who could tell what was inside that shadow? What if the woman were really a leper? Or perhaps she was a wraith, or Death herself, come to lead the procession to the grave.

Maruxa closed her eyes and gripped her prayer beads tightly. She knew too many stories to chill the marrow on long winter nights. She tried to shake the feeling that one of them was sitting beside her on a bright spring afternoon.

There was a stirring from within the cowl. A voice came from its depths, soft and mellifluous.

"Do you know *Jherusalem, grant damage me fais?*" the woman asked. "I've always loved that song."

"We . . . we know a version of it," Maruxa answered, flustered to hear a human voice from this mysterious shape.

"Perhaps you would sing it for me tonight," the woman said. "I can only pay you with my prayers."

"That will be sufficient," Maruxa answered. "There will be someone else willing to toss us a coin."

She waited for a response, but the cowl dipped down again to rest on the woman's knees.

The ferry hit the opposite shore with a thump and they all stood. Maruxa had assumed that the other three men who had crossed with them were lords of some sort, but when they didn't immediately strut to the front to be let off first, she revised her opinion. They were all rather dark, like the men of her region, and seemed to be related. But two were bearded after the manner of the Jews, and the third was clean-shaven, with only a week or so of stubble showing. The youngest one had a nice smile as he offered her his arm to steady her jump to the riverbank.

Solomon next reached toward the pilgrim in black, but was rebuffed. The woman steadied herself on the rope stretched across the river to guide the ferry and swung from it to the bank. Her sleeves slipped back to her elbows, revealing strong brown hands and arms. Solomon watched, fascinated, fighting the urge to stretch out his hand and pull back the hood to uncover her face.

Eliazar recalled him to duty. "Let's get the packs back on the horses," he said as they led the animals ashore, "then see if we can find a place to shelter us."

"As soon as that's done," Hubert added, "I'm going in search of Catherine."

"You'd have an easier time if you asked for Edgar," Solomon suggested. "Not many tall, Saxon-blond men in Le Puy, I'd imagine."

Hubert made a face. "Edgar. Yes, you're right. And if I don't find Catherine with him . . ."

Solomon laughed. "Don't imagine impossibilities, Uncle. There's no place else she would be."

When the abbot of Cluny travels, the entourage is something akin to that of a king. He takes along his own cooks and secretary, a number of lay brothers to see to the animals and the packing and unpacking, several priests, an infirmarian with his herbs and simples for sudden illness, a pair of laundresses, a number of guards, ostlers, friends from among the monks, as well as other prelates. He also takes a treasurer to pay the tolls he can't bargain away and a cellarer for wine both sacred and mundane, as well as a steward to be sure the abbatial table is not found wanting. Finally, among the group are several small boys, called *garciones*, who run errands, carry messages and generally get in everyone's way. For this pilgrimage, there were over sixty people in the abbot's entourage to attend and be attended to. Brother Rigaud and Brother James had been put in charge of keeping them all organized.

"Have beds been found for everyone?" Brother Rigaud asked on the day of their arrival at Le Puy.

"Sleeping places, at least," Brother James answered. "The bishop has, of course, provided rooms for Bishop Stephen and Abbot Peter. You and I and the other monks will stay in the monastery dortor. The laundresses and the *garciones* have been given a place with the nuns. The lay brothers will have to make do in the field."

Brother Rigaud scanned the sky. It was unusually clear for spring. Good news for the brothers tonight, but it didn't bode well for the rest of the journey. Rigaud didn't trust missions that started out smoothly. One became complacent and therefore unprepared for the disasters that were sure to come.

Brother James agreed with him. The two were strikingly dissimilar in looks, Rigaud slightly built with a fringe of hair that had once been red, and James of medium height but strong-featured, with a severe tonsure that left only a thin, steel-grey circle around his scalp. But they were one in spirit, each striving to create order in a world he knew was bent on chaos.

Brother Rigaud sighed. "I should check to be certain that the provisions have been properly unloaded. At the last stop, one of the lay brothers stored the holy water and chrism with the cook pots, as if they were some sort of spice for the meat sauce."

Brother James nodded. "One can never be too vigilant. I shall go and supervise the setting up of the camp for the brothers. The sleeping area should be more centrally placed. I have noticed that a number of the women of these towns have no respect for the brothers' monastic status. They seem to think that because the lay brothers don't shave their beards, they have taken no vow of chastity. The temptation offered by such women might prove spiritually fatal to a man allowed to make his bed too far from the support and guidance of his friends."

The two men parted, each intent on his own duty. Brother James set out for the field near the monastery that had been allotted to the lay brothers. His thoughts were totally occupied with the organization of the sleeping arrangements in relation to the drainage of the field and other sanitary considerations. He hoped the land would be of a proper slope that he would not have to decide between the health of the men's souls and that of their bodies.

The woman at first simply passed through his vision without registering on his mind. But something—a gesture, the tilt of her head—made him stop and turn, blessing himself in panic. He saw only the edge of a skirt vanishing around a corner.

Brother James closed his eyes. A ghost, it had to have been, or a trick of the light. She was dead, long ago. Cruelly and horribly slain. It was impossible for her to be here now. *With God all things are possible,* he amended. But he saw no reason for God to have resurrected her. Not her.

No. He took a deep breath. It's only the pilgrimage, the people, he thought, those old knights who still wore their swords. He'd been in the cloister more than twenty years now. Being once again among the worldly simply brought back too many memories. That was all it was, a memory rooted out from his mind and accidentally rerouted past his eyes.

He blessed himself once again and without realizing it, muttered a charm from his childhood meant to keep away bad dreams. He forced his thoughts and his feet back in the direction of the job at hand.

Brother Rigaud was having his own vision from the long-ago. His path had taken him past the pilgrim hostel just as one of the guests was coming out.

"Rigaud!" the pilgrim cried. "Rigaud, you old bastard! I can't believe it! You here, as well. Saint Patrick's pulsating purgatory, it's good to be all together again."

Rigaud was forced to stop as he was caught in the grip of a

bear hug by a man a head taller than he. Feebly, he tried to push away.

"*Benedicite*, Gaucher," he said in resignation. "I take it from the cross on your cloak that you have become a pilgrim. I suppose it's never too late. And what you mean by 'all together again,' I fear to even ask."

Gaucher ignored his old comrade's lack of enthusiasm. "The four of us, of course," he answered. "Now all five! Wait until the others see you."

"The others?" Rigaud cringed. "Hugh. Rufus. You can't mean old Norbert is still alive?"

"A lot more so than you!" a voice boomed from behind him. "Look at you, face as smooth as a girl's and skirts to your ankles. You look a fair *fanfelu!*"

Rigaud wriggled himself out of Gaucher's grasp and started to back away. "You can't say things like that to me anymore, Norbert," he said evenly. "I have become a man of God, and when you insult me, you insult Him."

Norbert shook his head. "You never were much sport, Rigaud," he said sadly. "Come along, hike up your skirts, come in and have a few bowls of ale with us."

"Yes, come in, Rigaud!" Gaucher slapped him on the back, causing the monk to inhale sharply, swallowing a passing fly.

"I'll not come in and I don't want to see the others," Rigaud insisted when he had stopped coughing. "I have repented my life with you and I fervently wish never to see any of you again, not in this world or the next."

"Save your wishes for something else, old *compaing*." Gaucher raised his hand for another backslap, then took pity on his friend. "We're all going to be together from here to Compostela, and if we reach Saint James, you can be sure we'll all meet again one day in heaven, our sins washed away."

Rigaud continued moving away from them. "If Our Lord intends such a thing," he shouted as he left, "it is a certain proof that His mercy is greater than mine. But I don't believe that's where you really intend to go. I know what you're after! And I won't be a part of it. I warn you both, stay away from me!"

With that, he turned, lifted his robe to avoid tripping and ran as if all the demons of the air were flying after him.

Norbert and Gaucher laughed. "I wondered if Abbot Peter would drag old Rigaud out of his cell for this trip," Norbert said.

"I wonder what threats he used," Gaucher replied. "It was the last trip to Spain that sent him into the monastery."

"Rigaud always did have the *pendons* of a rabbit," Norbert said. "We were fighting a holy war, after all."

"Yes—" Gaucher's face twisted at the memories "—I know. But why, if it was so damned holy, do I still have nightmares about it?"

Norbert looked him up and down in scorn. "You don't drink enough," he answered. "Let's start taking care of that. Now."

The overwhelming sense of terror had passed and Edgar was now feeling more than a little embarrassed to have made a fool of himself in front of Catherine and the other pilgrims. He only half-listened to her stream of comments as they walked, searching instead for some alteration in her tone that would mean she had lost all respect for him.

"Edgar, don't look, but over by the water trough there are three men barefoot and wearing chains around their necks and waists," she was saying. "What do you suppose they could have done? Edgar?"

"Hmm? Oh, almost anything, I'd imagine," he told her, "from murder to sacrilege to unnatural lusts."

"Unnatural . . . like what?" she asked.

Edgar looked down into her deceptively guileless blue eyes. He smiled. There was no trace of scorn in them, although he saw a bit more amusement than scholarly inquisitiveness in her expression.

"Perhaps we can find a copy of Seneca's *Naturales Quaestiones*," he said. "There's a passage in there that might give you some suggestions."

"Oh, Hostis Quadra and the mirrors," she said.

"Catherine!"

She had the grace to blush. "I found it at Saint-Denis," she explained. "I was reading about light and reflections. I didn't know what was coming."

Edgar bit his tongue. They hadn't been married long enough for him to respond to that. "Well, then," he said finally, "as long as you weren't assigned it at the Paraclete."

"I don't think that part would interest the sisters very much," Catherine considered. "But in the monks' copy, that page was very well thumbed."

Edgar surrendered.

Fortunately, just then a voice called out, "There she is!"

Catherine turned toward it. "Father!" she cried and ran to his arms.

Halfway there, she stopped. She had seen Eliazar and Solomon with him. Who was he supposed to be here, a Christian or a Jew? Would her recognizing him cause him to be exposed? Hubert saw her indecision.

"Come here, *ma douce,*" he said. "I have missed you so."

She threw herself at him, forgetting for the moment that she was no longer eight years old. "Did you bring my blue *bliaut* with the daisies on the hem?" she asked. "And my extra shoes? And a new pair of *brais* for Edgar?"

"I should have known," he laughed. "You aren't hugging me, but the packages I've brought."

Edgar came up behind her more slowly. Hubert nodded to him. "She's looking well," he told his son-in-law. "*Diex te saut.*"

Edgar smiled. That was the most approval Hubert had ever given him, a tacit recognition that perhaps Catherine hadn't made a mistake in marrying him.

Solomon's greeting to Edgar was much more friendly. "Pilgrimage seems to agree with you," he said. "With any luck, you won't have to go all the way to Compostela to have your prayers answered."

"Catherine and I do believe that we have to help the saint all we can," Edgar grinned. "But I think we'll finish the pilgrimage just the same." His expression changed. "Perhaps then the Lord will give to us without taking away so soon." He looked out into a future too much desired to hope for.

Solomon waited a moment for Edgar to return. "So," he said, "where have you found lodging? Uncle Eliazar and I have a room with some friends, but I think Hubert plans on staying with you. Is there space?"

"The hostel is packed to the rafters," Edgar said, "but they always seem able to squeeze in another body."

Solomon wrinkled his nose. "Sounds very cozy."

Edgar was puzzled. "Are you coming with us on this journey?" he asked.

"For a while," Solomon smiled. "My uncles have some business to transact, and I . . . well, you could say I'm on a pilgrimage, too. We'll see you tomorrow."

Although the hostel, no more than a large barn with a loft partitioned for sleeping and an enormous hearth on the floor below, was full, somehow the new pilgrims were fit in. The *jongleur* and his wife expected no more than a small space of floor and were not disappointed. As the woman in the black cloak made her way across the room, people edged out of her way until she found a corner all to herself. Edgar had given a coin to the hostel keeper to save them a place in another corner, and they managed to make room for Hubert there as well.

"This will not do." The voice was not loud, but authority carries better than volume. "Goswin, I understood that you had found me a room."

"I'm sorry, my lady," the guard told her. "The town is full. There wasn't a room to be had, even with the nuns. We have made a bed for you in the loft and hung the curtains. Aymo and I will stand watch all night."

There was a pause.

"Very well." Griselle's eyes flicked about the room, taking stock of the people there. From the corner near the fire, where the knights had settled, Rufus of Arcy leered at her and lifted his cup. She raised her eyebrows. He lowered the cup.

Catherine watched her, admiring the cut of her *bliaut* and

the rich color of the *chainse* underneath. Even though this woman was in mourning, presumably for her husband, she had not abandoned her standards in her grief.

Catherine's hand found Edgar's, warm and living. Sometimes she just needed to be sure.

After sundown, the only light in the building came from the glowing coals in the hearth. The huge room never became completely quiet, but after a time, the talking and laughter were replaced by snores and the rustling of bodies in the straw.

Catherine slept well.

It was the aubade before dawn when she awoke. There were spaces now between the clumps of people on the floor. Others were already up, attending to prayers or ablutions. She stretched and eased herself to her feet, trying not to disturb either Edgar or her father. She made her way to the hearth, which still sent out some warmth. There was a man sitting next to it, his back against the wall, head drooping, cup beside him.

Catherine didn't notice the cup until she knocked it over. A trickle of wine ran out, wetting the hem of her skirt.

"Oh, I'm sorry, my lord," she said, righting the cup again and placing it by his hand.

He didn't stir.

He was unnaturally still. Catherine had seen many a man sunk too far into a wine flask to awaken, but she knew there was always some sort of movement. Nervously, she touched his hand. It was cold and flaccid.

Oh, dear.

She made her way back to her corner and found Edgar already awake. She sat down next to him and put her arms around him.

"Do you see the man over there by the fire?" she asked. "It's the knight from Vézelay, the one who ran into me outside the church. The poor old thing seems to have died in his sleep."

Four

*Le Puy, Sunday in Albis, April 26, 1142; Commemoration of Saint
Marcellinus, pope, apostate, penitent.*

*Quum, ergo sacrificia . . . pro baptizatis defunctis omnibus offerunter,
pro valde bonis gratiarum actiones sunt, pro non valde malis
propitiationes, pro valde malis etiamsi nulla sunt adjumenta mortuorum
qualescunque vivorum consolationes sunt.*

Therefore, when sacrifices . . . are offered for all the baptized dead,
they are, for the very good, acts of thanksgiving: for those neither
good nor bad they are propitiations: for the very bad they are of no
help to the dead, but are of some consolation to the living.

—Hugh of Saint-Victor
De Sacramentis Septem
Liber II, Pars XVI, Cap. VI

*R*ufus, Hugh and Gaucher looked down upon the body of their fellow knight and longtime companion. Rufus gave Norbert's leg a push with his boot. Dead. No way around it.

"I told him he was too old to come along," Hugh said.

"We all did," Rufus said, "but when did the old bastard ever listen to us?"

"Now one of us will have to go back and tell his children," Hugh sighed.

Gaucher spoke for the first time. "Why?" he asked.

"Well, they'll have to know where he's buried and start Masses for his soul, and his property will have to be divided," Hugh answered. "The usual reasons."

"We'll send a messenger," Gaucher said. "We can't turn back now. And we *must* stay together."

The other two looked at him in suspicion. Hugh moved closer so that the others in the room couldn't hear. "Now don't start all that nonsense about someone following us, Gaucher," he said. "What happened in Vézelay was just some pot boy's *tricherie*. Norbert was at least seventy. He'd had his three score and ten, and God sent the Angel for him. That's all."

"Perhaps," Gaucher said. "But he was fine yesterday."

Rufus hadn't taken his eyes from Norbert's body. He let the others argue over his head until they wore themselves out.

"I agree with Gaucher, we should send a messenger," he said at last. "Norbert looks to me as though he gave the Angel a hell of a fight for his soul. I don't like it. It makes me want to have friends about me in case whatever took him should come again."

They all forced themselves to look at Norbert's face, now stretching into a rictus. Hugh felt something pulling at his own lips. He looked away. "I see nothing untoward," he insisted. "You're getting as bad as Gaucher, Rufus."

But he had seen it. They all had. Even in the vacancy of death, there was an aura of hatred around Norbert. The way his right hand lay, as if going for his sword, his head thrown back and teeth bared. Hugh had seen him like that before, hugely alive and on his feet, dealing out cruel death to others. It was true. Whatever had come for him, Norbert of Bussières had fought it to the last spark of his soul. . . .

"Yes," Hugh said at last. "A messenger might be enough. We shall continue the pilgrimage together."

Edgar had been more resigned than surprised when Catherine had told him of finding the knight's body. She had a gift for such discoveries. So he was greatly relieved when he and Hubert had gone over to the hearth and realized that this must be a natural death. They were sorry, of course, and offered to come with the man's companions to say a prayer at his grave, but hundreds of people died on a pilgrimage, some of the illness they had set out to find a cure for, some of disease contracted on the road or from accidents or brigandage. This poor old man seemed merely to have succumbed to time.

Edgar returned to the corner, where Catherine was stuffing their belongings into the packs. "The journey was simply too much for the man," he told her. "We'll say a paternoster for him tonight."

Catherine nodded. "He seemed rather frail when we saw him at Vézelay," she said. "He was so determined not to admit to his infirmities. Ah well, he would have confessed and been absolved before he left his home. It must be a very peaceful way to die."

"May we all be so fortunate," Hubert added from behind Edgar's shoulder. "I presume you two are going to the pilgrims' Mass today. I'll see that our horses are being looked after, find Eliazar and Solomon, and meet you afterward in front of the cathedral."

He paused. "I'm coming with you, you know," he said. He looked at Catherine, but it was Edgar he was speaking to. "If you have no objection."

"We would be glad of your company," Edgar answered. "Will Solomon and Eliazar be in our party as well?"

From his tone, Hubert could divine nothing. He should ask Edgar straight out, he told himself, but he was a coward. Who should he be on this journey? What did his son-in-law want him to be? Hubert turned to Edgar and found himself facing a pair of grey eyes that were like a fog over the thoughts of the man inside. He wondered if Catherine knew how well her husband could hide his true feelings.

She interrupted their stare-down.

"I think we could all ride together," she said. "I remember there were often mixed parties of Jews and Christians among the merchants on the road. But we should find separate places to stay at night. That way, we can avoid questions that might lead to scandal."

Edgar and Catherine exchanged a glance, and it hit Hubert with the force of a weight hurled from a trebuchet that Edgar's eyes changed when they looked at his daughter. Even more startling was the change in hers. She and Edgar communicated in a way that made him ashamed to watch.

Catherine smiled and took her father's arm in both her hands, as she had when she was small. "Will you travel with us as my father," she asked, "or do you prefer to be with your brother and nephew?" She rested her chin on his shoulder. "Either way, I shall love you."

Hubert swallowed. "I am Hubert LeVendeur, merchant of Paris, member of the *marchands de l'eau,* supporter of the Church, and your father. I would like to stay with you."

Catherine kissed him in delight. "Then we would be honored to have you join us on our way to Saint James."

Mondete Ticarde, late prostitute of the town of Mâcon, uncurled herself from the straw she had slept in. She brushed bits of it off the back of her cloak and reached underneath to re-move a piece that was stuck to her thigh.

"Enjoy the bed, Mondete?" Giselle stood at the top of the ladder to the loft.

"I've slept in worse." Mondete didn't look up. "Did you enjoy mocking me at the ferry yesterday?"

Griselle finished climbing up. The guards and the maid were attending to her packing and she wanted amusement. "Not really," she shrugged. "It was that *questre*, the ferryman, who infuriated me. After all, my pilgrimage is as genuine as yours, perhaps more so."

She went over to Mondete and took a bit of the cloak be-tween her fingers, testing the material. "It's good wool, care-fully dyed." Griselle was impressed. "What do you have on underneath it, a silk shift or a hair shirt?"

"Neither," Mondete answered. "But how did you know me? No one else has. I haven't shown my face since I started out."

"I'd know your hands anywhere," Giselle answered. "Even without all the rings." She looked down. "You have ugly feet but the most exquisite hands."

Beneath the cloak, Mondete flinched. Too many men had commented on her hands and what they could do.

Griselle went on. "You've come down a great deal since we first met."

Mondete picked up her small bundle and stamped her bare feet on the floor to shake off the last of the straw.

"But I believe I've ascended a great deal since we last met," she said. "And what of you, my pure Griselle, married to a man fifteen years your senior who couldn't even give you children? Do you expect me to believe you never betrayed him?"

Griselle recoiled as if slapped. "Saint Melanie's stillborn son!" she exclaimed. "No, I don't expect you to believe any-thing I say. Why should you? But it's true. I never did. I never wanted to. I loved Bertran more than my life, or my soul. He died in battle, far away from me, alone and unshriven. I'm going to Compostela for the remission of his sins, not for my own."

Mondete's head dipped. "Then may both our petitions be graciously received," she said. "I would rather you didn't speak to me again, Griselle. You're part of a life that I would rather forget."

Griselle's mouth tightened in anger. "Very well," she said. "If I had ruined my life as thoroughly as you did yours, I would want to forget it, too. I only came to speak to you as an act of charity in the first place."

The voice from within the cowl was dry. "And it was only in charity that I answered you."

"You have to at least give him a Mass, Rigaud," Gaucher told the monk. "We can't just bury him here without a proper ceremony."

"I don't care what your duties are to Cluny," Hugh added. "You owe Norbert as well, and it's an older obligation."

Brother Rigaud was backed into a corner of the narthex of the cathedral with the other two looming over him. He squirmed but could see no way around.

"I'll see what I can do about it," he promised them. "What did Norbert leave to Saint Peter in his will? Did he ask the monks to say Masses for him?"

"We're not talking about Cluny, Rigaud." Hugh leaned closer. "We're talking about one low Mass from one little monk for the soul of his friend. What will it cost you?"

"We'll all attend," Gaucher said. "You can impress us with your Latin."

Rigaud gave in. "I don't believe that a Mass will do him any good, though," he warned. "He still had to repent before he died."

"Perhaps he did, Rigaud," Hugh said and stepped back. "He was the one who insisted we all go on this pilgrimage."

Brother Rigaud lifted his face to catch the cool air that found its way into the space Hugh had left.

"If he did," the monk said with certainty, "it wasn't because he wanted to save your souls. If anything, it was to have one last chance to ensure your damnation." He held up his hands at their protest. "It doesn't matter. If a Mass won't rescue him, it still may help us. It would be a mockery of my conversion if I didn't at least try."

"Fair enough," Gaucher said. "The monks here will bury him, and we've sent word to his children. We'll expect you to say a prayer with us tonight."

"You ask too much, Gaucher." Rigaud suddenly stopped caring what they would do to him. "A Mass, yes. In my own time and place. But I won't pray with you. I'm not one of you now. I wish to heaven I never had been."

They let him push his way out between them. When he had left, Hugh leaned against the wall, watching the flow of pilgrims through the doors.

"Do you think it's the tonsure that does it to them?" he asked Gaucher.

"More likely the bed," Gaucher answered. "Too narrow."

"If I remember rightly, Rigaud could find a way to fit two in a very narrow space," Hugh said.

Gaucher laughed. "But they squealed so, like pigs at slaughter."

He stopped laughing. He didn't want to remind himself of pigs. It did seem that they had eluded the trickster who had been following them, but Gaucher still felt as if he were being hunted by something. This whole journey had been Norbert's plan, even though he himself had willingly become involved. Perhaps it would be better if they forgot the whole thing.

Hugh had been thinking the same. He sighed. "We took an oath, Gaucher," he said. "Once a thing's been sworn to, you can't go back on it."

Gaucher nodded. "I know. I wouldn't break a vow if all the devils and wolves of Hell were following us." He shivered. "It's just that I have the feeling they are."

The only trouble with following the party of the abbot of Cluny was that it moved so slowly. The loaded horses couldn't be forced to hurry. Nor could those who were walking the route barefoot. It would be better to set out ahead of Peter's caravan, but then there was the danger of getting too far ahead and losing the protection of the guards and the extra people.

Solomon, Hubert and Eliazar spent much of the morning debating the matter. Finally, they decided to stay in the rear with most of the other pilgrims, at least as far as Conques. Solomon was worried that they would be stopped on a mountain road at sundown, far from any village, hostel or even likely campsite.

"It's this route I hate," he muttered, looking to be sure Catherine was out of hearing distance. "There'll still be places blocked by snow or treacherous with ice. And not enough grass to feed the horses yet. The monks will have taken all the best of everything before we arrive anywhere. I say we get our own guards and go on ahead. A night in the mountain wind can kill as thoroughly as wolves or bandits can."

Hubert sighed. Solomon's advice should be given more weight than his years would allow. The young man had spent the past ten of them traveling so that Hubert and Eliazar wouldn't need to. It startled Hubert to remember that his nephew was only twenty-six. The lines on his face were from the elements, not age, and perhaps from what he had seen and had been forced to do in order to return alive from his sojourns in alien lands.

"Perhaps farther along we can join a more swiftly moving group," he told Solomon. "When the roads meet at Moissac, it should be easier. For now, you'll simply have to resign yourself to being surrounded by penitents."

Solomon gave him a look that would melt chain mail. Then his face changed as he noticed something over Hubert's shoulder. Hubert twisted his head to see what it was.

"Oh, no," he told Solomon. "Don't even think it. I know you. You're only fascinated by the cloak. Don't be an idiot, boy. Underneath all that she's probably toothless, aged and riddled with disease."

Solomon watched Mondete stride across the open field the lay brothers had camped in. She appeared neither old nor infirm. Nor did she seem meek and remorseful. If anything, there was a tremendous self-assurance in her walk. He did feel pulled to her, but Solomon didn't think it was just the allure of feminine mystery. It was true that he wondered what her face was like, how her body curved under the dark robe. But more than that, he wanted to know how she seemed so certain. What had she discovered that allowed her to move like that, as if there were a path unrolling wherever she stepped, leading her directly to the Truth?

He wanted to talk with her, ask her, make her tell him how to find the Way she followed. It never occurred to him that it might be simple acceptance of faith in Christ. He had seen too many Christian pilgrims. They were humble before their Savior. No. Whoever this woman was or had been, she was taking a different pilgrimage. Solomon desperately needed to know where it led.

Ignoring his uncle's warning, he followed her.

Mondete saw the young man from the corner of her eye. When he had offered his arm to her on the ferry, he had seemed innocent enough, but experience had taught her that the ones who appeared the most guileless could be the most cruel. She increased her speed, then slowed, realizing that it was better for him to catch up to her here in the open, under the eyes of the monks. Without looking back, she could feel him closing in on her.

"Lady."

He sounded out of breath, or frightened. The voice was soft, not what she'd expected. The form of address was one she hadn't heard used without mockery for many years. Not knowing why, Mondete stopped.

Solomon was surprised when she seemed to turn and wait for him. He had gone after her on impulse, drawn without reason. Now that he had to speak to her, he had no idea of what to say.

The sleeves of the robe fell over her hands. The hood was deep, covering her face. Solomon looked at her toes. They were human, at least. He wasn't sure about the rest of her. She stood before him motionless, the spring breeze not even ruffling the folds of her cloak, the sunlight all around but not touching the darkness that was Mondete. He felt that they were no longer on the earth. The order of society had no more meaning.

"Lady," he repeated, "what is your pilgrimage?"

There was a long stillness. Finally, she spoke. "I seek forgiveness, of course." Her voice was tired and full of contempt.

"What do you want God to forgive you for?"

He was startled when she laughed. "Don't you think it's evident?" she asked.

"No."

She was silent again. This dark young man wasn't what she had expected. But that only made her warier. Whatever his devices, he would not trick her into trust. She wrapped her arms tightly around herself, gathering the material in layers against her skin, guarding against him.

"If you don't know what everyone else does, then you're either a fool or even more evil than I," she said. "Now, leave me alone."

She turned and continued on her way.

Solomon watched her. Leave her alone? No. He couldn't do that. He'd heard her voice. That was enough. She knew. He was positive. She had looked outside the world. All the numbers and approximations of truth that the scholars gleaned from the ancient books were irrelevant for her. She had gone past them. If he had to follow her through the ring of fire around the equator and down onto the underside of the globe, he would, until he convinced her to give up her secrets.

"Desfaé mesel!" he cursed himself. He wished again that he had never crossed the Pyrenees or met those men entrapped in the paths of the stars. His life had been so much more pleasant when he had simply thought everyone but himself an idiot and searched the world for nothing more than a good meal, untainted wine, and a warm, soft body next to him in bed.

Catherine had noticed that Solomon was quieter than usual; he hadn't teased her about anything since he arrived. That was most unlike him. But she was too worried about Edgar to concern herself with her cousin. She turned the matter over and over in her mind, her annoying voices making the situation worse with their comments.

He must have known there would be mountains, she thought. *Why didn't he tell me he couldn't do it?*

How do you know he can't? the voices chided.

I've no right to ask him to, Catherine told them. *I'm the one who had the dream, who insisted on taking this route.*

No, you're not. Lord, those voices were smug! Edgar decided. He knew what it would entail. He's giving this offering freely, not just for the children you might bear, but for your own safety as well. Did you ever think he might be afraid of losing you? He wants to do this. Stop whining.

Catherine halted the rabbit chase in her head. Losing her? She hadn't thought of how he would feel if she died. After all, she wouldn't be there to see his grief. Odd. She had always known that if his life ended, so would hers. But what if she were the one to go first? There was a whole other side to this problem to consider.

She went to find him.

He had finished loading the packhorse and was busy whittling a green stick while waiting for the rest of the party to resume the journey. She came up and kissed his cheek.

"Edgar," she said, "what would you do if I died?"

He didn't take his eyes from the stick. "Go home and marry a blonde," he said without a beat.

He looked up and grinned at her. For a second, his smile faltered. That tremble told her all she needed to know.

Catherine grinned back. "I feel the same way about you," she said. "Now, when are we going to leave?"

Edgar sighed. "The abbot's party left some time ago. Your father and uncle told me we would set out with the next group. To be safe, they want at least fifteen people, but not many more."

"I wish that the *jongleur* and *jongleuse* would come with us," Catherine said. "It would be nice to have music on the road."

"I thought you liked my singing," he objected.

"But I've heard all your songs," she answered. "Not that they aren't wonderful, of course. Especially the Saxon ones I can't understand a word of."

"I love you, too," he said.

Catherine decided not to mention mountain roads again.

She got her wish for music, though. When the group assembled for the trip to Conques, the *jongleur* and his wife were part of it. So were the remaining three knights and Griselle of Lugny, along with her guards and maid. There were also four men from Germany who had started out in Spier seven weeks earlier. They came from a village that had been saved from a fire by the intercession of Saint James; the villagers had elected these four to undertake a pilgrimage of gratitude.

Behind them, close enough for safety but too far for conversation, Mondete Ticarde walked alone.

When she noticed Solomon among the party, Mondete had hesitated, then shrugged. She didn't know if he were seeking spiritual or only carnal knowledge from her. It didn't matter. She had no intention of giving him either. As the days passed without any further confrontations, however, she began to study him. She learned early that he and his uncle were Jews, under the protection of Abbot Suger of Saint-Denis and traveling with a Christian merchant and his family. That didn't concern her, although there had been strenuous debate among the other pilgrims on the matter the first day out. If the abbot of Saint-Denis associated with these people, she could, too.

What she couldn't understand was how she could feel him looking at her when she knew he was staring at the road ahead. It infuriated her. He was a boy, really, ten years younger than she, at least. His eyes in his dark face were surprisingly green, and they did not look on her with lust.

Why not?

Mondete forced her thoughts back to her prayers.

Gaucher and Rufus were highly amused to discover that it was Mondete hiding under the hood; it gave the trip some spice.

They both remembered her well from Mâcon. Of course it was wicked to try to tempt someone away from a life of repentance, but they each had privately resolved to try. Rufus was considering wagering with his friend as to who would be first to break her resolve.

"I wonder if she can still ring the bells in her earrings with her toes," Rufus mused as the three knights rode together.

"Of course she can't. She doesn't wear jewelry anymore," Hugh reminded him.

The other two shook their heads. No wonder Hugh's wife had entertained so many troubadours. Gaucher had often thought that she had died of the tedium of having to sleep with Hugh.

"Hersent, I need my gloves."

The men all turned their attention to Griselle of Lugny. She looked straight ahead as she waited for her maid to rummage in the pack. So far, she had spoken little to anyone besides her servants. Gaucher took the opportunity to pull up beside her, cutting in front of Hubert and forcing him to stop as well.

"May I be of service, my lady?" said the knight.

"At the moment, I am capable of putting on my own gloves," she told him. "Should that change, I will remember your kind offer."

He tried again. "I hope the gloves are warm enough. The weather is changeable this time of year. It's been unusually warm, but tomorrow we could have sleet."

Griselle gave him a look reserved for puppies that have not yet learned to contain themselves when held in one's lap. "I have sufficient clothing for the variations in climate," she said. "So unless you are offering to regulate the weather for me, I doubt you can be of use."

"I only wish to serve," Gaucher responded huffily.

"I shall keep it in mind should one of my servants be incapacitated," Griselle said.

She took the gloves from the maid and kicked her horse into movement, leaving Gaucher behind. He returned to his friends.

"I hate widows," he said. "Give them control of a bit of property and they lose all respect."

"Oh, I don't know," Rufus said. "I can remember one or two who showed me a great deal . . . of respect."

It had been impossible for Hubert not to overhear the exchange between Gaucher and Griselle. He had been put to some discomfort to avoid laughing out loud. It was good to hear a woman who could so easily deflate the swollen arrogance of a man like Gaucher. His Catherine had the intelligence to parry words, but not the inclination to humble her opponent. Hubert wondered what a woman like that would say if he approached her. She could probably destroy him in three sentences.

Nevertheless, he was very tempted to find out.

Catherine walked between Edgar and Solomon, each man leading a packhorse. The day, the sixth since they left Le Puy, had been gentle and the road along the river valley, smooth. She felt so content that it seemed wrong. A pilgrimage shouldn't be pleasant.

"We should be in Conques by tomorrow night," Edgar said. "They say the town is built into the side of the hills, like the monastery we stayed at last night."

Catherine gave him a quick appraisal. All the villages here were tucked along the valley, but the monks had chosen to carve their retreats out of the cliffs and perch them far above the rivers. So far, Edgar had shown no discomfort at climbing up to them, but she kept a close watch on him all the same.

"I've always wanted to see the reliquary of Saint Foy," she said. "It's supposed to be covered in jewels."

"I've never understood the penchant you people have for decorating the bodies of your relics," Solomon said.

Catherine fought back her annoyance. Her cousin would never be converted by anger. "It's to honor them," she explained. "Nothing more. Don't you do that to the boxes that hold your holy books?"

He didn't answer. By that alone, Catherine knew she had scored a point. Although . . . she couldn't be sure. Solomon had not regained his former careless attitude. If anything, his mood seemed to deepen every day. He hadn't goaded her into a real fight since the journey began. It was such unnatural behavior from her cousin, whose greatest delight from childhood on had been teasing her into incoherence, that she began to wonder if he were ill.

They camped that night near the priory of Saint Marcel, where the party from Cluny was staying. It was at the end of the Gorges du Tarn, the cliffs jutting up sharply from the Lot River. Tomorrow they would have to turn southeast and cross the Ouche and the Dourdou, following another valley to Conques.

There wasn't much space for them to set up camp. The land sloped upward almost as soon as it left the river. Catherine was pleased that she didn't have to go very far to fetch water. Edgar, Solomon and two of the Germans managed to catch enough fish to feed the party. Eliazar's eyes lit when he realized that Solomon had caught trout and not allowed any of the Christians to touch it. It would be good to have proper food again.

Maruxa and Roberto paid for their dinner with stories. Mindful of the reason for the journey, they recited lives of the saints. Then Maruxa sang the song Mondete had requested: *Jherusalem grant damage me fais.* It had always puzzled Catherine. It was supposed to be a lamentation for the Holy City, but it seemed to be more of a song of lost love. She was well aware that earthly love is only a shallow reflection of divine love and that the terminology of the two were interwoven, but this song seemed firmly rooted in the corporeal. Perhaps she just wasn't spiritual enough. The voices of the singers were passionate:

> *Quant me remembre del douz viare cler*
> *Que je soloie baisier acoler,*
> *Grant merveille est que je ne sui dervee*

Catherine moved closer to Edgar and leaned her head on his shoulder. " 'When I remember your sweet face that I have so often kissed and caressed, it is a wonder that I have not gone mad,' " she repeated. No, it was not religious fervor that she felt. In the darkness, Edgar took her hand and set it on his lap. Catherine smiled. It was evident that he shared her interpretation of the song. She thought of how nice it was that they had found a spot a little away from the others to sleep tonight.

They had climbed to a sheltered ledge surrounded by trees and laid out their blankets. Edgar tied branches together and leaned them against the rock face to protect them should the weather change.

"I don't think it will, though," he said. "Everyone told us it would be freezing and drizzly here, but it's been warmer than Paris."

"Almost anything would be." Catherine had endured her share of springs in Paris and the rheum and chilblains that went with them.

"No one can see us from here. Do you think it's mild enough to sleep without your shift on?" Edgar asked.

Catherine started untying the drawstring at her neck. "As long as you can think of some other way to keep me warm," she told him. "From your reaction to the music, I'm confident you can come up with something."

It was late into the night, between moonset and sunrise, that Catherine awoke to the sound of a great roaring. For a moment, she couldn't remember where she was. The sound was like a thousand waterwheels turning at once. Then from below, there were shouts of alarm. The roaring grew louder. It was coming from farther up the valley, the route they had traveled the day before.

"Edgar, what is it?" she cried as he stood to look.

"Saint Columba's creaking curragh!" Edgar said. "The river! It's pouring out of the gorge. Catherine, stay here." He started down the hillside, pulling his shift over his head as he went.

From below, the sounds of confusion and panic were increasing. People had been awakened by icy water splashing over their faces. Those nearest the river had no chance even to

stand as the sudden rush encircled them, pushing them downstream with the flow.

Catherine struggled into her clothes. "Edgar!" she called.
"Wait! Edgar! Where is my father?"

As she ran down after him, stones and branches cutting her
feet, Catherine tried to think of a saint she could beg for help—
but all she could feel was anger at heaven for its cruel way of
reminding them who was in charge.

Five

At the southern end of the Gorges du Tarn. The cusp of dawn, Saturday, May 2, 1142; The Feast of Saint Athanasius, stubborn bishop and exile.

. . . et simul imbres cadant, flumina increscant, maria sedibus suis excita procurrant et omnia uno agmine ad exitum humani generis incumbant.

. . . and at the same time the rains will fall, the rivers flood, the seas will rush forth wildly from their beds and all as one concerted force will concentrate itself upon the destruction of the human race.

—Seneca, *Naturales Quaestiones*
Book III, 27. 1

*E*dgar, sliding down the hill, had met Hubert hurrying up. "Don't let her follow!" Edgar had yelled. "Where's Solomon?"

"We were all camped on high ground," Hubert panted, "but at the first roar, he leaped up and went off in search of that *jael*. I came to find you. Eliazar is taking care of the horses and moving the luggage up to the priory."

"I don't understand this," Edgar shouted above the roar. "It hasn't been raining. Why should the river suddenly flood?"

"Ask the Almighty," Hubert shouted back.

"After I find Solomon." Edgar continued his slide.

Hubert found Catherine half-dressed, trying to negotiate the slope without falling. He took her firmly by the elbow and led her back up.

"Father, there are people down there who need help," she remonstrated.

"There's little we can do now," Hubert told her. "Those who were carried away in the first rush are beyond our help, and everyone else is wandering about in soggy confusion. We would only add to it."

"Then what is Edgar doing?" Catherine asked, still prepared to descend into the maelstrom.

Hubert hesitated. "Your cousin ran off after that *engieneuse* in the black shroud. Edgar has gone to find him and bring him back."

"Did you see where she was camped?" Catherine asked.

Hubert shook his head, not in denial, but in worry. "Among the rocks at the water's edge," he said. "The dampest, most uncomfortable place possible."

"But then she would have been—" Catherine stopped.

"He won't find her," Hubert said. "It's too late. I tried to tell him. The first rush came like a just-opened millrace, sweeping everything before it; then the force of the water subsided. But it's still high, and slowly rising again. I'm afraid the road up to the priory will be covered by the time there's enough light to see it. However, it's no longer gushing. Don't worry, *ma douce*. Edgar is in no danger, and I hope Solomon has more sense than to jump into floodwaters."

"Then we can only wait." Catherine sat down.

If the emperor of Byzantium had appeared at his side selling the gilded fingertips of Saint John Chrysostom, Hubert could not have been more surprised. Catherine suggesting patience?

"Are you ill, daughter?" he asked.

She looked up at him with a sad smile. "No, Father, and not pregnant again, either. Just intimidated, I think. We tempted fate. We were enjoying something that is supposed to be an act of expiation." She sighed. "But it does seem a cruel trick. Don't you think God could give us more gentle lessons?"

Hubert had no answer for that, so he sat next to her, and wrapping a blanket around her, held her as he had when she was little and he could explain everything.

Abbot Peter had not been awakened by the tumult down below. He had finished saying the Night Office and Lauds with the community of Saint-Marcel and was spending the brief time before Prime going over a copy of the instructions he had left for the management of Cluny in his absence. The cell he had been given was solid against the cliff wall, and no sound from the world intruded.

So he was surprised at the rapid knock at the door and the disheveled appearance of Brother James.

"Are our people all accounted for?" Peter asked when the monk had explained the situation.

"As far as we can tell," Brother James said. "But the pilgrims who camped in the valley are in disarray. Several of them were caught by the flood and carried away. We don't know if they are living yet or not. Some of those who managed to save themselves have lost what little they brought to survive the journey."

"Find out from the prior the state of the supplies of Saint-Marcel," Peter said. "Then you and Brother Rigaud go down and discover the degree of the need. We must at least provide these people with bread. And send Brother Savaric to me."

Brother James left at once and went to fetch Brother Savaric, the almoner. Normally, Savaric handled only the charitable activities of the monastery, but for this trip he had been given charge of all the funds. James explained again what had happened while all those above slept.

Brother Savaric blessed himself. "Those poor souls," he said. "I'm sure we can find enough to clothe them again, at least. I shall consult with the abbot on how the aid may best be distributed. Will you and Brother Rigaud report your findings to me at once?"

"Of course."

Shortly after that, the two monks made their way down the path from the priory to the river. They could see that the current was much stronger than it had been on the previous day. It rushed now over rocks that had provided a place for campfires the night before. From the scum and debris, it was also clear that the water had once been much higher. People were standing in stunned groups or disconsolately scraping the mud from the belongings they had salvaged.

Brother Rigaud was surprised to find that he felt relief upon seeing that Gaucher, Hugh and Rufus were among the survivors. But that relief did not extend to giving a warm welcome when Gaucher rushed up to him.

"We can't find the Lady Griselle!" the knight greeted him. "No one remembers where she was last night. We think she's been drowned."

"If you mean Griselle of Lugny," Brother James told him, "she and her maid were given shelter in the priory guest quarters last night. Her late husband, Bertran, willed all his property to Cluny at her counsel, with the proviso that Lady Griselle be allowed the use of it until her death. We consider that means she is under the protection of the abbey at all times."

"She argued the point most forcefully herself," Brother Rigaud said. "The woman should have been an advocate."

Gaucher's shoulders sagged. He ought to have known that the damned woman would have found herself a dry bed. And the news that her land would go to Cluny at her death was most disappointing. Still, he brightened; she wasn't that old, a few years past thirty, he guessed. A man could spend his last years quite comfortably in her care—if he could get around her cutting tongue, Gaucher reflected as he returned to tell the others.

The monks continued their survey of the damage. They concluded that three people were missing: two of the Germans and the woman known as Mondete Ticarde. Others had suffered some loss of goods or had their clothing soaked in mud, but were otherwise unharmed.

Brother Rigaud approached a man who was helping Maruxa, the *jongleuse*, scrape off her blankets. Next to them, her husband was making a forlorn attempt to blow silt from his pipes. Brother James followed his companion a few paces behind. The man straightened as they came up to him and smiled cautiously through his greying black beard.

Eliazar was used to being polite to monks; he spent enough time dealing with the abbey of Saint-Denis. But new clerics always made him nervous. Sure enough, the second brother gasped in revulsion when he saw Eliazar, averted his face before Eliazar could even get a look at it, then pulled his cowl down to his nose and retraced his steps to get as far away as possible. Brother Rigaud looked after him in puzzlement, then remembered his mission.

"The abbot of Cluny sends his condolences," Rigaud told the three. "He wishes to know what he can do to aid you."

"I and my companions escaped harm." Eliazar said, "but there are others here who could use the loan of dry clothing and some help in cleaning their own."

"We could use a hot meal as well," Maruxa added.

Her husband merely continued blowing glumly into the pipes.

Rigaud finished the rounds of the survivors on the bank. He found Brother James attending to the remaining Germans. "What did you run off for?" Rigaud asked. "I thought we were doing this together."

Brother James pulled Rigaud aside. "Do you think that man saw me?" he asked. "They can curse you with their eyes, you know."

"Who?" Rigaud asked. "The players?"

Brother James lowered his voice to a rasping whisper. "That Jew, of course," he said. "The man with the beard. What is he doing, traveling with honest Christians on a holy mission?"

"Jew?" Rigaud repeated. "Was he? I had heard there were two of them sent by Abbot Suger. I haven't seen them. How did you know what he was?"

"By the smell, of course," Brother James answered. "If Suger is protecting them, there's nothing we can do, but I would stay away from him and his coreligionist. They're dangerous, deceptive people."

"So I've heard," Brother Rigaud answered. "Very well. Have you finished questioning the pilgrims as to their needs?"

"Yes, we can take the list to Brother Savaric at once," Brother James answered. "We should make haste. Charity ought never be sluggardly."

Maruxa gave the blanket Eliazar was holding one last thump with her hand. "There," she said. "I'll beat it again when the mud has dried. That's the best I can do for now. Thank you."

Eliazar helped her fold the blanket. Roberto put down the pipe with a forlorn sigh.

"At least we saved the *vielle*," he said. "That isn't so easy to replace."

"Cheer up, *m'aucel*," Maruxa said. "We have our voices yet, our stories, our hands to keep the rhythm and our feet to dance. We will survive much more easily than others."

"We always do, don't we?" Roberto smiled. "Very well, no more long faces. Although . . ."

All three of them looked at the place where Mondete had been sleeping. The flat rock on which she had lain was just visible under the water.

"Poor thing," Maruxa said, crossing herself. "She had no chance. *Sieur* Eliazar, has your nephew returned?"

"Not yet," Eliazar replied. "I share your fear for the poor woman. Wrapped in that heavy garment, she could not have been able to save herself. But Solomon wouldn't listen. He's obsessed with her. Thinks she's hiding the wisdom of the ages under that cloak."

"How strange," Maruxa said. "I believe that all that lay inside it was Mondete and her sorrow."

Eliazar looked downstream where Solomon had gone and Edgar had followed. He saw no sign of either of them.

"I hope my partner's son-in-law can convince him to come back," he said. "We mustn't delay too long here. Once we're through the gorge and onto the plain, we'll be out of danger from floods."

"Yes," Roberto said. "Then we can return to worrying about wolves and robbers."

Eliazar left them still sorting out their things. He considered going after Solomon and Edgar, but decided that it would simply mean one more person missing. Farther up, he could make out the figures of Catherine and Hubert. Perhaps from their vantage point, they could see if the other two were on their way back. He went to join them.

Edgar had caught up with Solomon easily. His friend was moving slowly along the edge of the water, scanning both banks for some sign of Mondete.

"Solomon, come back with me," Edgar said when they met. "The force of the river was too strong. Everything will have been carried miles downstream. You won't find her, at least not alive."

"I will," Solomon answered. "One way or the other."

"We need your help," Edgar pleaded. "Everything is in confusion."

"It can be nothing to the turmoil I feel," Solomon answered. His eyes never left the water's edge.

Edgar opened his mouth to argue further, but realized that Solomon would not be persuaded by reason. He and his cousin, Catherine, were alike in so many ways. They both believed themselves to be fortresses of rational thought, but all that logic withered when opposed by passion. Passion for a person, an idea, an answer, it didn't matter what. When they were in the grip of it, there was nothing to do except try to protect them from the worst of the consequences they were certain to face.

"Very well," Edgar told Solomon. "The sun has barely raised itself over the edge of the gorge. The road, what's left of it, follows the river. We can still be at Conques by nightfall, where there is a proper pilgrims' hostel. If you don't see us on the road, meet us there. Otherwise, all four of us will come looking for you. You'll have no rebuttal to Catherine's scorn then, nor will I protect you from it."

"Thank you, Edgar." Solomon paused for a moment to take his friend's hand. "If I don't find her by the time the Lot meets the other rivers, I'll know she's lost forever. But I must be sure."

"I don't understand your fascination with this woman," Edgar said.

"Don't say it," Solomon said. "She's nothing but a *jael* who's finally repented her licentiousness, and hides her face only because she's become old and ugly. That's what those old men say, and the Lady of Lugny as well. I don't believe it. And I won't believe she's drowned."

"I never said that you would," Edgar told him. "At Conques by nightfall. Be careful."

As Edgar made his way back, he shook his head at this new madness in Solomon. Up until now, he had thought Catherine's cousin always able to counter his intensity with his logic. Solomon had never studied philosophy but he had long been

a classic cynic, never trusting anything enough to take it seriously. What had happened to him on this last trip to Spain?

Catherine's unnatural display of patience lasted only until the
sun was fully up. By that time, as much order as possible had
been restored and the pilgrims had been fed by the monks of
Saint-Marcel. By the haste in which the parties formed Catherine knew she wasn't the only one eager to leave the narrow valley behind.

"What's keeping Edgar?" Hubert asked. "Solomon
couldn't have been that far ahead of him."

"Perhaps we should start now and meet him," Catherine
suggested.

"No," Hubert said. "Everyone isn't ready yet. Lady
Griselle's men are still loading her packhorses. If he isn't here
by the time the party sets out—"

He stopped. Catherine had spotted the flaxen hair of her
husband among the cluster of people milling about on the road
below. She was halfway down the slope before Hubert could
finish his sentence. He started after her, then noticed that there
was no dark head next to the fair.

Eliazar had found Edgar also, and as Catherine and Hubert
approached, the two men seemed to be having a strong dis-
agreement.

"You should have dragged him back by the belt of his
brais," Eliazar was saying. "Hubert, did you hear this? Edgar
found that idiot and then let him go wandering off like some
poet in a song, hunting for his true love."

"I couldn't force him to return, sir," Edgar said. "And I
don't think he's looking for love, not this time."

"Whatever he thinks it is, a good short yank on the back
of his *brais* would bring him to his senses," Eliazar grumbled.
"I only hope we don't lose days searching the riverbank for
him."

No one was in a better mood as the pilgrims set off again,
this time following closely behind the party from Cluny. There
was little talking and only an occasional mournful toot as

Roberto continued to work on his pipes. As the sun rose higher, many of the party gave off steam when their wool clothing began to dry. They looked like bewildered sinners rescued in the Harrowing of Hell, back in the world but still bearing the stigma of their punishment.

Catherine made no objection when Edgar shifted their packs to Hubert's horse and hoisted her onto their own. She used the vantage point to take an inventory of her fellow travelers.

The two remaining German men were tight-lipped but determined to continue. They agreed that the loss of their comrades was simply part of the price exacted for the saving of their town. To turn back might only bring further disaster. Catherine felt that this was bad theology. But even knowing the correct doctrine on the matter hadn't kept her from a feeling that everything in life was a matter of reward and punishment, of covenant made and honored or covenant broken and betrayed. Like Gaucher, Hugh and Rufus, like the German townsmen, like Mondete, she had taken a sacred oath to complete the pilgrimage. If she failed through her own weakness, she could hardly expect Saint James to make any effort on her behalf.

Catherine sighed and turned her attention to Griselle. Having spent the night in a comfortable guest room at the priory, and having had her hair combed and then braided with ribbons by her maid that morning, the Lady of Lugny looked radiant. Catherine noted her own rumpled clothes and terminally tangled hair and had a brief struggle with envy.

Never mind, her voices told her. *She is a poor lonely widow. You have a perfectly nice husband who's every bit as disheveled as you at the moment. Charity, child.*

Odd how those voices could give her such good advice and still sting with irony. Catherine watched as the "poor lonely widow" refused conversation first with Gaucher, then with that Rufus, his nose as red as his beard had once been. Griselle seemed relieved when Hubert happened to draw up beside her. He said nothing to her beyond a perfunctory greeting, then looked straight ahead as they rode.

Father is more considerate of her than I am, Catherine thought. *It's very kind of him to save her from unwanted attentions.*

As they began to climb the road up to the town of Conques, Catherine tried to keep the worry from growing. They had seen no sign of Solomon when they left the banks of the Lot to follow the ravine of the Dourdou. He wouldn't have followed the river farther. They passed by holes in the side of the limestone cliffs, many as large as doors.

"Father," Catherine called, causing Hubert to start. He had been occupied with thoughts that didn't involve his daughter.

"Father," she said again, "are those hermitages? Could Solomon be in one of them?"

"I don't know why he would have bothered seeking any shelter before nightfall," Hubert answered. "And most of those caves are used to store cheese and wine and suchlike. They're cold and damp all year 'round. Hardly a welcome refuge."

Still, Catherine examined each dark opening carefully as they passed, hoping that her cousin would magically emerge from one of them.

They finished the long climb to the town just before sundown. The golden light was enhanced by the warm sandstone walls and buildings. Despite her worry for Solomon, Catherine felt herself becoming excited at the thought of being able to worship at the shrine of Saint Foy.

Edgar was walking along more briskly as well. Catherine thought it was because of his nervousness on the narrow path along the steep cliff falling to the river below. But then she realized that he was humming and saw that his face was alive with anticipation.

"I didn't know you had a particular devotion to Saint Foy," Catherine said.

Edgar looked up at her, puzzled. "I don't. I have my own saints."

"Then what are you so eager for?" she asked, hoping he would say it was the night ahead with her.

"Haven't you heard about the tympanum here?" He asked.

Of course. Catherine firmly quashed her disappointment.

"It should face west, if the church was built properly," he continued, not noticing her lack of enthusiasm. "If we can get up there just as the sun is setting, that will be the best time to study it."

He startled the horse by pulling on the dangling reins. They moved past the other pilgrims and in among the party from Cluny.

Catherine sighed in resignation. When she first met Edgar, he was a student pretending to be an apprentice stonecarver. But now she knew that the real pretense had been the student. Edgar had been born an artist. It wasn't his fault that he came from a noble family in that almost-mythical Scotland. He had studied, trained to become a cleric, tried to be enthusiastic at the prospect of spending his life as abbot of the family monastery, or Bishop of St. Andrews, but his hands would always search out something to carve: wood, stone, ivory.

Catherine touched the delicate ivory cross at her neck. Edgar had made it for her and been too ashamed to tell her the work was his own. At first she had felt strange about this craftsman's trade that he loved so much. But not anymore. At some point without realizing it, she had come to love him so much that anything he did seemed wonderful to her.

All the same, she wished that it had been the prospect of a night in a real bed with her that had hastened his step.

"I've heard that the Last Judgment is one of the best in France," Edgar said.

Catherine felt a flicker of interest. She had a nebulous memory about the Hell at Conques, a recollection that real people were portrayed on it: abbots who had despoiled the property of the abbey, a lord who had tried to encroach upon land belonging to Saint-Foy. And there were always inventive punishments for the usual run of sinners. She couldn't see the tympanum in the same way Edgar did, but still, it might be worth the visit.

Griselle was suspicious when the merchant from Paris began to ride alongside her. She wasn't inclined to speak to such people . . . although she had heard someone mention that this Hubert LeVendeur had married into a fairly good family of Blois. That might make him acceptable at least as a dinner companion. But what had happened to his wife? Not that it was of any matter to her. Griselle of Lugny had only one desire: to fulfill her husband's unfinished goal, let his anguished soul find satisfaction for the terrible wrongs done to him, and then to join him in Purgatory.

Now, perversely, she wished that Hubert would talk to her.

Gaucher and Rufus amused themselves on the journey with reminiscences, greatly expanded and wildly embroidered, of their years together and nights apart.

"And there were those Saracen twins in Narbonne." Rufus leered at the memory. "Wanted to know if I was as red all over as my beard. What could I do but show them?"

"You slept with Saracens?" Gaucher asked in mock horror.

"Not a wink," Rufus answered.

"Good man," Gaucher said. "Always have to be vigilant with the enemy."

"Sword always unsheathed and ready to attack," Rufus agreed.

Hugh turned to them with a sour expression. "I thought this journey was to do penance for our sins, not to glory in them," he said.

Gaucher and Rufus stared back at him, all innocence.

"We were simply remembering our battles against the infidel," Rufus said.

"All of which were victorious," Gaucher added solemnly.

Hugh snorted and moved away from them, almost knocking over Roberto, who was walking behind him, still fussing with the clogged flute.

"Watch where you're going!" Hugh shouted. "Stupid man."

He stopped and peered down at the startled *jongleur*. "Have we met before?" he asked.

Roberto shook his head decisively. "My wife and I are returning from Troyes," he said. "We joined your party at Le Puy."

"Your wife." Hugh turned his attention to Maruxa, who modestly pulled her scarf closer across her face. "I don't know, both of you seem familiar. Are you sure you never entertained at Grignon? I was castellan there for many years. My wife always had a soft spot for musicians."

"No, never," Roberto said earnestly. "I'm quite sure."

"Strange." Hugh moved on, and a moment later forgot them.

Maruxa lowered the scarf with shaking fingers. "He doesn't remember," she whispered. "He couldn't. Anyway, he never knew the truth. Who would have told him?"

"Saint Vitus's twinkling toes!" Roberto tried to catch his breath. "Yes, I suppose you're right. But I wish now that we'd waited for another party. I don't like having him searching his memory every time he looks at us between here and Astorga."

Maruxa took his hand. "I don't want to wait. I want to go home. Don't worry. We'll simply stay out of his way."

"And how will we do that and live?" Roberto asked her. "What if we're asked to perform again?"

Maruxa thought. "We'll simply have to sing something new and hope that Sir Hugh still has no ear for music."

Between the terror of the previous night and the long journey that day, everyone was moving more slowly up the last steep incline to the gate of the town of Conques. Catherine had dismounted so that the packs could be distributed between the two horses. Even Griselle had consented to walk to spare her palfrey.

The gate was too low to allow a mounted rider admittance anyway. The monks were not so otherworldly as to allow pillagers easy entrance. The pilgrims went in one by one, following the abbot of Cluny, who was being given a ceremonial welcome.

Catherine was so tired that she noticed little of the beauty of the town, built in narrow steps up the side of the cliff, with giant chestnut trees in new leaf casting long shadows over the streets. She just wanted to find a place to wash and rest. The rows of vines along the path they trod gave her hope that the monks might have wine to share.

When they came to the parvis of the church, Edgar gave a cry of delight. Catherine looked up. The tympanum must be everything he had hoped for. She gasped.

In the full light of the setting sun, the images within the porch of the church were incredible. Brightly painted reliefs of Christ giving judgment, the saved sitting demurely at His right hand, the damned doing much more fascinating things at His left.

But Catherine realized that it wasn't the sculpture that had caused Edgar's joy. He wasn't even looking at the tympanum, but beneath it.

For, sitting on the stones beneath the entrance to the church of Saint Foy was Solomon, and sitting next to him, directly under the Mouth of Hell, was the dark shape of Mondete Ticarde.

Six

Conques, just after sundown, Sunday, May 3, 1142; The Feast of the Invention of the Holy Cross.

Hodie misericordia et veritas obviaverunt sibi, et multitudo miserationum Domini in peccatricem feminam refusa est. Filius enim Viriginis, peccatricis et menstruatae manibus attrectatur, Deumque Dei Filium mulier infrunita contingit.

Today mercy and truth have met one another, and the multitude of God's mercies have been poured out upon the woman of sin. For the Son of the Virgin is touched by the hands of a sinning and unclean woman and the unfit woman touches God, the Son of God.

—Nicholas of Clairvaux
Sermon for the Feast of Mary Magdalene
PL 185: 1, 213

I had my eyes on the river and nearly ran into her," Solomon explained to Catherine and Edgar as they sat under one of the chestnut trees and ate the bread given them by the monks. "She was limping along the road in front of me. I don't know how she survived, how she managed to pull herself from the river. Her cloak was soaked. It must have been as heavy as armor."

"She told you nothing?" Edgar asked.

"Wouldn't say a word," Solomon replied sadly. "Wouldn't let me touch her. She's hurt, I know. She must have been badly bruised, at the least. Catherine, can you do something?"

Catherine looked over at the unmoving figure. The people entering the church for Vespers flowed around Mondete as they would a stone in the path. No one bent to speak to her. No one attempted to remove her. Catherine felt a moment's fear that if she tried to touch Mondete, her hand would vanish into the darkness. She shook the thought away as unworthy of her education.

"I'll help her . . . if she'll let me," Catherine told Solomon.

She got up and brushed the crumbs from her skirt to the birds waiting around them. Then she slowly made her way to Mondete. She stopped in front of the figure, hoping that her presence alone would bring some response. Nothing. Catherine knelt and hesitantly laid her hand on the woman's arm.

"Mondete?" she said softly. "My name is Catherine. My husband and I are also pilgrims coming from Le Puy. We thought you had been drowned in the river. It is a wonder you survived. Only a miracle could have saved you from that torrent."

From deep within the folds, Catherine heard a distinct snort.

"Our friend Solomon said that you were limping. You must have been dreadfully battered by the water and rocks," Catherine continued. "I'd like to help you. Are you in pain?"

There was no response at first. Then . . .

"In pain?" Mondete seemed to consider the question from far away. "Yes, young Catherine, I am always in pain. And you cannot help me."

"But," she added as Catherine stood, "you are kind to ask. I was not badly used by the river. My bruises will heal. I have had worse."

"If you wish, you may ride our horse until you're able to walk with more ease," Catherine offered.

There was another silence. Catherine wondered again if there were really a person inside the cloak, or merely shadows and an echo of someone who had once lived.

Mondete rose in one seamless movement. She wavered and a strong brown hand gripped Catherine's shoulder for an instant. "I thank you," Mondete said, "but I am not worthy of your charity. Good night."

With that, she strode, limping only a little, down the main road, then turned left into one of the steep and narrow passageways that led from one level of the town to another.

Catherine returned to Edgar and Solomon. "Maybe you're right about her knowing some great secret," she told Solomon. "I've never encountered anyone so completely still within herself. It's not just the cloak."

She shivered. Edgar got up and put his arm around her. "Let's go on to the hostel while there's light enough to find it," he said. "If we don't get a bed there, we'll have to sleep in the galleries of the church. You need a warmer place than that. You're worn out."

"So are we all," Catherine sighed. "Solomon, don't try to seek out Mondete anymore. She frightens me."

Solomon opened his mouth to protest, then closed it. "Not tonight, anyway," he assured her. "We've barely begun this journey, though. I must have her answers somehow, before it can end."

He kissed her good night and left for the house where he and his uncle had found a room.

Catherine leaned against Edgar. "Solomon frightens me, too," she said. "He seems almost a stranger now. Oh, Edgar, you won't change when I'm not looking, will you?"

He smiled at her. "Shape-shifting is not one of my talents, *leoffaest*. And even if it were, the old story says that the shifter can never change in the eyes of the one who holds his heart."

Catherine's body relaxed in his hold. She turned her face up to his. "Will you tell me that story tonight, before we go to sleep?" she asked.

"The ending is sad," he warned her.

"Then tell me only the happy parts," she answered, "and I'll finish it my own way as I dream."

If she dreamt that night, Catherine didn't remember it. She awoke with her cheek against Edgar's warm back and feeling perfectly happy. She reached around to tickle him. He grabbed her hand as it moved.

"I'm already awake," he whispered.

"Do you think anyone else is yet?" she whispered back hopefully.

Around them, a general rustling destroyed their hopes.

"Oh, well." Catherine reached for her shift and wiggled into it under their blanket. Then she got up and felt for her *bli-aut*. As she picked it up, she heard a soft thump. She looked down at the floor and squealed.

"Edgar! A rat!" She kicked at it, and it rolled a little. "It's dead!"

By now everyone in the room was looking at Catherine, half-dressed, her hair tangled, poking at a dead rat with her bare toe. She glared back at them.

"Whoever did this, it's not funny!" she said.

There was a chorus of indignant denial. Edgar, by now having pulled on his *brais* and thrown his shift over his head, bent down to examine the corpse.

"There's a piece of something in its mouth," he said. "It looks the same color as your *bliaut*."

Catherine didn't want to get any closer to the rat. Instead, she examined the hem of the *bliaut*. There was a stain on one section of it, a reddish brown, like wine or blood. In the center of the stain, a hole had been gnawed out. Catherine looked from the hole to the rat.

"Do you think it was killed because it ate the stain on my skirt?" she asked, showing the fabric to Edgar.

He looked at it and then at the rat. "Well, Catherine, you do step in some odd things," he said at last. "Never mind. The monks should thank us for ridding the hostel of one more bit of vermin. I'll throw it in the midden. Then I want another look at the carvings on the church."

The town and the monastery at Conques had been maintained for pilgrims ever since the body of Saint Foy had been brought there almost three hundred years before, through the agency of Saint Foy herself and the stealthy cunning of the monks who stole her from her original home. The site of Conques was so difficult to reach and hard to keep supplied that it was only the determination of the pilgrims to pray at the shrine of the saint that allowed the monastery to continue in prosperity. In more recent times, Conques had become an established stop on the way to Santiago de Compostela. Shopkeepers reminded visitors of this with scallop shells carved over their doorways, and pins, honeycakes and felt badges in the same design for sale at their stalls.

Catherine wanted a pin, even though Edgar said it was poorly made and would fall apart in a month. "When we get to Compostela, you can have a real scallop," he promised, "with the cross of Saint James painted on it. I'll even get you one made from silver, to hang around your neck."

"Very well," she answered. "We can put it on a hook above our son's cradle, to keep him safe."

Edgar's jaw clenched. Ever since Master Abelard had interpreted Catherine's dream, she had been calmly certain that it would come true as long as they followed the Way of Saint James to the end. He wished he could be so sure. Edgar didn't like the icy fear that touched him when he thought of what might happen to Catherine if the journey proved fruitless, in every way.

"Why don't we just buy a candle today?" he suggested. "And leave it in thanksgiving for surviving the flood."

"That's a good idea," Catherine said. "I've been thinking about that. I have formulated a theory as to how such a sudden inundation might have happened."

"Really?" One eyebrow rose in amused doubt. "Pray, Master, expound."

"Great minds must become used to scoffers," she answered, then spoiled her dignity with laughter. "I would tell you eventually, so you may as well resign yourself to listening now."

"You have my complete attention," Edgar said as he paid for the candle and they moved on to the next stall.

"Well—" she took a deep breath "—as I recall, the mountains all around Lyon were still covered in snow. When we reached Le Puy four days later, the snow did not come as far down the mountains. Now, it seems to me that several people commented on how unusually warm it has been this spring. The snow melts into the rivers. In the warmth, it may have done so more rapidly than usual. The water behind dams and mill-races would then rise more quickly. What if someone upstream did open a millrace, or the rush of the snow water was too much for a dam—wouldn't that cause a sudden overflow of the river, even without rain?"

She waited. Edgar pursed his lips. "I suppose it could," he said at last. "Where did you get the theory?"

"Some part-Seneca, some part-Marius, some part from the evidence of my own eyes," Catherine answered.

"They're beautiful eyes," Edgar said.

Catherine smiled. "You can't think of an argument to refute me, can you?"

He was spared the ignominy of admitting her right by the arrival of Hubert.

"I have consulted with the rest of the party that came with us from Le Puy," Hubert told them. "We are all agreed to stay together for now and leave as a group when the abbot does, to-morrow morning."

"Good," Catherine said. "If we have a whole day in one place, I'm going to try to find a trough to wash shifts in."

Edgar was already heading for the church.

"He can spend every moment of daylight just studying the carvings in there," Catherine told her father, looking after Edgar fondly.

Hubert sighed. This desire to work with his hands—mak-ing carvings like some journeyman—wasn't appropriate for a man of Edgar's background. Ah, well. He was young yet. Per-haps he would outgrow it. But Hubert had no intention of en-couraging his son-in-law in such foolishness.

"My favorite torment in the Hell is the poacher being roasted by the rabbits," Catherine continued. "What's yours?"

"I hadn't thought," Hubert answered, startled. "I didn't re-ally notice."

"What's the matter, father?" she asked. "Something is wor-rying you."

"The journey," he said too quickly. "Your safety. Solomon's strange behavior. I have many things to occupy my mind."

"Of course," she answered, not quite believing him, al-though the reasons he gave were quite enough.

Griselle of Lugny passed by on her way to the church, ac-companied by her maid and guards and followed by Gaucher and Rufus. Behind them, Hugh trailed, looking exhausted. Catherine wondered if any of the knights would survive the pil-grimage. They all three seemed less robust than even the week before, and the most difficult part of the journey was still be-fore them. The death of their friend must have disturbed them more than they acknowledged.

"It's disgusting the way those men drool over her," Hubert

said as Griselle stopped to adjust her veil and both the knights hurried up to her to offer assistance.

Catherine laughed. "I doubt she's in any danger from them. The Lady Griselle seems well able to manage men."

"Yes," Hubert agreed, "she does."

Catherine caught an odd tone in his voice, but as she opened her mouth to ask him what he meant, he changed the subject.

"How much money did you have changed?" he asked. "What's the state of your shoes? Eliazar says the cobblers here charge too much. You can do better in Figeac, if they'll last that far."

They began to discuss mundane matters attendant on any journey, and Catherine forgot to question her father concerning the Lady Griselle.

Hugh of Grignon was not interested in joining the chase for the person and property of Griselle of Lugny. He had had enough of that when his wife was alive. Most of his land had been settled on the two older sons that he knew were his, and the rest of the children she had presented him with had been parceled off to convents, monasteries or useful marriages. What little property he had left, he had deeded to Saint Peter for the good of his soul.

He should have retired to Cluny at the same time, he thought; but he had been coerced to come on the trip by Norbert's persuasiveness and the feeling that there was another reason the old knight wanted to return to Spain. This pilgrimage plan was nonsense. Hugh didn't believe he had been that evil in his life. Not for the past thirty years or so, anyway . . . and before that, only in the way all warriors are. Nothing God would have much minded, he reasoned. Nothing, except that boy.

Hugh shuddered. Why should he remember that now? It was so long ago and in another country. And almost everyone who had been there was dead.

"Hugh!" Gaucher called. "We're going to negotiate with

the monks here for a jug or two of better wine. Do you want
some?"

For a moment, Hugh couldn't remember where or when
he was. His mind had leaped in panic to another time, when
Gaucher had suggested much the same thing with terrible results.

"No," Hugh answered. "I don't mind the wine they give us
with our bread."

"You would if you knew what they made it from," Rufus
laughed. He stopped. "Hugh, what is wrong with you? You've
been even more gloomy than usual today."

Hugh caught up with his friends, who had left Griselle to
her devotions. He waited until they were on the path to the cave
where the monks stored the wine and safely above anyplace
where someone might overhear.

"I found something in my pack last night," he whispered
to them.

"I hope it wasn't as messy as what was left in mine at Vézelay," Gaucher said.

"No, but more frightening to me," Hugh answered.

He reached into his pilgrim's scrip and drew out a ring. It
was made of gold and had once had been set with a large stone.
Now there was only a gaping hole in the metal, like a missing
tooth. They all three stopped to look.

"Why would anyone give you a ring without a stone in it?"
Rufus asked.

"Don't you remember?" Hugh answered. "Either of you?"

He held out his left hand. On the first finger was another
ring of gold. This one had a large rough-cut emerald in it.

"Oh, yes," Rufus said. "That's right. You got the ring as
booty, but you took only the stone. I've forgotten why. But this
can't be the ring it came from originally."

"I would swear it is," Hugh said. "Gaucher was right. Some
one of our old enemies is stalking us. He's taunting us with
signs from our past."

"That's nonsense," Rufus said. "What has an empty ring
to do with pig parts? And who here would know anything

about us? Do you even remember where you got that emerald?"

"In Spain," Hugh said softly, seeing it all again. "At the siege of Saragossa. Fighting the Saracens."

"There," Rufus said in triumph. "And you think some Saracen lord has decided to go on pilgrimage with us?"

Gaucher had been listening with amusement to Hugh's tale, but now his forehead creased in worry. "Why not?" he asked. "The men in the party of Bishop Stephen . . . have we really looked at them? Many of them are Mozarabic Christians. I can't tell them from Saracens, can you?"

"Who would know we would be traveling with the Cluni-acs?" Rufus protested. "And anyway, I didn't see any of them at Vézelay. I tell you, someone dropped the ring into Hugh's pack by accident. Someone else thought to play a stupid joke on Gaucher. The events have nothing to do with each other. Ever since Norbert died, the two of you have jumped at every shadow."

Hugh did not appear convinced, but Gaucher straightened his shoulders and shook his white-and-golden hair like a lion rising to hunt. "We are going back to the places of the deeds of our youth," he said. "Our minds are much in the past. It's not surprising that the past should awake to greet us. Whichever, I do not intend to turn coward at this time of my life. I am continuing to the end of the journey, whatever it may be."

Rufus looked at him sourly. "That's the sort of speech I'd expect from Hugh here. Why don't you just say, 'Damn all the bastards. We don't surrender'—like you did at Saragossa?"

Gaucher threw his head back and laughed. "You're right, *vieu compang*. Damn them all! On to Saint James!"

Catherine had found a place to wash their shifts and stockings as well as certain other articles necessary to women. She hung them in the sun from a branch of the tree by the church and went to sit next to Edgar, who had been cross-legged before the figures on the tympanum all morning.

"One of the townswomen told me that they might have a display of the relics tonight in honor of the abbot of Cluny," she remarked. "I'd like to see Saint Foy outside of the grillwork in the church. They say her reliquary is exquisite. And, of course, I want to venerate her from as close as possible."

Edgar nodded, not really hearing. "If only I had a scrap of parchment and a pen," he lamented. "I don't know if I can remember it all clearly."

"You will; you always do," Catherine said as she studied the work. "I think I know who all the damned are. But I can't recognize all the saved. They look too much alike. There's Charlemagne, I suppose, and those others must be his family. And some hermit with Saint Peter, and the usual assortment of local martyrs. I wonder who that is in the corner."

"Arosnide," said a voice from over her shoulder. "The monk who went to Agen to steal Saint Foy and bring her to Conques."

Catherine turned and saw Roberto and Maruxa, their *vielles* as usual in leather cases strapped to their backs.

"The sculptor should have given him a more prominent place," the *jongleur* added, "considering the prosperity he brought to the town."

"But only through the kindness of Saint Foy," Catherine said. "And she isn't here at all, is she?"

"Yes, she's kneeling there, see? Have you found the angel who speaks Arabic?" Maruxa asked.

That got even Edgar's attention. "Where?" he asked.

They pointed to one of the angels on whose wing there were lines that Catherine had assumed were decoration.

"It is said that a number of workmen came from Spain to help with the building of the church," Roberto told them. "Some were Moslem, although they didn't mention it. One of them left that."

"How do you know?" Edgar asked.

"What is he saying?" Catherine asked at the same time.

"I can't read it," Roberto admitted, "but I've seen the same design in my travels and been told that it means something like 'May Allah bless and keep you.' "

"Is Allah one of their gods?" Catherine asked.

"That's their name for the one God," Roberto said.

"I thought they worshiped many gods: Mohamet, Apollo, others I don't remember," Catherine said.

"No, just the one," Roberto told her. "Our beliefs confuse them as well. They think we have many gods because of the shrines to the saints. And they can't understand the idea of the Trinity."

"Where did you learn all this?" Catherine asked.

Maruxa put her hand on her husband's arm in warning. "We travel many places, wherever we are paid," she explained. "Years ago we visited some of the courts of the caliphate. Other entertainers told us stories. We live by stories. It's important to have new ones from time to time."

"It's also important to know something of the beliefs of the people you travel among," Roberto added. "Tread on a local custom and you can find yourself dead."

They all returned to the contemplation of the figures over the doors.

"That knight falling off the horse there," Maruxa said. "Is he supposed to be Anger?"

"Pride, I think," Catherine told her.

"I've never seen anyone fall in that position," Roberto said. "With his head down and his legs straight out. And the way the demon with the spear is aiming, it looks as though he's about to be spitted right up his—"

Maruxa kicked him. Roberto looked at Catherine in apology. Catherine sighed. "What is it about me?" she asked. "I know where the spear is pointed. You don't need to be delicate."

"We heard you were from the convent," Maruxa explained. "A few days on the road and no one has secrets anymore."

"Except Mondete Ticarde," Catherine said.

There was another silence.

"There's no secret to her life," Maruxa said at last. "She was concubine to a lord who eventually tired of her. He passed her on and on and on, until she ended on the streets of Mâcon. But that's only the outside. What she is now and why she's with us, that is a mystery."

"Not one, I think, that will soon be unraveled," Roberto said.

Catherine sighed. She only wished Solomon would agree.

The next morning was startling in its brightness. Catherine awoke with her mind still glowing from the candles around the golden reliquary of Saint Foy the night before. When she came out of the hostel, the sunlight hit her with a harshness that made her want to duck back inside.

Edgar had much the same feeling. "Your uncle said we should get wide-brimmed felt hats in Moissac for the journey into Spain," he said, "but perhaps we should buy them now."

Catherine agreed. "I'm not used to the world this bright," she complained. "It hurts my eyes."

The hats made her laugh. They both looked silly in them, like peasants in the vineyards. But the shade hers gave was enough to stop her from squinting. And she needed to see the way clearly as they descended to the valley, crossed the still-high Dourdou and then climbed up the other side.

At the old chapel of Saint Roche, the party stopped for water. Looking back across the valley, Catherine could see the town of Conques. It seemed so remote, as if it had sprouted buildings and trees out of the rock the night before.

"Edgar," she said, her gaze roaming the hills and woods around them, "I wonder if the sunlight is affecting my mind. I keep feeling that we've wandered into one of your stories and that dragons and giants will suddenly swoop out of the forest, or that half-human trees will begin to sing and lure us from the path."

Edgar was doing his best to avoid looking at the view that so enchanted his wife. He wished Catherine would stay farther from the edge of the road. There was no need to imagine dragons. In one form or another, they were all around him.

Solomon, passing by, pulled the reins of her horse, bringing Catherine back to the center of the path. "There are no dragons in France anymore," he said with certainty. "Your saints drove them all away. But there are still wolves and wild boar and wilder men. So stop dawdling, Catherine."

Instead of being annoyed, Catherine rejoiced at Solomon's querulous tone. That was more like her cousin's usual mood. Perhaps the sunlight had awakened him from his fascination with discovering the secret of the universe.

The mild weather, and the fact that they were well above the river now, seemed to raise everyone's spirits. Maruxa and Roberto played a dance tune from their region that made even the horses move more briskly. The three elderly knights were telling stories of their exploits, each tale grander than the last, to any who came near enough to listen. Occasionally one of them would glance at the Lady Griselle, to be sure she hadn't moved out of hearing distance. The two remaining Germans were enthralled and begged for more.

Behind them, Hubert and Eliazar rode intent on their own conversation. If they approached the knights too closely, Hubert would give a sour look and slow down until they had dropped back.

Ahead of them all was the splendor of the entourage of the abbot of Cluny. At the very end as usual, Mondete walked alone.

Solomon seemed to have learned his lesson. Every now and then he checked to be sure the woman hadn't fallen too far behind. But he offered no help. Neither did anyone else.

By that afternoon the party had reached another meander of the Lot River. By common consent, they went a few more miles until the plain broadened and they found an area well away from the water to camp. As Catherine shook out their blankets, getting rid of the last of the dried mud, she thought how strange it was that such a short time ago they had all nearly been swept away by raging waters. Yet now they were in another place behaving as if it had been years ago.

It was something about the pilgrimage itself, she realized. She and Edgar were going in the hope of life, but so many others—the knights, Mondete, the German townsmen, even Griselle—were prepared for death. If they escaped it today, there was always the chance it would meet them tomorrow. Therefore, Catherine reasoned, disaster must not affect them the way it would if it had occurred on their doorsteps.

In the convent, Mother Héloïse had scoffed at those who went great distances to reach the shrines of saints or the sites of the passion of Christ. Life was enough of a pilgrimage for her. Staying in one place when her whole being longed to be somewhere else was as arduous as anything that might face them on the way to Compostela.

At least Catherine hoped so. They had barely begun the journey and already three people had died. By Solomon's reckoning, it would take two more weeks at least to reach the other side of the Pyrenees and another four or five weeks before they arrived at Compostela. And then, *Deo volente*, there would be the long road home.

"What have I got us into?" she murmured.

Fortunately, her musings were interrupted by Edgar. "Catherine!" he called. "Come down here. You have to see this. Maruxa and Roberto can walk on their hands!"

Catherine decided to worry later.

Maruxa had tied her skirts up the middle with her scarf, making billowy pants to tumble in. Roberto caught her heels as she turned upside down and then vaulted her over his shoulders. She landed in a somersault, then sprang to her feet to cheers from the group circled around them. Even some of the monks had come from the separate camp of the abbot to watch.

The noise finally reached the Lady Griselle, resting in the tent her guards had set up for her. She sent her maid to find out what was happening. When she and then the guards didn't return, Griselle decided to go see for herself.

As she left the tent, she was startled to find a man at her side, offering his arm. Not Gaucher or Rufus, but that merchant, Hubert. Her first impulse was to ignore him. Then she looked at his face and changed her mind.

"Thank you," she said, in a voice no one had heard since her husband died. "It's kind of you to help me."

"I am honored to be of service to you," Hubert answered.

They said no more until they reached the place where the *jongleurs* were performing. Then Hubert lowered his arm, bowed and left her to rejoin his family.

"That was very thoughtful of you, Father," Catherine said. "All her servants had deserted her."

Eliazar was more observant. He waited until the performance was over, then took his brother aside. "Are you mad?" he asked quietly. "Her guards will kill you, if those idiot knights don't. And what will your daughter think, you and that woman while Catherine's mother is still alive? You have a wife; it doesn't matter to the others that she's shut up in a convent."

"Eliazar, I only gave the lady my arm, not my soul," Hubert answered.

Eliazar wasn't convinced. "The least you could do is find a nice Jewish widow," he muttered.

"If we meet one taking a pilgrimage to Santiago, I'll offer her my arm as well," Hubert promised.

Eliazar spat on the ground. "Between you and that nephew of ours, I'll not survive this trip and then you can have my widow, if you want one so badly."

Hubert sighed. He reflected, as Catherine had, that the journey had scarcely begun. He, too, wondered just what he had got himself into.

The moon was near to setting when Catherine opened her eyes. The Milky Way, the *Via Lactea* of the Romans, arched across the sky, a pathway leading to the shrine of Saint James. Catherine would have liked to lie quietly under its glow, but she knew what had wakened her. Just once she'd like to sleep through a night without having to find a chamber pot. As she started to get up, she remembered where she was.

"Oh, no," she moaned.

There was nothing for it. She'd have to find a nice clump of bushes and hope the grass wasn't too prickly. At least the night was chilly enough that she was sleeping in her clothes.

She eased out from under the blanket, trying not to let the cold air in to awaken Edgar, and stumbled to the edge of the campsite. She found a hollow fairly well sheltered from wind and the eyes of anyone awake, checked the slope, raised her skirts and squatted.

That was when she heard something in the bushes.

Her first thought was that it was a wild animal. The growl sounded a bit like a wolf's. A small, not very fierce wolf. A wolf making funny, high-pitched yips in the back of its throat. A wolf that said, "Oh, oh, yes, more . . . more! Ohhh . . ."

Oh, dear.

Catherine considered her options. She was hardly in a position to sneak away. Waddle, maybe. No, she wasn't even sure she could do that. She really couldn't stay like this much longer. She had waited too long before getting up in the first place. She vowed that she would stop drinking wine in the evening, but it was too late for that now. As she let go, she hoped the couple wasn't downhill from her.

They didn't seem to notice anything. As Catherine started to ease herself up, the man gave one last, gurgling cry and then was silent.

Catherine crouched again.

After a moment, she heard the rustle as someone made a path out of the thicket. Through the branches, Catherine caught a glimpse of a dark, hooded figure.

No wonder Mondete didn't think she deserved my charity, Catherine thought with a stab of disappointment. *She hasn't repented her life at all.*

She was terribly curious as to who the man was. He hadn't appeared yet, probably waiting until Mondete was safely back to camp. Then it struck her that it might be Solomon. It hadn't sounded like him, but the voice had been muffled.

Catherine didn't want to know. She couldn't face her cousin after hearing that cry. On reflection, whoever it was, it would be hard to look at that person in the same way again.

Not caring anymore if she were heard, Catherine backed out of the clump of bushes and hurried across the field to the comfort of her warm husband.

The next morning, Catherine wasn't sure if she had been dreaming, but the bits of grass on her feet indicated that at least part of the experience had been real. She thought of telling

Edgar, but it didn't seem right. It was Mondete's salvation that was at stake. She would just have to find a time to try to discuss it with the woman privately.

The thought was not appealing.

They had finished packing and loading the horse for the day in a pattern that was becoming increasingly routine when they heard a commotion from the other side of the camp. Along with everyone else, they hurried to see what it was.

The shouting grew louder as they approached; then there was a wail of grief that tore at Catherine's ears and heart.

"NO. . . !" The one word seemed to go on forever, and then to echo across the plain . . ."NO. . . !"

Then she realized that there were two cries, lamenting together.

She couldn't see over the heads of the people, but Edgar was tall enough. "What is it?" she asked him.

"Gaucher of Mâcon and Rufus of Arcy," Edgar said. "They're the ones screaming. Move, Catherine, they're coming this way, carrying something."

Catherine moved aside as Gaucher and Rufus came out of the thicket, carrying the body of Hugh of Grignon.

She didn't want to look. She wasn't going to look. She looked anyway. She had to know.

This wasn't a natural death. Hugh's throat had been cut wide open.

Involuntarily, Catherine's hand went to her own throat. It appeared that now she would have to tell someone about Mondete Ticarde.

Seven

Near Figeac, Wednesday, May 6, 1142; The Feast of Saint John before the Latin Gate, on the occasion of his surviving a bath in boiling oil previous to his exile on Patmos.

Deus qui diligentibus te misericordiam tuam semper impendis et a servientibus tibi in nulla es regione longincus, dirige viam famulorum tuorum illorum in voluntata tua, ut te protectore et te perducente periusitie semitas sine offensione gradiantur.

O God, you who always grant your mercy to those who love you and are in no place far from those who serve you, direct the paths of these servants of yours in your will, so that they may, without offense, walk the paths of justice with you as their guide.

Liturgy of the Pilgrimage
Missal of Vich 1038

*V*enerable Father." Brother James bowed to Abbot Peter. "It grieves me to have to report this, but there was a murder last night among the pilgrims. One of the men wandered only a little away from the campsite and was apparently set upon by brigands. The others are in a panic. They're begging you to allow them to travel among us under the protection of our guards rather than following behind."

The abbot considered the information, his forehead creased in thought. "Brigands, you say?" he asked. "Didn't the pilgrims set a watch?"

"They say they did," Brother James answered.

"Yet no one saw or heard the men who attacked their comrade?"

Brother James had just dealt with a crowd of hysterical people, all talking at once and all apparently thinking it was up to him to do something. He hadn't stopped to ask many questions.

"I don't know, Lord Abbot," he answered. "No one mentioned it. His companions say he was robbed, however."

"His companions might have killed and robbed him themselves," Peter suggested. "Was the murdered man a dependent of Cluny?"

"I'm afraid so," Brother James sighed. "His name was Hugh of Grignon. He deeded us property and two mills for his soul and that of his wife and asked for burial among us."

"Well, that won't be possible now," Peter answered. "See to it that he's taken to our priory at Figeac and buried there. If his relatives protest, tell them that the honor is the same. Saint

Peter will hear their prayers whether the man lies in the Au-
vergne or in Burgundy."

"And what of the guards for the pilgrims?" Brother James
asked.

Peter studied his fingers for a moment. "There are several
women in that group," he said at last. "More than usual and
younger than usual. I will need some sort of guarantee that they
not be allowed to wander among the monks or lay brothers. If
they swear to that, tell the pilgrims they may camp within the
circle of our guards. Tell two of the guards to ride behind
them, but only if the pilgrims can keep up with us. We can't
wait for people determined to make the trip on their knees."

"Thank you, Lord Abbot." Brother James bowed again. He
turned to go.

"Brother James," Abbot Peter added.

The monk turned back. "Yes, Lord Abbot?"

"I want you to be sure that this was done by robbers from
the woods and not by other members of the party. Aren't there
also two Jews among them, with a letter from our friend, Abbot
Suger?"

"This is true, my lord," Brother James said. "I've seen
them. But devious as those people are, I can't believe they
would be so stupid as to commit murder like this. They know
they would be among the first suspected."

"It may have been done in anger," Peter said. "The man
might have insulted one of their practices or reneged on a debt.
Or, as I said, his own companions may have killed him and
placed the blame on brigands. Or, finally, it may be just as it
appears, a killing for gold by the outlaws in the forest. I rely
on you to discover the truth of the matter. Get Brother Rigaud
to help you."

Brother James reflected that the venerable abbot did not
suggest how he was to find the truth. But all the monk said was,
"Thank you, Lord Abbot. With God's help, it shall be done."

Catherine stewed all morning, trying to decide what to do. Perhaps the person she had seen wasn't Mondete. She had had
only a glimpse of a cloak in the night. She had assumed it was

the prostitute on the basis of the activity she had overheard. Or, Catherine considered, the man with the woman might not have been Hugh. She didn't know when the knight had been killed. He might have come to the bushes sometime later for the same purpose Catherine had and been attacked then. If the brigands had come up quietly behind him, he might have had no time to call for help. And who went armed to the privy?

But, she flipped again, there was that awful gurgling sound. Catherine's experience was limited, but she didn't think the sound was normal in carnal activity. Edgar never gurgled. The rustlings she had listened to from dark corners and through bed curtains when she was a child had never ended in gurgling. Occasionally in gasps, giggles and moans that made her curious, but nothing worse.

And what about the blood? If he had been on top of Mondete and she slit his throat, then the woman would have been awash in gore. She couldn't have just casually gone back to her pallet and to sleep . . . unless she had simply wrapped herself up in the cloak.

Saint Ida's arrogance! Why did she have to think of that? Catherine realized that she didn't want Mondete to be a murderer, or a whore either, for that matter, for Solomon's sake, if not for the woman's own. Still, the questions had to be reasoned out logically. It wouldn't do to accuse someone unless she were very certain. But if she were certain, then her duty was clear.

There was only one way to know. She went to find Mondete.

Pilgrimages don't stop long for death. Once the body has been cared for and prayers said, it's necessary to move on. When a vow has been made to visit the saints, it cannot be broken and ought not be delayed. Therefore, the pilgrims were already preparing to continue the journey, albeit with more seriousness and a greater sense of dread than before.

Mondete, having less to pack than anyone else, was sitting on a stone in the field, waiting. Not far from her, seated on the grass, was Solomon. He didn't notice Catherine coming up behind him.

"Some of it is in Ezekiel and Isaiah," he was saying, "but other parts of it have been passed down from master to pupil for a thousand years. Only, no one seems to have the whole of it. I can only find pieces, and they won't fit together."

Mondete made no response. She may have thought that if she ignored Solomon, he would get tired and go away. Catherine knew him better than that.

"You've found a sliver of the Truth, all on your own," Solomon continued. "If you tell me what it is, I might be able to finally make the picture whole. You may have the piece of knowledge I've been looking for."

Mondete swung around on the rock. Catherine tried to see if her cloak was stained with blood, but there was so much dirt from the road and dried mud from the river that it was impossible to tell. The woman raised her hands in exasperation. Her nails were long and filthy, but Catherine saw no trace of blood there, either. She didn't think Mondete could have washed herself enough to remove any signs of murder and yet leave her nails like that.

If Mondete saw Catherine staring at her, she gave no indication of it. All her attention was on Solomon.

"What must I do to convince you that I have no secrets?" she asked. "I am only what they say I am, a *bordelere* and a *meretrix*, who would spread her legs or anything else for anyone with money, including you."

Solomon wasn't impressed. "Then why are you here?" he asked. "What happened to change your life?"

Mondete dropped her hands. "Others will tell you that, too. Perhaps I got too old, or became diseased. Perhaps I smelled the sulfur of Hell in some man's sweat and suddenly feared for my soul. What difference does it make to you?"

Solomon rubbed his forehead as if it ached. He closed his eyes tightly, then opened them again. "I don't know," he said quietly. "It just does. I don't wish to torment you. But there is something; I feel it. You may not even be aware of what it is."

"You're wrong," Mondete answered. "You sense nothing more than desolation. That's all I can give you, and *I* sense that you already have enough of that of your own."

Solomon didn't answer. Nor did he move. Mondete pulled her hands and feet back inside her cloak.

Catherine decided not to bother them now.

"The rings are gone, Gaucher," Rufus said. "I looked in his pack and his scrip. Nothing else is missing." His voice was shaking in panic.

"The thieves may not have had time to take more," Gaucher answered. "Stop trembling so. You look like a man with quartan fever."

Rufus bridled in anger. "Don't pretend you're not afraid, Gaucher. I saw your face when we picked up poor Hugh."

Gaucher looked away, then back. His face was stern. "It's hardly the first time we've seen a man with his throat cut, or a friend slaughtered," he said firmly. "We've become soft living in our keeps with no real fighting to do."

"First Norbert, now Hugh," Rufus said. "Pig balls in your pack and that ring. I can see Hugh prizing the stone out even now. He broke a blade-tip on it. But I can't remember the hand it was on."

"It doesn't matter," Gaucher insisted, running his hands through his hair. "We're the only ones alive who were there then."

"How do you know?" Rufus asked. "Anyway, you're forgetting Rigaud, if you can call what he's doing now living."

"I don't think he slipped out of his cloister and came down here on the chance that Hugh would pick that moment to empty his bladder," Gaucher sneered.

"I don't mean that he killed old Hugh," Rufus answered. "Only that there could be someone else, maybe one of the guards or the lay brothers. You said there could be a Saracen hidden among the men Bishop Stephen brought with him."

"I don't know anymore what to think or who to fear," Gaucher sighed. "But we have to go on, are we agreed on that?"

"Yes," Rufus said. "But I'm wondering now, if we can even find it after so long, maybe we shouldn't try to sell it. It might be better for our souls if we simply gave it back or made an offering of it to Saint James."

"Don't go on about your soul, Rufus," Gaucher answered. "It's too late for that. Norbert spent years preparing for this. We aren't going to fail him now."

Edgar had been waiting impatiently for Catherine. "What kept you?" he asked. "Your father and Eliazar are ready to set out."

"Is Solomon with them?" she asked.

"No, but he'll catch up; he always does," Edgar said. "I was worried about you. Are you all right?"

"Yes," she said. "No. I don't know. I'll tell you all about it tonight."

Edgar knew that mood. He didn't press her. "We'll be in Figeac by evening," he said. "We can get our shoes resoled and maybe find a private corner with a mattress."

Catherine smiled. He always knew how to cheer her. "Even more, I'd like to find a bathhouse," she said, fingering her greasy braids. "The only thing good about having hair this filthy is that the curl is pulled out of it. Your hair could use washing as well, you know. I would be happy to do yours at the same time as my own."

Edgar smiled. Catherine had ways of cheering him, too.

Brother James was shocked by Brother Rigaud's reaction to the news of the murder.

"You knew the man?" he repeated. "Why didn't you tell me that you'd fought alongside Hugh of Grignon?"

"Why should I?" Rigaud answered. "It's from a life I wish to forget. I renounced all of that when I took my vows. Do I ask you about what you were before you came to Cluny?"

"I've never made a secret of it," James bridled.

"Nor did I," Rigaud said. "But I saw no reason to give all the names of the men who were my companions or my friends. That was more than twenty years ago."

"But they knew you, you said?" Brother James asked. "They approached you?"

"They tried to," Rigaud answered. "I repulsed them, consigned them to Hell unless they joined me in my conversion. They laughed at me, of course. So you can see that I'm not the person to question Gaucher and Rufus concerning Hugh's death."

James scratched his chin, where the dark beard was again in need of a razor. "I would think you'd be the best one to question them," he said. "They couldn't lie as easily to you. However, let me try at first. I'll tell you their replies and let you judge their veracity. In return, I want you to speak with that merchant from Paris and his Jewish friends."

Rigaud rubbed the back of his neck. Ever since Gaucher had slapped him on the back at Le Puy, there had been a kink in it. "But, Brother James, if Hugh was killed by one of the *ribaux* that lurk in the woods, what is the point of questioning any of these people?" he asked.

Brother James put his hand on Rigaud's shoulder. "Because the abbot has told us to," he said, "and obedience is our first duty."

Rigaud shook the hand off in annoyance. "You might have said that in the beginning," he complained. "Of course I shall start at once. Since the group is now traveling among us, I can question the traders as we ride."

"And, since they are now among us," Brother James replied, "it's all the more important to make sure that none of them is a murderer."

The idea made Brother Rigaud's right palm tingle with the sort of itch that can only be soothed by the pressure of a tightly held sword. He blessed himself hurriedly instead.

"May the Lord aid us in our search for the truth," he murmured.

"Amen," said Brother James.

The route to Figeac was an easy one after the steep up-and-down of the previous several days. They rode through a wide valley in which the road was well maintained and the forest often interrupted by clusters of homes and cleared fields. Gradually, the mood of the pilgrims began to lighten. Sheltered now more securely under the wing of Saint Peter and in the bright spring sunshine, they felt less fear of the terror stalking by night.

Eliazar considered the questions of the monk, Rigaud, to be no more than the usual nuisance. He was used to being the first questioned when anything nefarious happened.

"No, I didn't know the man," he said. "We don't come from Burgundy, but Paris. My nephew and I are traveling with my partner, Hubert LeVendeur."

"And why are you with this man?" Rigaud addressed Hubert.

"My daughter and her husband wished to make a pilgrimage to the shrine of Saint James," he explained. "Abbot Suger has business for me in Spain, so with the permission of your abbot, we joined the party. The other pilgrims are all strangers to us."

"But why with this man?" Rigaud asked suspiciously. "Why would a Christian have a Jewish partner?"

"For a number of reasons," Hubert answered. "Including their contacts in Spain. If Abbot Suger has no objection, why should you? It's not unusual, especially here in the south."

"I was not objecting," Rigaud said. "Merely asking. My duty is to assure the abbot that the ones who murdered and robbed Hugh of Grignon are not still among us."

"Then do your duty," Hubert said. "We have no more wish to travel with a murderer than you do."

He turned away from Rigaud and resumed his conversation with Eliazar.

Rigaud drew himself up in anger. "How dare you turn your back on me!" he said, grabbing the reins of Hubert's horse and jerking them so that Hubert was forced to turn back. "You've clearly spent too much of your time among these stiff-necked unbelievers. You've forgotten the respect you owe the Church and her servants. I am not one of your apprentices to be ignored or ordered about. How dare you treat me like this! How dare you!"

His voice rose with each sentence, becoming a shriek that alarmed Hubert and caused those nearby to stop and stare at them.

"Good Brother," Hubert began, "I had no attention of offending you or insulting your order. I merely—"

"Merely dismissed me like an errant pot boy!" Rigaud shouted.

"I thought you had finished with us," Hubert said, flustered at the intensity of the man's reaction. "I humbly ask your pardon—" he swallowed—"as one Christian to another."

Rigaud had stopped his tirade long enough to notice the people around him. With a great effort, he managed to control himself.

"I accept your apology—" he said "—as a good Christian ought. But the next time I have questions for you, I expect to be given every courtesy and the respect due me."

"Of course," Hubert said, fists clenched.

He and Eliazar waited until the monk had ridden on, back to his companion at the front of the procession. Eliazar chuckled.

"I don't believe our pious friend likes laymen of any sort," he said. "But you were unconscionably rude to him. What made you turn your back like that?"

Hubert shook his head. "I have no idea," he said. "The monk said nothing meant to be insulting. I think I became angry for you. Or at myself. We're brothers. We should be treated in the same fashion."

"Forgive me, Hubert," Eliazar said, "but I don't think this would be the right moment to renounce your baptism. As the elder brother, I would counsel you to wait until we are not surrounded by monks."

Hubert grimaced. "It's being surrounded by them that makes me feel a coward for not admitting who you are."

"Trust me," Eliazar said. "There will be a better time to become a martyr. Let's wait until then. Now you have other responsibilities."

Hubert looked ahead, where Catherine and Edgar walked, arm in arm. "As usual, brother," he sighed, "your advice is sound."

Brother James thought he was having somewhat better luck with Gaucher and Rufus. They seemed eager to tell him all about Hugh, praising his exploits in various sieges, his devotion to the abbey of Cluny, his generosity to the poor and to his friends. They were loud in their certainty that their friend was on his way to heaven at this very minute.

"Poor old Hugh had no enemies," Gaucher mourned. "Kind and gentle, always at his prayers."

"We should have mounted a party to scour the woods for whoever slew him," Rufus added. "What sort of *mesel* kills a man with his *brais* down?"

"Were they down," Brother James asked, "when he was found?"

"Around his knees," Gaucher said, shaking his head. "Saint Sergius's stone chicken! It's a shameful way for a warrior to die."

"It seems strange that he didn't hear his attackers approaching," Brother James commented.

The other two looked at each other.

"Ah, well, poor old Hugh was getting a bit deaf with the years," Rufus said. "Not so he couldn't talk with you. But a branch crackling underfoot, he might have missed that."

This seemed to satisfy Brother James. "And all that you say is missing is a ring?" he asked.

"Yes, he wore it always," Gaucher told him. "All the rest of his worldly goods were given to his children or to the Church before we left."

"If this ring were found again, would you know it?" the monk asked.

"Of course," Rufus said. "We both would. Gold, with one large emerald. A very simple design."

Brother James bit his lip. "If necessary, we will search the belongings of the other pilgrims for it," he said. "Including yours. Would you object to that?"

"Of course not," both men said instantly.

"Thank you," James told them. "I will report my findings to the abbot and ask him how we are to proceed. It may well be that your friend was killed by those lawless men who infest the forests. But there are some matters here that I don't understand. No one else reported seeing or hearing anything?"

"Not to us," Gaucher said. "Perhaps your religious garb will cause someone to come forth with more information."

"Perhaps," Brother James said. "I will continue searching and speak with you again later."

"Anything we can do, you need only ask," Rufus assured him.

Brother James continued riding down the line of pilgrims. He wasn't happy with the answers he had been given, although they sounded truthful enough. He discounted the tales of Hugh's sanctity. Every man is a saint to his friends after his death. But there was something odd about the manner of both Gaucher and Rufus. If they hadn't been such battle-hardened knights, James would have sworn the men were terrified. Anger he could understand if their comrade had been killed by bandits, but not fear. Were they afraid of being caught in their lies?

James resolved to have the party stopped and all luggage searched before they arrived at Figeac.

He passed Griselle of Lugny. She would certainly object to such an indignity. So would the German townsmen. Perhaps he should consult the abbot before making the decision. His mind was taken up with the problem as he passed Catherine and Edgar. He barely glanced at them in the road below until Catherine chanced to look up. Brother James's jaw dropped.

"Lord Jesus, save me!" the monk cried. "*Deus in adjutorium meum intende!*"

It was the ghost he had seen at Le Puy.

Catherine smiled at him. "*Domine, ad adjuvandum me festina,*" she said, automatically giving the response to the verse.

That was enough to convince him she was not of this world. In life, his ghost would never have spoken Latin. Brother James decided to wait a while before continuing with his investigation. He was shaking too much from this second encounter to think clearly.

Catherine watched as the monk wheeled his horse about and returned to the front of the procession.

"How very odd," she said. "The poor man must have felt suddenly ill. I should have asked if he needed help."

"The monks have an infirmarian with them," Edgar said. "That's probably where he went so quickly."

"Yes, of course." Catherine spoke slowly. "He seemed very familiar. Have we met him before?"

Edgar had been going over the order of the saved on the tympanum at Conques. He wanted to be sure he remembered the exact placement. He hadn't really looked at the monk.

"No, I don't think so," he said. "These monks all tend to look alike after a bit. The tonsure, the robes, the same food, the air of holiness, you know."

"Oh well, I don't suppose it's important," Catherine said. "When you have the tympanum clear in your head, I want to tell you about what I heard last night. I think that perhaps I should have stopped the monk and told him, but it's rather embarrassing."

"Then walk closer to me," Edgar told her, "and tell me now. If you don't want to repeat it, I'll go to him for you."

So, leaning her head on his shoulder as they walked, Catherine explained about her midnight experience. Although his lips twitched once or twice, Edgar didn't laugh. When she finished, she was surprised by how tightly he was holding her.

"*Leoffaest*," he said, "how do these things keep happening to you? I suppose we should say something, but . . ."

"I know," Catherine said. "I think it was Hugh of Grignon and Mondete Ticarde, but what if I'm wrong? I don't want to accuse her unjustly."

"But we can't let a murderer go free, either," Edgar said. "There must be a way to find out more. After all, even if Mondete has returned to her profession, why would she kill the man?"

"Perhaps he threatened her," Catherine suggested.

"Did you hear any threats?" Edgar asked.

"I told you everything I heard," Catherine said. "It was the gurgle that worried me."

"Yes," Edgar said. "And you saw no signs of blood on Mondete's hands. I wonder. You never heard the woman's voice?"

"No, just breathing."

"Perhaps it wasn't a woman," Edgar said.

"Oh." Catherine spent a minute absorbing that.

"It would be easier to cut a man's throat from behind," she admitted. "I remember some interesting marginalia in a manuscript Father borrowed for me once. In that position, one could kill someone and not become covered in blood."

Edgar looked at her. "Someday, *carissima*, you must give me a list of what you've read," he said. "In any case, we are agreed that we need more information."

"But how are we going to get it?" she asked.

"I think we've been spending too much time on our own reasons for taking this route and not enough on getting to know our fellow pilgrims," he said.

Her eyes lit. Even though the matter was serious, she had to admit that it added some interest to what was certain to be a long journey.

"Where shall we start?"

The Lady Griselle was startled when Brother Rigaud approached her. She lowered her veil over her face at once.

"How may I help you?" she asked.

"My lady, the abbot wants you to know that he is very concerned about the unfortunate death last night," Rigaud said. "He has asked Brother James and me to assure ourselves and you that this horrible crime was not committed by anyone among the party."

"That is most kind of him," Griselle answered. "While there are some unusual people in this group, I cannot imagine any of them wishing to murder. After all, we are traveling for the good of our souls. Who would be mad enough to risk eternal damnation at such a time?"

"I agree that it would be an insane act," Rigaud answered. "So you neither saw nor heard anything suspicious last night?"

"If I had, I would have called my guards to investigate," Griselle told him. "That's why they are with me."

"Yes, of course." Rigaud was beginning to feel foolish. He didn't care for it. "And you know of no reason for anyone here to murder Hugh of Grignon?"

"No one anywhere," she answered. "I barely knew him, but his reputation was blameless. After his wife died, there was no gossip about another marriage, or even of a mistress. I believe that all his children are doing well. He seemed a totally inoffensive man."

Rigaud thought of the Hugh he had known twenty years before. Griselle's estimate was true, and yet it seemed such a poor summation of a man's life, that he had committed no offense. He wished that he could discover something dark and horrible, just to keep Hugh's memory alive. But he didn't believe he would. Not Hugh. The man had been too much of a coward to be evil. He'd needed the coercion of his friends just to have a little fun.

And even then, he hadn't liked it much.

Rigaud thanked the Lady Griselle and went to give his report to Brother James.

"Roberto," Maruxa whispered as they walked, "those two monks are asking people about the death of Hugh of Grignon. What are we to tell them?"

"Nothing," Roberto answered. "They won't bother with us anyway. Why should they?"

"But what if someone remembers us?" Maruxa asked.

"Then we'll say we forgot," Roberto said firmly. "It was a long time ago. We travel to so many places. Why should there be anything memorable about Grignon?"

"You were right. We should have waited to set out," Maruxa muttered. "There are too many people from that area among the pilgrims here."

"Well, we didn't," Robert said in exasperation. "And no one has recognized us so far. Even if they did, why should I want to kill Hugh of Grignon? It would make more sense for him to murder me."

"That's true," Maruxa said. "And the one who is really to blame is already dead, may her soul writhe on a red-hot bed of coals, forever in torment."

"Amen," said Roberto.

Eight

Figeac, Wednesday, May 7, 1142; The Feast of Saint Mastidie, Virgin of Troyes, whose deeds have been lost to time.

Unde si bonum est Iherusalem ubi steterunt pedes domini visitare, longe melius est, caelo ubi ipse facie ad faciem conspicitur, inhiare. Qui ergo quod melius est promittit, quod deterius est pro meliore compensare non potest.

Therefore, if it is good to visit Jerusalem where the Lord's feet stood, far better is it to long for heaven where he is seen face-to-face. Therefore, whoever promises that which is better cannot reckon what is poorer to be the equal of that which is greater.

—Peter the Venerable
Letter 51, to the knight, Hugh Catula

*C*atherine, I couldn't understand a word that cobbler said," Edgar complained. "That was never French."

"Something like it," Catherine said. "Queen Eleanor speaks it and she has no trouble being understood. There are a few strange words and the pronunciation is different, but I can usually make it out. Don't worry."

Catherine continued looking through the felt-maker's tray in front of his shop, next to the one where they had left their worn shoes. The felt-maker had used scraps of leftover material to create souvenir badges showing the dove of Figeac and the shell of Saint Jacques. He was doing so well with them this year that he was considering setting his daughter and son-in-law up in a stand by the abbey church of Saint Sauveur. He had already looked into making an arrangement with Arnauda, the baker who supplied the workers at the half-built church with bread and sweet *gastels*, for the space next to her cart. The felt-maker loved pilgrims.

Edgar wasn't interested in shopping. He wanted to go to the church and watch the masons at work. Catherine looked at him in pity.

"*Carissime*, doesn't it hurt you to watch work that no one will ever let you do?" she asked.

"A little," Edgar said. "But there's a certain joy just in learning how it's done, in seeing the stones raised and fit just so. All the tools and machines and men moving together to create this wondrous edifice. It's beautiful."

He stopped. "You don't understand, do you?"

"Yes," she said slowly, "I do. At least I understand that this gives you the same feeling I have when I listen to Master Gilbert lecture or when I can make sense of all the numbers in Father's account book. It only saddens me that I can't see the craft the way you do, that I'll never share it with you."

Edgar had no answer for that. He knew of no way to give her the excitement he felt when watching the men at work on the monumental building. He could no more explain the deep contentment he had when carving a bit of wood into a shape that had before existed only in his mind.

Catherine laughed at his expression. "It doesn't grieve me all that much," she said. "We share other things, don't we? Now go to the church and enjoy the afternoon."

Catherine wandered through the shops a bit more after he left. She didn't really need to buy anything, but looking at the wares gave her time to think without having to talk with anyone.

Edgar had agreed that something should be said to someone about Catherine's midnight expedition, but neither one of them were sure whom to tell.

Catherine knew that her reluctance to speak with the monk sent by the abbot had to do with the way she felt about Mondete Ticarde. It would be so easy to accuse a reformed prostitute, and Mondete would have so little chance to defend herself.

"If only I could be sure," Catherine muttered as she examined a row of bright ribbons.

The vendor looked up. Catherine shook her head.

This wouldn't do. She needed to know more, but who could she ask about Mondete? Not the other knights. They had already made it clear that they had known her quite well, but Catherine didn't think they would discuss particulars with her. The Lady Griselle? Perhaps not. There was something about the woman that made Catherine feel that she had dirt on her face and a tear in her stockings. Griselle wouldn't gossip casually with someone so far beneath her. But who else would know?

The answer came to Catherine.

Of course. How stupid not to have thought of her first: the invisible woman, Lady Griselle's maid. Always silent, always in attendance. She would notice much more than her mistress did. She would hear the best gossip. Catherine tried to think of her name. She didn't remember ever hearing it.

Now the only problem was to find the woman apart from her mistress and then gain her confidence. But where would Lady Griselle go without her maid? Certainly not to church. The maid always went with her, never more than a step away. Griselle was such a stickler for propriety that Catherine feared she didn't even go unaccompanied to the privy.

There must be something inspirational about shopping. As she looked over the lengths of cloth at the scarf-makers, Catherine thought of something a lady would leave her maid to do alone. She was looking at a length of bright yellow cloth, with a pattern worked in red at the edges. Catherine fingered her own scarf, dingy now from the elements and too many washings. Wearing something new would make her feel less like a peasant next to Lady Griselle, whose clothes were always clean and scented with lavender, as if freshly taken from the clothes chest. Catherine suspected that Griselle had even brought a gauffering iron to pleat the sleeves of her *bliaut*.

Somehow Catherine couldn't imagine Griselle bent over a washtub. So who would be the one most likely to see to it that the fine linen shifts, silk scarves and woolen *bliauts* were kept spotless? Was Lady Griselle likely to waste an afternoon in such work? Of course not. That's what maids were for.

Catherine decided that her father should buy her the scarf as a reward for her cleverness. She told the woman at the shop to wrap it up to be paid for that afternoon.

"It never occurred to me that a pilgrimage would be so hard on my clothes," she commented to the woman. "They become faded and dirty so much more quickly than at home. And my stockings! I washed them at Conques and they should be done again. Where do the women of the town do their washing?"

"At the river, of course," the woman answered. "Where do the women of Paris do theirs, at the bathhouses?"

Catherine was tempted to say yes, that then one could wash body and clothes all at once, but she refrained. Instead, she thanked the woman, promising to return for the scarf.

Now she only hoped that the Lady Griselle had not brought so many pairs of stockings that she didn't need to have them washed.

After questioning the pilgrims, Brother Rigaud and Brother James had conferred and decided that there was no apparent reason for any of them to have murdered Hugh of Grignon.

"You are quite certain that neither of your old comrades could have had a part in it?" James asked.

Rigaud was. "Gaucher and Rufus are lecherous, gluttonous and bibulous," he said, "but they would never slit a man's throat in such an undignified and cowardly manner."

"No one else in the party seems to have known him well. No one has accused anyone else," James said. "That alone is unusual. I searched the belongings of the *jongleurs* and they had no rings."

"As you requested, I went through the boxes of the Jews," Rigaud added. "They protested, of course, but I told them it was on the orders of the abbot. The younger one had a knife strapped to his arm that he insisted was for preparing game according to their laws while traveling. I didn't believe him, but the blade, I think, was too thick to have made the clean cut in Hugh's neck. He wasn't good at hiding his anger at my questions, either."

"They're all arrogant in their stubbornness," James said bitterly. "And these men are under the protection of Saint-Denis. We can't accuse them without absolute proof."

"Without a witness or the missing ring, I don't see how we can get it," Rigaud said sadly. "I believe we should tell the abbot that we have concluded that Hugh was killed by robbers stalking the group. We've promised to hire more guards at Moissac. There's little more we can do to help protect the other pilgrims."

Brother James scratched his chin worriedly. "I suppose that would be best," he said. "I wish I felt more sanguine about it, though. I can't conquer the feeling that there's a murderer traveling with us."

Rigaud shrugged. "On a pilgrimage, there are many kinds

of sinners. Perhaps you sense the guilt of old murder in some-one."

"Perhaps," James said. "But something about this slaying just doesn't strike me as being the work of the *ribaux*. They would have taken his clothes and boots as well as his jewelry, don't you think?"

"Not if they were in a rush, afraid of being seen." Brother Rigaud put a hand on James's shoulder. "If I, who was also his comrade, am satisfied that Hugh's death was at the hands of the men of the forest, why should you doubt it?"

"I don't know," James answered. He thought for a mo-ment, then shook himself as if that would shed the worry. "It's certainly not as if the man were anything to me," he added. "I have more than enough to concern myself with."

"Precisely," said Rigaud. "For instance, there have been complaints again that the priests the bishop of Osma brought with him are not conforming to our usage in the saying of Mass. We really must have this settled before it breaks out into open warfare between them and the rest of our brothers."

Brother James was pleased to have something important to deal with again.

Catherine found the women of Figeac to be more than happy to share the stone trough at the river's edge and give her a bit of their *leissive*, a mixture of wood ash and caustic soda, to rub into her laundry before soaking it. The laundresses traveling with the monks were also there, two widows in their fifties who had decided to devote their remaining years to caring for the linen of God's servants, knowing that when they were too old for work, God's servants would care for them. But there was no sign of Griselle's maid.

There was no point in wasting the opportunity, however, so when her stockings and old scarf had sat long enough in the trough, Catherine took off her shoes and her long *bliaut*, tied up the skirts of her *chainse* and waded into the water with the others, who were busy pounding the dirt out on flat rocks and rinsing the clothes in the flowing water.

As she stood to wring out the stockings, Catherine caught

a name from amidst the babble of the women talking as they worked.

"I heard that, too," one of the women was saying, "but I won't believe it's really Mondete unless I can see her face."

"Don't you think she could have repented?" the other woman asked.

From the black robes they were washing, Catherine realized that these were the laundresses from Cluny. She hadn't thought of them as sources of information; they were even less noticed than the maid. But it made sense that they would be native to the region around Cluny, where Mondete came from as well. Despite the pain in her feet, turning blue in the cold water, Catherine slowed in her work and waited for the answer.

"Repented of what?" the first laundress asked. "What else was she supposed to do, starve? After what they did to her, Mondete's parents could have at least taken her back in and arranged for her to marry or enter a convent."

"It's one thing to be the concubine of a rich lord," the other woman objected. "There's some advantage in that. But when you've lain with every man in the keep, from the knights to the stable boy, how could your parents even own you?"

"If they were the ones who sent you there in the first place, I think they'd have to," the first woman snorted. "Giles and Theoda traded her for a piece of land. They knew when they sent her to him that Norbert liked 'em young."

Catherine started in surprise and let go of the stocking, then had to splash after it as it floated downstream. Norbert!

In retrieving the stocking, she had missed part of the conversation: ". . . always did well by them, especially if it was a boy." The first laundress was speaking again. "Her parents were counting on that, too."

Catherine understood enough. Poor Mondete! Sold to Norbert and cast off by both him and her family when she proved barren. Catherine wondered how young she had been. She knew the arrangement wasn't uncommon. Often it was a way for a woman to marry into a better life when the lord gave his old mistress and a castellany to one of his supporters. Or he at least provided for the raising of his bastard children.

Catherine's thoughts echoed the comment of the first laundress: What did Mondete need to repent of, then? What choice had she ever been given in her way of life? Of course, she may have taken to it. If she had enjoyed prostitution, then it was certainly sinful.

Catherine's pity for the child Mondete slipped on a new thought. Perhaps her pilgrimage wasn't penitential at all. Perhaps Norbert of Bussières hadn't died as peacefully and naturally as they supposed.

It was then that she remembered what had made the stain on the hem of her skirt—the stain that the rat had gnawed a hole in. It was from the last of the wine in the cup she had kicked over. Norbert had drunk most of the contents of the cup. Norbert was dead and so was the rat. Mondete had been sleeping in the hostel that night.

"By the fatal bear bite of Saint Euphemia!" Catherine muttered as she gathered up her laundry. "Why does it always come back to Mondete?"

Hubert wasn't pleased to find Edgar alone, gawking at the stoneworkers at the church.

"Where's my daughter?" he asked without further greeting.

"Shopping," Edgar said without moving. "Watch out!" he cried suddenly.

Hubert looked at the church. A basket of building bricks was swinging wildly halfway up the wall as the man in charge of the hoisting crane at the top struggled to replace the rope that had slipped out of the groove. They watched the workers scatter from beneath as the basket reversed and bricks came flying down.

Edgar exhaled in relief. "Someone could have been killed," he said. "There has to be a safer way to do that."

Hubert regarded his son-in-law with skepticism. "Such as?"

"A net over the bricks, with weights at the corners to keep the basket from tilting and to make it harder for the bricks to fall out," Edgar answered promptly.

Hubert had to admit that there was some merit in this idea.

He also knew what the master mason would say if some idle watcher were to come up and suggest it.

"I think we should find Catherine," was his only comment. "You've entertained yourself enough for the day."

Edgar followed sadly. He knew there was no way he could ever please his father-in-law. He had been trained for nothing Hubert could approve of. Once he had rashly promised to go to Montpellier to study law, in the hope that this skill would be useful to a merchant. Hubert hadn't mentioned it again and Edgar didn't want to remind him. But he wondered if that might not be the only way to earn some respect from the family he had married into.

They met Catherine as she came up from the river. Her feet were still bare and now bright red from the chafing of the water. Her head was uncovered, her dark braids coming undone. She clutched a damp wad of clothes in her arms and her teeth were chattering, more with excitement than with cold. Hubert turned to Edgar.

"Look at her! This is what happens when you go off and leave her on her own!" he shouted. "Can't you take better care of her than this?"

Catherine was so angry that she dropped the laundry. "Father, don't talk to him that way!" she shouted back. "I'm not a baby who needs a nurse. I'm a married woman and I can care for myself."

Edgar said nothing. Glaring now at his daughter, Hubert didn't notice, but Catherine knew the silence meant that her husband was angry. Edgar compressed his lips like that only to keep fury from exploding. She would rather he let it out, shouting like her father did. Then she would know if he were furious with Hubert for berating him in public or with her for thinking he couldn't defend himself.

She bent over to pick up the stockings and scarf. There were bits of grass and dirt sticking to them now. She shook them out, partly to disguise the fact that she was shaking as well.

Without speaking, Edgar took Catherine's elbow and led her roughly away. Hubert didn't move. Watching them go, he had an unsettling sense that he had just done something that would take a long time to repair.

Catherine waited until Edgar's jaw unclenched and he began to breathe normally again. Then she shook free from his hand. He seemed surprised that he had still been holding her arm. He took a deep breath.

"I suppose I've made a fool of myself," he said.

That was the last thing Catherine expected him to say. "I thought you were going to tell me I had embarrassed you," she answered.

He glanced sideways at her, trudging next to him with her skirts trailing in the path and the tip of one stocking dangling over her arm. Despite himself, he began to laugh.

Catherine blinked hard several times to keep back tears of relief. His silent anger frightened her more than she dared say. There was no way to counter it. Her own volatile temper was the same as her father's, a flare and then spent; Edgar's temper was like ice, growing and hardening throughout a long winter.

He stopped and took her in his arms, squeezing the laundry between them. "I'm sorry," he whispered.

She wasn't sure for what. "You're getting wet," she answered.

He moved away slightly, then hugged her again. "I don't mind," he said.

Catherine turned her face up to him. He kissed her nose. She smiled.

Summer was coming. Even on the moutains, the winter ice was melting.

The next morning they set out once again. This time when Catherine looked around, she noticed new faces among the pilgrims.

"Are there people from Figeac also going to Compostela?" she asked Maruxa, who was walking beside her.

"No, but there's a party from Burgundy that has just returned from a side trip to pray at Rocamadour," the *jongleuse* answered. "They petitioned the abbot to let them join us."

"That will be good," Catherine said. "We'll have more protection from bandits now."

"Roberto and I are always glad of a new audience," Maruxa added.

"Did those monks come back to ask anything more about the death of Hugh of Grignon?" Catherine asked.

"No." Maruxa's voice became wary. "Why should they? Everyone knows it was the *ribaux*. One of them told me that they only questioned us because Abbot Peter didn't want any of Hugh's family to say the matter had been dealt with too lightly."

"I see," Catherine said.

Maruxa seemed disinclined to further conversation. She moved away from Catherine and fell back to walk again with her husband.

So there would be no more questions about Hugh's murder. And no one had thought to wonder about the death of Norbert. Catherine knew she could keep silent; she had said nothing to anyone but Edgar so far. She wasn't sure if she would have the courage to stand up before Peter the Venerable, abbot of Cluny, and tell him that she thought she might have overheard a man being murdered while she was crouching behind a bush emptying her bladder. The tale of the rat seemed even less likely to be believed, although not as embarrassing to relate. And even if Mondete had had a reason to kill Norbert, why would she also murder Hugh?

Catherine walked more slowly as she pondered these things, falling behind Edgar and Solomon, who were involved in a discussion of their own as they led the horses. Suddenly she realized that she was walking next to the wrong horse. She looked up and found Lady Griselle's maid staring down at her in amusement.

Catherine was glad she had decided to wear the new scarf, even though yellow and red were not exactly appropriate colors for a pilgrim. It drew attention from the increasingly bedraggled state of her second-best *bliaut*, which hadn't been cleaned since she left Paris.

"I've been watching you," the woman greeted her.

Catherine started guiltily, even though she couldn't think of anything horrible she'd done recently.

"You must find traveling very tedious," she replied, "if you find me of interest to watch."

The maid laughed. "I do indeed find it tedious, but no more so than staying at home. That's why I'm grateful to your father for entertaining my Lady Griselle and thus allowing me a morning to myself."

Catherine looked at the riders ahead of them. Yes, Griselle was keeping pace with her father, while Eliazar had moved ahead. She couldn't hear what they were saying, but suddenly Hubert laughed. The sound was oddly disquieting. Catherine hadn't heard him laugh like that since before she had gone to the convent. It had been so long ago that she had forgotten what he looked like when happy.

"Don't look so worried," the maid said. "I can assure you that Griselle has no intention of seeking a replacement for her dead lord."

"Of course not," Catherine answered. "That hadn't even occurred to me. And my mother isn't dead. She's . . . ill, and has retired to the convent of Tart. The sisters care for her very well there."

"Yes, I had heard something of that," said the woman. "Do you then manage your father's household?"

Catherine thought about this. She supposed she did, what little of it was managed. Since her mother left, Hubert rarely had anyone in to dine with them. Many nights were spent at the home of Eliazar and Johannah. She and Edgar were so absorbed in each other and their problems that she hadn't noticed her father's growing melancholia.

She sighed. "Not as well as I should," she admitted. "But we live in Paris and don't have the responsibilities that the mistress of a castellany would have. My name is Catherine," she added.

"Yes, I know," the maid said.

Catherine waited.

"My name, I'm afraid, is Hersent," the maid told her.

"Oh," Catherine said. How embarrassing. She knew the fable; everyone did. Hersent was the name of the she-wolf ignominiously raped by the fox. It was part of a very popular series of tales. What had the woman's mother been thinking of? "I'm very pleased to meet you," Catherine added. "Are you also traveling as a pilgrim?"

"Not really," Hersent answered. "Like my lady, I owe it to the memory of my husband. But if any grace is added to my soul because of my patient endurance of the journey, I will not be ungrateful to Our Lord."

Catherine shaded her eyes to look up at Hersent. She saw a woman about fifteen years older than herself, perhaps thirty-five or so. She had rich blond hair and light brown eyes. Her lips were thin, as was the bridge of her nose. This made her seem more disapproving than her behavior with Catherine indicated. Cautiously, Catherine decided that she might like this woman.

"How long have you served Lady Griselle?" she asked.

"Only since her husband died," Hersent told her. "Before that, I had my own home, small though it was. But my husband was killed in the same battle as hers, and our eldest son married and wanted our house. So Griselle took me in."

"I didn't learn where this battle was," Catherine said. "Were they fighting in the Holy Land?"

"Hardly," Hersent said. "Although Queen Eleanor seems to think it is. No, they were good vassals, helping King Louis and his wife keep her patrimony in Aquitaine. Last summer's campaign. So far as I know, no one has made a song about it. I don't even know if it was successful. Only that I got no reward from it."

"So you are also going to Compostela for the sake of your husband's soul," Catherine said.

Hersent smiled. "Not really," she said. "Oh, I say a few prayers for him. He wasn't such a bad husband, as they go. No, it's Griselle who truly grieves. I believe she means to enter a convent upon our return. Don't be deceived by her attire. She weeps for him every night."

"Will you go to the convent with her?" Catherine asked.

"I don't think so," Hersent answered. "I've made other plans."

Catherine started to ask what they were, but Hersent interrupted.

"I am being signaled to attend," she said and urged her horse forward through the line to where Lady Griselle was beckoning her.

As she left, Catherine realized that they had fallen to the end of the procession. Only Mondete was behind her.

The day was mild and calm. There was a perfume in the air from some flower she didn't recognize. The road was soft, the hills bright with the first green of the year.

Leaving Mondete to her thoughts, Catherine hurried into the wake Hersent had left and a moment later caught up with Edgar and Solomon, who were still arguing. She put her arm around her husband's waist and tried to adjust to his longer stride. He slowed a bit and absently kissed the side of her head, then returned to his discussion. Someone in the party was singing *Ave Maris Stella* in a fairly good bass.

Perhaps she was wrong and old Norbert had died naturally. Perhaps poor Hugh had been waylaid by bandits, and the lovers she had heard were no one she knew. Catherine wanted to weave a crown of daisies, not to poke into other people's misery.

This was not a day to think about death.

Gaucher watched Hubert riding next to Griselle. He frowned. "Where are her guards?" he muttered. "That's the sort they should be protecting her from."

Rufus scratched at a flea bite under his chain mail. The rings cut into his skin. Damn thing chafed enough to drive him mad. Tomorrow he would leave it off, he decided. Then he turned his attention to Hubert and Griselle.

"She's baiting us, old friend," he told Gaucher. "You know how women are. When they get bored, they try to set us against each other, then watch the fun."

Gaucher's eyes narrowed. "Do you think so?"

"Certain of it," Rufus said. "Ignore it and she'll be bored with him, too, soon enough. Look at him. Got a paunch like an innkeeper's. Probably never lifted a sword in his life. What would she want with a man like that?"

"What did Hugh's wife want with all those poets?" Gaucher asked rhetorically. "And I understand the merchant's rich."

"So will we be, when we find the treasure," Rufus reminded him. "And now we only need to divide the profit between the two of us."

"That's true." Gaucher gave him an appraising look.

Rufus decided that he would continue to wear the mail shirt, however much it might chafe.

That evening, clouds began to move in. Remembering the sudden flood the week before, by common consent the pilgrims climbed the narrow paths up to a row of holes in the side of the cliff overlooking the River Celé. On this ascent, even Catherine was nervous. The rocky trail was too much like that of her dream. She, Edgar, Eliazar and Solomon found shelter in the first empty cave they came to.

"The horses won't fit in here," Hubert said. "We'll have to unload them and take them back down."

"Yes they will," Edgar said from inside. "It widens once you're past the opening. Hurry. We need to get a fire started before the sun sets."

Catherine was glad of the warmth the horses would give off in this dank place. She wondered who, or what, had slept here last. At the moment, it didn't matter as long as they didn't return tonight. Because of the good weather and growing daylight, they had walked farther today than ever before. All she wanted was to be allowed to lie flat and close her eyes.

"Catherine." Solomon touched her shoulder. "Catherine, Mondete didn't follow us up."

"You know she doesn't like to camp near other people," Catherine answered, feeling for a level place to lay her blanket.

"It's going to rain tonight," Solomon said. "Before, she was always at least within sight of the rest of us."

Catherine felt as if a stone had just been laid on her stomach. "You want me to convince her to come stay with us, don't you?" she asked her cousin.

"Yes. I'd go, but she won't listen to me. She thinks I'm mad," Solomon said.

"So do I," Catherine told him. "But as a good Christian, I must try to help her."

"I don't care why you do it, just bring her back here," Solomon said. "Please. Before it gets dark."

Even with the thunder clouds, twilight was long. In the grey evening, Catherine set off back down the narrow path. Solomon came behind her, promising to wait at the foot of the trail for them.

"She won't come, you know," Catherine said again.

"Just try," Solomon answered.

They could see her now, a black shadow by the side of the river. As Catherine approached, Mondete took something out of her knotted sleeve and vanished behind a bush growing out over the water.

Catherine paused. She could wait until Mondete had finished.

Several minutes passed and Mondete did not reappear. Catherine began to worry. She might be ill. She might have fallen into the river.

Just as Catherine reached the riverbank, Mondete reappeared. Catherine froze in terror.

In her right hand the woman held a straight razor. Even in the dim light, Catherine could see it gleam. Mondete took a step toward her. Catherine opened her mouth to scream.

Mondete stopped, puzzled.

Catherine stepped back, her hands up to defend herself. Mondete looked down at the razor, seeming to realize only then what had frightened Catherine so.

"I won't hurt you," she said. She wrapped a cloth around the blade and tied it back inside her sleeve. Then she held up her hands. "See? Empty," she said.

Catherine took another step back. "Is that what you killed Hugh of Grignon with?" she asked.

"What?"

"Solomon! Help!" Catherine called. Then she said to Mondete, "I heard you that night, with Hugh."

Mondete wavered. Her hands shook. "No," she said. "I don't know what you mean. I've killed no one. Why should I?"

"I know about Norbert, too," Catherine said.

"Norbert! Oh, Holy Mother, defend me!" Mondete cried.

"Why would you carry such a thing, but to kill?" Catherine demanded as Solomon came running.

Mondete sank down upon the stones. "For this, young Catherine," she said.

Mondete lifted her hands and pulled back the cowl.

Nine

Somewhere between Figeac and Moissac, Friday, May 8, 1142;
Commemoration of the appearance, with building plans, of Saint
Michael the Archangel at the site of Mont Saint-Michel.

*Tercio quoque, cum apud cenobium beate semperque virginis Marie,
cognomento Meleredense, demorarer . . .*

The third time [I saw the devil] I was staying at the convent of the
blessed and ever-virgin Mary at Moutiers-Sainte-Marie

—Ralph Glaber
Historia Liber Quintus

$\mathcal{B}$ehind her, Catherine heard Solomon's startled cry. She was too shocked to make even a sound. At first, in the grey light, she thought Mondete a skeletal ghost, fulfilling her worst nightmares. Her hand went up instinctively to cross herself, to plead for the protection of the saints. Then she realized that the reason Mondete looked so deathlike was because she had no hair, not even eyebrows. Her head shone pale under the clouds, her cheeks hollow in a face emaciated with fasting.

Moving closer, Catherine saw that Mondete had cut herself recently in her tonsuring. There were fresh and half-healed nicks scattered over her scalp. The woman faced them both with defiance.

"Now do you understand?" Mondete looked from Catherine to Solomon.

"No," Catherine said. "I mean yes, I see why you have the razor, but no, I don't know why you did this to yourself. Even the nuns only cut their hair short."

Solomon said nothing. He slowly moved forward until he was standing just behind Catherine.

Mondete pulled the cowl back on. "Assume that this is part of my penance," she said. She prepared to resume her place among the rocks.

Solomon brushed past Catherine. "Wait here," he said to her. He went straight to Mondete and knelt beside her. She buried her covered face in her knees.

"Why can't you leave me be!" she wept. "Didn't you see me? There is no mystery, no great knowledge. Only ugliness and anger."

Solomon bent closer to her, his lips almost touching the edge of the cowl. "I see nothing ugly," he said. "And I, too, am fueled by anger. I'll not torment you any longer with questions, although I still believe you have the answers hidden within your heart. But unless you propose to die before you've finished your pilgrimage, please give up this self-torture . . . at least long enough to sleep in the warmth tonight, safe from the storm."

Mondete was still. It seemed to Catherine that even the river stopped to hear her answer.

From inside the cowl there was a sniff. "Wouldn't you fear that I would cut your throat as you slept?" she asked.

Solomon gave an unamused laugh. "No more than anyone else in this group might."

Mondete looked up, letting the hood again fall back to her shoulders. He could just discern the outline of her features in the darkness.

"Come up with us." He stood and held out his hand.

Very slowly Mondete reached out to him, her hand turned palm upward, as if begging. Solomon laid his hand over hers and their fingers curved together.

The wind grew stronger as the three of them made the climb back up the steep cliff to the cave. They entered just as the rain began, a biting torrent on their backs. Edgar was crouched at the entrance, coaxing a small fire to stay lit despite the wind in the entry. He stood when he saw Catherine and hugged her in relief.

"I was just about to go down after you," he said.

"You were?" Catherine eyed him skeptically.

Edgar wished she had never found out how he felt about these high, narrow trails. She had been alternately overprotective and superior each time they had encountered any sort of rise in the land. It was a situation they would have to resolve soon.

But not tonight. Edgar turned to Mondete and bowed. "Allow me to welcome you to our fortress, lady," he said, indicating the rest of the cave. "Although the accommodations are not those of Paris, you will allow that it is secure from the elements."

Mondete, her cowl once more covering her face, said nothing. She released Solomon's hand and made her way to the darkest corner, where she sank down, resting her back against the rough wall.

They all stared at her for a moment, then returned to their business as if she weren't there. Eliazar wrapped his phylacteries about his arm in preparation for evening prayer.

"At home," he said, looking around the damp cave, "Johannah is lighting the candles and saying the Sabbath blessing. When I came back to the house from the synagogue, it would seem as if I were already in Eretz Israel. She makes the desert of our exile bloom. I miss her. Solomon, come pray with me."

Solomon hesitated, then took the phylactory his uncle was holding out to him. They stood together and recited the evening prayer. Hubert watched them, his lips moving occasionally as he recognized a word.

Catherine waited until they were done to root in the bags for bread and dried fish. She then warmed some beer in a crock over Edgar's fire and crumbled both bread and fish into it to make a thick potage.

"About all this southern beer is good for," Hubert muttered as he sniffed the pot. "Can't drink the stuff."

When the soup was ready, Catherine ladled it into their shallow wooden drinking bowls. Then she set the remainder in front of Mondete.

"Do you have a spoon?" she asked.

For answer, Mondete untied her right sleeve and pulled out a flat piece of wood. Edgar frowned.

"I can make you a better one by morning," he said.

"I don't deserve a better one," Mondete answered as she scooped up a glob of the potage.

Edgar thought, then said, "It would be an act of charity on your part to allow me to carve you a spoon. You would save me from the sin of idleness."

Mondete continued to eat. When she had finished, she licked the wooden piece clean and handed it to Edgar. "It's rare that I'm given the opportunity to save anyone from sin," she said. "Thank you."

She moved closer to the fire. Outside, the rain came down in a steady sheet, cutting them off from the rest of the world.

Edgar had taken out his knife and was singing one of his Saxon stories quietly as he carved. Catherine sat next to him, admiring the skill in his hands. The others watched the fire settle into coals and prepared to sleep. Eliazar got up before all light was gone to make sure the horses were tethered securely for the night.

When he turned around, he found Mondete standing behind him, her cowl once again pulled back to reveal her face. Eliazar's eyes widened at the sight and his hand moved swiftly to ward off evil.

She stared at him intently, but not meeting his eyes. Eliazar wondered if she were hunting for lice in his beard.

"Do you love your god?" she asked abruptly, looking up.

"What?" he answered, staring into her deep brown eyes. "Of course. And there is only one god. He is yours as well."

Mondete brushed this aside. "I don't understand this," she said. "You people are reviled and despised throughout Christendom. You have been driven from your own land and you are denied advancement in other lands because of your faith. You are shunned, beaten—sometimes killed—and your god does nothing to save you. How can you still trust him? How can you love him?"

Eliazar smiled sadly. "Those are old arguments," he told her. "We are in exile for our sins perhaps, or as a test of our faith, just as the Holy One, blessed be He, tested Job. We live among you, enduring your scorn, as witnesses to the Truth. When He is ready, we will be returned to Israel."

"But," she persisted, "how can you love someone who would treat you so?"

"Faith," Eliazar answered. "He brought us out of Egypt and home from Babylon. As long as we stand firm in our faith, we will one day be rescued from this exile as well."

"Faith," Mondete repeated. "Yes. That's the answer the priests give me, too. I thought . . . I had hoped . . ."

She shook her head and moved away from him, back to her place by the wall. She curled down into her cloak, turned her back to them and said no more.

If Catherine had thought that Mondete's revelation and acceptance of their company would make her more friendly, she was quickly disabused of the idea. The storm blew through in the night, and the next morning was washed as clean as Eden. When Catherine awoke to the raucous calls of a thousand birds, Mondete had already slipped out of the cave and was back down by the river.

"Was she really here last night?" she asked Edgar.

"She took the spoon with her," he answered, "but the shavings I made are still here. Do you think she used her razor to kill Hugh of Grignon?"

"I don't know," Catherine said. "Why would she? From what the women at the river said, she might have had a reason to wish Norbert dead. Perhaps Hugh also hurt her in some way, but how could we find out? Who would tell us?"

"From their talk, I had the impression that the other two pilgrim knights knew her far better than Hugh did," Edgar told her as he finished lading their horse. "They were mocking him for his lack of interest in carnal matters."

"He may just have been less inclined to brag," Catherine said as they left the cave. "He must have had some interest to have been lured to his death, if that was what I heard. Edgar, do you want me to lead the horse down so you can have both hands free?"

"No!" Edgar said.

He went out into the sunshine. The narrow path was still muddy from the night's storm. Over the edge, the drop was directly down to the riverbank. He took a deep breath.

"Catherine, you must stop treating me like a child," he said. "Yes, I don't like high places. But most of the time I can walk along them without screaming. It was only that once, when the crowds were so thick that I thought they might push me over, that I felt that terrible panic. It isn't something that happens every day. Do you understand?"

"Yes." But she still walked on the outside.

Edgar sighed again. "Catherine, isn't there anything that you're afraid of, against reason?"

"Yes," she said. "Losing you. It terrifies me. If you went over the edge, I would follow you."

He stopped in the middle of the path, took her hand and kissed her fingers. Catherine blinked tears onto her cheeks and he kissed those, too.

"Saint Agatha's amputated tits!" someone behind them shouted. "Can't you do that somewhere else?"

Catherine blushed and wiped her eyes. Edgar grinned at the irate face of one of the pilgrims who had joined them in Figeac.

And another normal day began on the Way of Saint James.

Peter, abbot of Cluny, waited patiently at the gate of the priory where he and his party had been sheltered the night before. He was not looking forward to the day's journey. His digestion was never good, due to frequent fasting, and he feared that even his gentle white mule would be too much for him to ride this morning. He also had awakened with a slight chill and now was worried that a return of the sweating sickness was coming on. He had been plagued with it since his trip to Italy years before, and he prayed it would not keep him from completing the journey.

Bishop Stephen of Osma, standing next to him, noticed the shiver and moved back a pace. "Are you well, Venerable Abbot?" he asked.

Peter nodded. "A bit of trouble with my bowels, that's all."

The bishop stepped closer again, reassured. "The rain seems to have blown over," he remarked. "A good day for travel."

"Yes," the abbot agreed. "If the weather remains fair, we should be in Moissac in less than a week. I hope that the messenger you sent to the emperor will be awaiting us there."

"I'm sure he will be," Stephen answered. "The Emperor Alfonso is most eager to meet you. He will have sent the man back directly with instructions as to where he will receive you and your party."

The ostler brought the mule and the bishop's horse. Peter mounted gingerly, feeling his stomach roil with every move-ment. Oddly enough, apart from the unpleasantness of his reaction to the food, Peter enjoyed traveling. He was looking forward to Spain and, among his other goals, hoped that he could actually meet a Moor. It would be a fitting accomplish-ment if he could effect, by his example, the conversion of the infidel.

As they set off, the abbot's mind wandered to the Jews from Paris who were in the party of pilgrims. He didn't like know-ing they were there. It bothered him even more that they were under the protection of the abbey of Saint-Denis and not to be interfered with. Not that he would do anything to harm them, but he hated knowing that the infidel living in their midst were allowed such freedom. Perhaps, somehow, during the jour-ney, he could persuade them to recognize the Truth and sub-mit to baptism. It had happened before.

Peter felt a twinge in his stomach but resolved to bear it, as he did the other weaknesses of his body, as an offering to the Lord. Brother Bernard had made up the potion recom-mended by Dr. Bartholomew on his last visit to Cluny, but so far, it was having no effect.

Brother Rigaud rode up alongside him.

"Are the lay brothers all accounted for?" Peter asked.

"Yes, Lord Abbot," Rigaud answered. "They are all well. None has uttered a word of complaint about conditions on the road. However, one of the *garciones* is causing some trouble. He is inclined to tease the younger boys, especially those who miss their mothers."

Peter, who still grieved for his mother, set his face sternly. "Have the boy brought to me this evening," he said. "I will see to him personally. Now, has there been any other problem among the pilgrims?"

"Nothing of any consequence, Lord Abbot," Rigaud replied. "There are two lepers among the group that joined us at Figeac. Their keepers have been told where they may go and warned that any attempt to mingle with the others or to bathe upstream from them will cause them to be immediately ex-pelled."

"Good. And there is no more information on the death of your old comrade?" Peter asked.

Rigaud hunched his shoulders as if trying to slide off the stigma of his former life. "No, my lord," he answered. "Brother James and I have concluded that it was done by outlaws. There have been no more incidents."

"Very well." The abbot grimaced at a sharp pain in his lower stomach. "You may go. Send Brother Bernard to me. Tell him I need more of the digestive potion."

Brother Rigaud did as he was bid. When he had delivered the message to the infirmarian, he did his best to lose himself among the other black-robed monks. But his old friends, Rufus and Gaucher, spotted him easily and made their way to him, one riding along each side.

"Glad to see that you don't sit your horse like a monk," Gaucher said. "It infuriates me the way they ride slumped over with their legs dangling. A stiff wind could throw them off."

"Peter of Montboissier doesn't look like a bag of flour," Rigaud responded. "The abbot rides as well as any knight."

"I'll give you that," Gaucher conceded. "It's in the blood. Seems a pity to waste all that skill on a cleric."

"Do you want something?" Rigaud stared straight ahead, hoping they would vanish.

"Your company, *vieu compang*," Rufus laughed. "You re-alize that there are now only three of us left."

"Two," Rigaud said firmly. "I have abandoned the world."

Gaucher pursed his lips, looking at the sky as if expecting a letter from heaven. "I see," he said. "Then you have no more interest in the parcel we left at Najera?"

Rigaud looked sharply from Rufus to Gaucher and back. "You mean you never returned for it?" he asked in disbelief.

"Norbert felt it wasn't safe," Rufus said. "But this year he decided that it was time to take the risk, before we all died and it was lost forever. Think what it's worth, Rigaud! After all this time, no one alive will remember where it came from. The bishops of France and Burgundy will fall over each other to have it."

Rigaud bent his head and was silent for a long time. When he looked up again, his face had changed. It was stern and somehow stronger than before.

"Of all the sins I have committed in my life," he said, "that is the one that grieves me most. If your intention is to ransom this to the highest bidder, then I will tell everyone just how we came by it, whatever it may cost me."

"What do you mean 'how we came by it'? It was rescued from the Saracens," Rufus said. "There was no sin."

"We risked our lives to redeem it from their sacrilege," Gaucher added. "It's ours now."

"We stole it from Christians," Rigaud answered, "and slaughtered them to do it. You know that well."

"We didn't know they were Christian until it was too late." Gaucher lowered his voice, making sure no one had overheard Rigaud's outburst. "They looked and dressed just like the Saracens. How were we to know? And I'm still not sure they weren't lying to save their lives."

Rufus leaned over, one hand pressed against Rigaud's shoulder. "And I don't hear you repenting of what you did to that boy we caught that day," he whispered. "That gives you no qualms? Does your noble abbot know about it? Do you confess *all* your sins, old friend? And if so, do they let you near the *garciones*? Or was the prospect of being so close to all those fresh young men what brought about your conversion in the first place?"

Rigaud whipped around angrily, knocking Rufus back so that he almost toppled out of the saddle.

"Consider the state of your own soul, Rufus!" he hissed. "There are far blacker stains on it than mine. I took a vow of chastity when I entered the monastery and I have remained chaste. Not that it is any of your concern. Pilgrimage! *Quelle merdier!* I knew that none of you had any contrition for your heinous deeds. I knew it from the moment I saw you at Vézelay."

"What?" Gaucher now reached over and gathered Brother Rigaud's cowl in a tight grasp. He lifted the furious monk halfway off his horse. "What were you doing at Vézelay?"

"I was sent to accompany Abelard's son," Rigaud said. "I saw you all, praying so devoutly all night and then drinking yourselves insensible the next day. Your pilgrim badges and staffs didn't fool me. Now, for the last time, understand that I will not help you in your wickedness. I'll do everything I can to stop you."

Gaucher lifted him further. Rigaud set his jaw and prepared to be thrown to the ground.

"Gaucher," Rufus warned, "people are watching."

Slowly the knight loosened his hold on Rigaud. "They won't always be," Gaucher assured him. "If you want nothing more to do with us, so be it. Rufus and I will trouble you no more. But I would advise you to keep proper monastic silence concerning this matter, or you may find yourself truly leaving this world."

Gaucher signaled to Rufus and they rode forward, forcing the monks on foot leading the packhorses to make way for them. Rigaud watched them until they rounded a bend in the road, Gaucher's blond stripe of hair gleaming in the sunlight.

"There must be a way to stop them," he murmured, "without the abbot learning the truth."

Ignoring the curious glances from the brothers around him, Brother Rigaud bent his head, praying fervently for a way out of the horror that he had thought left behind when he entered the gates of Cluny.

They came at last out of the narrow valley, past the point where the Celé River joined the Lot again. The land was now gentler. It had been tamed centuries before and instead of tangled forests teeming with wild men and monsters, there were orchards of apple and peach trees in bloom, and row upon row of vines. There were more pilgrim refuges along this route so that it was no longer necessary to camp in caves or on the river-bank.

The days passed without any further incident. Mondete continued to trail behind the rest of the group, but she now tolerated Solomon's presence beside her. For his part, he rarely spoke, not to Mondete or anyone else. Catherine worried about this. She had the feeling that his spirit was off on some other pilgrimage while his body continued to travel with them.

In her concern for Solomon, Catherine didn't notice how much time her father was spending with the widow Griselle. To the annoyance of Gaucher and Rufus, Hubert rode next to her almost every day, entertaining her with stories he had learned in his travels or discussing the possible uses for the small estate she had inherited from her husband.

"Since it will be the property of Saint Peter when I die," she explained, "I can do little to improve it without the permission of the monks."

"I doubt they would object to anything that brought in more profit," Hubert said.

"I'm not so sure," Griselle answered. "I know they are very strict about cutting down the woods. The abbot is looking ahead to timber for his building program. Also, I had thought to put in a water mill, but there was some question about what it would do to the fishing farther downstream. My, the sun is bright today. It seems fiercer the farther south we go."

She signaled to Hersent to bring her broad-brimmed hat.

"My poor husband was born in Spain, you know," she said. "He was dark, like you. He told me that the summer was very cruel there. He was grateful when his uncle died without heirs and he could come to live in Burgundy."

"His family was one of those that settled in Spain after Alfonso the Sixth drove back the Saracens?" Hubert asked.

"Not exactly," she answered. "His father was also a knight and a younger son. There wasn't enough property to divide. Bertran's father went with Alphonse Jordan of Toulouse to fight the Saracens and then married a woman whose family had converted."

"A Saracen woman?" Hubert was shocked.

Griselle drew herself up proudly. "Her family was from that of one of the caliphs," she told him. "I have always thought it thrilling, like something from a tale of the heroes of the past. There is always a brave pagan woman who converts to the true faith for the sake of love."

"Yes," Hubert said sadly. He wondered if he could have convinced Madeleine to abandon her Jesus and all His saints and convert to the true faith. But he knew that there had never been enough love in her for that, only obedience to her father's choice and a certain fondness that had come with the children and fled into guilt when so many of them died.

"Don't you agree?"

"What?" Hubert jerked back to the present. Griselle was looking at him expectantly. What was he supposed to be agreeing to? "Oh, certainly, certainly," he said quickly.

"You don't think it would be too much of a miracle to hope for?" Griselle asked.

"Oh, no, not at all," he answered in confusion. "All things are possible with God's help."

"Yes, I suppose so," Griselle said slowly. "But it seems rather odd that He would make someone like Mondete the instrument."

Now Hubert was completely lost. "Mondete?" he said. "Instrument of what?"

"Bringing that Jewish man to baptism, of course," Griselle answered sharply. "What did you think I was talking about?"

Since Hubert had had no idea, he wisely, if belatedly, kept silent. He doubted that either Solomon or Mondete were intent on converting the other. The only point at which their beliefs met seemed to be at the depth of their individual misery. Hubert smiled an apology and tried to steer the conversation back to something safe, such as the cost and availability of genuine Byzantine embroidered silk.

Edgar was only marginally relieved when they came out onto the river plain. He knew that worse mountains awaited them. Solomon had told him of his winter treks across the Pyrenees. Even allowing for exaggeration, there were very likely a number of steep and narrow trails with precipitous drops. Catherine's dream of falling off a narrow ledge haunted him far more than it did her. Edgar had studied dreams. He knew that even true sendings were often couched in metaphor. It might not be a real bridge that collapsed, but a symbol for a test of faith.

Edgar's trouble was that crossing a real bridge over a chasm was the strongest test of faith he could imagine.

"Edgar, look!" Catherine poked a pungent branch under his nose. "Lilacs! Isn't it beautiful here?"

Edgar pulled his mind away from the mountains. He looked around and admitted that the land was indeed beautiful. Catherine's arms were full of the lilac branches. Whatever did she intend to do with them? He asked.

"I don't know," she admitted. "At home, we would dry the petals, mix them with lavender and orrisroot and use the potpourri to keep moths from the linen. I suppose I'll have to throw them away. I didn't think. I just smelled the perfume and wanted to have the flowers. Perhaps we'll pass through a village and I can give them to someone there."

Edgar smiled at her disappointment. "I'll tie them together for you," he suggested, "and we can leave them at the next shrine we pass, as an offering."

"Yes, that would be appropriate," Catherine said. "You know, whenever someone speaks of the 'odor of sanctity,' I always have imagined lilacs."

She buried her face in the blossoms, inhaling the rich scent. "Do you think that's foolish?" she asked him.

"No," he said.

She looked so happy. He hadn't seen that much hope in her since they lost the first child. If lilacs could give her back that air of possibility, if they could remove the grief from her eyes, then Edgar was willing to grant them leave to run riot in heaven.

Perhaps the mountains wouldn't be as dreadful as he imagined.

Maruxa didn't fear the mountains. She had crossed them before. All that mattered to her was that they lay between her and home and the children she hadn't seen in six months.

"Do you think Diede is old enough to come with us next

time?" she asked Roberto as they stopped with the others to rest in the noonday heat.

Roberto sighed. "Old enough, yes, but I wish we could apprentice him to a safer trade than ours. Or that we could find a place to stay permanently. I'm getting too old to wander about."

Maruxa put her hand on his shoulder. "You're as strong as ever," she assured him. "It's only seeing that man again that's upset you. Stop worrying. Now both he and his wife are dead and their wickedness with them. No one else knows what happened."

"I wish we could forget it," Roberto said. "And how do we know that Lord Hugh didn't tell one of those other men?"

Maruxa didn't want him thinking in that direction. "Why should he have?" she asked. "That would mean admitting he had been cuckolded."

"Yes, of course," he said.

He got up and stretched out the kinks in his back. Maruxa exhaled in relief. She'd kept the secret nearly ten years now. Roberto had confessed what he had been forced to do and she had forgiven him. But she had never had the courage to say what had happened to her. She had tried not to think about it, but seeing Hugh and his companions had brought the nightmare back, as fresh as the morning after.

They would be at Moissac soon. They could find another party to travel with. Maruxa couldn't stand the constant fear that one of the remaining knights would remember them. She couldn't bear wondering if Roberto had learned the truth and decided to take his revenge on Hugh of Grignon.

Roberto held out his hand to help her up. Maruxa took it and stood, feeling the ache in her back that told her it was almost her time of the month. One more thing to cope with.

As they passed through the field of lilac bushes, Maruxa thought of how overpoweringly sweet the odor was. It made her want to retch.

Ten

Moissac, the abbey of Saint Peter, Saturday, May 17, 1142;
Commemoration of the landing of Saint Tropez, noble Roman, martyred
under Nero, who later relocated to the south of France.

*Quid dicamde lectione? Cellam sine lectione infernum reputo sine
consolatione, patibulum sine releuamine, carcerem sine lumine,
sepulcrum sine respiramine. . . .*

What should I say about reading? I consider a room without
reading to be a hell without consolation, a gibbet without relief, a
prison without light, a tomb without a vent. . . .
—Peter of Celle,
On Affliction and Reading 8–13 PL 202

*W*hat do you mean, the emperor can't meet with me in Pamplona?" Abbot Peter rose from his chair to face the messenger. "It's at his invitation that I've made this journey."

"Yes, my Lord Abbot," the man replied, "but our gracious emperor is at this moment personally conducting a siege of the Almoravid stronghold at Coria. He had hoped to be able to present you with the souls of the citizens for baptism, but they are more reluctant to surrender than we supposed and he fears he will not be able to join you for another six weeks."

Peter walked around the messenger, who wasn't sure whether to turn respectfully or stand motionless while being inspected.

"You have been at this siege?" the abbot asked.

"Yes, Lord Abbot." The man stared straight ahead. "I ask pardon for the state of my clothes. I rode from dawn to sunset for a week to bring you this message."

"Very well." Peter waved the man out. "Someone will see that you are fed and given a place to rest. I'll send for you when my reply to the emperor is ready."

When the man had left, Peter paced back and forth across the chamber that the local abbot had vacated for his use.

"Well, Pierre," he asked his secretary, "what shall I do? I could go on to Compostela and meet the emperor upon my return, assuming he brings his siege to a successful conclusion."

"That would be one possibility," Pierre answered. "Of course, your appearance at Compostela might be taken to indicate a preference for one episcopal candidate or the other. However, you might also take this opportunity to cross over

into Catalonia and visit our establishments there before heading west. No abbot of Cluny has made an appearance there for
at least forty years."

"Exactly what I was thinking." The abbot sat again. "It's all
too easy for remote dependencies to become lax in their observance. It's only proper that I use this gift of extra time to inspect them myself."

"I'm sure the monks will be overjoyed at the prospect of
your arrival," Pierre told him.

The secretary took out his wax tablet and prepared to com-
pose a draft of the letter to the priories.

"Begin with Sant-Pere-de-Casseres," Peter said. "Tell the
prior that I will also go to Comprodon and Clarà, the roads permitting. Inform Alfonso's messenger of this and have word sent
to me at Casseres when he has concluded his siege and is ready
to meet with me."

"Of course, my Lord Abbot," Pierre said, scratching the
information on the tablet in his own form of shorthand.

As he wrote, he thought of something. "What about all the
pilgrims who have been following us?" he asked the abbot.
"Most of them won't wish to continue with you if you're making such a long detour."

"That can't be helped," Peter answered. "They should be
able to make other arrangements from here. The route is well
traveled."

"I will arrange for those who are from our area to be informed." Pierre made a final note with his stylus, bowed and
left the room.

Peter of Cluny wasn't annoyed at this change in plans. It
made excellent sense to make a personal visit at the Catalon-
ian priories. It was important to keep the ties between the
mother house and the dependents strong. He did wonder if the
time might be better spent staying at one Cluniac house and
having the priors come to him. But it seemed wiser to show his
concern for his far-flung children by going there himself. It
would also be more difficult for them to cover up any irregularities in their observance or accounts.

He wished he had thought to remind Pierre to see if any

translators of Arabic had been found. That project should continue in spite of the emperor's delay. Peter knew that souls were not won by siege, but by persuasion. And how was he to persuade the Saracens to give up their religion if no one knew what it consisted of?

Catherine loved the new abbey church at Moissac, with its interior freshly painted in bright patterns of stripes and flowers. As usual, Edgar spent most of his time studying the tympanum and commenting on the technique used to sculpt the figures there.

"Those patterns are new to me," he told Catherine, pointing at the *roseaux* along the bottom of the tympanum. "I wonder if they were also done by Moorish artists."

"What I want to know is why those rats are running around the edges," Catherine said. "I can't think of any biblical reason for them."

"I have no idea," Edgar said. "Why don't you find someone to ask?"

Catherine took that to mean she had shared his interest long enough. Edgar could sit for hours imagining how the figures had been formed. His interest fascinated her, but her mind didn't function in that way. The artistry of the work was important to her only in the ability of the creator to make the story come alive. Not understanding the symbolism of the rats irritated her. She would be very angry if she found out they were there simply because some apprentice only knew how to carve rats.

Catherine left her husband at the church, knowing that he wouldn't have moved at all when it came time to retrieve him. She wandered down the row of shops leading up to the abbey. She paused for a moment to look longingly at a pair of earrings made from beads and bits of polished glass, laid out on a bed of black felt.

"I know a shop you'll like better than this," a voice whispered in her ear.

Catherine turned around. "Are you trying to lure me into

a tavern, *Sieur?*" she laughed. "Solomon, what are you doing away from Mondete?"

"She went into the church," Solomon explained. "At that door, my devotion ends."

He tugged on one of her braids. "Do you want to see the shop, or not?" he asked. "It's down a twisting side street. You'd never find it on your own."

"And what could be for sale that I'd trust you to lead me there without one of your tricks?" Catherine knew from long experience how Solomon loved to tease her.

He smiled and said one word.

"Books."

Catherine felt as if she had been fasting for a month and someone had just said the word "bread." Her mouth dropped open and she swallowed to keep from drooling.

"For sale? To anyone?" she asked in disbelief. "Like in Paris?"

"Not on such a grand scale," Solomon answered, "but a nice selection nonetheless. At least in number. I have no idea what's inside them."

Catherine took his hand. "Take me there," she said, "and I'll tell you."

Brother Rigaud was more than a little relieved at the news that they were going to Catalonia.

"Now, if only Rufus and Gaucher leave me alone until we depart," he muttered to himself as he and Brother James checked the robes of the monks for holes or tears. If they were now going to move east and pass through Toulouse, it would be a good place to buy replacements before confronting the rigors of the trek over the mountains.

"What about boots?" Brother James asked. "Have you asked any of the brothers if their shoes need resoling? I don't want anyone going lame because of a misplaced desire for asceticism."

"Yes, it won't do simply to ask them," Rigaud sighed. "I'll have to take a look at each man's clothing."

Brother James gave Rigaud a sharp glance. "Are you sure you wouldn't rather someone else did that?" he asked.

"Of course not," Rigaud answered, purposely misunderstanding. "No task is too menial for the Lord's servants."

Brother James shrugged. If Rigaud was willing to perform the task, he should be grateful. After all, despite rumors of Rigaud's life before entering the monastery, there had been not a whisper of any impropriety since then.

"Very well," he said. "Have you heard when we are to leave?"

"Not for a few days," Rigaud answered. "We'll have time to get things sorted out here."

James looked at him quizzically. "Are you eager to see Spain again?" he asked.

Rigaud's face clouded. "No," he answered. "I fear it, somewhat. There are memories I would not awaken. But that's cowardly. And I have vowed obedience to my abbot. I'm more afraid of breaking that than of any memory. After all, it's likely that my apprehension is groundless. I haven't been there in more than twenty years. Everything is probably different."

He spoke too quickly, the words falling on top of each other. James wondered how horrible the memories could be.

Brother James closed his eyes. Nothing could be worse than the specter who had been haunting him since Le Puy. He knew now that she was one of the pilgrims from Paris, but how had she come by that face? He remembered the tale of the dissolute pilgrim priest whom the devil had come to in the guise of Saint James. The priest had already repented and Satan feared to lose the man's soul to God and so, making the penitent believe it was God's will, he convinced him first to amputate the most sinful of his parts and then to cut his own throat. The prayers of the other pilgrims had caused the true Saint James to bring the man back to life, but Brother James did not remember anything about the lost organ being replaced. It seemed a large price to pay for having been deceived. But it was certainly a stark warning against trusting in visions.

Was this woman also the Great Liar in the form of someone he had loved? He had considered confronting her, but now he was to be spared that decision. In a few days he would head for Catalonia with the abbot, and the woman and her family would continue on through Gascony to Navarre.

Perhaps his prayers had already been answered.

Catherine admitted that she never would have found the bookshop on her own. It was only a small room, next to an atelier where vellum and parchment were prepared and sold, not far from the tanneries. The reek of the chemicals used in the preparation of the material made her eyes water. She was grateful when the door shut behind them.

"Back are you, young man?" a voice came out of the gloom. The room was lit only by a small oil lamp. "Brought your sister, I see. I don't have anything for ladies. Nothing with gold letters or pictures. A few compendia and a lot of pages that can be scraped and reused. This is a place for scholars. I already told you that."

"Yes, I know," Solomon answered. "She'd like to look anyway."

The man gestured his permission.

Catherine inhaled the scent of ink and leather and felt a sharp pang of longing for the convent and days when study had been her main occupation. She reached for the nearest book. It was crudely bound between boards and not well stitched. Nevertheless, she held it lovingly and, opening it, moved closer to the lamp.

"It's not in French, *ma douce*," the bookseller said. "I told you."

Catherine ignored him. She ran her finger along the line. "Lactantius," she said finally. "On *the Death of the Persecutors*." She turned a few pages. "What else is bound with it? Some Gregory, a few passages from Augustine. Where did you get this?"

"From one of those wandering students," the man said. "Needed to sell his text to continue his studies. Also thought it would be too heavy to take over the mountains. A lot of them do that. Or sell their books on the way back when they discover they haven't enough money to get home again."

He got up and took the book from Catherine. "Now, that's

enough of your playing, both of you," he said. "I know very well that she can't read. I don't know why you thought it would be funny to make me think she did. What did you do, look at the book first and then tell her to recite it back?"

Solomon grinned in unholy glee as Catherine's eyes flashed and her chin went up. "I am not accustomed to being disbelieved," she said with deceptive restraint. "Therefore, I will excuse your rudeness and prove my honesty. You give me something and I'll tell you what it says."

"Done," the man replied.

She didn't know how much at that moment she sounded like the Lady Griselle.

The bookseller rooted about in a pile of vellum pieces. They were irregular or stitched together from scraps, the sort of thing students often bought to make a permanent record of their notes.

"I don't know how you thought to fool me," he said as he searched for something difficult. "You didn't even look as though you were reading. You didn't say a word. Your mouth hardly moved."

Catherine bit her lip. She had learned the art of silent reading because she had opened a book so often when she had been told to do something else. It wouldn't do to be caught reading when one was supposed to be sweeping.

"Put the words in front of me," she demanded, "and I'll say each one clearly for you."

"I'm looking," the bookseller replied. "Now, you stand back, young man. I don't want you seeing this and giving her some sort of signal."

Solomon laughed and covered his eyes. The man pulled a page from the bottom of the pile, looked at it, gave a grunt of satisfaction and handed it to Catherine.

"There," he said. "See what you can make of that."

Catherine took the page and held it to the light. The writing was crabbed, the writer using every bit of space, every possible abbreviation. She squinted.

"I thought so," the bookseller said, reaching for the vellum.

"Just a minute," Catherine moved closer to the light.

"*. . . celesti celum omne penetranti, celestis munus voveo, quad in-tegritatem scientie in se complectitur. . . .*"

She looked at Solomon in excitement, not noticing the bookseller's look of disbelief. "I don't know this work," she said. "It's some sort of treatise on the motions of the stars."

Solomon came to attention. "Who wrote it?" he asked.

"It doesn't say." She scanned the page. "Whoever wrote this, though, seems to have studied with someone who could read the language of the Saracens. *Dicitur Arabici magistri.* 'It is told by the Arab masters.' "

"How much do you want for it?" Solomon asked the man.

But the bookseller was angry now. "I don't know how you're doing this, but I don't like being the butt of anyone's joke."

He snatched the vellum back from Catherine and studied it himself. "You can't have read this so easily!" he shouted. "I can barely make it out."

"Perhaps you were not as fortunate as I in choosing your teachers," Catherine shot back. "I have studied with Master Gilbert de la Porrée and Master Peter Abelard."

The man's eyebrows rose. "I never heard of Master Gilbert," he answered. "And it's easy for you to say you learned from Abelard, now that he's dead."

"What?" The room seemed to freeze around Catherine. "That's not true. He has retired to Saint-Marcellus, in Burgundy."

"He died three weeks ago," the man told her. "Messenger just arrived at the abbey. One of the monks was in a day or two ago and told me. Now, now, sweeting! Don't go on so. Did you really know him?"

He had reason to be alarmed. Catherine had fallen against the table and was bent over it, sobbing. Solomon rushed to her and made her lean against him. He glared at the bookseller.

"If this is some cruel deception," he said, "I swear I'll cut your tongue out. She was raised at the Paraclete, by Héloïse herself. She can read better than you. And now you've broken her heart. Well, stop gaping like a tide-bound fish and get her some wine or something!"

"There's a tavern three doors down," the bookseller said. "Wait here." He hurried out.

Solomon helped Catherine to a bench, swept parchment from it and sat her down. Sitting beside her, he patted her shoulder. "Cry all you like, Catherine," he said, "but that old fool may be wrong, you know. It's only hearsay."

"No," Catherine gulped. "We knew it when we saw him last, Edgar and I. He didn't expect to live much longer. It's only . . . poor Mother Héloïse!"

She wept some more, wiping her eyes and nose on his sleeve, then realized what she'd done and apologized.

"Don't worry," he said. "There's been worse on it."

The bookseller returned with a ewer of wine.

"We didn't bring our cups," Solomon said.

"Never mind," the man said and brought out his own, wiping it with a blank sheet of parchment, then filling it and handing it to Catherine. "Drink the wine slowly," he warned her. "There's no water mixed with it. I'm sorry, young woman. I didn't mean to grieve you so."

She nodded her understanding and took his advice about the wine, which was rough and strong. After a few sips, she gave the cup back.

"We should be going," she told Solomon. "I don't want Edgar to learn this from a stranger."

"Yes, very well," Solomon said. "But first, please, will you look for any other pages in this same hand? I need to know what's in them, where they came from."

He turned to the bookseller. "Who did you buy this from?" he asked. "I'll pay whatever you like for it, and for any others she finds."

"That's no way to trade," the man said. "There may be a few more pieces in the pile. I got them from some northerner, English or German, I think. He was on his way back from Toledo. Said he needed enough money for a good Christian whore."

"And how much was that?" Solomon asked, pulling out his purse.

"Depends on what you want her to do," the man answered.

He gave Catherine another apologetic look, but she was busy among the pages and hadn't heard him.

"How much?" Solomon repeated.

"Ten sous of Narbonne," the bookseller told him finally. "Or four of Troyes. Have you changed your money yet?"

"Here." Solomon counted out the coins. "Did you find any more, Catherine?"

"Yes, a few." She held them up. "But there seem to be some missing. I'm not sure. I need time to look at them properly."

Solomon took the pages from her. "Six of them," he counted. "Is this all you bought?" he asked the bookseller.

"No, there were ten, I think, but Abbot Peter's notary was in yesterday and took a number of pieces to be scraped and used again. The other four might have been among them. I didn't look. It's not quality material."

"All right, we'll buy what there is." Solomon took back a coin. "Catherine, are you feeling well enough to walk back to the hostel?"

"Yes," she said, "but take me to the church instead. I need to find Edgar. Now."

The man rolled up the pages, tied them with a string, and with more apologies, showed them out. When they had gone, he refilled his cup from the ewer and drank the wine in one draught.

Catherine felt numb as Solomon led her back up the twisting road to the church. She ought to rejoice that Master Abelard had at last found peace after so many years of physical and intellectual torment. She told herself that. But all the time, she was aware that there was a hole torn in her universe that couldn't be repaired. It was as bad as if she had lost her father.

Solomon was struggling between the knowledge that he should respect her grief and the fierce desire to know what was written on the pages. What astronomical secrets had this student learned? How far had he gone to find a master? How could he have been so degenerate as to sell what he had learned for a night of lust?

That led his mind to other speculations, but he quickly returned to wondering what might be written on the smudged pages. He could read in French and Hebrew but had no Latin, and all the abbreviations made it impossible to even sound words out. Catherine and Edgar were the only Latin scholars he knew well enough to ask for help. He knew it was selfish, but he hoped they could overcome their sorrow enough to be of use to him.

As Catherine had expected, Edgar was seated just where she had left him, staring up at the carvings on the tympanum. She began crying again as she knelt beside him, and it was several minutes before he understood what had upset her so. He crossed himself and bowed his head.

"We should go in and pray for his soul," he told Catherine.

She took his hand and they went inside the church. Solomon watched, knowing that for the moment he had been forgotten. He didn't mind. He had known Abelard, too. The master had been an extraordinary man in many ways, not the least of which was his understanding of and sympathy for the plight of the Jews.

"*Baruch atta Adonai,*" Solomon said quietly. "Even though the man was a misguided infidel, Lord, take care of him. There must be a place for such a one in Your garden."

Hubert and Eliazar had their minds only on business. Moissac was a confluence of rivers and trade. Merchants on their way from Italy and the East passed through as well as Norse traders coming down with furs and amber to sell in Spain. Mozarabic and Jewish merchants waited here for those who preferred not to cross the mountains but wished to buy goods from Al-Andalus and Africa. The streets near the abbey were crowded with inns, boot-makers, money changers, wine-sellers, brothels, and suppliers of anything else a traveler might need.

"I don't like to see you weighted down with all those packages," Eliazar said to his brother.

"Tomorrow you can carry them," Hubert said firmly. "Or we can hire someone. I won't coerce you to carry anything on the Sabbath."

"You couldn't," Eliazar said. "But that doesn't mean I want you to, either."

"This is an old argument," Hubert sighed. "Be grateful that I'm young enough to carry the load for two."

They trudged along until they reached the inn where Hubert had found them a whole room to themselves. Eliazar shook his head. "Such extravagance!" he told Hubert. "One room for the five of us!"

Hubert went up the narrow stairs and dumped the boxes on the bed. "I'm hoping that three of us will find a reason to come in late," he said. "With all that camping and staying in hostels, it really will be a miracle if Catherine and Edgar are able to give me a grandchild."

Eliazar laughed. "You underestimate your daughter and her husband. They manage these things better than you think."

"Perhaps," Hubert said. He sorted out the packages as to owner, then set the piles on the floor and sat heavily upon the bed, causing a cloud of dust to rise from the coverlet.

"What am I to do with this son-in-law?" he asked Eliazar. "He shows no talent for trade. He obviously has no future in the Church. He sold his land to give Catherine a dower. All that seems to intrigue him is the work of common laborers: masonry and machines and carving designs in bits of wood and ivory."

"His talents have proved useful in the past," Eliazar pointed out. "He was able to pose as a goldsmith and keep us from being accused of stealing Christian relics."

"And how many times will that happen?" Hubert asked.

"Never again, I hope," Eliazar answered. "But there must be other ways he can be of service."

Hubert ran his hands through his graying black hair. "Don't you think I've tried to find some?" he said. "I know how the boy feels. As much as they despised my profession, Madeleine's family at least had to be polite to me because I brought them wealth. And I have been angry and rude to Edgar more than once. I forget that his family is, if anything, better than Madeleine's. Do you know what I fear most?"

Eliazar shook his head. Hubert looked at him bleakly.

"I am terrified," he said, "that Edgar will decide to take Catherine back to his people. Scotland! The end of the world. You've seen the students in Paris, dressed in belted skirts with no *brais*, just their ugly knees showing. I can't let my daughter live among savages!"

Eliazar stood and patted Hubert on the back.

"There now," he said. "Kings have done worse. But why should it come to that? If the boy wanted to study *Torah*, you would support him, wouldn't you? Why not let him learn masonry and machines? Perhaps Count Thibault will hire him to design siege engines. Or some bishop will have him oversee the building of his cathedral. That's a lifetime of employment."

Hubert still looked glum. His stomach rumbled.

"That's it," Eliazar said. "Hunger has put your humors out of balance. Come along and eat with us. The brethren from Toulouse are traveling with their own cook. We'll have real food tonight!"

Gaucher and Rufus had also found congenial lodging. They judged any inn on two things: the quality of the beer and the absence of fleas. In this case, they decided to put up with the fleas.

"I haven't tasted anything this good since we left Mâcon," Rufus said as he lowered the bowl and wiped his mouth. "Why do you think they can't make decent beer here in the south?"

"Too many heretics," Gaucher answered. "You need absolutely orthodox methods to make beer properly."

Rufus accepted this as logical. "Have you seen Rigaud?" he asked. "I'm worried about him."

"What for?" Gaucher asked. "What can happen to him? He says he doesn't play with boys anymore. And if he's caught at it, they'll only make him pray harder."

Rufus belched loudly in disgust. "I don't give a damn what he does with boys," he said. "He can poke it up a cow, if he wants to. I'm worried about him keeping his vow of silence to us. He seems to think we're about to commit sacrilege."

Gaucher leaned back on his stool and toppled over. He

righted himself and poured another bowl. "So he'll pray for our souls," he said. "I don't mind."

"What if he decides to confess to the abbot instead?" Rufus asked.

"He wouldn't!" Gaucher said, shocked. "He swore a sacred oath!"

"That was before he became a monk." Rufus peered into the pitcher, then upended it over his bowl.

Both men stared at their beer in silent contemplation. Gaucher looked up first, his forehead creased in the attempt to resolve a theological paradox.

"Rigaud took the oath with us first, didn't he?" he demanded. "He can't break it just because he's joined the Church. It would even be worse then. Who would trust a monk who didn't keep a vow?"

Rufus wasn't convinced. "I don't know. They don't have the same kind of honor we do." He stared at the bits of herb floating in the beer as if waiting for them to form the answer.

"I think," Gaucher announced, "that we need to ask him, just to be sure."

Catherine had finally stopped weeping, but she felt drained of more than tears. Edgar guessed what she was thinking.

"*Leoffaest*," he said, "your being at the Paraclete when Abbess Héloïse heard the news would not have been a comfort to her. There is some grief that cannot be consoled."

"I know," she answered, thinking of the tiny graves they had left behind and of how little comfort anyone had been able to give her. "Astrolabe will go to her."

"And when we return, we can go see her as well," Edgar suggested. "By then, the first pain will have died and she may want to speak of him to friends."

"He was no heretic," Catherine said firmly. "God knows that, if the pope doesn't."

"Yes," Edgar said. "I have no fear for his soul."

They were walking slowly back to the inn at twilight. The shops were boarded over, the tables taken in. Lamplight glowed through cracks in the doors. The dust of commerce had settled and the air was clear. Catherine leaned her head on Edgar's shoulder.

"We'll tell our children about him," she declared. "I won't have him forgotten even though his work was condemned."

He turned his face and blew at the curls escaping from her scarf. "Abelard won't be forgotten," he promised. "All of us who loved him will make certain of that."

At the inn, they found the Lady Griselle eating alone at one end of a table. At the other end, her guards and maid sat with their dinners and made sure no one came between them. When Griselle saw Catherine and Edgar, she smiled at them to join her.

"It's so difficult, keeping a sense of rank on a journey like this," she explained. "And don't you go on about all being equal before God. In His house there are many mansions, and I don't expect to be in one with some *villein* with filthy feet. Are you quite well, my dear?"

This last was addressed to Catherine, who smiled and said she was simply tired. Edgar went to fetch their cups and spoons and get some food. Catherine sat across from Griselle, who was wearing a shimmering green-silk *bliaut* over a white-linen *chainse*. At her shoulders were gold brooches in the shape of hunting dogs with tiny rubies for eyes.

"I don't know how you stay so fresh under these circumstances," she told Griselle in honest admiration. "I feel as if everything I put on becomes soiled instantly."

"One learns the art of it after many years of marriage to a warrior," Griselle answered, patting her smooth scarf. "Hersent is an excellent servant. She came to me as a child and I had the training of her before she married. We often traveled with my husband. We even accompanied him on some of his campaigns."

"Have you been to Spain before?" Catherine asked. "My father tells me that your husband was born there."

Griselle bent over her soup, gracefully sipping a bit of it. "No, Bertran never spoke much about his home there," she said. "His parents had died and there was no one for him to go back for. It always made him sad, so I didn't ask much."

She took another sip, then smiled brightly at Catherine. "Your father is a dear man, isn't he?" she said. "He's been very kind to entertain me as we ride. I'm a little vague on his family connections, though."

"They were merchants in Rouen," Catherine said guardedly. "He also lost his family when he was young and was raised by a fellow merchant, a friend of his father's. He settled in Paris before I was born."

"And your mother is of an irreproachable family of Blois, I understand," Griselle continued.

Catherine thought of her bombastic and apparently immortal grandfather. "Irreproachable" was not the first adjective that came to mind.

"We have allodial land granted us by Charlemagne himself," she said proudly, neglecting to mention how little of it was left. "My sister, Agnes, is currently living with our relatives there."

She wanted to ask Griselle about her own family and if they were of a lineage old enough to share a table with Catherine, but convent manners prevailed. Edgar returned with the soup and bread. They ate quickly and excused themselves to go upstairs.

"How long do you think it will be before Father and Uncle Eliazar come in?" Catherine asked as Edgar helped her out of her clothes.

"Long enough, I hope," he answered.

The next morning, the entire inn was awakened not by roosters, but by shouts and screams of panic in the street below. Hubert stumbled from his bed and stuck his head out the window.

"What is it?" he called down. "Is the city being attacked?"

"Yes!" a man shouted back up at him. "But not by the infidel. The devil himself is among us. There's been a murder at the altar of the church."

Eleven

The abbey church of Moissac, Sunday, May 18, 1142; Commemoration of the martyrdom under Diocletian of Tecusa, Alexandria, Claudia, Euphrasia, Matrona, Julitta and Phaina, strong-minded seventy-year-old virgins.

Reconciliatio ecclesiae benedictae fieri potest aqua lustrati communi; reconciliatio vero ecclesiae consecratae fiat aqua ad hoc benedicta secundum leges liturgicas; . . .

The reconciliation of the church that has only been blessed can be done with ordinary holy water, but the reconciliation of an actually consecrated church must be done with water blessed for this purpose according to the liturgical laws.

Codex Iuris Canonici
Canon 1177

This was done by nothing human!" Brother James exclaimed.

Abbot Peter shook his head in denial, horrified at what he saw before him. "The impulse may have been demonically instigated," he said, "but I have no doubt that the hand was human. The man who did this shall be found and brought to me before sunset tonight. Do you all understand that? Now, I want this mess cleaned and the church reconciled at once. I will not allow even such an atrocity to prevent me from serving Mass."

He strode out through the door to the cloister, leaving Brother James and the other monks to deal with the remains.

For a long while, no one dared move closer. The only sound was the murmur of prayers. Finally, Brother James approached the grotesque form draped over a sawhorse that workers had left in the transept.

"He mustn't be left like this for everyone to see," he said.

"But how are we to move him?" one of the monks asked. "We should send for the lay brothers."

"No, even they shouldn't be allowed to witness one of our order in such an improper position," James snapped. "Now, help me!"

They came forward timidly, all staring in a combination of revulsion and horrid fascination. The very stiff body of Brother Rigaud lay propped over the sawhorse. His feet barely touched the floor on one side. His hands seemed braced against it on the other. They were spattered with blood, which was still dripping slowly from the spear-point coming out of his throat.

His robe had been pulled up to his waist, and the other end of the spear was protruding from between his buttocks.

"Improper" was the least one could say about his position. That he was dead was a given.

"But how . . . how will we get it out?" Brother Felix asked.

Brother James stopped. He wasn't sure what would happen if they tried to pull the spear out. He wasn't even sure which end to pull from. Nor did he have any idea of what Rigaud's body would do if they tried to lift him with the spear still stuck through him.

"We'll leave that problem to the infirmarian," he decided. "For now, let's see . . . one of you lift him by the legs, and you, Brother Vulgrinus, take his shoulders from the other side. Turn him so that the body can be put on the litter."

"Someone will have to get the spear out," Brother Vulgrinus said as he attempted to lift the body without causing further damage. "We can't bury him like this."

Brother James heartily wished that they could, and as soon as possible. Thank the saints Rigaud hadn't been murdered in the cloister. At least out here in the church, anyone might have killed him. But if word of the method used became known, the scandal would be horrendous. There were enough ribald stories about effeminate monks for most people to gladly believe that Rigaud had come to the church during the Great Silence for an assignation and been killed by his lover.

It certainly appeared so, James thought. How else could one explain such a humiliating position? One would hardly lift one's robe and bend over politely for a stranger with a spear.

As the brothers managed to get Rigaud's body onto the litter and lifted it to carry him out, Brother James stopped them.

"That's odd," he said as he knelt before the point of the spear. It protruded from Rigaud's throat like a serpent's tongue. James realized that the tip had been broken off, leaving a slight fork. Had it snapped within the body—against a bone, perhaps? But that wasn't what puzzled him. The wound was actually wider than the end of the spearhead, which had completely exited the body, leaving the gaping hole where blood was just now starting to coagulate around the shaft of the spear.

James stood up, brushing dust from his knees. "Thank you," he told the monks. "You may take him away now."

He went back to the sawhorse and knelt next to it, examining the pattern of blood on the floor. He certainly wasn't an expert on death, the way the former soldier, Rigaud, had been, but he had seen his share of violence. It seemed to him that there should be more blood. It should have gushed not only from the wound, but from Rigaud's mouth, too, as his vital organs were punctured. Brother James had no idea who he could ask about such a thing. At the very least, he decided, his observation must be brought to the attention of the abbot.

While everyone else at the inn was discussing the morning's discovery in delighted consternation, Catherine returned to their room. Though sorry for the monk, she was more relieved that for once she hadn't been the one to find the corpse. She was much more interested in deciphering the astrological notes that Solomon had bought the day before. When the mattress and covers had been taken from the trestle bed in their room and stored for the day, she spread the pages out on the board, trying to find their order and a clue as to who had written them and under what circumstances. Solomon hovered over her impatiently.

"It's all in the same hand," she told him, "but done in different inks, and the size of the letters differs even within each page. I believe these were intended to be personal notes, from lectures, perhaps, done at various times. The treatise certainly isn't in any form to be circulated. He may have made a clean copy before he sold these."

Solomon leaned over the pages and tried to follow her finger as she pointed out the various sections of the work. Most of it meant nothing to him, but here and there he was able to piece together a series of letters that made sense.

"Isn't that word 'angel'?" he asked.

"*Angeli*. Angels, yes." Catherine squinted as she read the

passage. "This part isn't about the stars. It's about the power of words. What's it doing in with this?"

Solomon fidgeted while she deciphered the words.

"Oh, I see," she said at last. "He says that using the secret names of God and calling upon the angels by name can be efficacious in controlling the weather, but only if the words are said with the correct motions and when the stars are favorably positioned. There's a note in the margin saying that he had tried the formula recommended by his master but it wasn't successful. Then there's a digression about the importance of knowing the correct pronunciation of the names."

Solomon picked up the parchment and stared at it as if he expected tongues of fire to leap from it. "Does it say what the names are?" he asked.

"Not that I can see," she said. "At least not on this page. The rest seems to be a lecture on how to calculate the most auspicious times to cause earthquake and flood."

She looked up. "Solomon, I will not help you if you intend to use this to destroy people."

"Catherine!" he said, shocked. "I don't want to cause earthquakes or even a mild spring rain. I'm not interested in making things happen. I want to know why they do. I want to know what the Almighty One wants from me, why He has left us amidst our enemies, and when the Messiah will come."

"And you think the answer is on these rough bits of parchment?" Catherine tried not to laugh. He seemed serious.

His shoulders drooped. "I suppose not," he admitted. "But there might be a key. One word. A number. Something. Does it give the name of the master he studied with?"

"I don't know," Catherine said. "I need more time to read through this. It doesn't appear so, but sometimes people will hide such information in the text as a puzzle. You know, it would be easier if I could work alone for a while. Why don't you go see what everyone else is doing? Didn't someone say that it was one of the Cluniac monks who had been found dead in the church? That may delay the abbot's departure."

"We don't need to travel with him," Solomon answered,

still looking with longing at the writing. "From here on, there will be a number of caravans we can join."

"Solomon!" Catherine said. "Go away."

"Ah!" Comprehension flooded his face. "I'm hindering you. Why didn't you just say so?" He patted her head in an avuncular manner that irritated her even more and went out.

It was afternoon now, and the street market was crowded with people using their day of rest to shop and gossip. In one corner of the church square, Maruxa and Roberto had joined forces with another traveling player. They were providing music and pantomime to accompany his story. It was a local tale that the audience knew well, full of magic and battles against the Saracens. Roberto was the doughty Christian warrior, and Maruxa the Arab princess who betrays family and religion for his love.

"Odd how they're always princesses," a voice said at Solomon's elbow.

He turned and smiled. It was Hersent, Griselle's maid. She smiled back.

"Well, it does seem strange to me," she continued. "Princesses today seem to marry only where their families tell them. Of course, it may have been different in the time of Charlemagne."

"So you think that a Saracen woman today wouldn't defy her family to marry a Christian?" Solomon asked.

Hersent knew he was laughing at her, but she answered the question seriously all the same.

"Of course a Saracen woman would," she answered, "or a Christian woman if it were the other way around. It happens all the time. But not likely a princess. That could cause a war. And where would a princess see a man alone? A serving girl or a tradesman's daughter, they would often meet men who were infidels, especially in this area. They would see their masters or their fathers treat these men with respect. Yes, I could believe that in such a case, love might result."

"You sound quite certain," Solomon said.

"It happened to the parents of Lady Griselle's husband,"

Hersent told him. "His father was a Frankish knight, his mother the daughter of a Saracen silk merchant in Narbonne. He converted to Islam when they married, he said, and they settled in Saragossa. But he secretly taught her the Christian faith, and even though their son was mutilated in the way of the infidel, he was also baptized. When Saragossa was taken by the Franks, the knight returned to the True Faith openly. It's fortunate that he did or Lord Bertran could never have inherited from his father's family."

"What happened to the Saracen woman?" Solomon asked.

"She was baptized as well," Hersent said, "but she died during the siege. It was very sad."

She was silent for a moment, biting her lip. "I've said too much," she muttered. "You won't tell Lady Griselle what I've told you, will you? I didn't learn it from her, but from my husband, who served Lord Bertran for fifteen years. My lady would be furious if she knew I were telling strangers about him."

"There was nothing in your tale that would take away from the honor of Lord Bertran or his family," Solomon told her. "But I promise not to speak of it. Where is your mistress, by the way? I don't recall ever seeing you without her before."

Hersent indicated the basket on her arm. "Lady Griselle is resting," she explained. "I've been sent out for supplies—soap, needles, wine, a few other things."

"Resting? Is she ill?"

"No, only tired," Hersent said. "Griselle often spends most of the night praying alone in her room. When she summoned me this morning, I could see that her bed hadn't been disturbed. All night on her knees. And people mock her because she doesn't choose to dress in sackcloth."

The music stopped and coins were tossed to the performers. Hersent suddenly remembered that she had been told to return quickly. She nodded good-bye to Solomon and vanished into the crowd.

Solomon longed to return to the inn and make Catherine read every word of the leaves of parchment to him, but he knew he hadn't given her enough time yet. He wandered along the

booths, looking idly at the wares. He was hoping he'd find
Edgar there someplace, not merely to have a friend to talk
with, but because he was fairly certain that if Edgar went back
and interrupted Catherine's work, she would be all too inclined to be distracted from it.

Rufus and Gaucher stood at the door of the church, waiting
for it to be reopened after the purification. Both of them had
put on their mail shirts under the pilgrim robes and each had
a knife at his belt.

"Do you think they'll let us see him?" Gaucher asked his
companion.

"Don't know," Rufus grunted. "What good will it do?"

Gaucher bent closer so that no one else could hear. "This
can't have anything to do with us," he said. "How many people even knew we had all fought together?"

Rufus kept his hand on his knife hilt. "Only one needed
to know," he said. "You, for instance."

Gaucher drew back. "Or you."

Rufus shrugged. "Or me," he admitted. "But there's no
other explanation for what's been happening to us. Think of
it. All of us survive the wars, live to better than three-score
years, then within a month, three of us die, two by violence.
Someone, some old enemy, is stalking us."

Gaucher started to deny this as preposterous. Then he remembered the bloody pig parts, the sudden reappearance and
loss of the emeraldless ring, the other insults. They all could
be coincidences, even the deaths of Hugh and Rigaud. But . . .

"But who?" he asked. "Why now? And why in such a cowardly manner? Our enemies were all soldiers, knights like ourselves. They would challenge us openly, not sneak around by
night to catch us alone and unarmed."

They thought of how very unarmed Hugh had been, and if
the rumors were true, Rigaud even more so. Rufus edged
around so that his back was against a pillar.

"Do you think the abbot will suspect us?" Gaucher worried. "I didn't like the questions that Brother James asked when
Hugh was killed."

Rufus picked his nose, then examined his finger as if the answer could be divined from what he found there. "But we were together last night," he said finally. "We can take the oath to that. Of course, I can't say what you did after I passed out."

"I fell on top of you," Gaucher reminded him. "The pot boys had to drag us up and throw us in bed. Didn't you wonder how you got there?"

Rufus rubbed his nose again. "I had hoped that I'd managed to get there on my own," he sighed. "But then, the pot boys can also swear that we were in no condition to be out murdering poor old Rigaud."

"Unless one of us was dissembling," Gaucher said.

There was a creak behind them as the doors to the church swung open. The crowd pushed forward and swept the two knights in with it. The bell rang, calling the faithful and the curious to Mass.

Catherine paid no attention to the insistence of the bells. She barely heard them. Her attention was totally captured by the writing before her. Usually when she was reading, she would find common phrases, quotations from the scriptures or the Church fathers that she could recognize, even if all the letters and symbols of abbreviation weren't clear. Often she would be able to name the writer within a few lines.

But this contained nothing she had ever seen before. It didn't seem to be a copy of another manuscript, or even lecture notes drawing on sources she knew. It was full of words that she guessed were Latin transliterations of Hebrew or Arabic. From what she could decipher, it did seem to be a guide of some sort to hidden knowledge. There were various groups of words with directions as to when and where and with what gestures one should say them. The trouble was that she was neither sure of her understanding of the directions or of what was supposed to happen when they were followed.

What if this were a guide to calling up demons?

"*Oleth, lothen, ethat, edim, eliyad, hachim, atarpha,*" she whispered nervously, her finger following the words on the page.

Catherine looked around for a sudden manifestation. She sniffed the air for the tang of brimstone and sulfur. With an exhalation of relief, she went back to the work.

Of course she hadn't been standing in an olive grove at midnight with Venus in Scorpio, wearing a white-linen robe. But Catherine always felt that power lay more in words than in anything else. She had taken a terrible chance. Edgar would be furious if he knew.

But Solomon wouldn't. Her cousin would run out and buy a white-linen robe and check astrological tables to find out when Venus would next pass through Scorpio.

And what might he summon to himself then?

Catherine was in torment, split between intellectual honesty, her own passion to know, and terror for both the soul and the life of her cousin.

What could she tell him?

It was afternoon before Edgar returned. He found Catherine sitting exactly where he had left her that morning. And she thought him obsessed with the designs on the church! She rose to greet him and swayed, dizzy from being seated for so long. He put his arms around her and she kissed him with her hands held out away from him.

"My fingertips are black from following the lines on the page." She showed him.

"So is the tip of your nose," he informed her. "And your chin and forehead. You look like one of the painted Highlanders at home. And this is just from reading! I'm amazed you were ever let near a clean piece of vellum at the Paraclete."

He spit on the edge of his sleeve and wiped her face as best he could.

"Thank you, *carissime*," she said. "I left a smudge on your cheek from my nose when I kissed you."

When they were both reasonably clean, Catherine asked what was happening outside.

"The man found murdered in the church was apparently one of the monks whom the abbot sent to investigate the death of Hugh of Grigmon," Edgar told her.

"Are they sure he was murdered?" Catherine asked.

Edgar told her of the condition he was found in. Despite Brother James's desire to keep the method of the slaying secret, such news always manages to escape.

"Oh," Catherine said after she had envisioned Rigaud's position all too clearly. "That does seem to indicate murder. Do they have any witnesses? Do they know when it happened? Was it someone in the cloister or someone from outside?"

"I don't know the answer to any of that," Edgar said, "but . . . something does worry me about the position Brother Rigaud was found in."

"I was thinking that, too," Catherine said. "The similarity struck me at once. I might not have remembered it clearly. But if you agree . . . you studied the tympanum at Conques more seriously than I did."

"The knight being spitted as he fell from his horse," Edgar said.

"Not to mention the hunter on the stake being carried by the giant rabbits," Catherine mentioned. "But any number of people who live in Moissac must have been to Saint-Foy and seen the carvings. Or someone could have thought of it independently."

"Yes," Edgar said slowly. "Still, it does seem strange that it should be a monk who has been traveling with us who was killed."

"No, it doesn't," Catherine said with a decisive foot stamp. "People always die while traveling. It's dangerous. Everyone knows that. Weather, disease, accident, bandits. We were warned of all these things. Why should anyone comment if three men die on a long and arduous journey? Not to mention the poor Germans lost in the flood. That certainly had nothing to do with the party from Cluny."

"Catherine?" Edgar looked at her worriedly. "This isn't like you. You're the one who feels that she has to find the truth, no matter what the cost. And as far as I know, only you have connected all three deaths in your mind. And now you won't pursue it? What's wrong?"

Catherine pushed the pieces of parchment aside and sat on

the plank that would be their bed that night. Edgar sat next to
her and she turned to half-curl onto his lap.

"I'm afraid," she said. "There's something wicked, something evil, about these deaths. I fear that this time the price of
the truth may be more than we can afford to pay."

Brother James was admitted to see Abbot Peter and the local
abbot later that afternoon. He had made his examination of the
church before it had been scrubbed and doused with holy
water. He had also, with much distaste, examined the remains
of Brother Rigaud. He was not happy with what he had discovered.

"Have they found the one who committed this sacrilege?"
Peter of Montboissier did not waste time with pleasantries.

"Not yet, my Lord Abbot," Brother James answered. "We
haven't found anyone who saw Brother Rigaud leave the cloister, nor any witness to who might have been in the church waiting for him."

"Surely there was someone sleeping in the porch?" Abbot
Peter asked.

"Yes, my lord, several pilgrims and beggars," James answered. "But all whom we have questioned so far claim to have
slept through until the bells sounded for Matins."

Peter frowned. "Are you implying that someone came in
from the cloister to kill our poor Brother Rigaud?"

James swallowed. He wasn't sure what he was implying, but
he would be damned if he let the blame for this fall on his order.

"It's possible," he said, "that the murderer came into the
church during the day and then hid in the shadows at nightfall.
But that still doesn't explain why Brother Rigaud was there
when he should have been in bed."

James waited, then made a decision. "I am aware," he added
carefully, "of the dissolute nature of Brother Rigaud's existence
before he was converted to our way of life. Is it possible that
he may have been tempted beyond his power to resist?"

He braced himself for a torrent of denial and anger that he
should say anything so unkind about a fellow monk. Abbot
Peter only sat quietly, considering the matter.

"Who can say at what point temptation becomes more than we can bear?" Peter said. "In all the years he was at Cluny, there was never a breath of such scandal about Brother Rigaud. I even trusted him to watch over the *garciones*. He was touched with my faith in him and never abused it. I would prefer to find another answer."

"So would I," Brother James said. "Even if Rigaud did falter in his vow of chastity, I see no reason for the object of his affection to kill him. Why meet with him at all? I fear there is more to this than may be understood in the short time we have before we leave."

"You suspect someone?" the abbot asked.

"No, my lord," James answered. "Not one particular person, but I do believe that Rigaud's death is connected to that of his old companion-at-arms, Hugh of Grignon, which would indicate that it is one of the pilgrims who is responsible."

"Do you have any proof of this?" Peter asked. "I thought the two of you had decided that the other murder was done by the *ribaux*."

"We did, but that was before Rigaud died," James said. "The horrible method of this murder indicates a personal hatred. I know of nothing Brother Rigaud could have done since he entered Cluny to occasion such animosity. Therefore, I can only conclude that it was the result of some deed committed in his secular life—perhaps something he and Hugh of Grignon did together."

"And that would lead back to their other comrades," Peter said.

The abbot of Saint-Pierre, who had been silent up to this point, heaved a great sigh. No one from his house would be suspected in this horror. He thanked Saint Peter, Saint Stephen and the Virgin. The abbot had looked forward to the visit of the head of Cluny and the bishop of Osma. Now all he wanted was for these High Church officials to leave him in peaceful autonomy.

Brother James would have liked to accuse Gaucher or Rufus, or both, of the murder, but he had already checked and it appeared that they had not left their room the night before.

But there were others among the pilgrims who hadn't been accounted for. Those *jongleurs*, for instance. Roberto and his
wife had been among those sleeping in the porch of the church.
Roberto could have crept in with no one noticing. There was
more than one possibility. He told Abbot Peter as much.

"I quite agree," Peter said. "You have a fine grasp of logic.
Your early training was excellent. I consider it a great blessing
that we were able to save you to ourselves."

"Thank you, Lord Abbot," James answered. "Now, what
do you wish me to do next?"

James wasn't pleased with the answer.

That night Catherine and Edgar dined with the Jewish traders
from Toulouse. Eliazar had explained to the men that they
were the children of his partner and friend, and the couple was
welcomed cautiously.

"You look like a Slav," one of the traders said to Edgar.
"Are you from Rus?"

"Scotland," Edgar answered.

They all looked down, expecting bare knees. "My husband
prefers to dress in the French fashion," Catherine said proudly.

Edgar felt insulted, but he was used to swallowing his pride.
There were times in the early days in Paris when it had been
his only dinner.

The discussion revolved around the difficulties of trade, the
debates between scholars, and the scandals of families from
Catalonia to Baghdad. Finally, someone mentioned the murder of the monk.

"Any reason they can blame us for it?" The man who spoke
was named Aaron. His family had lived in Narbonne and then
Toulouse for nearly a thousand years. His face bore traces of
every race that had passed through, from the Greeks to the
Franks to the Visigoths to the Arabs. As far as he was concerned, the only line he came from was Abraham's.

Eliazar poured another dipper of fish stew onto his bread.
"Who can say?" he said. "If they find no one else, they can always accuse us. But I see no reason for them to. I spoke to the
man only once."

"That might be enough," Aaron said darkly.

They sat around a campfire not far from the bank of the Tarn River. The stewpot was balanced on coals at the edge. Catherine thought it very cozy, but the way the men tended to start and turn at the sound of every splash or twig snap reminded her of the danger always present. She wondered what would happen if someone decided that the monk's death was the fault of the Jews. If a party from the town descended on them now, would they spare her? She felt sure that Edgar could not be mistaken for anything but a Christian, but she knew that she and her father looked as if they belonged with the others. Catherine was darker than some of the men there, one of whom even had bright red hair, a gift from a Visigothic ancestor.

She had noticed the way they looked at her and her father, and then at Solomon, enough like her to be her brother, but no one said anything.

Talk had drifted from the murder to the journey.

"The Lady Griselle informed me today that Peter of Cluny isn't entering Spain by way of Navarre," Hubert was saying. "She was wondering if I knew of anyone going by way of Roncevalles. She has two men-at-arms with her."

His comment was greeted with silence.

"Griselle is a woman who would speak for us if there were problems with the Edomites," Eliazar added.

"Loudly," Catherine added.

"Is she so fond of Jews?" Aaron asked.

Solomon thought about that. "She certainly hasn't avoided us," he said. "Her maid tells me that Lady Griselle's husband was half Arab. Perhaps she's inclined to tolerance."

"I don't think so," Catherine said.

They all looked at her. She could see that they weren't used to being contradicted by a woman who was also a Christian. But she was too accustomed to arguing with Solomon to stop now.

"The Lady Griselle is determined to reach the shrine of Saint James," she continued. "I believe that she will defend anyone willing to help her to that goal."

"It comes down to the same thing," Eliazar said. "You have

guards but more wouldn't hurt, especially now that we're about to enter the country of the Basques. They have no allegiance except to their own people."

The other men considered this but refused to make a decision until they had spoken privately.

"We don't plan to set out until the day after tomorrow," Aaron said, as spokesman. "If you wish to come with us, and if the pilgrims promise not to try to proselytize, we'll consider allowing you to join us."

They walked back to the town in the misty spring twilight. Fog was crawling up from the river behind them but it was still too light for a lantern. Catherine and Edgar walked with their arms around each other, well-fed and content. Solomon followed them. All at once he gave a startled exclamation. Everyone stopped.

"What is it?" Edgar asked.

"Nothing," Solomon said. "I thought I saw someone, but it was just a pile of wood, distorted in the mist."

"I had forgotten how much you hate fog," Catherine said. "Come walk with us."

Solomon came up beside them and Catherine linked her free arm in his. She could feel the tension in his body and tried to think of something to say to ease it, but her head was full of the charms and spells she had been reading all day. The fog came in wisps like stretched fingers, curling around the trees and lying in wait at hollows in the path. Catherine thought of the words she had dared to whisper. They were supposed to be the names of the seven spheres above the earth.

What if they were the names of demons of the air instead? What if she had in her ignorance called them into form? The cold damp stroked her neck and she shivered.

"Put up your hood, *leoffaest*," Edgar said absently.

Catherine did. She clung more tightly to the men on either side of her. *Saint Genevieve*, she thought, *please make there be no demons in the night. Please bring me back safely to your city.*

Surely the patron saint of Paris would want to bring her child home again!

They reached the inn without incident and went immediately to bed. The next morning was bright and clear. Catherine woke early, stretched her arms and crawled over Edgar to get out of bed. Her father and uncle were still snoring, but Solomon had already wakened and dressed.

"Want me to walk you down to the privy?" he asked her.

"Let me get my shoes and *bliaut* on first," Catherine whispered back. Since they all shared a room, she had slept in her shift so that she was at least partially covered.

They stopped at the outhouse behind the inn and then wandered around to the front. The sun was climbing and the heat growing. It promised to be a warm day.

They were sitting on a bench in front of the inn, sharing a slab of cheese, when the guards came. With them was a man in ragged clothes and bare feet. He pointed at them.

"That's the man!" he shouted.

The guards moved forward and lifted Solomon from the bench, the cheese still in his hands.

Twelve

Moissac. Monday, May 18, 1142; Commemoration of the Blessed Alcuin, student of the Venerable Bede, teacher of Charlemagne and his daughters.

Cur haec igitur versa vice mutentur scelerumque supplica bonos premant, praemia virtutam mali rapiant, vehementer admiror, . . .

Why, therefore, these things are switched, and the penalties of the wicked are visited upon the good while the rewards of virtue are seized by the wicked, I wonder greatly.

Boethius,
The Consolation of Philosophy,
Book Five

$\mathcal{A}$s the guards lifted the astonished Solomon from the bench, Catherine screeched and launched herself at the one nearest her.

"Let go of him!" she shouted, kicking the guard and pulling his arm. "Put him down at once!"

"Catherine, don't!" Solomon yelled at her as the men tried to drag him away. "Get Uncle Eliazar! Call your father!"

She paid no attention but continued flailing her arms and feet upon the increasingly irritated guard.

Solomon made no attempt to fight. He knew official force when he saw it. He also knew what would happen to him if he spilled Christian blood. So he made no move for his knife. His experience had been that most of these things were taken care of with an exchange of gold . . . but let the townspeople become involved and he would find himself hanging from an oak tree before the terms of his release were arrived at.

"Catherine!" he shouted again. "Stop that! You'll hurt yourself!"

The guards had now managed, despite Catherine's efforts, to tie Solomon's hands behind him. A crowd was starting to form, and night-capped heads were poking out of windows all up and down the street.

"What's going on?" someone called down. "Have you caught him? Is that the man who murdered the monk?"

Solomon's heart sank. He turned to the guard being pummeled by Catherine. "Whose men are you?" he asked. "Is this about the dead monk? Is that why you've been sent?"

"We're Lord Geraut's guards, but in service to Abbot Peter

for the time being," the man answered. "I don't know what
they want you for. Will someone get this woman off me?"

"I've tried," Solomon said. "She never listens to me. Is this
beggar, here, accusing me of killing the monk?"

"That's for the abbot to say," the guard replied as he
twisted away from Catherine's knee. "*Aiee!* That hurt, young
woman!"

His patience exhausted, the guard thrust out a gauntleted
hand and Catherine dropped to the ground.

"You didn't have to do that!" Solomon protested.

"I just winded her," the guard assured him. "I'll be bruises
all over tomorrow from what she's done to me."

Solomon nodded in unwilling sympathy. "Take me to the
abbot," he told the guard. "I'm innocent of any wrongdoing,
so I have nothing to fear from him. These people here, however, I have no such faith in."

So, leaving Catherine sitting dazed in the street, Solomon
practically led his guards to the abbey, where he would at least
be safe from the mindless violence of the crowd.

"Saint Felician's nails and pincers! Get out of my way!"

Catherine looked up. The people who had been encircling
her moved back. Her father pushed through them, looming
over her, dressed only in his shift. He held out a hand to help
her up.

"Are you hurt, child?" he asked as he pulled her to her feet.

She shook her head. "They took Solomon." She shook
with anger. "I couldn't stop them!"

"The abbot sent the guards to capture the monster who
committed murder in the church," a woman from the shop
across from the inn explained to Hubert. "Then this hellion attacked them! Is she yours?"

Hubert put his arm around Catherine's shoulders. "She
certainly is," he said. "I'm only sorry I wasn't here to defend
our friend as well. I'm proud of her."

The woman glared at him. "It may be that you'll all hang
from the same gibbet," she said. The thought seemed to satisfy
her and she left.

The rest of the crowd was also dispersing, some to work, others to wait outside the abbey for word of the punishment of the murderer. Hubert took Catherine back inside the inn.

"Father, they'll kill Solomon." She was still shaking in anger. "What are we going to do?"

"Put on our clothes," he said. "Our best clothes. Take our letters of safe passage from Abbot Suger and show them to the abbot. See how much gold it will take to set Solomon free."

"That's all?" she exclaimed. "What if they torture him?"

"He won't confess to something he didn't do, no matter what," Hubert said, hoping it was true. "But while he's in the hands of the Church, they won't do more than question him. We have to free him before he's turned over to the town authorities."

They had reached their room. Inside, Edgar and Eliazar were busy packing their belongings. Edgar held up the pages Catherine had been working on.

"I don't know where you and Solomon got these," he said, "but they must be destroyed before someone from the abbey is sent to search the room."

"Oh, no!" Catherine cried.

Eliazar agreed with Edgar. "It's more of Solomon's madness. All those astrological symbols. Burn them at once. Do you want us charged with necromancy as well as murder?"

"But I haven't finished reading them!" Catherine said.

"Catherine, are you mad?" Edgar asked. "We aren't just talking about Solomon's life. All of us could be implicated if they think sorcery is involved."

"Well, then," she said, "how are we to burn them? There's no fire in the room."

She was right. They all looked around for a method of destroying the parchment pages. It had been too warm the previous night to even have a fire on the hearth in the common room. Cooking was done at a bakehouse in the next street.

"Give them to me," she told Edgar. "We'll have to hide them for now."

She knelt on the floor and began to go through her pack.

She pulled out a bundle and began rolling up the parchment tightly.

"What are you doing?" Hubert asked. "If our things are searched, they're sure to find them."

"Perhaps not," Catherine said. She began unrolling the bundle. "It depends on how fastidious the searchers are."

The pieces of cloth were clean but covered with old brown stains. Catherine put the parchment in the center and rolled the menstrual rags around it. From the expression on the faces of the three men, it was the last place anyone would want to check.

"Hurry, Catherine," Eliazar said. "Your father and I have to go negotiate for Solomon."

"No," Hubert said. "I think only Edgar and I should go. This is a time when it would be better to have Christians to stand up for him."

"But he's my nephew!" Eliazar said.

"And mine," Hubert reminded him. "In a case like this, we can't rely on the protection of the king or Suger. We're not in France now. Also, Abbot Peter is not well-disposed toward Jews. He's taken out a number of loans from them. Unless you can promise him remission of his debts, I doubt he would listen to you graciously."

"What about me?" Catherine asked.

"Absolutely not!" Edgar and Hubert said at once.

Before she could protest, Hubert raised his hand. "One—" he turned up his thumb "—women are allowed to give evidence, but you have none as to where Solomon was last night. And you can't stand surety for him. Neither can Eliazar. Edgar and I can."

He waited for her to explode, but she simply stared at him.

"Two—" he held up his first finger "—it has often been remarked how much you and Solomon resemble each other. Would you have more questions added to the accusations?"

Catherine sighed and shook her head.

"Three," she finished for him, reciting as by rote, "you love me and don't want me put in danger."

"Well, that too," Hubert agreed. "But more important, I don't want to remind anyone that Edgar is part of our family."

"What?" Edgar was outraged. "*Godes micellic palstr!* How dare you? I have endured much from you for Catherine's sake, but this is going too far! Who are you to refuse to admit me to your family?"

"No one," Hubert answered, deflating Edgar's wrath into flat confusion. "And that's why you must come with me to speak for Solomon."

"I don't understand," Edgar said.

Hubert looked uncomfortable. "I am too used to thinking of you as some student who has bewitched my daughter," he said.

"More the other way around, I think," Edgar interrupted.

"Perhaps," Hubert conceded. "Nevertheless, I forget that in your own country, you are a nobleman. You are accustomed to being treated with a certain deference. And though you usually hide it, you have an arrogance that comes only with being well-born and knowing it."

"Come to the point," Edgar said. He was still angry.

Hubert smiled. "Exactly. I've been rude to you, and you've taken the insult for Catherine's sake. I apologize. It was wrong. For now I need your name and your arrogance if we're to save Solomon and continue our journey. Peter of Montboissier comes from an old Auvergnat family. He is a great lord of the Church but was born to be a secular lord as well. I know that in his eyes I'm simply another trader. He might not be inclined to trust my oath. Yours, Edgar, he would have to take. You are his equal."

Catherine looked at her husband. His clothes were plain, his tunic still unbelted. His boots were good leather, but scuffed from the journey. He hadn't brought valuable chains or rings on the pilgrimage, and rarely wore them anyway. She wasn't sure he could convince the abbot of his identity.

Edgar wasn't either. He rubbed his chin. "I need a shave," he said. "I need a bath, probably a delousing."

"We all do," Hubert said. "It's one of the hardships of travel. But that won't make any difference. Go in your pilgrim garb. He'll know the quality of the material. He misses nothing."

"Of course I'll do anything I can for Solomon," Edgar said. "I will even offer myself as pledge. He's my friend."

Catherine hated being left behind when something was happening, but saw the sense in her father's argument.

"Then hurry!" she told them. "Get dressed. Edgar, at least wear a clean tunic."

Eliazar followed Edgar and Hubert down into the street. "I'm going to the brethren from Toulouse," he told them. "If you can free Solomon with words and promises, good. But we may need more than that. Aaron will advance me the ransom, and the community in Paris will repay him. I'm going now to tell him what has happened. When one of us is accused, we all are."

Catherine rubbed her jaw. It was sore and swelling from the blow the guard had given her. It had been foolish of her to attack him with only fists and feet.

Everyone else had gone to do something to help. They had left her with little more than an absentminded kiss or a pat on the shoulder. Catherine sat amidst the hastily stuffed packs and tried to think of what she could do.

The idea that Solomon would sneak into a church in the middle of the night to murder a monk was preposterous, of course. He wouldn't enter a church for any reason.

Well, he had once, Catherine remembered suddenly. A ruined church, it was true, but it went counter to everything he believed in. He had done it for her, because she was in danger. He'd saved her life. She owed him more than to simply sit and wait while other people worked for him.

With no clear idea of where she was going, Catherine put on her shoes and arranged her head scarf neatly. She fastened the belt over her plain *bliaut* and went out to find a way to repay her debt to her cousin.

Catherine hadn't gone far when she had to stop to let a group of riders pass.

"Halt!" a familiar voice ordered.

Catherine shaded her eyes with her hand and looked up at the Lady Griselle, glittering as the sun behind her caught in the jewels of her earrings.

"I heard they took your father's friend to the abbey," she said.

"Yes, we fear he's to be accused in the death of the monk," Catherine said. "Can you help?"

"I'm going up there to try," she answered. "They may not be willing to listen to me."

"Do you have any evidence?" Catherine's heart rose. "Did you see him elsewhere that night?"

"Hardly." Griselle seemed shocked. "I was keeping vigil all night in my room for the soul of my poor Bertran. But I am also my husband's heir. That means I can at least vouch for the man's character before the abbot. I believe it to be good, despite his fascination with poor Mondete. Many men seem to share that failing."

"It's kind of you," Catherine answered.

"Bertran would have wanted me to," Griselle said simply. She and her entourage rode on.

It annoyed Catherine even more that a stranger could help her cousin and she couldn't. Uselessness was making her frantic. She was afraid even to go to the church lest someone see her face and associate her with Solomon, to his cost.

She felt a great desire to smash something.

"*Persequar inimicos meos, et comprehendam illos,*" she muttered as she walked along, hands clenched. "*Et non convertar donec deficiant.* 'I shall go after my enemies and I will catch up to them and not turn back until they are vanquished.' "

Psalms had so many wonderful uses. "*Confringam illos!*" Catherine said more loudly as she walked farther from the town. " 'I shall strike them down!' *Nec poterunt stare!* 'Nor will they be able to stand!' "

It had always helped release her feelings to shout the warrior psalms when she was angry, often while performing another penitential task set her by Sister Bertrada, her special bane in the convent.

She had reached the riverbank and had not yet come up with any workable plan to free Solomon. She picked up a handful of pebbles and threw them in the water, one by one, still chanting anathema to her nebulous enemies.

"And I'm considered mad."

Catherine stopped. Mondete had come up behind her silently.

"I don't consider you any more mad than I am," she told the woman.

Mondete sat on a boulder thrown up by the river. "I don't find that a firm endorsement of my sanity," she said. "I was looking for you. I have a question."

"For me?" Catherine was leaning to Solomon's opinion that Mondete knew everything but refused to tell. What could she want Catherine to answer?

"Yes. I was wondering if it would do more harm than good if I told the abbot that Solomon was with me all Saturday night." Mondete pushed back her hood. Sweat glistened on her pale scalp. "What do you think?"

Catherine tried not to look at the bald head, but to consider Mondete's words. "Were you really with him?" she asked.

Mondete smiled. "Yes. I never met a man so persistent in his wish to simply talk with me," she said. "It's a novel experience, so much so that I doubt I'll be believed. Do you think it will be the worse for him if instead of killing a monk, people simply think he was having *la covine* with a Christian whore?"

Catherine thought. "Either way, someone will want to hang him," she decided.

"That's what I feared," Mondete said. "So what's being done to free him?"

Catherine told her. When she heard Griselle's name, Mondete raised her eyebrows, or would have if she hadn't shaved them off.

"I never had much use for Griselle of Lugny," she said. "Her devotion to her husband always seemed her only virtue. To his credit, I don't believe he ever came to me, so the devotion may have been mutual. But I'm surprised that she would go surety for a stranger."

"She said her husband would have wanted it," Catherine explained.

"Did she now?" Mondete said. She put her hood back up and stood. "I'm going back to the church to find out what's happening. Do you intend to vent your wrath upon the water the rest of the day?"

"It's better if I stay here." Catherine threw in another pebble. "Will you tell them where to find me?"

"If you wish." Mondete left her.

Catherine picked up another handful of pebbles and started another angry psalm recitation.

Solomon was more afraid than he dared show, or admit to himself. He had been in worse situations. There had been that time in Hungary, for instance. The girl had sworn she had no brothers. She didn't tell him about the uncles and five large male cousins. He had managed to escape that with no friends to help and with all his vital organs intact. This was nothing.

So why was it so hard to keep from shaking?

He stood in the anteroom to the abbot's chamber. The area had been cleared of guests to allow space for the questioning. High-backed chairs with padded arms and cushions had been placed for the abbots and Bishop Stephen, but at the moment, there was no one in the room but himself and the guards. They waited a few moments in silence, one of the guards shifting constantly from one foot to the other.

"Here, you keep watch," the guard finally said to the other man. "I can't hold it anymore. I'll just go water the abbot's garden and be right back."

"What if he attacks me?" the other guard asked.

"What's wrong? You still limping from what the girl did to you?" his friend jeered. "This one doesn't look any tougher."

He wasn't the first person to assume that because Solomon was slender and fine-boned, he was weak.

When the man had gone, Solomon studied his other captor. The man was a trained fighter, he was sure. But it would be easy to take him by surprise and then escape. The leather bonds at his wrists were loosening already. He could be out of them and gone before the guard realized what was happening.

It took every bit of self-control he had not to run.

What held him wasn't the thought of the swords of the guards or the fear of being hunted down and hanged. It was knowing that if he ran, his uncle would pay the price. Freedom wasn't worth it.

He did wish that something would happen soon, though.

The remaining guard was still rubbing his thigh, where Catherine had kicked him. "*Bordelere*," he muttered. "A bit to the left and she could have done some real damage. Who is she, your wife?"

"Just a friend," Solomon answered.

"Ah, some tavern slut," the guard sneered.

Solomon had been baited much more skillfully than this. He just smiled at the man.

"I said, she must be some weaver's whore," the guard continued.

"Not even that," Solomon said cheerfully. "I think she prefers tanners and dung collectors."

"And which one are you?" The man seemed really curious.

"Ah, I was just eating with her," Solomon answered. "For that, she prefers men who smell better."

The guard's eyes narrowed. He was about to ask another question when his partner reappeared. "That's better," he informed them, though no one had asked. "Thought I'd fertilize the cabbage while I was about it." Having conveyed that information, he fell silent.

At last the door to the abbot's chambers opened. Peter of Cluny, Stephen of Osma, and the abbot of Saint-Pierre entered and took their places. They were followed by two monks, one carrying a writing tablet. The other one stepped forward to examine the prisoner.

"Is this the man?" he asked the guards.

"This is the one the beggar says he saw enter the church last night," the guard attacked by Catherine said.

"I see." The monk stepped up to Solomon. He was built with the same whiplike slenderness as the man he faced, his natural gauntness further aggravated by fasting. He was only a fraction shorter than Solomon. His brown eyes bore into Solomon's green ones with frightening intensity.

"I'm Brother James," he announced. "And you are one of the filthy Jews polluting the pilgrims who travel with us."

Solomon's jaw tightened. This man was much more proficient than the guard at baiting him.

"My name is Solomon," he answered as calmly as possible. "My uncle and I are from Paris and are engaged in trade for Suger, abbot of Saint-Denis. We have letters to that effect."

"I am aware of that," Brother James told him. "That is the only reason you were allowed to accompany honest Christians. And this is how you repay the kindness of Saint Peter? To murder one of his monks?"

"I have killed no one," Solomon answered. "If you know anything about my people, you would be sure that we would never enter a church voluntarily, not for any reason."

He winced, remembering the times he and the others of the community had been herded into a local church to hear someone preach to them in the hope of effecting a mass conversion.

"The beggar saw you!" Brother James put his face close to Solomon's and spit the words.

"He was mistaken." Solomon moved his head back and looked more closely at the monk. "Do I know you?" he asked.

Brother James stepped back in confusion. "Your conscience may know me," he said proudly, "as the one who will discover your sins and make you pay for them."

Solomon shook his head. "My conscience has never met you, I'm sure," he said, "but your face is that of someone I should remember."

He seemed more concerned about that than about the charges against him.

Abbot Peter leaned forward in his chair. "Do you understand why you have been brought here?" he asked.

"A beggar sleeping in the narthex thinks he saw me enter

the church last night," Solomon replied. "I wasn't there. My friends will be coming soon, I hope, to vouch for me."

"Were they with you last night?" Peter asked.

"No, Lord Abbot," Solomon answered with a half-smile. "I was with a lady, I'm afraid. I would not wish to damage her reputation merely to save my life."

The guard smothered a guffaw. The abbot looked at him. "Nothing, Lord Abbot," the man said quickly. "Dust in my throat."

Bishop Stephen leaned over to Abbot Peter and said something behind his hand.

"I agree," Peter said. "Brother James, has anyone come forward to speak for this man? Are any of his people here?"

Brother James went to the door and asked the question of the monk stationed on the other side. The two conversed for a moment, then Brother James returned, apparently annoyed.

"I understand that the Hebrews of Toulouse who are here in the city have offered to pay his ransom, if necessary. They also deny his guilt. Also, there are some Christians here to stand witness to his innocence."

The door opened and Edgar, Hubert and the Lady Griselle were led in. They all bowed to the abbots and the bishop.

"My lords." Hubert spoke first. "I am Hubert LeVendeur, a merchant of Paris and a member of the *marchands de l'eau*. This man has been a trusted messenger for me and for Abbot Suger of Saint-Denis for many years now. He is honest and responsible. I will take the oath that he is innocent of any wrongdoing."

"Of course you know who I am," Griselle said. "I have no business or social connection with this man, yet I also believe him to be innocent. I have traveled with him for some weeks now and know him to be as near to a courteous knight as is possible for one of his faith. I will also swear to his innocence and stand for him, as the widow of Bertran de Lugny."

Peter looked at Edgar. "And you are . . ."

"My Lord Abbot," Edgar said, "I am Edgar, son of

Waldeve, lord of Wedderlie in Scotland, grandson of Cospatrick, earl of Northumberland, descendant of Alfred the Great, king of the Saxons, and kin to David, king of Scotland."

Griselle and Hubert tried to hide their surprise. The abbot of Cluny regarded Edgar gravely.

"Are you on the continent only for a pilgrimage to Saint James?" he asked. "Your French is quite good for a Saxon."

"I am going to Compostela, Lord Abbot," Edgar said, "but I have been studying in Paris for several years and have known Solomon for some time. While I am unknown in Moissac, there are many in Paris who know my lineage. Master Abelard could have told you my name. And I have been received by Héloïse, abbess of the Paraclete."

"Really?" Peter leaned back in his chair and pursed his lips. "There aren't many who have seen Héloïse in the past fifteen years. What color are her eyes?"

"Her eyes?" Edgar was taken aback by the question but answered without hesitating. "Brown, my lord, large and as deep as velvet, the saddest I've ever seen."

The abbot was silent for a moment. Then he nodded. "I will accept your oath," he said.

He turned to the guards. "Where is the beggar who accuses this man?"

The guards looked at each other nervously. "I don't know, Lord Abbot," the first said. "Our orders didn't include keeping him. We were only told to take him with us this morning to point out the prisoner."

"Haven't seen him since we took this man," the other chimed in. "Last I noticed, he was back at the inn."

"Brother James?" Abbot Peter asked the monk. "I was told that we had a witness to the murder. Where is he?"

"I . . . I don't know," James answered. "He came to me this morning with his tale. I presumed he would be here to repeat it for you."

Bishop Stephen had been following the French discussion with difficulty. Now he stood up and twisted a kink in his back.

"*Do I understand,*" he said angrily in Latin, "*that we've sat half the morning to judge a man whose only accuser is a vanishing beggar?*"

Edgar's face lit. "*Sic est,*" he said. "Your guards have detained my friend on the word of a man who not only has no one to vouch for him, but who hasn't even the courage to make his charge in front of the one he accuses. I demand that Solomon be released at once!"

"But he has no one who will swear to having been with him last night!" Brother James protested. "And he's a Jew!"

Lady Griselle dismissed him with a wave of her hand. She approached Peter and knelt before him. The silk of her *bliaut* swished against the rushes on the floor.

"No one saw me last night either, my lord," she said. "I was in my room alone. Does that mean I murdered your poor monk? And as for Jews, the town is full of them. At least this man admits to his faith. There are many who pretend to be good Christians while hiding black hearts and heretical beliefs."

Hubert had to control himself to keep from gasping. Who was she speaking of? What did she know?

Griselle gazed imploringly at Abbot Peter, her hands clasped so that the gold of her wedding band caught the light. "If you seek the killer," she continued, "I suggest you look closer to home. The reason may lie in the life your monk led before he took his vows. Or in a vow he broke."

Peter's face was grim as he held out his hands to Griselle. "Rise, my daughter," he said. "The rushes must be cutting into your skin. Your argument has much merit to it. I will consult with my brothers as to our decision."

Edgar's smile grew as he followed the brief Latin discussion. Both the other abbot and Bishop Stephen were of the opinion that their time had been wasted. They said so curtly and rose to go. Peter stayed only to speak with Brother James.

"Release him at once," he told the monk. "Then report to me after Tierce."

He left.

The guard was somewhat chagrined when he went to untie Solomon's bonds and found they had already fallen off.

When they were once again out in the sunlight, Solomon allowed himself a long, convulsive shudder.

"All I want right now is a vat of wine and a dipper," he said. "Preferably in a town on the other side of the mountains."

Edgar laughed shakily. "I won't even ask to share it with you," he said. "Men have been hanged before without a reliable witness."

"Was your grandfather really an earl?" Solomon asked. "Or was that to impress the abbot?"

"He was," Edgar said, "but it's all gone now. And so is he. I don't think the abbot was all that impressed in any case. Scotland is too far and Cluny has no houses there. It was Griselle who tipped the balance in your favor, I believe."

"I do, too," Solomon said. "I was amazed to see her there. Why would she risk her honor and land for me? I can't begin to thank her, but I must try."

Edgar lowered his voice and there was a hint of laughter in it. "Well, I have heard that she likes dark men."

"Yes," Solomon answered slowly, "but I don't seem to be what she had in mind."

They gaped with wide eyes as Hubert bowed over the hand of the Lady Griselle, then offered to assist her to mount her horse. He started to bend with hands cupped for her to put her foot in, but instead, she laid her hands on his shoulders and allowed him to lift her up by the waist onto her saddle. She seemed to lean against him more than was necessary for good balance. Hubert held her rather longer than courtesy required.

"Saint Eulalia's cold modesty!" Edgar exclaimed.

Solomon whistled. "I wonder if Catherine will approve of the price of my release."

Edgar grabbed his arm. "Not a word, Solomon. One hint, one bit of teasing, and I'll give you to that malevolent monk myself."

For once, Solomon was completely serious. "Don't worry,

old friend," he said. "I wouldn't be the one to tell her this for all the gold in Genoa."

As they left the square before the church, Solomon saw the hooded figure standing in the shadows. He put his finger to his lips and shook his head.

Mondete slipped away to the riverbank to tell Catherine that Solomon was safe. Then she sat next to the river for a long time watching the water swirl around rocks and roots. The motion was reflected in her troubled heart.

Brother James was both furious and frightened. The beggar had been so sure in his insistence. The man had come to him willingly with his tale. James hadn't been fool enough to pay him more than a sou, with the promise of much more when he had told his story to the abbot. What could have happened to him? And then all those people standing up for that Jew! Who would have thought that an English lord and the Lady of Lugny would be willing to stand surety for a man like that? Now what was he going to tell the abbot?

He scratched at the door and a voice bid him enter. The abbot was busy dictating letters to his secretary, Pierre. He didn't look up when Brother James came in.

"Send a copy of that to Cluny and another to the abbot of Santa-Maria de Najera," he told Pierre.

Pierre nodded and began gathering up his writing material.

"Stay a moment," Peter told him. "You may need to add something for Brother James to take."

James blinked. Peter frowned at him. "You made us appear foolish this morning, Brother James," the abbot said. "The honor of Saint Peter deserves better."

"I ask your pardon, Lord Abbot," James replied. "I still believe that the accused man had something to do with the death of Brother Rigaud."

"Really?" Peter said. "I can find no basis for that conclusion. I'm more inclined to Lady Griselle's suggestion that we look at Rigaud's life previous to his entering Cluny. There was no reason for him to be in the church at that hour. He must have gone to meet someone he knew."

"Or perhaps to save the soul of someone who lured him there by falsely asking for conversion," Brother James said angrily.

"Perhaps." The abbot was not convinced. "But even in that case, there would have to be a reason for asking Rigaud particularly. Or do you believe the Jews are now so mad as to vilely murder clerics at random."

James grudgingly admitted that this was unlikely. "I will find the one who did this," he insisted.

"Oh yes, you shall," Peter replied. "I believe it must have been one of the group of pilgrims who set out with us from Le Puy, perhaps one of his old companions. But there may be someone else who knew Brother Rigaud in his former life. Apparently, all of them have decided to continue together among a larger group leaving tomorrow."

"Tomorrow? But that's not enough time!"

"I agree," the abbot said. "And I need to set out at once for Toulouse and then to our houses in Catalonia. Therefore I have decided that you, along with a few of the lay brothers and one or two of the other monks, are going to accompany them. I'll meet you at Najera, and I expect you to have Brother Rigaud's murderer with you in chains. Pierre will give you a note of safe conduct. Now I am going to prepare for Tierce."

With that, he and the secretary left the room. Brother James stood by the open door feeling as if he had just been catapulted into Hell.

Thirteen

Saint-Jean-Pied-le-Port/Donibane-Garazi, at the foot of the Pyrenees.
Thursday, May 28, 1142; The Feast of the Ascension.

Hymnum canamus glorie
hymni nunc/ personent,
christus novo nunc tramite
ad patris ascendit thronum.

Let us sing the hymn of glory
Now the hymns resound
Now Christ by a new path
Ascends the Father's throne.

Hymn for the Ascension
Molesme Breviary

$\mathcal{D}$espite the company of his brother monks and the protection of the guards, Brother James felt terribly exposed on the
road to the mountains. When he had entered Cluny over
twenty years before, he had vowed never to set foot in the
world again. Only the direct order of Abbot Peter had induced
him to leave the safety of the monastery. Now he was back in
the world with a vengeance, jostled by all the rabble that ac-
companies any group of travelers or accosts it on the road. And
there was no abbot to protect him.

With the traders from Toulouse, there were now about
thirty Jews in the group. Every morning and evening, James's
nerves were grated with the sound of their prayers. No matter
how far away he stayed, it seemed that the wind brought the
dreaded chanting to him. He would try to stop up his ears with
his own prayers, but the melody of the Hebrew slithered in
every time he stopped for breath. How was he supposed to discover a murderer in all this mob and with such distraction? The
Jews worried him more than Brother Rigaud's killer did. What
was the loss of one's life compared to the loss of one's soul?
Of course, there was always the possibility that those men
might wish to rob him of both.

James did his best to stay out of sight in the center of his
party, sending the lay brothers to barter for food or to arrange
sleeping quarters. But he was still afraid. He knew that the time
would come when he would have to do more than watch from
a distance.

In contrast, Brothers Deodatus and Bruno, who had been

assigned to travel with him, were delighted with the variety of people and scenery.

"I thought the mountains of the Morvan were impressive," Deodatus gasped the first time the fog lifted and he saw the Pyrenees looming ahead, "but they're nothing but gentle hills compared to this. Are we really going to climb over?"

"We'll go through the pass at Roncevalles," James explained, "but I assure you, it will seem as though we've climbed the highest of them."

"Roncevalles!" Bruno was just as excited. "Will we see the rock that Roland split?"

"No doubt," James answered.

Deodatus looked at him worriedly. "Forgive me, Brother James, but are your bowels functioning properly? You seem melancholic."

"My system is in excellent order," James replied coldly. "And I hope yours is, too, for this is not a journey to the market at Mâcon. You'll need all your energy and all your faith to reach Pamplona, on the other side of these monsters."

"You've taken this trip before, then?" Bruno asked.

James pulled his cowl down over his face. "Yes."

He bent his head as if praying, and they finally left him alone.

Solomon was so shaken by his recent escape from hanging that he was even more subdued during the ensuing days. Catherine was surprised at how much she missed his teasing. Edgar also grew more quiet as the most difficult part of the journey neared. If there were to be a place where the road ended in a sheer cliff and a narrow bridge, he believed it would be somewhere amidst all those crags and precipices. Catherine could think of nothing to say about it that wouldn't annoy him. So she only waited and worried.

The weather had brought a constant spring drizzle, and everything was wet through. The hard bread they had bought in Moissac had maggots in it that dropped squirming into the hot water as the bread was crumbled, or coiled from the top if

they poured hot wine over it. Twice the party had been challenged by robbers. The guards fended them off easily, but the
events reminded everyone of how dangerous a pilgrimage actually was.

"It will be worse when we get to the other side," Hubert
sighed. "The Basques there have no treaty with anyone and
consider all travelers theirs to plunder."

"We've all made the journey safely before," Eliazar reminded him. "The first time I took Solomon with me, he was
only twelve. A poet in Saragossa fell in love with him and
wanted to buy him from me. The man was furious when I
wouldn't sell. That was the worst situation I've ever encountered."

"Depraved Saracens!" Hubert said.

"Well, no, the poet was one of us," Eliazar admitted. "Life
is different in Spain."

"Yes," said Hubert after a moment, "I remember. That's
why I had to come on this journey with Catherine."

Gaucher and Rufus added nothing to cheer the group.

"We should have taken the Somport Pass," Rufus grumbled. "The road is easier and better kept up. Saint Margaret's
demonic dragon! My joints feel as if all the red-hot nails of the
martyrs were being shoved through them. If that package isn't
where we left it, Gaucher, and this agony is for nothing, I swear
I'll finish my sins by cutting your throat."

"Keep your voice down, Rufus," Gaucher said. "And stop
complaining. Your spirits will improve once we're into Spain
and the sun shines again. Remember, now there are only two
of us left to share the profit."

"I never forget it, old friend," Rufus answered. "That's
why I sleep every night with a knife in my hand and a solid wall
at my back."

"As do I, old comrade," Gaucher assured him. "But we're
letting death taunt us. After so many years of laughing at it, we
mustn't be cowards now. And the more I consider it, the more
I believe that there can't be any connection linking the others'

deaths. Norbert died of age, Hugh from the knife of a *braban-tine*, and Rigaud most likely at the hand of an angry lover."

"All three are still dead," Rufus said. "And if no one person killed them, I can only believe that we're under some sort of curse, or even divine punishment."

Gaucher crossed himself rapidly. "If that's so, then our swords are useless."

Maruxa gazed at the mountains with longing. To her they were nothing but another obstacle between her and her adored children. She sighed and wondered if her shoes would last the distance. At home, Roberto could stitch new soles onto them, but here, they would have to pay outrageous prices to have someone else do it.

She laid out their remaining provisions on her cloak. There wasn't much left. Lately people had been more careful with their donations. They were beginning to realize just how much farther there was to go.

Hersent came over and knelt next to her. "My Lady Griselle wishes to know if you're too proud to take a pair of her cast-off hose," she said. "The color has faded and there are holes near the top, but they are warm."

Maruxa held out her hand. "My life doesn't allow for much pride. Give her my thanks and tell her I'll remember her in my prayers."

Hersent gave her the stockings but didn't seem inclined to leave. "I understand you come from Astorga," she said.

"Yes, both of us," Maruxa answered. "Do you know it?"

"No, I've never been to Spain before," Hersent said. "My husband fought there once, but nearer to Saragossa, I think."

Maruxa nodded. "There were many battles in that land. My husband, Roberto, was born in Saragossa, but his father grew weary of the constant fighting and moved his family to Astorga. Was your husband in Spain with Lord Bertran?"

"No, years before. Ghyso was only a squire then, and the country fascinated him." Hersent smiled. "He told me so many stories that I feel it will all be familiar when I see it."

"It's very different from what people in the north believe," Maruxa said. "We have so many songs about the battles between Christians and Saracens, but half the time the lords of both faiths are fighting among themselves and making alliances with those who should be their enemies."

"Yes, that's what Ghyso said." Hersent shook her head. "That's why Lord Bertran was so useful to the kings he served, for he spoke the language of the Saracens and understood their customs."

"There are many like that where I came from," Maruxa told her. "And since we all dress much the same, it's difficult to know what religion a stranger is. Many of the northerners get themselves into trouble by not understanding that. You should be careful."

"I'll remember. Thank you." Hersent got up. "I have other commissions from my mistress. I must be going."

Maruxa watched her, not sure why the maid had stayed to talk in the first place.

"By the way," Hersent said before she left, "that's true of those who come north from Spain as well. They can meet disaster through ignorance of our ways. But you already know that, don't you?"

Maruxa gaped at her in sudden terror. Hersent did not look back.

When the maid had gone, Maruxa took the stockings and ripped at them until there was nothing left but a pile of shredded yarn.

They spent several days in Saint-Jean, preparing supplies and repairing equipment. The village had been built recently by the king of Navarre specifically to attend to the needs of pilgrims and traders. Goods were priced accordingly high. Money changers did a thriving business, as did sellers of old clothes and boots. The prices for these latter were quite reasonable, as long as one wasn't particular about what had happened to the previous owner.

Even though it was the height of the season for traffic over the mountains, Solomon had found a place for them to stay in the end of a room at an inn set next to a mountain stream. The music of the water bounding over the rocks lulled them to sleep, and Catherine's dreams were all gentle.

Solomon had even managed to get a curtain hung across the corner where Catherine and Edgar slept. It was a luxury not often come by on the road. Catherine was thrilled not to have to sleep in her clothes . . . and even more so that Edgar didn't have to either.

"How did you manage it?" she asked her cousin.

"I've been here before." Solomon tried to control his smirk.

"Ah, you are a friend of the woman who owns the inn." Catherine understood. "I thought she greeted you with exceptional enthusiasm."

"Let's say that she was happy to know that Edgar was your husband," Solomon said.

"And she has no protective brothers?" Catherine laughed.

"No one." He seemed uncomfortable. "She's a widow with no children. Her husband brought her here from Navarre. He left her the inn when he died. I keep telling her she should marry again. With no family here, she needs someone to watch out for her interests."

"And why haven't you applied for the job?" Catherine teased. "It's the perfect life for you—a beautiful woman and a constant supply of wine."

"Ah well, she has higher standards." Solomon's lips tightened slightly. "Didn't you hear what she called me when we arrived?"

"No, it was just a torrent of sound to me," Catherine admitted. "Until she switched to something like French."

" 'Yuda,' " Solomon told her. "I'm her pet Jew. Maya is a good Christian. She'll go to bed with me, but as for marriage . . ."

Catherine opened her mouth to make a suggestion but stopped herself. They had been through this often before. Solomon knew what she had been about to say.

"I'm not converting for her sake," he said firmly. "What sort of person would give up his place in heaven for the enjoyment of human pleasures?"

"Some have converted for less," she answered. "But I know you aren't one of them. You must come to belief honestly, through grace and your own reasoning . . . though I wonder if the grace might come to you if you ever found someone you really loved."

Solomon pulled on her braid, a signal that the conversation was over. "That is something I may never find out," he laughed. "But the search is so much fun."

That evening Catherine found Mondete sitting on a rock jutting out into the tumbling stream. "You do love running water," she commented.

"It's strange, isn't it?" the woman answered. "It's not as if I lived in a desert. But there's something about the water, especially in the heights. It's so cold and clear and untroubled. Long ago, they say, there were creatures living in the streams, like mermaids in the oceans, but the saints drove them all away. I never understood why. Their souls couldn't have been very evil, not so much as those of the men who hunted them."

She trailed her hand in the foam as the stream spilled over a log just above the surface. Catherine sat near her.

"I don't think the creatures were driven away," she said. "I think that perhaps they were convinced to come out of their streams and accept baptism. Then they no longer needed to live submerged. The water of life was with them always."

She couldn't see Mondete's face, but the tone of her answer told Catherine her opinion of that theory.

"You should have stayed in the convent, young Catherine," Mondete said. "Pretty stories like that are only for the cloistered. I think the river maidens were driven away by the missionaries because they had no sin, no part in the curse of Eden. They needed no savior. They were already as pure as the water. So there was no place for them among us."

This idea opened up intriguing intellectual explorations for Catherine, but she reined them in. Mondete wasn't interested in debating the nature of humanity or redemption.

"You've repented, changed your life, and are doing

penance," she said instead. "Those will restore purity. Look at the *vita* of Saint Mary the Egyptian. Her sins of the flesh were all forgiven when she washed herself in the River Jordan."

Mondete turned and lowered her hood to look at Catherine more clearly. "What book have you lived in all your life, girl?" she asked in exasperation. "I'm not repenting sins of the flesh. I've committed none."

"What? You mean you weren't a whore?" Catherine blurted.

"Oh yes, that I was," Mondete assured her, "since I was given to old Norbert in the first month after I became a woman . . . almost twenty-five years and hundreds of men ago. Maybe thousands, I don't know."

She stopped herself and looked at Catherine with curiosity. "Tell me," she said, "in confidence, how many men have you had?"

"Me?" Catherine was shocked. "Only Edgar, of course. That's all. Truly!"

"And you enjoy the act, don't you?" Mondete pressed. "Of course one is allowed to in marriage, as long as it's only to engender children, and that's the only reason why the two of you do it, right?"

Catherine blushed, but felt she had to be honest. Mondete had answered her blunt question truthfully. It would be wrong to dissemble now.

"No, it isn't," she said softly. "When I look at Edgar, when he touches me, all I want is to be one with him, so close that not even death could tear us apart. I want children because that's the only way in this life that the two of us can be one. But if Saint James doesn't grant this, and even if I know there is no possibility of a child, I'll still long for the times Edgar's body is with mine and greet them with joy."

Mondete's head snapped back as if Catherine had slapped her.

"I'm sorry," Catherine said. "I don't normally speak of such things. Forgive me."

Mondete took a deep breath. "No, I asked you and you

told me. It was an unforgiveable question. But you will agree that the sin is not in the act but in the lust, the giving way to carnality?"

"Yes, so we are taught," Catherine answered. "Where did you learn that?"

"Oh, Catherine," Mondete almost laughed. "When priests are unable to do anything else, they talk. I *know* my catechism."

This means of acquiring a religious education was not one Catherine had thought of. She was not so naive as to assume that all priests were chaste, but she hadn't considered that they might be both preacher and sinner at the same moment. Well, almost the same moment.

"I think I understand," she told Mondete. "Long ago, when the Visigoths captured Rome, the nuns there were raped by the soldiers. Saint Augustine wrote to the women that as they had not acquiesced in or enjoyed the experience, they were still virgins in the eyes of God."

Mondete was not impressed with Augustine's generosity. "They should have been crowned as martyrs," she said bitterly. "It's strange, you know. Can you think of one saint's life wherein she was threatened with rape and had to endure it? No, those women are torn with hot pincers and thrown to lions. They have their eyes gouged out and their breasts torn off, but they always die with their maidenheads intact."

Catherine tried to think of an exception. She couldn't. "Now I'm confused," she said. "If you mean that you didn't sin because you never *wanted* to be violated, that would make sense. But what has it to do with virgin martyrs?"

"Everything, Catherine." Mondete was shaking with the intensity of her words. "I would have been happy to be a virgin martyr. But no one gave me the option. Don't you think I prayed? I prayed to God and the saints. I prayed while Norbert was pinning me down and prying my legs apart, while he was slicing me in half with that horrible thing of his."

Catherine wanted to cover her ears, but she couldn't move. She was as fixed by Mondete's words as Mondete had been by Norbert's body.

"I prayed and then I screamed." Mondete's voice grew soft

and hollow. "I screamed and screamed, but no one came to save me, even though the keep was full of people. There was no angel to stand between me and shame. No hero to rescue me. No father to run home to on earth or in heaven. They had both abandoned me. Everyone had."

She turned her face up to Catherine's. Her eyes were dry and burning with emotions Catherine could sense but not share.

There was nothing to say. Catherine knelt on the stone and put her arms around Mondete, holding her until her shoulders relaxed and her head bowed into the folds of Catherine's cloak . . . and then they cried together.

Edgar was waiting for his wife back at the inn. "Your father tells me we'll start into the mountains tomorrow," he told her. "They were hoping for the weather to improve, but Aaron says that might not be for weeks. Is something wrong?"

He touched her arm and she pulled back. "Oh, Edgar," she said, "I'm sorry. Sometimes I feel terribly selfish." She leaned against him. "I am so lucky to have found you."

Bewildered, but too smart to question, Edgar kissed her forehead. "I'm glad you realize it," he smiled. "I think I've had more than my share of good fortune as well."

Catherine was grateful that he asked nothing more. She was still confused by Mondete's outburst. If the woman had hated the things she had been forced to do, there did seem nothing to repent of. So why was Mondete on the pilgrimage?

Had Brother Rigaud been one of the clerics who taught Mondete her catechism? Mondete certainly had reason to hate Norbert; and Hugh also lived near Mâcon and might have used her, as Gaucher and Rufus had. Could Rigaud have been another? Catherine refused to believe the conclusions that kept leering in her face. But logic told her that if she didn't want to suspect Mondete of having been the murderer, she had to find someone else who had a better reason to kill those three men.

The next morning was cool and still. The fog wasn't as thick and there was a golden tone to it that indicated the sun might burn through. As soon as there was light enough to find the road, groups started out. The small church on the edge of town was full of those asking one last blessing before facing this great challenge. Small offerings of candles or flowers, or coins worn almost thin enough to see through, were left next to the altar.

Edgar's fear of the steep path ahead was so great that he became unnaturally jovial, calling out to the others, laughing loudly at the slightest joke, making an uncommon amount of noise with the harness. Solomon, who had crept upstairs just before dawn, wasn't amused.

"What did you drink last night?" he demanded. "Or is it the air up here? They say that some men go mad from being so close to heaven."

Edgar sobered at that thought. "I can well believe it. Saint Anselm dreamt once that the throne of God was on a mountaintop. But I think it's more likely that the way to heaven from here is straight down."

"Your Saint Anselm dreamt of the Throne?" Solomon asked, suddenly awake. "What was it made of? What did it look like? What was it resting on?"

"Oh, Solomon, not now!" Catherine appeared, carrying her bundle of clothes. "Anyway, I don't think there was a description of the throne in his account of the dream. Now find a place for this, would you?"

Solomon took the bundle and began tying it to the rest of the packs with leather thongs, muttering all the while.

"*You* can go on forever speculating on the nature of the universe. *You* can spend hours spouting nonsense to prove that your three gods are really one, but if I ask one little question about the *merkavah*, then, 'Oh no, Solomon, it's not the right time, we're all too busy.' "

Catherine overheard him, as he intended, and laughed. "You're feeling better," she said. "I'm glad. I should thank our hostess for cheering you. We won't let that nasty Brother James near you again if he makes you such boring company. Has anyone even seen him since we left Moissac?"

"I did," Edgar said. "I think. He looks oddly familiar. I keep wondering where I saw him before."

"I had the same feeling," Solomon said, cinching the packs tightly. "And I don't want to know. I just don't want to see him again."

Catherine patted his back in sympathy. "You know, I don't think he likes women any more than he likes Jews. The few times he's passed me, he always turns away, crossing himself as if I were a demon about to pounce on him."

"Oh, would you, Catherine?" Solomon laughed. "It would be worth what he put me through to see him quail."

"Don't tempt her!" Edgar said. "I was nervous enough when you were taken. All I need is to have to defend my wife on a charge of demonic possession. Are we ready? Aaron just signaled that his party is leaving."

They crossed the stream that would soon become the River Nive and started up the path.

"I can't believe it," Catherine said to Edgar as they followed the long line of pilgrims. "Tonight we'll sleep in the hostel at Roncevalles and worship in the church built on the rock Roland split. We'll see where he and Olivier fought the Saracens. And after that," she told him reassuringly, "it will be downhill all the way to Compostela."

Edgar closed his eyes. "Catherine, haven't I explained? Down is much worse than up. When we're descending, I can see even more clearly how far I might fall."

The promise of sunshine was never fulfilled. The fog lifted to become a hard, biting rain, augmented by sudden gusts of wind whenever they rounded curves in the path. They went up and up and the earth fell farther away on their left, until only the occasional bleat of a wandering sheep was all that told them there was land at the bottom of the precipice.

Despite his terror, Edgar insisted on walking on the outside, keeping Catherine on the other side of the horse, nearest the mountain. When it was too narrow to walk three abreast, he still kept her on the inside as he led the mount.

He didn't speak, and Catherine was afraid to break his concentration with the wrong words. She didn't tell him how much she wanted to look over the edge. Clouds were drifting far below them, swirling about and giving glimpses of rivulets and what might be tiny settlements. She thought of Mondete's river maidens. If they hadn't been driven away but stayed and married humans, then this was the sort of place she could imagine them living. It was so frustrating not to be able to climb down into the valleys to see if it were true.

Looking up into a tree overhanging the road, Catherine was startled to see a face looking back at her, upside down. It was just the sort of person she had been imagining: half-human, half-spirit, with skin so white it was almost blue, great eyes of grey, like Edgar's, the color of the storm. But instead of the fine blond Saxon hair of her husband, this apparition had long straight braids as black as Catherine's own.

She started to cry out, but the face vanished, leaving her to wonder if she had created it herself from her daydream.

They stopped once to rest and eat, although there was no way of telling if it were morning or afternoon. Partway up the long climb, there was a huge stone cross, said to have been erected by Charlemagne in memory of Roland and the brave men who had died with him. Around it were hundreds of smaller crosses, most of wood, that pilgrims had pounded into the earth to mark their passing. Here the latest pilgrims leaned against the rock cliff and munched on hard cheese, washed down with raw wine that tasted of the untanned skins they carried it in.

Catherine wondered if the Lady Griselle had somehow managed to stay dry. It would have comforted her greatly to see those fine silks bedraggled with mud and the fur lining of Griselle's cloak matted and sticking to her skin. She told herself sternly that it was an unworthy desire. But it would have been so satisfying.

It was also not to be. Griselle was far ahead of them, traveling in the shadow of the monks and their guards. By the time the rest of the pilgrims arrived at the hostel, Griselle would have had time to put on dry clothing and have Hersent arrange her hair and sew her into a clean *chainse*. Catherine felt the drops trickle off the end of her nose and the ends of her braids and tried to remember that suffering willingly endured was good for the soul. But her mind kept drifting to hot soup.

She caught up to Eliazar, leading his horse just in front of them. "Do you think we'll be across by dark?" she asked.

"We'll have to be," he answered, pulling his hood closer to his chin. "Don't worry, sweet. If that *noisous* nephew of mine can get through here in one day when the snow is waist-deep, then we can do it despite a bit of wet."

Catherine knew mendacious reassurance when she heard it, but resolved to try to believe it all the same. She slipped back to Edgar and took his hand.

"How are you?" he asked.

"Wet to the skin, chilled to the bone, and the sound of the squelch in my boots is enough to induce hysteria," she answered. "How are you?"

"About the same," he said. "What shall we think of to make the journey less unpleasant?"

Catherine started to smile, then remembered Mondete. In part, she wished the woman had never said a word to her. It made her ashamed to be loved and cared for and to take such joy in the body of a man when other men had done unspeakable things to Mondete.

"Now what?" Edgar asked with a trace of impatience. His feet were cold and wet, too.

Catherine squeezed his hand, although her fingers were so numb she could hardly feel it. "I'm sorry," she said. "It's something I have to think through. Perhaps when we're dry again, and warm and alone, I'll tell you about it."

"If all those things ever happen," Edgar sighed, "I'd rather we didn't settle in to a long discussion."

The light stayed the same forever, Catherine thought. No morning or noon, only fog. They had been walking steadily uphill since the beginning of the world and they would go on climbing for all eternity. Even though she hadn't seen it on a church sculpture, she was sure that endless walking in inclement weather must be one of the torments of Hell.

Suddenly she heard cries from far ahead. "What is it?" She clutched at Solomon. "Are they being attacked?"

This was where the heroic rear guard of Charlemagne's army had been destroyed. Catherine could see all the brave knights in her mind. Was it happening all over again?

Solomon grinned. "No, silly. Put away your old stories and listen!"

The sound was distorted by the wind, but she soon realized that she wasn't hearing a clash of metal or the screams of wounded men and horses. It seemed strangely like . . . cheering. She looked at her cousin for confirmation.

"Roncevalles," he said. "Not far ahead at all. The hostel is just beyond it, on the lee side of the mountain."

Catherine and Edgar felt like cheering, too. After all her talk about seeing the site of the famous battle, her only vision as she urged herself that last mile was that of a roaring fire and her stockinged feet steaming before it.

The first thing she noticed as they reached the summit was the wind. The rain was being blown sideways, and the openings in cloaks were caught and pushed at until the people looked like giant wounded birds flapping wildly across the plateau.

It was not the scene Catherine had imagined.

Fourteen

The pass of Roncevalles in the Pyrenees, Friday, May, 29, 1142; The Feast of Saint Restitute, who was starved, chained, chased by Satan with a flaming sword, bitten by scorpions and finally beheaded. But, thanks to her guardian angel, she died a virgin.

Halt sunt li puiet li val tenebrus,
Les roches bises, les destreiz merveillus.
Le jur passerent Franceis a grant dulur.

High are the mountains and gloomy the valleys,
The rocks gray and brown, the narrow gorge awesome.
The French spend the day in great misery.
La Chanson de Roland
Laisse 66. 11 814–816

C aught and spun around by the wind, Catherine lost what little sense of direction she had. The ends of her scarf flapped across her face, stinging her eyes. The blowing rain made it impossible to see more than a step or two ahead. She had let go of Edgar's hand to grab her flapping cloak as they came out onto the plateau and now she couldn't find him.

"Edgar!" she cried, but the words blew back at her. "Edgar!"

She stumbled toward what she thought was the path, but found no one. All at once she tripped over a root and was thrown down a short incline and into a tangle of prickly plants. The stems were sharp and slippery and she couldn't right herself.

"Edgar!" she called again.

She tried to pull out of the gorse, but only slipped farther down. The angle became steeper, and she wondered how close she was to the edge of the plateau. She tried to dig her toes into the dirt but only kicked pebbles loose. Gritting her teeth against the pain of the thorns, she grabbed and pulled on one of the plants, which came up by the roots, spraying her face with mud. She could feel herself starting to slide again.

"Help!" she cried as she spit out bits of twigs and dirt.

"*Emadazu escua!*" someone shouted from nearby. "*Andrea! Emadazu escua!*"

A hand appeared in front of her face and she grasped it in both of hers. She heard her clothes tear as she was pulled up the slope out of the gorse and at last set on her feet.

"*Cer dembora icigaria!*" a man's voice said.

Catherine managed to unstick her scarf from her face and peer through the rain at her rescuer. Her eyes widened in fear and disbelief. It was the face she had seen in the tree on the road; pale as snow, hair straight and black as a raven's wing. Human, or demon?

The man saw her terror and held both his hands up in front of himself, open to show that he had no weapon. He was dressed in a rough wool tunic that ended above his bare knees. His boots were of thick, unshorn sheepskin, as was his vest.

"*Eman gaiten atherpean,*" he said, grabbing her hand again and pulling her in the other direction. "*Ez beldurric izan.*"

"No, let go of me!" Catherine cried. "What are you doing? Where are you taking me? Edgar!"

She tried to dig her heels into the ground, but only slid in the brown mud. The man stopped and looked at her in exasperation. "*Eman gaiten atherpean,*" he repeated slowly. "*Ez beldurric izan.*"

"I don't understand you," Catherine answered mournfully. "Please, help me find the others. My husband, my father."

He pulled on her again. "*Etorri, Andrea!*" He drew his knife. The rain slid easily across the sharp blade.

Catherine gave up and let herself be dragged wherever the man was going. "Saint Catherine, help me!" she begged.

The man stopped with a half-smile. "Catherine," he said. "*Cattalin.*"

"Yes, my name saint." With her free hand, Catherine pointed to herself. "*Cattalin.*"

"*Etorri, Cattalin,*" the man said, more softly. "*Ez beldurric izan.*"

He sheathed the knife, but didn't let go of her wrist.

Somehow, having managed even that much communication with the man gave Catherine the hope that he did not intend to hurt her. She followed with no further protest. They rounded a huge rock in the plateau and emerged from the wind.

"Catherine!"

She fell into Edgar's arms.

"Oh, *carissime!*" she said. "I lost you and couldn't find my way through the storm and then I fell and this man . . ."

She turned around. The man was gone. She stared for a moment at the place where he had been, then shivered. Edgar held her more tightly.

"I thought you'd gone over the edge," he said, trying to catch his breath. "I heard you cry out but couldn't reach you."

"I'm all right," she said. "The man in the tree pulled me off the mountainside."

Edgar turned her face up to his. Her teeth were chattering.

"*Leoffaest*, you sound feverish," he said. "We have to get you to the hostel at once."

"Edgar, you saw him, didn't you?" she asked. "The man who saved me?"

"There was someone," he said, "but I couldn't make out his face. I was only looking for you."

"Edgar, do you think it could have been Saint James?" Catherine was uncertain. "He didn't look like any of the descriptions of the apostle. It wasn't at all like my dream."

Edgar didn't answer, and Catherine was so worn that she didn't pursue the matter but let him guide her back to the trail. Solomon, Eliazar, Hubert, and oddly, Mondete, were waiting.

"No questions now," Eliazar decreed. "We must get out of this wind. We're no more than a mile from the hostel."

It seemed a thousand miles to Catherine as she walked propped up between Edgar and Solomon. She wished she could ride, but the time it would take to unload the horse and put her on it wasn't worth it. She was so cold now that she felt warm. At least the rain was washing the dirt from her face and clothes. She tilted her head and opened her mouth to get rid of the grit as well.

It didn't seem likely that the man from the tree was the venerable Apostle James, but he had seemed to appear out of nowhere to rescue her. Catherine puzzled over it. The event wasn't exactly like her dream, but they *were* in the mountains. The wind had been terrible, she had fallen, and the man had saved her. Could he have been an angel guarding the pilgrims? Did this mean that she didn't need to worry anymore about falling over the edge? Had the dream been fulfilled? Master Abelard could have told her, but it was too late to ask him.

She was so tired. Only the arms of her husband and cousin kept her from sliding down in the mud and falling asleep on the first rock she found that was above the puddles.

When they arrived at the hostel, it was already full of people. The building, made of stone blocks, was one enormous room with a loft running around the walls on three sides. The monks had strung lines from the railings of the loft and these were covered with drying cloaks and blankets. A fire was blazing in the huge hearth at the east end of the room.

As they came in, the abrupt change from freezing rain to steamy heat made all of them dizzy. Catherine clutched her stomach with one hand and her mouth with the other.

"Breathe deeply," Solomon told her. "I'll get you some wine to sip."

"Is everyone else here?" Hubert asked, his eyes searching the room for Griselle.

"Don't worry, I'm sure she already has the corner of the loft nearest the fire," Mondete said, guessing his intent.

"Do you think we can get closer to the warmth?" Edgar asked. "I'm worried about Catherine. You know how easily she gets sick."

"I'm stronger than you think," Catherine broke in. "And it's far too warm in here already. Saint Mary Magdalene's maggoty rags! The stench of this place is more than I can bear. I think I'd rather stay in the rain."

Solomon reappeared with the wine. He forced the wooden cup between Catherine's teeth and tipped, causing most of the liquid to run down the corners of her mouth . . . but enough got in to ease her shivering.

They managed to find a place near the wall under the loft and struggled out of their wet clothes and into dry shifts, at least. Most of the other pilgrims were in a similar state of undress. To Hubert, Catherine with her unbelted shift trailing the floor, her hair undone and tangled, looked about fourteen. For an instant, she was his child again, not some other man's wife. His alone to care for. Then Edgar came up with a blanket to wrap her in and she turned her face up to his. Hubert bit his tongue. The two of them were a world unto themselves; she was his no more. At least, whatever else this marriage might do to her, Catherine was happy.

It was enough, he told himself firmly; it was more than he had ever had.

Hubert's eyes continued to search the room. He still hadn't found Griselle. He knew that this was the only shelter until they descended to the base of the mountains. Even Aaron and his party were forced to stay in the hostel, grateful that the monks of Roncevalles were willing to allow them in. Finally, Hubert shrugged and tried not to worry. He hadn't the right to be concerned about the Lady of Lugny. She had probably arrived early enough to get a place in the loft, as Mondete had said, where it was warm and the straw both cleaner and drier.

As Hubert sorted out the wet garments to hang, he heard a familiar sound, the rattle of wooden dice as they landed on a board. It reminded him that not everyone traveling this route was a devout pilgrim, even those who wore the cross and carried the *bourdin* and scrip. He wondered why those monks the abbot had sent to investigate Hugh's death hadn't been more suspicious of the other pilgrims. Their questions had been aimed only at those who were obviously outsiders. How much easier it would be to pretend great repentance and devotion in order to take others off guard and slit their throats. One heard tales of it all the time. Why hadn't the monks considered that?

There was a shout from the circle of men kneeling over the dice. Hubert smiled. He could tell that a number of fervent prayers were being said.

"You find something amusing in this dreadful place?"

"After the storm and the fear that my daughter was lost, I find this shelter most congenial," Hubert answered.

He had known she was beside him, even before she spoke. The attar of lilies she wore was unmistakable. How did Griselle always manage to look so elegant? She might have just come down from her rooms in her own castle. Her hair was smooth, her face clean. The pleats in her sleeves looked freshly ironed. He felt like an ostler come in straight from mucking out the stables. Hubert rubbed his chin. He hadn't shaved since leaving Moissac. Griselle smiled.

"I can understand your feeling," she told him. "Especially your worry for your child. Bertran and I were not given that joy. I have often regretted it, but perhaps God was kind in also sparing me the grief so many have in their offspring."

Hubert laughed at that, but inside, he winced. The shot was closer to the mark than Lady Griselle knew.

"Would you care to sit by the fire?" he asked. "I can set up a stool for you."

"My guard is bringing one," she answered. "Perhaps you would care to set up one for yourself, next to mine. I would be pleased if you could tell me some more stories of your life in Paris. It might distract me from the noise and closeness in here."

"I would be honored," Hubert said.

His hands fumbled as he tried to fit the canvas seat over the tripod legs of the stool. What was the matter with him? Eliazar hadn't needed to remind him that Griselle was Christian and that Madeleine's retirement to a convent did not free him to remarry in any case. He knew it. Griselle was a good fifteen years younger than he as well, only a few years older than Catherine's brother, Guillaume. This was insane. He was deluding himself. She only wanted the company of someone harmless, someone to protect her from the attentions of Gaucher and Rufus. He had to be careful not to put any meaning to her smiles and half-lidded glances.

It would be all too easy to make a fool of himself.

From across the room, Eliazar watched. He knew that look of infatuation. He and Johannah rented out rooms to the students of Paris and he had seen it often. Usually the boys passed through the episode unharmed and returned to their studies and plans for a celibate life. But not always. It was bad enough to see a sixteen-year-old in such a condition. It was dreadful when it was his fifty-two-year-old brother.

Eliazar turned away. He was sorry now he had ever suggested that Hubert come with them. Instead of helping with the problems, he had become one of them.

Gaucher and Rufus were also appalled by the sight of Hubert and Griselle sitting together.

"The next thing you know, she'll be giving him sops of her bread and they'll be drinking from the same cup," Gaucher said.

"And you know what they say." Rufus was indignant. " 'Those that eat together will soon share a bed.' "

"She wouldn't demean herself so!" Gaucher said.

"Other women have," Rufus said. "Remember Hugh's wife."

Gaucher grunted. It was one thing to deceive one's husband with wandering players. At least they moved on quickly and some of the children turned out to be quite musical. One was the chantor at Saint-Lazare now.

"It's another thing to treat the man as an equal and flaunt your friendship before his betters," Gaucher finished the thought aloud.

"We need to do something about this," Rufus said. "It's indecent."

"What does she see in him?" Gaucher blurted. "His hair is thinning!"

Rufus ran his hand slowly over his smooth head. "It's well known that bald men are extremely virile," he said.

"Really? I thought they were just old and diseased," Gaucher answered. "No, wait. I ask your pardon, Rufus. We're letting ourselves be distracted from the problem of this low-born trader."

Rufus was suddenly aware of the ache in his joints, the fatigue in his heart. Perhaps Gaucher wasn't so far wrong. "What difference does it make?" he asked. "Once we retrieve the treasure, we can buy ourselves a dozen women, younger and more willing than Griselle."

"That isn't the point, Rufus." Gaucher raised his chin haughtily and glared across the room. "Would you let your daughter behave like that in public with a common workman?"

"I'd beat her silly," Rufus said. "Although the lordling she married is no prize, either."

"Do you know," Gaucher said slowly, "I seem to remember overhearing this Hubert LeVendeur shouting and hurling insults at our poor friend, Rigaud."

"You do? When?"

"The morning after Hugh was murdered," Gaucher said. "You were there. Rigaud was questioning him and that 'partner' of his, and suddenly the merchant started shouting and shaking his fist."

"Oh yes, now that you mention it, I do remember," Rufus said. "It's odd that Rigaud should die so soon after that and in such an unchivalrous manner."

"No honorable person would kill a man in such a way," Gaucher agreed.

"But one could expect no such honor from a man used to cheating people to make his living," Rufus finished.

They both smiled.

"I think it's our duty to report this to Brother James," Gaucher said.

"After which we'll be forced by honor to avenge the death of our friend."

On the other side of the room, Hubert said something that caused Griselle to laugh merrily. The sound didn't grate on the old warriors the way it had only a few moments before. Now they knew that Hubert LeVendeur would pay for his audacity.

Once Edgar was warm and sure that Catherine was taken care of, he became aware of the raging emptiness in his stomach. The bread and cheese they had brought with them from Saint-Jean were calling to him from the soggy packs. As he pawed through them, the door to the hostel opened, bringing the wind inside for a moment. Suddenly his nose was captured by a smell that seemed to emanate from paradise. It had been so long that it took him a moment to identify it.

Someone was roasting venison.

Edgar dropped the packs and joined the rush to the door. Outside, the ravenous pilgrims followed the scent to a smaller building nearby. Next to it was a fire pit, and above that, a whole deer was roasting. A collective groan of ecstasy arose from the pilgrims.

Then the groan turned to one of dismay as someone cried out, "But it's Friday! We can't have meat!"

Edgar's heart sank. It was true. How could the monks who kept the hostel do this to them?

Catherine, barefoot, with a blanket thrown over her head and shoulders, had followed Edgar out. "Oh, no!" she moaned. "Meat! What sort of hideous temptation is this?"

"Meat," Edgar echoed. Then he snapped out of his dream. "Catherine, you have no shoes on! Get back in there! I'll find out what this is all about."

Catherine hadn't even noticed. Her body had been deprived of red meat for so long, what with Lent and then penitential fasting, that the scent of it sent out a call stronger than any other need.

One of the men tending the fire caught her eye. Catherine gasped. He smiled. It was her rescuer.

"Edgar!" she said. "That's the man in the tree! Do you see him?"

"Ah, yes. Basque, perhaps a guide," Edgar said, still focused on the venison. "I don't think he's Saint James in disguise."

One of the other pilgrims overheard him. "Maybe not," he said. "But if it means we can eat that deer tonight, I'll believe he's Saint Gilles, offering us his pet doe for dinner. It would be irreverent to turn him down." He had already taken out his knife, to cut a slice as soon as the meat was within reach.

"Catherine, I think you should have some," Edgar said. "It's well known that women need red meat more than men do."

Catherine turned back to the hostel with a sigh. "No. It's likely just another test, one more temptation to overcome. If there's any left tomorrow, I'll eat it as soon as the sun is up. I promise."

Edgar agreed sadly. This was not a trial he had expected, which made it all the more likely it was intended. The Great Trickster loved undermining the resolutions of the faithful in just this way.

Many of the other pilgrims agreed, but not all. There was a thick cluster around the fire, and every turn of the spit was greeted with groans of anticipation.

Brother James heard the commotion from the small priory where he and Brothers Bruno and Deodatus were staying. He asked one of the monks of Roncevalles what was happening. The monk laughed.

"Some of the shepherds of the region have brought us an offering," he explained. "They do that from time to time. The pilgrims are always most grateful. Many of the poorer ones have never eaten fresh game, at least not to admit to. It's a rare treat for them to dine as well as the great lords; it reminds them that Our Lord makes no distinction of earthly rank."

Brother James was outraged. "You allow these barbarians to corrupt honest pilgrims with red meat? And on a fast day as well! What sort of shepherds are you?"

"Ones who believe that their flock needs material sustenance as well as spiritual," the monk retorted. "Nor are we too proud to take any gift the forest sends."

"You should be," Brother James answered. "This would never happen at Cluny. And if you won't prevent the pilgrims from eating this tonight, I will."

The monk of Roncevalles wasn't swayed. "I can't stop you from preaching to them, if you must," he said. "But if you try to come between them and the first red meat many have seen in years, then I will stop you. And you'll be grateful I kept you from being killed. Hunger may give visions to some, but most people are only driven to desperation by it."

Brother James was so overpowered by his wrath that he forgot his resolve to keep in the shadows while observing the suspects in Rigaud's death. Even if he had given himself time to reflect, he would have considered the danger to himself unimportant next to his duty.

Rufus and Gaucher had no qualms about a nice slice of venison, whatever the night. They had broken worse rules. But the sight of Brother James bearing down on the crowd around the fire reminded them of their higher mission.

"Brother James!" Rufus called. "A moment, please! We have information that might be of interest to you."

James stopped. He had to convince the people not to yield

to the temptation of gaining a full stomach. But these men were wealthy and had been soldiers of Christ. He owed them some courtesy. Reluctantly, he came over to them.

"Don't worry," Rufus told him. "There'll be plenty of meat left. We've just remembered an incident that may have some bearing on poor Rigaud's unnatural death."

They proceeded to explain.

At first James was annoyed that they assumed he was as eager for the venison as they. Then, as their story progressed, he was too excited to chastise them.

"Do you mean the merchant who spoke for that Solomon person?" he asked again. "The one who made me look a fool before my abbot?"

"I don't know about that," Gaucher hedged. "Hubert is certainly in business with Solomon and his uncle."

"But Lady Griselle was a witness as well," James said. "They could hardly have suborned her."

"Ah, but that is even worse!" Rufus shouted. He looked around, then lowered his voice. "We believe she didn't speak for the man voluntarily. This merchant from Paris may have ensorcelled her."

James was pleased with the accusation against Hubert, who was not attached to Cluny in any way and who associated with known infidels. He would be a perfect prisoner to present to Abbot Peter. But recent experience had made him cautious.

"Have you proof of this?" he asked.

"He and Griselle are sitting together at this very hour," Rufus said, "talking and laughing and drinking in a most unseemly manner. He's probably put some kind of potion in her wine."

"I'll question the man, of course," James said. "And your evidence does make me suspicious. But I can do nothing without some form of proof. I've observed the Lady Griselle and she doesn't appear to be under the influence of any sort of necromancy. She is most regular in her attendance at the sacrament and in her devotions."

"You mean you'll do nothing?" Gaucher was outraged.

"Not without the accusation of an eyewitness," James said

patiently. "Now, if you'll excuse me. There are people here about to commit the sins of fast-breaking and gluttony. I must help them find the strength to resist."

He left Gaucher and Rufus standing open-mouthed in the rain.

"Now what do we do?" Rufus asked his friend.

"Find an eyewitness," Gaucher answered. "Or find evidence of the crime. There must be something."

"But, Gaucher—" Rufus wiped his head with his sleeve "—I thought we'd decided that Hugh and Rigaud were killed by the same person who played those tricks on us at Vézelay. Hubert wasn't there then. And why would he want to murder Hugh?"

Gaucher raised his eyes to heaven. "Saint Appollina's double somersault into the flames! What are you talking about? The man is clearly some sort of sorcerer, probably not even human. He can do anything he wants. Did you ever think that he might be stalking us for the treasure? If it's of value to us and the Church, what do you think it would be worth if he gave it to his master, Satan?"

Rufus felt his head aching with the effort of following all this. From being an upstart who had stolen Griselle of Lugny from them, Hubert had become an emissary of the devil. It seemed to make sense, but Rufus wasn't sure.

"I think I need a large slice of venison, preferably from the shoulder," he declared. "And a skin or two of wine. Then I'll decide if I want to do battle with this servant of evil, or just run like hell."

James's attempt to convince people who had lived for weeks on bread, cheese and various suspect things floating in broth to renounce a real piece of meat was a complete failure. As the monk of Roncevalles had warned, James barely escaped martyrdom.

He was not in good humor as he went back to the priory and answered the benign greeting of the monk there with a most unbrotherly bark. "What kind of salvation do these people think they'll find?" he shouted at Brother Bruno, startling him from meditation.

"You know our venerable abbot says that the only true pilgrimage is one that renounces the world forever," Bruno answered. "There are traps and snares in every path. Too many
of these poor people apparently believe that merely reaching
Santiago de Compostela will be enough to remit their sins. So
one more sin before the end of the journey must not seem too
much to them. And in my experience, hunger is harder to resist than lust."

James sat on the bench next to Bruno and leaned against
the wall, eyes closed. He could resist hunger, thirst, lust, and
usually, pride. But there were times when he felt the lure of despair too much to endure. He had been back among laymen for
only a few weeks and he didn't think he could bear another day
of it. He was haunted by living ghosts, mocked by those he tried
to preach to, and had done nothing to fulfill his directive from
Abbot Peter. He had lost his courage and was terrified that he
might also lose his faith.

The only way to regain both was to face the terrors.

Tomorrow night, when they reached the Augustinian
monastery and hostel at Larrasoña, he would question this
merchant and find out just what his relationship had been with
Rigaud, as well as what it was presently with Lady Griselle.
James was sure that one who would consort with and protect
unbelievers could do anything. But why? And why were
Gaucher and Rufus so eager to blame the merchant and the lady
but not forthcoming enough to give a valid reason?

James suspected that the knights knew a great deal more
than they had told him. He wondered if they had used their
time in Spain doing more than fighting the Saracens. What if
they had had some sort of business transactions with Hubert
and then reneged? In that case, wouldn't the old men be in as
much danger as their former partners?

Brother James let his head thump against the wall. This was
an impossible task. People moving about all the time. Not
enough information on the lives and characters of accusers or
accused. One had to step carefully in this morass. He could feel
Despair's cold fingers tightening around his heart.

"*Quare tristis es, anima mea? Et quare conturbas me?*"

James opened his eyes. Brother Bruno was reciting softly, saying the words as if he really wanted to know the answer. " 'Why are you sad, my soul? And why do you trouble me?' "

Strange, Brother James thought. *Even after all these years, the psalms still don't sound right in Latin.*

The next morning, the sun shone brightly, welcoming the pilgrims for their descent into Navarre. There were still patches of mud, and those experienced in travel knew that the road down is often more treacherous than the one up. But there was a general air of excitement and a feeling that the worst was over. Catherine even caught Mondete humming as she shook out her cloak and took out her spoon and bowl.

When she realized that Catherine was watching, Mondete stopped at once. The cloak gave a slight shrug. Catherine bent to hide her smile.

Edgar had procured a small piece of venison the previous night, and the two of them had shared it as soon as they awoke. While doubtful about the propriety of eating any meat under the circumstances, Catherine had to admit that she felt more energetic this morning than she had since they left Paris.

When the packs were ready, she waited out by the hostel door while Edgar and Hubert went for the horses. Even though the day was cloudless, the wind still whipped through the trees surrounding the slight valley in which they were sheltered. Catherine leaned against the pile of bundles and watched as the other groups set off. What could be keeping them? The merchants from Toulouse had already gone, taking their guards. Others followed after them.

Edgar arrived with Eliazar, leading the horses.

"Where's my father?" Catherine asked.

Eliazar grimaced. "The Lady Griselle stopped him to ask his advice or some such nonsense."

"And Solomon?"

"Went to find that Basque hunter," Edgar told her. "He was muttering something about getting another guard."

Solomon came back before Hubert did. He nodded to Eliazar, who seemed relieved.

"What is it?" Edgar asked.

"I wanted to see Catherine's savior," Solomon answered. "It occurred to me that he hadn't been properly rewarded for saving her life."

"That's true," Catherine said, embarrassed. "I didn't even know how to say thank-you."

"We came to an understanding," Solomon said. "I hope. My knowledge of their language is not complete."

"You're sure he's the right one to deal with?" Eliazar asked.

"No." Solomon tucked his purse back inside his tunic. "But if he is, we should have no trouble the rest of the way through Navarre. Besides what I paid him, I think he feels protective of Catherine. He told me not to let her fall anymore."

"You mean he's going to come with us as a guard?" Catherine was puzzled.

"No, Catherine," Edgar explained. "I think Solomon means we just paid him so that we wouldn't need guarding from him and his men."

"He's a bandit? But he was so nice." Catherine still didn't understand. "He brought the deer."

Solomon was about to explain the intricacies of Navarrese customs when Hersent hurried up to them. "Come at once!" she said. "Those idiots are accusing *Sieur* Hubert of sorcery and murder! And they're trying to convince Brother James to let them hang him!"

Catherine stood stunned by the news. "That's impossible!" she whispered, unable to get her breath.

"This has gone far enough." Eliazar stated grimly.

Solomon had never seen his uncle look like this before. Eliazar showed no fear, but pure, righteous anger. Sparks seemed to fly from his eyes. Moses breaking the tablets couldn't have been more wrathful.

They followed Hersent to the priory gate. Outside stood Hubert, held firmly by Gaucher and Rufus. His cheek was swollen and cut. Brother James faced him, shouting something, but they were too far away to make out the words. The other monks from Cluny watched in confusion but did nothing to intervene. To one side, the Lady Griselle stood, wringing her hands. When she saw them, she ran to Eliazar and clutched his arm in supplication.

"They've gone mad!" she said. "They say I can't swear for him because I'm under his influence. They've found proof that Hubert killed Hugh, they say. It's all horrible. You have to stop them!"

"Proof? What proof?" Eliazar paused.

"A ring, with no stone in it," Griselle said. "Gaucher insisted on searching him and found it in the bag at his belt with his knife and spoon."

Catherine gasped. Eliazar seemed uninterested.

"Did he now? I'm not surprised." He continued walking.

"Uncle!" Solomon caught his other arm. "Let me go get help. We can't stop them alone!"

"Oh yes I can." Eliazar reached the group. Hubert saw his face and shook his head.

"Don't—" he started.

But it was too late. Eliazar grabbed Brother James and spun him around roughly. He shook the monk in fury, shouting at him in rapid Hebrew. Then he switched to French.

"Jacob, you *questre!* You filthy *fils de lisse!* It's Chaim, you fool, little Chaim! I don't care what you are now; I won't let you murder your own brother!"

Fifteen

A moment later. No one has moved.

אַל תַּעֲלֹז נַפְשָׁם / הָאוֹמְרִים "תֶּאְשַׁם
צִיּוֹן" וְהִגֵּה שָׁם / לִבִּי וְשָׁם עֵינִי.

יהודה הלוי

May no joy come to those who jeer that guilty Zion in ruins must
lie. Not so. I know her innocence. She will always have my heart
and eye.

—Judah Ha-Levi

*L*iar!" Brother James spun around. "You were always trying to trick me. Chaim is dead!"

Still holding a stupefied Hubert with one hand, the monk pointed at Eliazar with the other. "Perfidious infidel!" he screamed. "You'd say anything to get me back, but I deny you and condemn you!"

Hubert seemed stunned. "Jacob?" he asked. "You? You can't be! How . . ."

Gaucher and Rufus were even more confused by the scene. Their glee at proving Hubert's guilt with the finding of the ring evaporated as their ally from Cluny suddenly appeared to be refuting accusations against himself. Gaucher stepped toward Eliazar, his hand on his sword hilt.

"Stay out of this!" he warned. "This has nothing to do with you, unless you and Hubert are also partners in murder. Then there'll be a rope for you, too, if you're lucky."

"Get out of the way," Eliazar said quietly, not taking his eyes off Brother James. "Jacob, let your brother go. He is your brother, I tell you. Chaim didn't die with our mother and sisters; he was taken and baptized and raised a good Christian. Look at him. You know who he is. Look at his daughter. You knew her from the start, but wouldn't believe it."

James and Hubert stared at each other, James in anger, Hubert in wonder. Gaucher stepped away from Eliazar. He didn't understand what was happening but knew that he had lost the attention of everyone present and doubted he could get it back unless he used the sword. He wasn't prepared for that, not yet.

He gestured to Rufus to come with him. They would have to wait for a better time. Rufus stayed where he was, fascinated by the scene.

Finally, Brother James released his grip on Hubert, who didn't move. The monk then turned his attention to Catherine, who was staring at him in horror. He held up his arm to keep her away.

"I thought you were a spirit," he said, "the ghost of my mother come back to reproach me for renouncing her. But even that wouldn't have turned me from my faith. There is nothing you can do to me to make me deny Christ."

"Why would I want you to?" Catherine asked.

Eliazar answered him. "Yes, every time I look at Catherine, I see our poor mother, too. You should have guessed who Hubert was from that alone. But you'll be pleased to know that Catherine's mother is a Christian and so is she. So spare her your hatred of your own people." His voice was thick with bitterness.

Brother James was just as intense. "Not my people, Eliazar. Not anymore. I have been reborn. My only brothers are those of Cluny."

"And your son?" Eliazar shot back. "You would have let Solomon be executed as well?"

Only Mondete, standing outside the circle as usual, had been watching Solomon. He might have been the ghost, white to the lips. She thought he was about to faint.

At the mention of his name, Solomon moaned, his head in his hands. "Uncle, what is this?" he pleaded. "My father's dead. He died just after I was born, drowned while crossing a river. You told me."

"So he did, Solomon; it was a horrible death," Eliazar answered without taking his eyes off the monk. "We said *Kaddish* for him. We sat *shiva*. Jacob ben Meïr died the day he shaved his beard, abandoned his wife and child, and went to the priests to be splashed by their filthy water."

"That's right," James said. "He did. That man no longer exists."

Rufus hadn't left with Gaucher. He had come to see a mur-

derer hanged and felt that the situation was getting too far away
from the original matter.

"Look, I don't know what you're all going on about," he
said plaintively. "I don't care which of you are dead or born
again, or if you're related to each other or not. We found
Hugh's ring in this man's purse and that's enough to convince
me he killed our friend. Now, if Brother James won't take him
into custody, Gaucher and I will. We can find enough people
to help us hang him."

"Where?"

"What?" Rufus looked around.

It was Edgar who had spoken. "Where will you find anyone
to help you? The others have gone ahead. There's no one here
but us and the canons. Do you think they'll assist in a hanging?"

"But we have the ring!" Rufus held it up. "Hubert the Merchant killed Hugh, and probably Rigaud, too. We have the
right to hang him."

"Someone put that in my scrip, I told you," Hubert insisted. "It wasn't there last night. You may even have dropped
it in when you were searching me. I had no reason to kill your
friend. I'll defend myself in any court."

Rufus was near to exploding. He gestured frantically at
Gaucher, who had come back, leading their horses. Gaucher
put a hand on his shoulder in an effort to calm him.

"We've clearly fallen into something more important to
these people than life or death." He looked from Hubert to
James to Eliazar in appraisal. "This knowledge might even turn
out to be of use to us. I think we should wait."

"But the ring!" Rufus protested.

Gaucher pulled him away from the others and lowered his
voice. "Yes," he whispered, "it was odd about the ring. The
merchant seemed honestly surprised to find it there. More
than you, even."

Rufus shot him a flash of malice. "You didn't seem unsure
about his guilt before. Or were you just relieved that someone
had been found to take the blame and draw interest away from
yourself?"

"I desire nothing more than the swift punishment of the

killer," Gaucher said. "But for my own safety, I want to be positive we've found the right one. At least now that he knows we
suspect him, this man is less likely to try to attack us, and we
can both be on our guard against him."

"What if he tries to flee?" Rufus asked.

"Then it will be an admission of guilt," Gaucher said. "And
we can track him down and administer justice with no questions. Remember, he's under the protection of Saint-Denis.
Abbot Suger is still a powerful man. We must be able to justify our actions."

Reluctantly, Rufus agreed. They returned to the group.

"Gaucher and I have decided that you're not a neutral
judge," Rufus told Brother James. "Therefore we will allow this
man to continue the journey under our surveillance, if he gives
his oath that he will answer the charges against him before
Abbot Peter when we reach Burgos."

James took a deep breath. He wanted to deny any prejudice
in the matter, but couldn't. He was still shaking. All these people, all these faces he wanted to forget. This was worse than
ghosts. This was the living past come to torment him.

He refused to surrender to it. He bowed his submission to
the knights, then turned to Hubert. "*Sieur* Hubert," he said
coldly, "do you take the oath like a Christian?"

"Of course," Hubert answered. "I have often. I *am* a Christian."

"So you say," James answered. "Then will you give your
word by the Holy Body of Christ that you will not attempt to
escape and that you will present yourself in Burgos and accept
the judgment of the abbot of Cluny?"

"Yes," Hubert answered. "I swear by Christ, the Virgin,
Saint Nicholas and Saint Vincent that I had no part in the
death of Hugh of Grignon or in that of the monk Rigaud, and
I will prove it by oath or by ordeal anywhere you like."

"I'll stand surety for him," Edgar said. "Do you doubt the
validity of my oath?"

James looked as though he wanted to, but he shook his
head. He had to get away from these people, especially from
the hard eyes of Solomon, whom he refused to think of as his

son. He continued shaking his head as he moved through the door of the priory, shut it and slammed the bar down with a firm thud.

Catherine wondered if everyone else were as dazed as she. That was the only explanation she could give for the way they all backed away from each other, not speaking, and returned to their packs and their horses as if nothing had happened.

Edgar and Solomon finished loading the animals. They didn't look at each other. Hubert let Eliazar guide him to his horse and help him mount. When they were ready to set out, Hubert only said one thing to his brother.

"You haven't called me Chaim in twenty years."

Eliazar smiled sadly but gave no answer.

They headed for the road leading them down into the kingdom of Navarre. Everyone was unnaturally quiet. Hubert rode slumped over, letting the horse find its own way. Eliazar watched him in silence. Behind them, Edgar and Catherine walked together, holding hands. They could find nothing to say either.

At the end of the line, Solomon led his packhorse. For once, he didn't seem to notice Mondete Ticarde, trudging next to him.

Mondete wasn't intimidated by the silence. "It seems you've found some of the answers you were seeking," she said conversationally.

The day was growing warm. She put her hood down. Then she came closer to Solomon and touched his arm. "I never understood what was so wonderful about truth," she said. "There have been many times in my life when I would have preferred a kind lie."

"My uncle didn't lie to me," Solomon said. "My father is dead. You heard him say so himself."

"That should be conclusive," Mondete agreed.

She inhaled as if preparing to say more, then shut her mouth, put up her hood and moved back to her old place at the tail of the procession.

Catherine didn't realize how tightly she was gripping Edgar's hand until he gently pulled her fingers away and shook his arm to restore the circulation.

"You have such an interesting family," he said.

"And I used to think we were quite usual," she answered. "Mother was always a bit more devout than most people, but otherwise . . ."

"Are you all right?" he asked.

"Oh, yes," she said. "I believe I'm becoming inured to sudden shocks. I don't particularly like the idea that Brother James is my uncle, but he doesn't seem interested in exploring the relationship either. No, what I'm really worried about is that ring. How did it get into Father's scrip? And why are we being suspected at all? None of us knew those men who died. But first Solomon is accused, then Father. Maybe next it will be you."

"It does seem strange," Edgar said. "As if someone were trying to turn the investigation as far from Cluny as possible. Perhaps it's time we started finding out more about our fellow pilgrims. It doesn't appear that Brother James, or Jacob, is in any condition to make a clear analysis of the situation."

When they reached the bridge at the River Urrobi, they found the Lady Griselle and her servants waiting for them. Catherine wondered when they had left the priory. She had been so fixed on what was happening that she hadn't even noticed Griselle leaving. It was odd that the woman hadn't stayed to watch the outcome of the drama.

"I don't believe you finished the tale you were telling me last night, *Sieur* Hubert," Griselle greeted him calmly. "I should hate to be deprived of the ending."

Hubert straightened out of his gloom. "I beg your pardon, my lady," he said. "I'm surprised to see you here. I believed that you wouldn't want to associate with me any longer."

"Really?" she said. "You were mistaken. Now, please tell me what happened after the wine was stolen by the Flemings."

Hubert's troubled heart flooded with joy. He hadn't expected this of Griselle. All the warnings and lectures he had given himself regarding her interest in him were totally forgotten. Inhaling her perfume, he felt his anguish evaporate. At least for the present.

"Ah yes, the Flemings," he said as he fell into place next to her. "They thought they would be safe in London, which is infested with their countrymen these days, but my partner and I knew a few tricks to match theirs. . . ."

Eliazar was left alone, walking rather than riding since it was the Sabbath. Griselle and her party, the guards riding nervously before and behind her, moved ahead of him. Ordinarily, Hubert would have walked as well, but he seemed oblivious to all but Griselle. While the sight of his brother so obviously infatuated filled him with dread, Eliazar was glad to be ignored for now. The company of his own thoughts was all he could stand.

This journey had become a disaster. He should have said something the moment he spotted Jacob. How could he have hoped they would be able to avoid each other? Hubert had been too young to remember his brothers who had left Rouen to study in Paris. Only Eliazar had known that Jacob had been ensnared by the preachers of the Crucified One. Eliazar shivered at the memory. Jacob must have been sneaking off to hear their sermons for months before he made his decision. Then, on a simple trip to the yearly fair at Provins, he had vanished. He had left behind two letters, one for his brother and one for his wife, begging her to join him in baptism. Eliazar had burned both missives, returned to Paris and told everyone that Jacob had died, drowned at a ford, his body washed away. The next year, Solomon's mother had died and he and Johannah had taken the child into their home to cherish.

After a while, he almost believed the story was true.

And here Jacob was risen from the lie Eliazar had created. What would happen now? Would Jacob denounce Hubert to the abbot? Could Jacob see his own baby brother hanged for murder? It was possible that Jacob would see it as a test of the sincerity of his conversion. And what of Solomon? What would this do to him?

Eliazar felt the world settle onto his shoulders. He wished with all his heart that Johannah were here to help him. In their

thirty years together, she had always been able to make the bur-
dens lighter.

Back at the priory, Brother James was in the chapel, pros-
trate before the altar. He had not been in such a torment of
spirit since he had made his decision to enter the monastery.
With flowing tears, he prayed for forgiveness, guidance,
strength.

"But first, Lord, please," he begged, "take away the faces
from my mind! I cannot bear them!"

Despite knowing now that she was Chaim's child, he could
only see his mother in Catherine's face. The beautiful, gentle
woman who had been killed by the soldiers of the god he now
worshiped. He thought that he had long ago managed to rec-
oncile the contradiction in his mind. Christ could not be held
accountable for all the evil done in His name. But every time
James saw Catherine, he felt that his mother's blood was on his
hands.

Solomon was even worse. James should have seen who he
was from the beginning. The man was all he had been himself:
arrogant, stubborn, belligerent, scornful of the Christian world
he lived in. No wonder James had felt an instant antipathy to
the son he had left behind.

He remained on the floor through the morning, until the
canons came in for None. The chantor conferred briefly with
the prior; then Brothers Bruno and Deodatus were asked to remove their colleague so that the recitation of the Office could
begin.

The two monks lifted James and dragged him to the cloister.

"How may we help you, Brother James?" Bruno ran to dip
a cloth in water to mop James's tear-streaked face.

"Tell us what has happened to bring you to this state," Deodatus begged. "Have you found out who killed Brother
Rigaud?"

James took the cloth and rubbed it over his face and head.
"The murderer. Yes, perhaps. I don't know! I don't know!"

"Brother Bruno, get the infirmarian," Deodatus said. "Brother James needs something to calm his spirit."

James shook his head and made himself stand. "No, Bruno," he said. "My spirit should not be calmed. I need to be overflowing with fire to finish my task. Forgive me, my brothers, for frightening you and for delaying our journey. We must leave at once if we're to rejoin the others at Larrsoaña tonight."

The descent in the sunshine was much easier than the climb in the rain had been, despite the warnings. The road twisted many times but led them gently into the kingdom of Navarre. Catherine didn't notice. For the moment, she had forgotten her own pilgrimage to ponder the meaning of the events of the morning.

Logically, as a good Christian, she should have rejoiced to find that this unknown uncle had converted of his own volition and gone so far as to become a servant of the Church. Hadn't she been trying for years to get Solomon to do the same? Why, then, was the revelation so upsetting?

It couldn't be because you love your Jewish cousin and loathe your Christian uncle, could it?

Oh, no! When those voices began to argue with her, Catherine knew she had gone too far into speculation. They always confirmed the one thing she had tried hardest not to face. Very well. Yes. Monk or not, uncle or not, she found Brother James/Jacob repellent. Rigid, humorless, unforgiving of others.

And he had been put in charge of discovering the killer of Brother Rigaud, and by extension, finding the one who had murdered the two knights.

That was what was really frightening Catherine. Whoever he was, whatever his past, did James hate her family enough to refuse to look elsewhere for the answer? Was he so eager to prove he had renounced his old beliefs that he would see his brother, his son, hang rather than admit that someone from the neighborhood of Cluny was responsible for these deaths? It would have frightened her even more to know that Eliazar was pondering the same questions.

Edgar was right. They had to find out more about how all

these people were connected. Everyone in their party seemed to have known each other, more or less, for many years. Even Maruxa and Roberto had passed through Burgundy several times in their travels. They must have learned all kinds of things about the people they had entertained. As someone had once told her, kitchen gossip is the most reliable. The *jongleurs* and the maid would have heard most of it.

Even though the journey that day was nothing to the day before, Catherine was exhausted by the time they reached the hostel. She let Edgar put her down on a blanket in the straw like one of the parcels and fell asleep before he had returned with their allotment of bread.

Edgar wasn't sleepy. After assuring himself that Catherine wasn't likely to awaken soon, he looked around for something to do. Solomon and Eliazar had gone to the camp where Aaron and the men from Toulouse were staying. Hubert was still entertaining the Lady Griselle. Gaucher and Rufus were sitting on opposite sides of a bench outside, eyeing with suspicion anyone who approached them. Edgar thought they wouldn't welcome his company.

He wandered about for a while, exploring the area around the Augustinian hostel. There were a few houses by the roadside, one clearly intended for providing the pilgrims with comforts that the canons declined to offer. Edgar wondered if decent ale could be found, but decided it wasn't likely. He felt a spasm of homesickness. It had been years since he'd had what he considered a proper bowl of ale. And the farther south he went, the worse the brewing seemed to be.

Perhaps he was tired. This sense of being an alien in a foreign land happened to him rarely these days. French came as naturally to him now as English, something that would horrify his father. He had friends here, and a family, albeit an unusual one. Of course, in Paris there were English friends as well. He missed John particularly. The cleric from Salisbury was a keen observer of people and would have been able to advise him on what to do next.

Finally, he wandered back to the hostel. Gaucher and

Rufus hadn't moved, but they had been joined by Griselle's maid, the one with the name Catherine thought so funny. What was it? Oh yes, Hersent. She was sitting at the end of the bench chewing on some bread that she dipped into her wine cup from time to time. The two knights were regarding her with something besides suspicion.

"My poor husband fought in Spain once," she was telling them, "before he became a vassal of Lord Bertran. I think they became friends because Ghyso also knew the country. He was a squire at the siege of Saragossa. Perhaps you knew him? When were you there?"

"It was more than twenty-five years ago," Rufus answered. "We haven't been back since. There was enough to do, keeping our own territory at home safe. I don't remember your husband."

"You never met Lord Bertran either?" Hersent asked. "It seems strange, when your lands aren't that far apart. He came to Burgundy after his father died, about twenty years ago. One would think you would have been called to fight together."

"I've heard of him, of course, but no, I don't think we ever did meet," Rufus answered. "You didn't know him either, did you, Gaucher?"

"No. From what I hear, the man was far too uxorious," Gaucher said. "He didn't often serve in person when he was required to send military help. Not but what I might not stay close to home if I'd had a wife like Griselle. Now that I've seen her, I understand better."

"They were devoted to each other," Hersent said. "He wasn't jealous; he just loved her too much to leave her alone."

"Unnatural," Rufus commented. "Sort of like this one." He gestured at Edgar, who came out of the shadows, embarrassed to be caught eavesdroppng. Rufus ignored his discomfort.

"Of course, your wife isn't bad either," he admitted. "Too dark for my taste, at least to marry, but she has an air about her. And since you're here, tell us, what was all that about this morning? Brothers, sons, everyone with another name? *Sieur* Hubert won't escape justice that easily."

Edgar stiffened. "As I recall, what happened was that you two accused my wife's father of murdering your friends."

"That's right." Rufus was unperturbed. "That *jongleur* fellow, Roberto, told us he'd seen Hugh's ring in the man's purse when the merchant emptied it to find some coins last night. We took the purse from him, searched it and found the ring."

Edgar was immediately alert. "Really? And how did Roberto know what this ring looked like?" he asked. "Why didn't he assume it was Hubert's?"

"Must have heard us talking about it," Gaucher answered him. "Both rings were taken, but Hubert only had the one without the stone."

"What?" Hersent stood up quickly, the wine splashing down her *bliaut*. "Both rings?"

"Hugh had one ring, with an emerald in it, part of some booty from Saragossa," Rufus explained. "And another one—"

Gaucher jabbed him in the side with his elbow. Rufus suddenly remembered that the ring without the stone hadn't been Hugh's and had only just reappeared.

"Your mind is failing with your years," Gaucher said. "He means that the emerald was missing from the ring when we found it yesterday. The merchant must have pried it loose and given it to one of his Jewish friends. Which brings me back to our original question. What was all that this morning with Hubert and Brother James? What did that trader mean, calling him Jacob?"

Edgar wasn't about to be pulled into that. "Perhaps you should ask Brother James," he said. "I still want to know how Roberto knew that the ring he saw was the one taken from Hugh."

"Perhaps you should ask Roberto," Gaucher answered.

"I intend to," Edgar said.

"Just remember that you're standing surety for your father-in-law," Rufus warned. "If he vanishes before we get to Burgos, you'll be hanged in his stead."

"We'll find out who really did this long before then." Edgar reined in his growing anger. "I wouldn't be so eager to start measuring the rope until you know whose neck it will circle."

Edgar turned his back on them and walked slowly to the door of the hostel, feeling the tickle of a knife-point between his shoulder blades with every step. But neither Gaucher nor Rufus made any move to attack him.

In their standoff, only Edgar noticed that Hersent had gone, leaving behind on the bench her bread soaked with spilled wine.

Edgar searched the hostel for Maruxa and Roberto, but didn't find them. It was possible that they had been asked to play for some other travelers, or that the canons had decided that as the two weren't genuine pilgrims, they weren't entitled to a place. The pilgrim shelters varied in their restrictions. Some were open to all, others allowed only pilgrims on foot without money, and made men and women sleep in separate rooms.

It was too dark now to search outside. Edgar only hoped that the *jongleurs* hadn't decided to leave the party now that they were over the mountains.

When he came back to their pallet, Catherine hadn't moved. As he took off his shoes and slipped in beside her, she stirred in her sleep to fit herself against his body, draping one arm across his chest. Edgar felt her breath on his neck and wished they were someplace where they didn't have to sleep in their clothes. He turned onto his side, and her warmth slid into his body.

He didn't feel homesick anymore.

The next morning at Mass, Catherine saw that Brother James had rejoined the group. He was assisting the priest from the hostel to distribute bread to the pilgrims. His face remained blank, as if he had never seen her before. Only when she raised questioning eyes to him, did he flinch and blink.

She tried to keep her mind on the journey, but the face of the monk kept intruding. He looked nothing like her father. The chins were different, and James was as gaunt as she was herself, while Hubert always appeared well fed. Catherine wondered if under his beard, Eliazar had a chin like James's. She couldn't feel connected to this man. She had known Eliazar and Solomon since childhood, even if the relationship had been kept from her, but Brother James was a stranger.

She wished she dared ask Solomon how he felt about it all. But he had refused to speak to anyone, even Mondete.

After Mass, the pilgrims started out again. If the weather held, they would reach Pamplona today, the home of the king of Navarre. The next day they would come to Puenta la Reina, where all the pilgrimage routes met. From thereon at this time of year, the Way of Saint James would be as crowded as Paris on market days, or so she had been told.

Catherine had fallen asleep without eating and then waited until late morning before getting the bread. As she left the hostel, she felt dizzy and stumbled against the Lady Griselle.

"I beg your pardon," she murmured as she was steadied.

"Not at all," Griselle answered. "Let me help you to your horse. Are you quite well, my dear?"

"I just forgot to eat," Catherine assured her.

"Fasting won't help you conceive," Griselle said. "I tried that, along with everything else. Sometimes it just doesn't happen."

"It does to me," Catherine said sadly. "All the time. But the babies never survive."

"Oh." Griselle paused, then said decisively, "all the more reason to eat. And perhaps Saint James will take pity on you and grant your request."

"Yes, thank you," Catherine said. "And thank you for your kindness to my father. I haven't seen him so alive in a long time."

Griselle seemed embarrassed. "Not at all. He's very kind to amuse me on the journey and to protect me from those *filz a frarine*, Gaucher and Rufus. Excuse me."

She waved to attract the attention of her guard, who changed direction to meet her.

Edgar set Catherine on the horse, and today she had no complaint. He gave her a hunk of cheese to nibble on but she had no appetite for it. She couldn't understand why she was still so tired. Sleep was all she wanted.

The road to Pamplona was hilly and rough. At the top of one steep climb, Catherine looked to her left and realized that they were again following a river.

"What it's called?" she asked.

"I don't know," Edgar answered. He looked around for someone who knew the area.

"Roberto and Maruxa." He spotted them farther up in the line. "Good. I was afraid they had left ahead of us. Catherine, you ask Maruxa about the terrain. I want to find out from Roberto what he knows about this ring."

Catherine could barely keep her head up, but she agreed to keep Maruxa busy while Edgar questioned Roberto.

The *jongleurs* seemed startled when Edgar and Catherine appeared. They had been trudging steadily up and down, not speaking to anyone. Roberto was softly playing his *fristel*, seven-tubed pipes. The tune was mournful.

"*Diex vos saut,*" Edgar said. "We were curious about the name of the river here. Do you know it?"

"The Arga," Maruxa said. "It flows through Pamplona. We'll follow it all the way to the city."

Edgar nudged Catherine.

"And then what?" she asked as Edgar lifted his arms to help her dismount. "After Puenta la Reina, how much farther will it be?"

Maruxa studied Catherine's face. What she saw there seemed to worry her. "At least two more weeks," she said, "and the land is empty in many places, and dry. There are ponds whose water is bad. You can see the bones of the horses that drank from them and died. The Navarrese direct the pilgrims there and then come and steal their belongings and skin the horses for the leather. Don't buy leather in Navarre."

Catherine nodded. "Very well. And then what?"

Maruxa put her hand on Catherine's forehead. "Are you well, *p'tite aucel?*" she asked. "You feel cool enough, but you don't seem yourself."

"I'm sorry." Catherine yawned. "I'm only sleepy. I can't seem to wake up today."

"You need a tonic," Maruxa said. "Let me see what I have in my bag."

In the meantime, Edgar had taken Roberto over to the side of the road. "I was told that you are the one who accused Catherine's father of stealing a ring from the man who had his throat cut near Conques," he said without preamble.

"I accused no one!" Roberto said indignantly. "I only mentioned that I had seen a gold ring with a hole where a stone would go when Hubert emptied out his purse to pay for his wine. That's all. It seemed odd to me."

"So you went at once to Gaucher and Rufus to tell them?" Edgar asked.

"No!" Roberto said. "I mentioned it only to Maruxa. They were at the table as well. They must have overheard."

"But you did see this ring?" Edgar asked. "You're sure it was before Hubert was searched?"

"Yes, the night before." Robert raised his hand. "I swear it. What reason would I have to lie?"

"I can think of several," Edgar said. "They paid you, they threatened you, or perhaps you simply remembered incorrectly."

"None of those," Roberto said. "By the callused palms of Santo Domingo the bridge-builder, I know what I saw, and it was just as I told you."

Edgar wasn't sure he believed the *jongleur*. But the man's sincerity was well-played. He would probably convince a court.

And if he *were* telling the truth, how had Hubert come by a ring belonging to Hugh of Grignon?

Sixteen

*The town of Puenta la Reina, where the roads to Compostela join.
Tuesday, June 3, 1142; Commemoration of the Blessed Isaac, put to
death by the Saracens in Cordoba in 834; no one is sure why.*

מִנִּי חֲצוֹת לַיְלָה פֶּרֶא רְדָפָנִי
אַחֲרֵי אֲשֶׁר רָמַס אוֹתִי חֲזִיר־יַעַר.
הַקֵּץ אֲשֶׁר נֶחְתַּם הוֹסִיף עָלֵי מַכְאוֹב
לִבִּי, וְאֵין מֵבִין לִי, וַאֲנִי בָעַר.

שלמה אבן גבירול

Since midnight I'm chased from place to place, pursued by the
desert ass; trampled by the forest boar. Everywhere harassed.
Keeping the end concealed only makes the pain worse. I suffer
ignorance, love, with no one to explain.
—Solomon Ibn Gabriol

*S*olomon sat on a tree stump and watched the world pass by. Pilgrims, traders, impostors and thieves, sick and well, rich and poor, speaking a dozen languages, everyone heading in the direction of Santiago. Solomon despised them all impartially. He squeezed the wineskin in his lap. Almost empty.

"Even you desert me," he told it reproachfully. It had been full when he sat down.

He had spent the last two days brooding and then decided that if he were going to feel this bad anyway, he might as well be drunk, too. So far, the wine hadn't helped.

He had wanted to find universal truth, not personal. What was wrong with him that the fates should trick him so cruelly? What had he done to deserve such shame?

After the first shock of anger, Solomon couldn't blame Eliazar for lying about what had happened to his father. To convert was the same as dying—worse, because there was no hope even of a reunion in the next world. Jacob ben Meïr *was* dead.

Solomon wasn't interested in James, the monk. He didn't want to see him again, much less demand to know how James could be so selfish as to leave his family, his community, his god. He had. The reasons didn't matter. What really terrified Solomon and drove him to empty the wineskin was that the seeds of apostasy might be lurking within himself. He had often been taken to task for not obeying the laws of behavior. He couldn't remember many of them. A teacher in Speyer had once told him that if he was committed to Israel in his heart, nothing else mattered.

Now he wasn't so sure.

He rolled up the skin to squeeze the last few drops into his mouth. There was just enough sense of self-preservation left in his sodden brain for him to stumble back to the inn before he passed out.

That was how he missed the arrival of two of the men he had returned to Spain to seek.

Catherine finally felt awake again, although her appetite had not returned. She was amazed and delighted by the variety of people here where all the roads blended into one. Even the fairs of Troyes and the Lendit didn't attract such a mixture. There were pilgrims from as far away as Hungary. There were Italians and Germans and Norsemen, English, Bretons, Lombards and, even more exciting to her, dark men wearing white robes and turbans.

"Do you think they're Saracens?" she asked Edgar.

"I don't know," he answered. "You remember Roberto and Maruxa explaining that even Christians and Jews dress in the Arab fashion here."

"It's all very confusing," Catherine said. "Not what I thought it would be. I worried that I wouldn't be able to understand anyone and now I find that half the towns were settled by the French after the Reconquest. I thought it would be easy to spot the Moslems, if they dared venture so far into Christian land, but many of the people here follow their customs and look just like them."

"If Solomon ever comes out of his melancholy, we can ask him about it," Edgar suggested. "He might know how to tell the difference."

Solomon had staggered by them a few minutes before without noticing their presence.

"I don't think that will be for some time," Catherine said.

The day was warm and sunny. Catherine and Edgar were glad to sit in the shade and watch the parade of diversity go by. This would be the last place they would stop for more than a night until they arrived at Compostela. Everyone else was bustling about making preparations for the next part of the trip. But Edgar and Catherine had done all they could. Now they only needed to wait until everyone else was ready.

One of the men passing by noticed Catherine watching him. He stopped, then signaled to the two men with him. The three came up to the couple.

"God keep you," the man said. He had light brown hair and a ruddy face. His accent was obviously Norman. Edgar stiffened, pulled his hat over his face and feigned sleep.

"And you," Catherine answered, seeing that Edgar wasn't going to. "May we help you?"

"I hope so. My name is Robert," the man said. "My friends and I have come from Barcelona. We were told that Peter, abbot of Cluny, would be passing through here soon."

"I don't believe he's arrived yet," Catherine told him. "But some of the monks who were with him are here now. They're probably at the priory."

She looked curiously at the other two men. One was blond and sunburned, the other dark, although his hair was lighter than hers, with red tints.

"Are you all from Normandy?" she asked.

"No," Robert said. "My friend, Hermann, is from Dalmatia. Do you know where that is?"

"Far to the east, I understand." Catherine hated being patronized. She addressed the third man. "Are you also Dalmatian?"

He gave her a wide smile and shook his head. Robert answered for him. "Mohammad is from Cordoba," he said. "We are students of geometry and astronomy. But we were told that the abbot of Cluny wished to engage us to translate the books of the Arabs into Latin."

This was the first Catherine had heard of it. "I am not in the abbot's confidence," she answered. "But I would welcome the opportunity to read your work when it is finished."

She ignored the look the man gave her at this statement. She was thinking of the pages of notes that she and Solomon had found. Geometers and astronomers. These men might know what some of the arcane symbols meant.

"Will you be staying here in Puenta la Reina to await Abbot Peter?" she asked.

"It depends on what we find out at the priory." Robert smiled and bowed to her. "Thank you, lady, for your kindness in aiding us."

It was only as they were walking away that Catherine realized she had finally seen a Saracen.

She nudged Edgar in annoyance. "You can't hide every time you meet a Norman," she told him. "They've overrun most of Christendom. And that man was a scholar, not a soldier."

"You spoke for both of us just fine," he said, pushing his hat back. "I don't mind."

Catherine understood his distaste for Normans, but it still made her uncomfortable. It had been nearly eighty years since the conquest, after all. She wanted to see this Robert again, when she was sure it was safe to show him the notes. Since Edgar refused to deal with the race that had taken over his country, that would make it more difficult for her to speak with the Norman scholar. Well, perhaps she could shake Solomon out of his misery long enough for him to go with her.

She settled back against Edgar's arm, wishing they never had to get up again. It seemed to her that they had been traveling forever, that she had never lived more than a day in one place, that Compostela was as far away as heaven and would take as long to reach.

But it was so nice sitting in the shade, being warm clear through, with the trees full of new leaves, and flowers everywhere. Catherine reflected that it was close enough to heaven for now. She closed her eyes and nuzzled Edgar until he roused himself to put his arm around her, then sank back into somnolence.

"Lady, kind lady," a voice whined above them. "A coin, for the love of Christ, a crust for a poor leper."

Catherine's eyes flew open. A person stood over them, its face covered, its arms and feet bound in rags. The hands were covered with sores and deathly white. Her hand went automatically to her scrip for a coin, less for charity's sake than to bribe the leper to keep away from her.

"Get away from her, Frolya!" Roberto knocked the leper to the ground.

Catherine and Edgar reached out to help him, then hesitated, remembering what he was. Roberto snorted.

"Frolya doesn't need your help," he told them. "His leprosy is painted on fresh every morning." He gave the man his hand and helped him up. "See?" he said, holding out his hand. There were smudges of red and white where the paint had come off.

"Sorry, Roberto," Frolya said. "Didn't know they were friends of yours."

He shambled off in search of more-sympathetic pilgrims. Catherine and Edgar stared after him in astonishment.

"Why would anyone pretend to be a leper?" Edgar asked.

Roberto laughed. "Frolya collects more in alms than Maruxa and I do for an evening of singing and tumbling. His family eats meat at least once a week, and he gave his wife a silver cross on a chain for her name-saint's day last year. He's as much an actor as I am."

"But he's taking money that should be given to those who really need it," Catherine complained.

"Perhaps, but it's an old custom here to get what one can from the pilgrims," Roberto said. "Think of it this way; would you rather Frolya took a bit of your money as a leper or all of it as a robber, and cut your throat as well?"

"Are those the only choices?" Edgar asked.

"In this town, yes," Roberto said.

"Then none of the beggars is truly in need?" Catherine was extremely perturbed. She had given as much as her father would permit all along the route.

"There are many who are," Roberto assured her. "Of course, they are often robbed in their turn. Once Maruxa and I found a blind pilgrim sitting in just his shift by the roadside. Thieves had set upon him and taken everything he had, even his staff."

"That's horrible!"

"I suppose," Roberto said. "They left him his life, and the canons at Roncesvalles gave him new clothes so he could continue his pilgrimage."

"Was his sight restored?" Edgar asked.

"Not that I heard," the *jongleur* answered. "Perhaps the only miracle he deserved was to finish the trip alive. Did you ever find out how that ring got in Hubert's purse?"

Edgar was surprised by the sudden change of subject. "No," he said. "When we asked him, he said he didn't notice it among the coins."

"How could that be?" Roberto asked. "I tell you, I saw it clearly."

"You might have," Catherine said. "Father doesn't see as well as he used to. In the dim light at the inn, he could have missed the ring. He often asks me to count out the price for him so he doesn't give too much."

"But you didn't that night?"

Catherine was sure she hadn't. "He was dining with Lady Griselle that night."

"That might account for her uncertainty when Hubert was accused," Roberto said. ". . . If he denied having the ring and she knew it had been there."

"She surely hasn't acted as if she suspected Father of murder," Catherine disagreed. "Perhaps she didn't notice the ring either."

"Perhaps we should ask her," Edgar said.

"I suppose we'll have to," Catherine agreed with reluctance.

Roberto sneezed.

"*Benedicite!*" Catherine and Edgar said together.

"Thank you." Roberto sniffed. "It's all these damned flowers. I hate spring."

Not far away, Gaucher and Rufus were having an argument.

"We'll be at Najera in less than a week," Gaucher protested. "You can't want to give up now. Not after waiting so many years."

"I don't know what the point is anymore, Gaucher," Rufus complained. "I came only because Norbert forced me to. He said he'd kill me if I broke my oath."

"Did he now?" Gaucher said. "That oath didn't die with Norbert, you know."

"Perhaps it's one I never should have made in the first place," Rufus answered hotly. "Back then, I thought I could do anything as long as I was fighting for Christ. But now I'm not so sure. I don't think we should sell it, if it's even still there."

"Are you proposing that we turn it over to some bishop or other for the good of our souls?" Gaucher's face showed what he thought of that idea.

"Why not?" Rufus countered. "We're a lot closer to the flames than we were thirty years ago. I need remission of my sins more than gold these days."

"You won't have either if you turn back now, old friend." Gaucher leaned closer. "What's your real fear? Do you think someone else is trying to keep us from retrieving the treasure? Does your *culet* pucker thinking of what happened to Rigaud?"

"Doesn't yours?" Rufus retorted. "Whoever did that was incredibly powerful. It seems to me there would have had to be at least two of them, one to spit him and the other to hold him down."

Gaucher thought about it. "But then you'd expect him to have yelled loud enough to awake the pilgrims sleeping in the narthex. I wish we'd been able to examine the body. What could Brother James know about violent death?"

"From what we heard at Roncevalles, Brother James has more to vex him than Rigaud's murder," Rufus grumbled. "I didn't understand all that talk about family and converting, but I wonder now if he might not ignore anything that incriminates those men from Paris."

"I wonder, too," Gaucher said. "I think it's up to us to find out more."

"And if the evidence leads me to you?" Rufus asked.

"Don't worry, Rufus." Gaucher gave him a thin smile. "If I were the one doing this, you would have died first."

Brother James greeted the three men from Barcelona with less warmth than was normal for a representative of Cluny.

"I have had no word from the abbot as to when he's returning," he explained to them. "We're waiting to hear the results of the emperor's siege of Coria."

"As far as I know, it still continues," Robert said. "Where is the abbot now? Perhaps we should go to him."

"He's moving from one of our houses to the other," James said. "You could easily miss him if you doubled back. But it's certain that he'll come this way. I would suggest that you travel with us as far as Najera and await him at our monastery there. You might begin the translation work at once."

Robert consulted with the other two men. "We are not simple translators," he told Brother James. "The abbot has promised us substantial inducements to abandon our examination of the movements of the stars for this undertaking."

Brother James was shocked. "You can't believe that the study of astronomy is more important than the refutation of heresy!"

Robert and Hermann seemed to consider this; then they both nodded. "What is forbidden today may be permitted tomorrow," Hermann said in thickly accented French. "But the stars do not change with the popes."

"But you're both clerics!" James was now outraged. He pointed at Robert. "You say you're a deacon of Pamplona?"

"Yes, and I must go there someday, when I can spare the time from my work," Robert said. "I assure you, Brother, that I am as devout in my own way as you. However, my studies are expensive. If the abbot wants me, wants all of us, to give them up, we need to gauge the weight of his money first."

Brother James was in dire danger of exploding. "Come to Najera," he said finally. "You will be paid your pieces of silver before you touch pen to parchment."

"Of course we will." Robert bowed to him. "Thank you for your time, Brother James."

The next morning, Solomon remembered why he rarely drank when he was miserable. "I'm going to die," he said.

"Not soon enough," Edgar told him cheerfully. "Here, drink a bucket of water and then throw up a few times. You'll feel better."

"Is that what you do in Scotland?" Solomon sneered. "We have much more efficacious remedies."

"Like cutting off your head?"

Solomon used both hands to support his. "That would be a good start. Where's Catherine?"

"She was up most of the night poring over those pages the two of you found at Moissac," Edgar told him. "Now she's waiting for you to become human again so that you can go with her to show them to this Robert of Ketton and his friend Hermann."

"Who?"

"Mages, I believe. They arrived while you were indisposed."

Solomon's red eyes opened wide for a second, then closed in agony. "I'm cursed," he said.

"That's a distinct probability." Edgar had no sympathy for him. "Considering the life you've led."

He stood and stretched. "Catherine's still asleep. I promised I'd try to find her some green vegetables. She saw some at the market yesterday but we had no money with us. Don't make any noise to awaken her."

"You have my word," Solomon said. "Stop shouting."

He sighed in relief when Edgar had gone and settled down to await the passing of his self-inflicted torment. It wasn't to be. A few minutes later, Catherine came down the ladder from the sleeping room.

"Solomon!" she cried. "Did Edgar tell you? I think I've deciphered enough of those pages so that we can ask those astronomers to expound the rest. Solomon? What's wrong?"

A shadow moved in the corner. Mondete unfolded out of it. "He needs a mixture of olive oil, myrrh and raw eggs," she said.

Catherine's stomach roiled at the thought, and Solomon gagged audibly. "Does it work?" he asked.

"I have no idea," Mondete said. "There are those who insist it does."

"I'll try anything," Solomon said. "Can you get myrrh here? I have to be able to go with Catherine to see these men."

"I'll do what I can," Mondete said and left.

"I didn't even notice her there," Solomon told Catherine. "Unlike you, she knows how to be silent."

Catherine started to reply sharply, then took pity on him. "Would you like me to tell you what I've found in these pages?" she asked. "I can speak softly."

"Very well, what are they about?" he grumped.

"Not all of it is clear, of course," Catherine began. "Some of the symbols are unknown to me, and the writer occasionally uses words in his own language, German perhaps. However . . ."

She bent down to peer into his averted face. Solomon opened one eye. "I'm listening."

"However," she went on, "most of this seems to be a series of lecture notes by a student of someone in Toledo who has studied the arts of astrology, necromancy, astronomy and something called 'algebra.' I'm not sure what that is, perhaps another way of foretelling the future. Or it might be the name of the master. It's not clear."

"Just tell me what is clear." Solomon lifted his head a fraction.

"He writes about new ways of charting the stars more accurately, especially the wandering of the planets, and deducing the ways we are affected by their temperaments. I'd say you were suffering from a confluence of Mars and Saturn in Pisces, myself."

"Very funny. What else?"

"There's a lot here about geomancy, how to set the points randomly so that they will be uninfluenced by the desires of the astronomer, and then a list of masters who have made up astrological tables to chart the results."

Solomon sat up carefully. He looked at the papers, trying to piece out familiar words.

"Yes, that's what they were talking about in Cardoba last winter," he said. "The Arabs have made great strides in perfecting the accuracy of the prognostications. What are the names of these masters?"

"I can't make them all out." Catherine pushed him aside.

"You're standing in the light. *Avois*, here are some: Abdallah, Alkindi, Alpharinus; then some Christian names, Gerard, Guillaume, Petrus, Bernardus. But the tables aren't here. Unless there is something in these symbols I can't read, I'm afraid it won't help you much."

Solomon smoothed the parchment with his hand. "Yes it does," he said. "It tells me that there is someone in Toledo who might help me."

"I see. Does that mean you will abandon us now for Toledo?"

Solomon looked up but didn't meet her eyes. "It might be better if I left, while that man travels with you."

"Do you mean your father?"

Now he did look at her. Catherine moved away. Solomon's green eyes were as hard as jade chips. "I mean Brother James, who seems determined to see that one of this family is executed." He sat down. "Did that woman go all the way to Jerusalem for myrrh? There's a stampede of horses in my head."

Catherine rolled up the parchment pages again. "Do you believe that you will waver in your faith because your father did?" she asked.

"Don't you want me to?" he countered.

"Not if you can't do it with joy," she said. "I have never denied that I pray for your eventual baptism, but not unless your heart and soul are converted as well as your body."

"And in the meantime?" he asked.

"I can love you for the man you are," she answered. "There's no possibility of my giving up the true faith, so no reason why I shouldn't continue to associate with you."

Solomon gave her a crooked smile. "And therefore no reason why I shouldn't stay with you and Edgar, at least as far as Compostela."

"None at all," Catherine said. "Ah, here's Mondete. If you're really going to drink that concoction she has with her, I think you should do it outside."

In the end, it was Catherine who left. The smell of the mess in the cup Mondete brought back was too much for her. She wandered down the main road to the church, not paying attention to the traffic, brooding about Solomon's dilemma.

"Catherine." The voice was soft and unmistakable. "When will you learn to watch where you're going?"

"Edgar! You've found new peas and lettuce," she cried. "I love you! Can we eat them at once?"

Her dormant appetite awoke roaring. Greens! It had been too long since she'd had anything but cabbage and roots.

"Here." He scooped up a handful of peas for her. "They're young enough that you can eat the whole pod. Don't worry. I have plenty, enough to share with the others."

She had been shoving them into her mouth like Golias at the table, but now she slowed, chewing ecstatically.

"You know, *carissime*, I think we should take some of these to Lady Griselle," she said. "And while we're enjoying them together, it would be quite natural to ask her if she happened to notice a ring without a stone in it among the coins Father spilled on the table the other night."

"Only you could move a topic from lettuce to rings," Edgar said. "But I'm willing to come with you and pretend it's a perfectly normal change."

Griselle received the offering graciously, although Edgar suspected that her interest in fresh peas was slight.

"How kind of you to think of me," she said. "Please, sit down. Hersent, pour some wine for Hubert's daughter and her husband."

They were settled into the small room that Griselle had once again managed to get for herself and her maid. The bed had been set up and hung with curtains, and Griselle had her own folding chair and pillow. The others sat on the bench provided by the inn to serve as both table and bed.

"I've been wanting to know you better, *ma douce*," Griselle told Catherine. "Your father has explained to me all of the history behind that horrendous scene at Roncevalles."

"He has?" Catherine nearly dropped the wine.

"Well, I had to coax it out of him a bit," Griselle smiled. "You must be very proud of him."

"Well, of course." Catherine looked to Edgar for guidance, but he seemed as bewildered as she.

"That Brother James is a dreadful coward," Griselle continued, "hiding in the monastery rather than staying among his former coreligionists and fighting for their souls, as Hubert as done."

Catherine was too stunned to answer. Edgar stepped in to save her. "I've heard my father-in-law give many an inspiring sermon," he said. "It would not be surprising to find the entire Jewish community of Paris coming to Notre Dame as one, clamoring to be admitted into the Church on the strength of his example."

He thought he had gone too far for credibility, but Lady Griselle smiled her agreement. "Greater miracles have occurred," she said. "And through far less noble men than Hubert. Do have one of these *gastels*." She passed them the plate. "There is an excellent baker in this town. So rare to find good quality in a place that provides for the needs of travelers."

The conversation continued along those lines for nearly an hour. Finally, Catherine realized that she couldn't find a way to introduce the topic of the ring. She was forced to surrender to a more worthy opponent.

"We must get back to our inn," she said, standing. "Thank you for the cakes and wine."

Griselle rose and kissed them both. "I hope you'll both come see me often, not only during the journey, but after I return to Burgundy."

They promised they would and made their escape gratefully.

"Catherine—" Edgar began, but she interrupted.

"Don't say it, Edgar. Don't even think it."

He didn't say it, but he couldn't help thinking that the Lady Griselle gave a very good impression of a woman trying to gain the affections of a future stepdaughter.

After they had left, Griselle sat for a while chewing pensively on a particularly tough pea pod.

"My lady?" Hersent was folding freshly laundered shifts.

"She doesn't trust me," Griselle said. "What does she think I mean to do, steal her inheritance? I know her mother's still alive. I couldn't marry some tradesman, in any case."

"He's a very attractive man," Hersent observed.

"He's kind," Griselle said. "And very sad, most of the time."

"And so are you, my lady."

"Yes," Griselle sighed. "That may be why I'm so fond of him."

"You wouldn't have let those men take him because of the ring, would you?" Hersent asked.

Griselle stiffened. "I never saw the ring they were fussing about. Gaucher and Rufus probably dropped it in Hubert's scrip while they were searching him. They undoubtedly bribed the *jongleur* to lie about it. Those are not men to be trusted. Remember that."

"I will, my lady," Hersent answered.

As soon as her chores were finished and Griselle settled for her afternoon prayers, Hersent went in search of Mondete Ticarde.

She found the woman still ministering to Solomon. "Now water, drink lots of water," she was telling him.

"Didn't you hear the warning?" he pleaded. "The water around here kills horses."

"That's not water from this river." She was implacable. "Drink."

She noticed Hersent beckoning at the doorway.

"Finish this ewer before I return," she ordered.

Hersent drew Mondete to an open space where no one could overhear them. "I need to ask you about those knights," she said.

"What for?" Mondete asked. "You're Griselle's maid, aren't you? Did she send you?"

"No, she has no idea I'm here," Hersent said. "I didn't know any of them before this journey, although I had heard of Hugh and Norbert, of course. Something is confusing me and I must know more about them. I understand you knew them all."

"More or less," Mondete said shortly. "Norbert had nothing to do with me after my fourteenth year. That was long ago, as you might guess. The others . . . Hugh came by once in a while, mostly to talk. It's common knowledge that his wife was more than he could handle."

"And the other two?" Hersent asked.

"Gaucher and Rufus. Yes." She hesitated. "I don't think anything I can tell you would be of use. If either one of them has propositioned you, don't believe him. They both like variety. Their tastes are exotic, to say the least."

She couldn't repress a shudder at the memory.

"Pigs!" Hersent spat.

"Just Gaucher," Mondete said. "Rufus only enjoys women, but he expects his whores to earn their payment. And he takes pleasure from their fear of him."

Hersent swallowed. "Did any of them ever talk to you about their time in Spain?"

"Only to brag," Mondete told her. " 'I slaughtered so many in battle. I won horses and armor. I stormed the gates of Saragossa and waded in blood to my knees.' They all go on about something. I rarely listened."

"What about Hugh? Did you see this ring that Gaucher and Rufus claim was his?"

"He had a ring with an emerald set in it," Mondete said. "I didn't see the one that was taken from Hubert. I don't know if it's the same."

"If you saw it, even without the stone, do you think you'd recognize the setting?" Hersent asked.

"I might. Why is it important? Do you think they put another ring in the merchant's purse and swore it was Hugh's in order to divert the blame from themselves?"

"Something like that," Hersent hedged. "If I can get it, would you say publicly whether or not it was the same as the one Hugh wore?"

"Yes, not that I'm considered a credible witness," Mondete promised.

"Thank you."

Hersent left and Mondete went back to the inn to see if

Solomon had managed to keep the water down. Considering the amount of liquid he had expelled, it was essential to add more to restore the balance of his humors.

The next morning, they set off again.

Even though they could all have separated now, joined other pilgrim bands or waited in Puenta la Reina for the return of Abbot Peter with his well-guarded retinue, none of them did. They all assembled shortly after dawn: Edgar and Catherine, Hubert, assisting Griselle to mount her horse, Eliazar among the party of merchants from Toulouse, Roberto and Maruxa, Gaucher and Rufus, Brothers James, Bruno and Deodatus with the three men from Barcelona, and at the very end, Solomon, trailed by Mondete.

Looking at them, Catherine thought how strange it was that they should cling to each other so when they all suspected that one of the group was a murderer.

Seventeen

Just outside Cirauqui, heading down the hillside toward the Roman bridge, Thursday, June 5, 1142; The Feast of Saint Boniface, né Winfrid of Devon, missionary to the Goths and destroyer of ancient oaks.

. . . inde Stella que pane bono et optimo vino et carne et piscibus fertilis est, cunctisque felicitatibus plena.

. . . then is [the town of] Estella, where the bread is good, the wine superb, meat and fish abundant and which is altogether full of delights.

—Aimery Picaud
Codex Callistinus,
C. III: *"De nominibus villarum itinerus ejus."*

$\mathcal{T}$he group of pilgrims making its way down the path from the village was much changed from the one that had started at Le Puy. Instead of the polite indifference of strangers or the careful politeness of neighbors, they were treating each other like members of the same family. A large, unruly one, it was true, subject to bitter hatreds and lengthy feuds, but connected nonetheless. They were now people who knew too much about each other.

Robert, the Englishman who had joined the party at Puenta la Reina, was puzzled by the obvious tension among the pilgrims. He made the mistake of approaching Edgar to ask about it.

Edgar only grunted and pretended to concern himself with a loose strap on one of the packs.

Catherine answered for him. "We've had a difficult journey," she told Robert. "There have been several . . . accidents. All of us are worn and quick to anger, I fear."

"Ah." Robert was intelligent enough to know he'd just been told to mind his own business—but not smart enough to resist making his next comment. "I understand you're some sort of scholar," he said.

"Some sort," Catherine answered. "I studied with the Abbess Héloïse, before my marriage."

"They say she teaches her charges Hebrew," Robert pried.

"I was taught a little," Catherine admitted. "Not enough to read the Pentateuch in the original, I'm sorry to say. Can you?"

"My Arabic is better," he said.

Something in the form of her answers seemed to reassure

him. It took him a minute to realize it was because the entire conversation had been in Latin.

"You wouldn't happen to know the meaning of the name of the town we just came through, would you?" Catherine asked him, this time in French.

"No, Basque isn't one of my languages," Robert said, also in French. Now that credentials had been established, Latin was no longer necessary.

"Nest of vipers," said a voice from the other side of the horse.

"Oh, Solomon," Catherine said. "I forgot you spoke Basque." She shivered in the desert morning. "Vipers."

She looked back up the steep hill to the few houses clustered tightly at the top. It seemed more innocent than the people who had just passed through. The name crystallized for her the feeling she had had since the revelation that Brother James had once been her uncle, Jacob. They were living in a nest of vipers, and there was no way to tell which ones were sleeping, and no safe path to tread among them. Catherine knew it was only a matter of time before one would strike again.

They others felt it, too. Ever since Roncevalles, Gaucher and Rufus had stuck together like jealous lovers, never leaving each other's sight for a moment. Watching them, Catherine wasn't sure if they were together for mutual protection or from mutual distrust. They slept back-to-back, and once, when she passed too near them on her nightly trek to the latrine, Catherine saw the motion of their hands reaching for their knives at the sound of her step, even though they appeared to be asleep.

The Lady Griselle had wilted like a rose browning at the edges. Catherine felt an unkind satisfaction that the rigors of the journey were finally telling on her. Her straight back slumped a bit as she rode, and even Hubert's company couldn't cheer her for long. She kept Hersent by her always, but rarely made any demands on her. Oddly, in such an atmosphere of suspicion, she allowed her guards to ride apart from her with those from Cluny and Toulouse, where the men relaxed and enjoyed themselves for the first time since the trip began.

Since the accusation at Roncevalles, Maruxa and Roberto

had distanced themselves from the others as much as possible. They played and sang at night only if asked, Maruxa once surprising Aaron by singing a secular Jewish song, written in Arabic. It was a story of love and longing, and even those who couldn't understand the words felt the emotion in her voice. But when they finished, the *jongleurs* picked up the coins tossed to them and retreated to their own corner.

Even among Catherine's real family, the tension was palpable. Hubert and Eliazar spoke to each other carefully, as if afraid to antagonize by a misplaced word. Solomon spent little time with them. He and Mondete seemed to have formed some sort of pact and now walked together, never speaking or touching. What sort of communication they had was beyond Catherine's ability to guess.

Brother James did his best to pretend that none of the others existed. Out of a sense of curiosity or family duty, she wasn't sure which, Catherine had tried to talk to him, but he had brushed her aside and refused to answer. He kept himself in the middle of a tight circle of clerics. Like Gaucher and Rufus, he acted like a man expecting a knife between his ribs.

Edgar, of course, would never be distant with Catherine, but there was an unspoken fear in both of them. It grew as they passed though Navarre and began to realize that the land wasn't a grassy plain running all the way to Compostela.

"I've never seen country like this," Edgar said. "It's as if some huge army has been through, ravaging and destroying everything, even the trees."

Catherine agreed. It was empty and bleak, with only dry, scrubby plants and great red rocks, the latter jutting out of the earth like giants buried alive. They both avoided mentioning the mountains in the distance.

" 'There were giants in the earth in those days,' " she quoted. "I always thought it was a metaphor. No one told us about this."

No one had mentioned the heat, either. It wasn't like the humid summers of Paris. This was a dryness that was carried on the wind and beat down from a cloudless sky until everyone felt that they were living in an oven. The sun followed them without mercy.

"We haven't brought enough water," Edgar worried as he emptied another skin.

"Father and Uncle Eliazar prepared better than that," Catherine assured him. "They have enough to get us to Estella. Actually, I think I should pour some more for you to wipe your face with."

He was clearly feeling the heat more than she. His normally pale face was red and damp beneath the wide brim of his hat. He was wearing only his shift, *brais* and shoes. The shift was stuck to his back with perspiration. Catherine went to the packhorse and untied one of the water skins. She wet her scarf and went back to Edgar. Solomon saw what she was doing and followed her.

"Don't use water," he told her. "Wine is better, some of that stuff from Moissac that's turned to vinegar. It's more cooling. Put some on his hands as well."

"On my hands?" Edgar suspected one of Solomon's jokes.

"I've seen it before," Solomon said. "You fair-skinned people can't take this sun. Ask that Hermann, traveling with the monks. You've noticed that he dresses like the natives here, all in white, with his head covered. But he also wears gloves."

Catherine had noticed. They were a thin version of the ones she used in the winter while working in the cold accounts room, with the fingertips cut out. She had thought it odd to wear such things while on the road.

"You can get gloves in Estella," Solomon told them. "Until then, vinegar."

They started to thank him, but he was already halfway back to his place at the end of the line.

Catherine stared after him. "Edgar, this is not one of the dangers I expected to encounter on the road," she said, not meaning the heat. "We can't continue with everyone coiled up in themselves, ready to lash out at whatever comes near. It feels like the night before a storm. I expect lightning at any minute."

But nothing happened as they silently crossed the Roman bridge at the bottom of the hill, skirted the town of Urbe and approached the River Salado.

There the party was forced to stop.

Standing on the bridge was a band of Navarrese Basques. They were armed with spears and knives. The guards with the pilgrims drew their weapons. Edgar stepped in front of Catherine protectively. Grateful, but curious, she peered around him.

She wasn't entirely surprised to see the man who had rescued her at Roncevalles. He noticed her and grinned. She pulled her head back.

"What do you think he wants?" she asked Edgar.

"I don't know," he answered, "but if it involves you, he isn't going to get it."

Catherine rather liked that sentiment. She wasn't used to being considered attractive, so she didn't seriously believe that the Basque leader would ask for her specifically. But it was nice that Edgar cared enough to think it possible. She looked around once more.

Aaron and Solomon had approached the leader. The guards didn't lower their weapons. They had been hired to defend the pilgrims and traders and were glad to have the chance to prove their worth. Their eagerness for battle seemed to give the Basques great amusement.

There was a brief conversation among the men, then nods of agreement. Aaron and Solomon went back to their groups to report.

"He says—" Solomon raised his voice enough that Brother James could hear as well "—he says that he has protected us from Roncesvalles to this river, which is the end of his territory. He has kept all his friends and cousins from robbing us, slitting our throats and stealing our women. This was harder than he expected and therefore he wants another ten *metcales* before he'll let us cross."

He stopped and waited for the uproar. To his astonishment, there was none. Griselle sighed and reached for the purse hung around her neck. Hubert reached for his also. Roberto fumbled in the bag at his belt, knowing that he had little to give but determined to contribute. Gaucher and Rufus conferred and then brought out their offering. Aaron was taking the collection from the resigned merchants. Only Brother James and the monks made no move to add a coin.

"These men call themselves Christians," James muttered. "They think that a poached deer can buy their way into heaven, then they turn around and steal from the Church and honest pilgrims. I will not add to such blatant hypocrisy."

Solomon ignored him, taking the money from those who offered and giving it to Aaron to count.

While they were waiting for permission to continue their journey, Brother James took the opportunity to lead his horse down to the river to drink. Catherine watched, waiting for someone to stop him. All the others assiduously looked the other way.

"Edgar, remember what they told us about the river?" Catherine whispered, "say something. The horse has done nothing wrong."

"Perhaps he'll drink it himself."

"Edgar! He's a man of God!"

"I think God should have something to say about that," Edgar answered. "Yes, yes, I'm going."

He started to follow the monk to the river but saw that Gaucher had preceded him. The knight was as shocked as Catherine had been, and for the same reason.

"Whatever you think of the man," he was fuming, "you don't harm his horse."

He caught at the bridle and jerked it back just as Brother James reached the river.

"What do you think you're doing?" James shouted, relieved to yell at someone.

"What's wrong with you?" Gaucher shouted back. "Don't you see the bones? The water here is poison. The Navarrese make a living off stupid pilgrims like you."

James glared up at the people watching the scene. He noted Edgar halfway down the slope and the rest simply staring.

"They all knew, didn't they?" he said softly. "They were hoping I would drink and die as well." His jaw tightened, then he took a deep breath. "I shall pray for them anyway, of course. And for you, Gaucher of Mâcon. Thank you."

He returned to his place in the procession, looking at no one. His face was expressionless. Catherine felt a sudden pity for him. She tried to suppress it. He had chosen to be what he was. But why? If only she knew what had brought about his conversion. James did not act like a man who had received divine grace and found peace; he was more as one who had always been fleeing from demons and hoped they couldn't find him at Cluny. But he was unprotected now, and the demons were catching up to him.

Perhaps that was what had caused these deaths. Servants of Satan were everywhere, it was said. In this wilderness, Catherine could almost hear the whir of their leathery wings. Her fingers touched the ornate ivory cross around her neck. No demons, please, she prayed.

The transaction with the Basques completed, the leader motioned for the band to step aside to let the party cross the river. It made Catherine nervous to feel them watching her as she passed by. She kept her eyes on the stones of the bridge.

As they reached the other side, there was a commotion behind them. Catherine turned around to see Solomon with his knife out, the point just touching underneath the chin of one of the Basques. Four others of the band were standing around him, knives out, ready to strike.

"What happened?" Catherine cried.

"That man came up behind Mondete and tried to find out what was under the cloak," Hersent answered. "I never even saw Solomon draw the knife. I imagine the Basque didn't either."

Solomon didn't react at all to the weapons nearly touching his skin. The Basque leader watched but gave no order. On the other side of the river, Hubert and Eliazar hesitated, knowing that Solomon would be dead before they could reach him. It seemed they would stand like that forever.

Mondete had been startled by the man trying to pull up her skirt. She had spun around to stop him, then been even more surprised at Solomon's response.

Now she was angry. She turned with her back to the pilgrims and faced the assembled men. Her fury was so forceful that slowly they were compelled to turn their eyes from Solomon and look at her.

"Curious, were you?" she said. "Of course. Why should you be different from any of the others? Very well. Why not? I'll show you. Just release my idiot protector."

They didn't understand her, but her next gesture was clear. She undid the brooches and opened her cloak.

After one glance at the scars on her body, Solomon looked away. The Basques lowered their knives, unable to look anywhere else. Some blessed themselves as they backed off the bridge to their own side of the river. Mondete refastened the cloak.

"Happy?" she asked tightly. "Was it worth the trouble? *Avoutres!* I curse you all! May your eyes burn forever, sleeping and waking. May you never find tears or salve to cool them. May all those you love run from you in fear of the flames in your wicked eyes!"

She didn't bother to see what they did next, but took Solomon's hand and led him away.

"When will you learn," she muttered when they had reached safety, "that I have no honor to defend?"

"Yes you do," he answered. "And if God allowed that to be done to you, then He's the one who should ask for forgiveness."

Mondete stopped. "Even among Jews," she said carefully, "I believe that idea is considered blasphemy."

Solomon's head went up sharply. He reached out and lifted the folds of her hood so that he could see her face. She didn't stop him but fixed his eyes with the flames in her own. They stood thus for a long minute, then Solomon blinked and exhaled.

"So that's why," he said. "This is your final test of God."

"Yes," she answered. "And you?"

He nodded slowly. "Yes. I hadn't realized it, but yes, that's what this is for me as well."

He lowered the hood, wrapping her once again in mystery. They started walking.

Everyone else had already turned away.

It was insane, Catherine thought, that they simply kept moving. No matter what happened or who died, they all moved on, drawn by some tidal force to reach the shrine of Saint James. She knew it was essential that they get there, but she couldn't think of anything beyond arriving. She tried to imagine Paris, her home, the child they wanted so much, but the images were vague and distant, with no emotions attached.

"Have we all died and not noticed?" she asked Edgar. "Things happen and we simply shrug and go on. What's wrong with us?"

"The wind," Edgar said. "It's so hot. It scorches the thoughts out until there's nothing left but the dust and the sun and the road. Even in my sleep, I hear it."

So it wasn't just her. Everyone was exhausted, constantly whipped by the weather, never in the same place long enough to rest. And tonight they would be in Estella, another place she had never heard of, in another hostel with dirty straw for a bed. Catherine knew she should make the discomforts an offering to the saint, endured in his name, but even her soul had gone numb.

They kept on walking.

Griselle forced her back to straighten. She had never in her life ridden astride for so long. It jarred her spine and made her legs ache. But if her suffering would lead to peace for Bertran's soul, then she was prepared to suffer. Not for one moment could she forget the purpose of her journey. She didn't worry about what would happen after Compostela. After that, nothing else mattered.

"Are you well, my lady?"

Griselle gave Hubert a wan smile. "Yes, certainly," she

told him. "A little worn, as are we all, but nothing more. I should be asking you the same thing. You've had more worries than I."

Hubert was touched by the concern in her eyes. "The accusation of those knights is not serious," he said. "Even if the *jongleur* gives witness that he saw a ring in my possession, they found nothing when they searched me. And you have said that you didn't see it. Your word will carry more weight than Roberto's . . . unless you think that I've bewitched you."

She laughed. "Gaucher and Rufus would like to believe that. Anything to explain why I refuse their advances."

It was on the edge of his tongue to ask if she would refuse his, but Hubert stopped himself just in time. Griselle tolerated him because he wasn't of her rank. Any improper behavior on his part would result in immediate action by her guards. There was nothing more to it, he told himself severely.

And yet she hadn't been repulsed on the discovery of his ancestry. Could it be that she was fond enough of him to ignore it?

He wished she would give him some sign.

The hot wind sapped them more than the cold rain of the north had. By the time they arrived at Estella, everyone was parched inside and out. Catherine felt as if her lungs had been put through a tannery. All she wanted was to immerse herself in liquid.

Edgar's mind had fixed on liquid as well, but he was hoping it would be fermented.

"Do you know what I would like?" he murmured. "To stay in a house in a real bed with sheets and a mattress instead of straw and a blanket. I want to eat from a loaf that hasn't gone stale and maggoty. I want a cup of wine that isn't tanning fluid or vinegar. Beer is too much to hope for. I want a hot soak in a deep tub with you."

Catherine smiled and took his hand. "You might as well wish we were back in Paris, for all the good it will do."

From the distance, the town of Estella looked much like the others they had passed through. It was set half on a crag and half

by the river below. There were the towers of churches and for-
tifications. As they approached, Catherine hoped for no more
than a flat place without vermin where she could lie undisturbed.

The first indication that something was different was when
the guard at the gate hailed them in French.

"Òc plan!" he shouted in Occitan; then, "Halt! Welcome,
pilgrims! The citizens of Estella wish you godspeed on your
journey and invite you to share their homes and meals. The
burgo franco is just down the street of San Martín. Keep your
eyes on the church above and you'll run right into it."

The guard assessed the composition of the group with prac-
ticed skill. "The Jewish quarter is on the other side of town,
on the hill below the castle. And for you monks, black monks
are you? The canons at the church will welcome you as they
did your abbot, Peter, who passed through here but a few days
ago and will await you at the abbey of Santa Maria in Najera."

They stared at him, slack-jawed with surprise and fatigue.

"What are you waiting for?" the guard jibed. "The gate is
open. Welcome!"

As they entered, Eliazar turned to Hubert. "Will you join
us?" he asked his brother. "Tomorrow night you can pray in
the synagogue with us."

Hubert shook his head sadly. "I must stay with Catherine.
This is the road I've chosen."

Eliazar followed Hubert's glance and wasn't surprised to
see, not Catherine, but the Lady Griselle. "The road you've
chosen leads to destruction," he said. "I say this not in anger,
but in concern, Chaim."

Hubert grasped Eliazar's arm. "I know it does," he said.
"But I will walk it all the same."

Solomon was making the same decision. "Do you want me to
come with you?" he asked Mondete.

She snorted. "To protect my virtue?"

"Then will you come with me?"

"Why? Experience tells me I'm just as likely to be propositioned by your people as mine."

Solomon sighed. "There are scholars here in Estella. Not

many, but some who have studied in Toledo. I thought you might like to question them."

He couldn't see her face, but her hand reached out and gently stroked his cheek. "There is nothing I wish to ask," she said. "Only God can answer me, and if He will not, then that is an answer as well. Spend the night with your own, my friend. I shall be safe. Your cousin will see to that, won't she?"

"Yes." Solomon hung his head. "I had intended to ask her."

"She has a kind heart," Mondete said. "She won't need asking."

Edgar felt that he had landed on the slopes of paradise. Every one of his wishes had been granted so exactly that he suspected sorcery. The bread was fresh, the wine ambrosial, the bed curtained and blessed with linen sheets, and the bath . . .

Catherine ducked her head under the water, coming up again with the clean curls a black tangle over her face and neck, tresses floating around her shoulders on the water.

"I should never have unbraided it," she said. "The comb will break in the snarls."

"I'll make you a stronger one," Edgar promised, catching at the strands. He parted the net of hair and kissed her, sliding his body against hers.

"Edgar, the *estuveresse* will be back in any moment," she protested.

"She'll have the sense to leave quietly," he answered.

Catherine should have thought of another argument, but she was betrayed by her own body. This tub was smaller than the one at the bathhouse at home. Here, she was able to brace her feet against the opposite side, resulting in an entirely new sensation.

Of course, she thought as excuse, *the marriage debt is a sacred obligation. It's my duty*—"Oh, God!" she moaned.

It was not a prayer.

Hubert had opted to stay at a guest house and pay for a room. Oddly, it was the same place Griselle had chosen. When

Catherine and Edgar left for the bathhouse, he watched them go with a sigh of envy. Griselle and her maid were going as well. He let his mind drift to the dimly lit, steamy cubicles, where in good weather the roof board was removed and one could lie in the cooling water and watch the stars come out.

He was marginally comforted by Griselle's promise to dine with him when she returned.

He sat at a table placed outside in the warm evening and sipped his wine. With no relatives around to worry about, Hubert allowed himself to relax. As far as he could tell, Brother James had given up trying to convict him of murdering the monk Rigaud. Brother James. Jacob. Try as he might, Hubert couldn't equate the older brother he barely remembered with this stern defender of Christianity. He felt no pull of kinship. As the days passed and James made no further attempt to speak with him, Hubert's only reaction was one of relief.

It was possible, he considered, that one or both of the knights had killed their old comrade. It was just as likely that the murderer was a stranger to all of them. It was no more than coincidence that Hugh had had his throat cut. Norbert had, perhaps, been poisoned. People die all the time. The pattern of fate is not a weave humans recognize. Only fools and scholars allow themselves to become snared in the attempt to follow the threads.

After two or three cups of wine, Hubert wasn't surprised to find Gaucher and Rufus sitting across from him, their own cups full and the wine pitcher nearly empty.

"We've deci-cided that you aren't trying to kill us," Rufus told him. He hiccoughed.

"We're not so sure about that Solomon, though." Gaucher was marginally more sober, but working to rectify the situation. "He's too handy with his knife."

Hubert had drunk too much alone with his thoughts to be cautious now. "Solomon's not had the experience you two have had," he told them. "No real battles, no charging at the enemy, *spear* at the ready."

Rufus bridled at that. "I never. Sword and mace, those

were mine. Only used my spear in bed." He leered and raised his eyebrows to be sure Hubert got the point.

"And Rigaud?" Hubert asked.

"Oh, he loved Spain," Rufus answered. "Smooth young boys for rent in every town."

"Rufus!" Gaucher knocked the cup away from his friend. The wine spilled down between the cracks in the table.

Rufus calmly set the cup upright and poured some more. "What's the difference?" he asked. "Poor ol' Rigaud is dead."

"That's right," Gaucher agreed.

Hubert was quickly losing the effect of the wine. "And of course things are different here," he said.

Gaucher nodded. "These infidels do many things that would horrify good Christians at home. The problem is that the Christians in Spain have fallen into heretical and decadent ways. They are almost Saracens themselves now. No one could be blamed for mistaking them for the enemy, could he?"

Hubert had no idea of what he was talking about, but he agreed.

"Even those clerics come to work for Abbot Peter dress just like the natives. Only their light coloring shows they're like us." Gaucher went on.

"Exactly," Rufus said. "And the boy was dark enough. How were we to know?"

His voice rose plaintively, carrying well across the plaza in the still evening. Gaucher stood, dragging Rufus up with him. "I think we should finish the wine in our room," he said.

Rufus allowed himself to be guided to the guest-house door. "We only rescued it!" he told the world. "How were we to know?"

Hubert heard the thumps as the two men tripped over stools and tables on their way to the stairs. Then he straightened up and prayed he wasn't as far gone as Rufus. Lady Griselle, newly washed, her golden hair braided and perfumed, was returning.

"Disgusting, drunken old men!" she greeted him.

Hubert looked around for a bowl of parsley or mint to clear

the wine from his breath. There was nothing. He would just have to try to avoid breathing into her face. He stood and bowed.

"The cook told me that he was preparing kid tonight, simmered in spices and goat's milk," he informed her. "I asked him to save you the most tender cut."

"Such a dear man you are," Griselle smiled.

Hubert smiled back, inebriated once again. He took her hand and escorted her to their table.

Catherine and Edgar stayed in the bathhouse until the water cooled and the hot wind of the day had become evening stillness. They lay in the water and watched the stars appear one by one.

"I don't believe that the movements of the planets can affect our lives," Catherine said as she watched the Twins form. "But there is something comforting about being so far from home and seeing them all there, where they belong."

"And there's the Milky Way." Edgar traced its path with his arm. "It's led us here and we have only to follow it to find our way home."

They were silent for a while. Catherine started to drift asleep.

"*Carissima?*" Edgar said.

"Mmmm?"

"What do you think frightened the men when Mondete opened her cloak?"

Catherine awoke with a start, splashing on them both and getting water in her nose. "I've tried not to think," she said as she climbed out, reaching for her *chainse*. Edgar helped her and she leaned against him, rubbing her wet hair on his shift.

"The more I know about Mondete's life, the more guilty I feel for complaining about my own," she told him. "The people we've seen on this pilgrimage: sick, lame, grieving, dying. I didn't know how much I had. I'm ashamed for bothering Saint James with my petition when there are so many others in far greater need than I."

"Yes," Edgar said. "We haven't been grateful enough for what we have."

He didn't add the thought that haunted him: that they would be asked to give up something more before they reached the end of the journey as a price for their complacency.

By the time they had dressed and managed to comb and braid Catherine's hair, it was well past Compline. Most people in the town were asleep, including the bathhouse attendant, who had kindly forgotten about them.

The stones of the plaza were still slightly warm under their feet as they went back to the guest house. The building was dark.

"I didn't realize how late it was," Edgar said. "I hope the door hasn't been barred."

They tried it; it wouldn't budge.

"Now what?" Catherine asked. "I'd rather not wake the entire household by pounding to be let in."

"I think there's a tree by the window to our room," Edgar said. "I remember noticing that the branches were low enough for a thief to get in that way. I was going to mention it to the owner."

They went around to the back. The moon, still in the first quarter, gave little light. They made out the outline of the tree and tried to see which was their window. Even in the warm night, all the shutters were closed against intruders, human or otherwise.

"I hate waking my father," Catherine muttered. "Coming in like this, I forget that we're a respectable married couple."

"He may forget as well," Edgar answered. "But there's nothing else for it."

He felt for a low branch to swing himself up by. As he did, something swung out of the dark, bumping into them.

"Oh, I beg your pardon," Catherine said, startled.

It swung away, and back again.

They both knew what swayed like that. There were gibbets on half the crossroads of Christendom, often occupied. Criminals hung for weeks to remind passersby of the fate of those who flouted the law. But this had been a private hanging.

Catherine closed her eyes. "Please," she begged, "don't let it be anyone we know."

Edgar knew he would have to find out. He climbed up onto the branch, took out his knife and cut the rope. Catherine looked as the body fell.

Even in the dim moonlight, she could make out the bald head and the bleached-out red beard. With his eyes bulging and his swollen tongue stuck out, Rufus still seemed to be leering at her.

Eighteen

Estella, very early the next morning, Friday, June 6, 1142; The Feast of Saint Philip, deacon, and his four daughters, prophets.

Astrologie fu aprés par quoi l'en fet en eutres leus, et les biens et les maus qui sunt present et a venir. Qui bien set ceste art, il conoist bien s'il a une grant chose a fere qu'il en est a avenir, ou s'il voit .ii. champions en un champ il saura biens lequeus vientra ou liqueus ert veincuz.

After this comes astrology by which one knows of other places and the good and evil events of the present and to come. Who knows this art well realizes that it is a great thing to foresee what is in the future, where if he sees two champions on a field, he will know which will be the victor and which the vanquished.

The Old French Pseudo-Turpin
Laisse 75, 11 1–6

I don't suppose there's a chance he committed suicide," Hubert said when they had roused him. "Perhaps from remorse at having murdered the monk? His hands aren't tied."

"That would be too easy," Edgar answered as he knelt to investigate the body in the light. He tried not to look at Rufus's face, distorted like a gargoyle's, or that of an imp in a scene of Hell. Instead, he examined the rope closely.

"Much too easy," he repeated. "Look at this knot. One could hang him by it from the tree, but there's no way it could have strangled him. And if his hands were free . . . here, move the lantern. Let's have a look."

Catherine had already knelt down and gingerly moved the flaccid arm outward to see if there were signs of Rufus having been manacled. "That's odd. He's wearing his tunic but not his shift. Shouldn't it be the other way 'round?"

"Catherine, you shouldn't—" Hubert began.

"Father, not now," Catherine answered. "This is important. Look at his wrists."

They all did. There were deep bruises on both wrists, but no mark from a rope. Catherine pushed up the sleeve. There, above Rufus's elbow, were more bruises, these clearly made by someone's hands. The pattern of a thumb ended in a deep nail cut that had bled and crusted.

"I don't understand," she said. "It looks as though someone shackled him and then held him down for good measure."

"And then choked him?" Edgar was doubtful. "It doesn't make sense, but I don't see any other explanation."

"But if one wanted to kill him, why choose such a complicated way?" Catherine wondered. "A simple knife would have been so much quicker, and more effective."

"Catherine!" Hubert stopped. "Never mind. You're quite right. I should be glad you've learned to put emotion aside and reason clearly in these situations."

"He's not someone I cared about, Father," Catherine reassured him. "I wouldn't be so dispassionate if it were you."

"Oh, thank you," Hubert said. "That's a great comfort."

Edgar had gone back to examining the head. "It appears as if he were somehow kept immobile in order to strangle him," he said. "There's the mark of another rope of some kind on his neck, much finer than this. That's what killed him, I'll wager. And there are bits of cloth on his tongue; I'd say he was gagged." Edgar sniffed. "*Ehuue!* He seems to have vomited at some point as well."

"There's no trace of it on his tunic," Catherine said. "Maybe it was earlier this evening. You've seen how drunk he gets . . . got."

"Well, I don't see how this can be put down to a random thief," Edgar said firmly. "Whoever did this wanted him to die painfully and slowly."

"Yes," Hubert agreed. The lantern shook in his hand. "Each one of the knights has died more horribly than the last. And now there's only one of them left."

Gaucher was not insensitive to this fact. As he stared down at the body of his last comrade, his face was drained of all emotion but terror.

"What if Rigaud was right after all?" he murmured. "We may be running from a Spirit bent on revenge. Then where shall I go to hide? If even the cloister couldn't protect him, then there's no hope for me."

He sat down heavily on the ground. "I'm doomed."

Hubert bent over him, curving the knight's nerveless fingers around a cup. "Hot wine and herbs, that's all," he told Gaucher. "To calm you and help you recover from the shock."

Gaucher drank automatically. As he lowered the cup, his eyes began to focus. "You found the body?" he asked.

"My daughter and her husband," Hubert said. "He was hanging from the tree here."

Gaucher looked up at the branch. "I always said he'd end up like this. But I thought I'd be beside him."

"We need to take him inside," Hubert suggested gently. "You don't want people gathering in the morning to stare."

"No, of course not." Gaucher didn't seem able to offer a course of action, however. He lifted the cup again and drained it, then carefully set it upside down on the ground.

"Father, why don't you go see if there's a place where the body can be laid out," Catherine suggested. "Take this poor man with you. Edgar and I will guard Sir Rufus until you return."

Hubert took Gaucher's arm and helped him to stand. Then he guided the knight back into the inn. Gaucher seemed to have aged twenty years. His step was halting and even the gold streak in his hair had dulled.

As soon as they left, Catherine took the lantern and set it close to Rufus's neck. Keeping her eyes from the distorted face, she touched the marks on the skin.

"You see how they're different?" Edgar asked.

"Yes. He was pulled up onto the branch with this one just at his jaw, the rope he was hanging from. But the one that killed him was different, thicker, though made of finer thread."

She saw a gleam in the light and bent closer, trying to pull the bit of rope out. It was so fine that she couldn't dislodge it from the swollen skin.

"I need a tweezers," she muttered. "I don't have a set, but the Lady Griselle might."

"You can't wake her this early," Edgar said.

"I know," Catherine answered, "but if I don't get it now, when will I have a chance? You don't have your bag of silversmithing tools with you, do you?"

Edgar produced them from a pouch at his belt. "I didn't want to leave them behind," he explained. "I thought that if we were forced to trade for food or shelter—"

"You don't need to apologize," Catherine said. "It was a

good idea. Now, isn't there some sort of thing you use to hold fine wire?"

He rummaged around in the bag and handed her a set of tweezers nearly as fine as that used by ladies on their eyebrows. Catherine picked carefully at the strand.

"I don't know what's the matter with me," she muttered. "I keep worrying that I'm going to hurt him. Edgar, could you?"

They switched places. Edgar took the tweezers and Catherine held the lamp, turning her face away as he prodded until he gripped the end of the gleaming material. With a sigh of relief, he held it up for her to inspect.

"Do you know what it is?" he asked. "It's even finer than gold thread."

"I think so," she answered, "but I don't believe it. There's only one person . . . yet it doesn't seem possible. Why?"

"The evidence is here," Edgar said. "We can't ignore it just because it doesn't fit with our theories."

"I know, I know," Catherine said. "But there's no reason. No reason to kill Sir Rufus, or to kill all the others. Even if we could find a motive, it's too preposterous to credit. Who could we tell?"

"Solomon and Mondete would help us find out the truth," Edgar said. "Unless you still fear that Mondete's responsible for this."

"I never wanted to think so," Catherine told him, "but she had good reason to hate Norbert, and she could have lured Sir Hugh out to the bushes for a tryst and then cut his throat with her razor for much the same reason. Even Brother Rigaud might have been one of those who visited her. Rufus certainly did. But for this deed, Mondete has no weapon."

"We have to prove it," Edgar said. "She would still be easy to accuse. I'm keeping this safe until we can use it." He carefully wrapped the evidence in a piece of chamois cloth and put it back in his pouch.

"Then we should find her and Solomon in the morning and show them what we've found," Edgar decided. "We must discover why all these men have been killed. Without that, we have nothing really, only guesses, It will be safer if all four of us do the questioning separately. We don't want anyone becoming suspicious."

"But we're in no danger!" Catherine insisted.

"Oh, yes we are." Edgar took her hand. "Especially if we're wrong about this."

They stood on either side of the corpse, hands clasped over it as if making a vow. "Catherine," Edgar began hesitantly, "promise me you won't go wandering about alone or with any of these pilgrims, whether you suspect them or not."

"I should make you promise the same," she answered.

"No, it's not the same for me." He grimaced. "It's that dream of yours. Even Master Abelard believed it to be a true prophetic sending. I don't know what lies between here and Compostela, but if you are destined to risk your life in any way, I'd rather be there. It's not just you, remember, but our son as well."

Catherine gave him a sharp look. Had he guessed? She'd tried so hard not to give any sign. The nausea wasn't so bad this time, but the aching and the intense exhaustion, added to the absence of the usual monthly pattern, made her fairly sure. She didn't want anyone to know yet—not until they had reached Saint James. She feared that Edgar would want her to stop where they were or return home. But that could bring disaster. They had to complete the pilgrimage as they had sworn to. She couldn't bear losing another child.

"I promise." She smiled to cover her nervousness. "To be honest, if I find myself hanging from the side of a cliff, I'd rather you were nearby to pull me back up."

Hubert returned with some men from the inn to bring in the body of Rufus of Arcy. As they bore the corpse away, Catherine wondered what sort of dreams Rufus had been sent. Had his fear been a premonition, or had he known why his companions were being murdered one by one? If only he had told someone. Now the search would be that much harder. And how was she to comprehend the passion that drove a person to such evil?

She almost felt that Rufus was sticking his tongue out at her in derision.

Inside, the commotion had awakened the rest of the people in the guest house. Lady Griselle's maid appeared at the top of the staircase, a blanket wrapped around her loose *chainse*.

"Are we being attacked?" she asked.

Hubert looked up. "Nothing to concern yourself with," he assured her. "Sir Rufus has met with an unfortunate accident. . . ."

"Don't speak nonsense." Griselle's voice came from behind Hersent's shoulder. "He's been killed, hasn't he? Just like the others. I thought we'd left this all behind in France. Hersent, wake the guards and tell them that from now on, they will sleep one at our door and the other under the window, as well as guard us both all day. We will complete our pilgrimage no matter what wickedness Satan puts in the path."

The two women vanished back into their room.

"Remarkable woman," Hubert commented as he returned to his attempt at making sense of Gaucher's rambling monologue.

"Only me," the knight kept repeating. "No one left but me. We meant no harm. We were protecting her, saving her from the desecration of the infidel. We didn't know he was Christian. How could we? Who's doing this? Only me. It's all on my shoulders now. What should I do? What should I do?"

He looked directly at Hubert, who had no answer.

"You need a sleeping draught," he told Gaucher. "In the morning, we can decide what's to be done."

Gaucher stared at him as if just realizing who he was. "Not you!" he shouted, standing abruptly. "You took Hugh's ring! Did you skewer old Rigaud as well? You're not what you seem. Neither is that other monk. You're all kin, you and the Jews and that monk. It's disgusting, twisted! You're all trying to steal it from us. I'm not a fool. I can see it now. You want to use it in your filthy rituals. But I'll stop you. The others didn't know what you were, but now I'm on guard. You'll never get it. Never!"

His hand went for his knife, but Hubert stepped back in time as Edgar came up from behind and yanked the weapon from the knight's belt, sheath and all. Gaucher whipped around to attack Edgar, tripped over a stool and sprawled on the floor.

The owner of the guest house lifted him gently. "There, there," he said. "Calm yourself. It's a terrible shock you've had, especially at your age. Don't worry. We'll take the matter to the lord's men in the morning. They'll discover who's to blame."

"Sir," Catherine interrupted, "you don't believe that my father . . ."

"Not at all," the landlord told her. "Not that I trust my judgment as to who's likely to be a murderer, having found that almost anyone is, but your father and I were up playing *tric-trac* until only a few moments before you came in. He had no time to kill anyone."

He paused. "You two, however . . ."

"Us? We were at the baths!" Catherine was astonished to be accused.

"So you say," the man replied. "Even this one—" he gestured at Gaucher "—could have gone up and climbed out a window to meet his friend. I only trust what I witnessed myself."

"Yes." Catherine swayed. The rush of energy that comes with shock had subsided and she was horribly tired. "You're very wise. That's all anyone can trust in this life. Edgar, will you help me up to bed?"

She barely managed to make it to the top of the stairs and fall onto the bed. Edgar wrapped the blanket around her and started to leave.

"No. Don't go," she said. "I'm frightened."

Edgar was eager to know what was going on downstairs, but he couldn't ignore her plaintive voice. Anyway, she'd be asleep in a minute and he could slip away then. He got under the blanket and wrapped himself around her.

Her breathing steadied and her body relaxed almost at once. He held her for a few minutes more, just to enjoy the warmth of her body and the smell of her freshly washed hair. Then he carefully eased out from under the blanket.

"Come back soon," she murmured. "And this time, take your shoes off before you get in bed."

Hubert and the landlord had managed to drag Gaucher up the stairs and dump him on the straw mattress in his room. They were standing at the foot of the stairs discussing what was to be done next when Edgar came down.

"Is Catherine all right?" Hubert asked.

"Just exhausted," Edgar said. "We've got to make her rest more without being obvious. She's doesn't want us to know she's pregnant again."

"What?" Hubert's mind spun quickly to this new worry. "She is? We have to stop at once. She shouldn't travel now."

"Our Lady did," Edgar reminded him. "Saint James told us to come to him. He'll protect Catherine as long as we follow his path."

Hubert had never believed in Catherine's dream. But for now, there were too many other problems to deal with.

"I've told the landlord about the other deaths," he said to Edgar.

The man nodded. "A fine group to bring to my door. Still, it does appear that it was one of your party who did it, and that spares me the scandal of having people fear they'll be robbed and murdered in my house."

"We've been trying to remember," Hubert said. "Rufus went out just after dark. Alone."

"Was he dressed then?" Edgar asked. "I mean, it wasn't just a visit to the outhouse, was it?"

"Yes, he had on a fine tunic that almost reached the top of his boots," the landlord said, "and a wide belt of brown leather with a big silver buckle. He looked like a man going to meet his *soignant*."

"Well, considering that the tunic was all he had on when we found him," Edgar said, "he must have met her. Where were the others?"

"Gaucher said his stomach was bothering him," Hubert said, "and from the fumes he was putting forth, I'd believe it. He went up early. So did Hersent and the Lady Griselle. I haven't seen the *jongleurs*. I don't believe they're staying here."

"But Rufus could have arranged to meet Maruxa some-where?" Edgar asked.

"Or anyone else," Hubert said. "That's the worst thing about each of these deaths. They're either a hideous string of totally unrelated murders or the work of someone guided by all the guile of Satan."

The landlord crossed himself. "It's always on a journey like this," he said, "that the *Aversier* tries hardest to wrest souls from the haven of the saint's shrine."

The three men were silent, each wondering what weapons they had at hand to fight against such evil.

The only emotion Solomon felt on hearing of the death of Rufus was relief. He and Eliazar had been far from the place, surrounded by brethren and friends. No one could lay this on them.

He did worry about Mondete, though. She had parted from him at the pilgrim's bridge and he had no idea of where she had decided to sleep. Now that he understood the real rea-son for her journey, he feared it would be the most unsafe and uncomfortable spot in town.

"You didn't see which way she went?" Catherine asked him.

"Illogically, I hoped she'd followed the rest of you Chris-tians," Solomon answered. "But even if she can't be accounted for, you say there's no way this death can be put to her, either?"

Catherine hesitated. "Not if Edgar and I are right about what killed Sir Rufus," she said. "But I would feel better if we knew for certain where she was last night and that there was someone who would swear to having seen her there."

"I'd feel better if I knew where she was right now," Solomon said in annoyance. All he had wanted was one night with his own people, eating proper food and sleeping without starting at every noise. One would think the world could move along peacefully without him for that long.

They were seated in the courtyard of the guest house. Edgar

and Hubert had gone with Gaucher to arrange for the burial. It was nearly high summer; Rufus wouldn't keep for long.

Griselle and Hersent had left early to worship at the church of San Martín and "to pray for the soul of the poor knight." The guards accompanied them without enthusiasm. Catherine hadn't seen Maruxa and Roberto yet. She surmised that they had found lodging among the natives of the town, who spoke their language. But there was no sign of Mondete.

"There's no point in looking for her in a place this size," Solomon decided. "We may as well wait here. And since there's nothing else to be done at the moment, couldn't you take another look at those papers from Moissac?"

Catherine had nearly forgotten about them, rolled inside the rags she hadn't needed to use lately.

"I suppose I can try to make out the writing once more." She got up reluctantly. "The brightness of the sun may make it easier. But don't you think it's more important to investigate what's happening now?" She paused. "Or do you think the notes contain some recipe for revealing the murderer? You know I won't help you if you intend to use the information to look into the future or to force secrets from people's minds."

Solomon rolled his eyes. "Catherine, why would I want to see the future? The present is quite awful enough. The stars may tell us such things, but it's not the secrets of men I'm looking for. I only want to know the mind of the Almighty."

Catherine blinked. "Oh, is that all? I understand. No wonder Uncle Eliazar thinks you've gone mad."

"Don't mock me, Catherine." His voice was low and terrifying. "Look around you. The world is full of insanity. Even when people aren't evil, they're selfish and stupid. I've been from Toledo to Kiev, to the villas of Rome and huts in the middle of unnamed pagan woods. Life makes no sense! I have to understand why."

Another voice in her mind echoed Solomon's words, a more elegant, rational tone, but with just as passionate a need.

"Master Abelard felt that way, too." Her eyes filled. "He taught us that one has to apply the rules of logic to the universe, that God is not arbitrary or cruel and so there must be answers if we can only find them."

"Yes, that's it," Solomon said. "And where better for the Lord to leave the answers than in the heavens?"

"However—" Catherine ignored his question "—Abbot Bernard says that it is *hubris* to assume that we can comprehend the divine plan. We will understand God only when we believe so strongly that we lose ourselves in Him and submit to His will."

"I've heard that one," Solomon told her. "I think it's nonsense. Why did the Almighty One give us the power of reason only to have us accept the absurdities of this world without question?"

"Are you asking me this?" Catherine was almost shouting. "Halfway across Spain, with bodies falling out of trees, vermin in our food and our beds, bandits on every road, and you want me to stop and explain Faith versus Reason? Maybe you *have* gone mad!"

She was so angry that she started to cry. Furiously, she wiped her cheeks with her sleeve, but the tears went on flowing. Solomon was immediately contrite.

"Catherine, I'm sorry," he said. "Here, use my sleeve. I didn't mean to upset you. I forgot about your condition."

"What! How did you know?" She looked down. "It's not evident yet, is it?"

Her sobbing slowed and he put his arm around her. "Of course it is," he told her. "First, you never cry when we argue. Second, you can't stay awake. The only other times I've known you to sleep when something interesting is going on is when you were pregnant. And last, green is not your natural color. Logic, my dear. You aren't the only scholar in the family."

Catherine made a fierce effort to regain her composure and keep her breakfast in place. "Your conclusion is correct, I'm afraid," she said, "but please don't tell Edgar. He worries so."

"Of course not," Solomon promised.

"Now, do you want me to get those notes?" Her expression told him that there would be no more discussion on the subject of her health.

"Later," he said. "I think that I should try to find Mondete, after all."

Mondete Ticarde might have found a more uncomfortable place to sleep if she'd been left to her own devices, but Maruxa saw her at the river's edge and called to her.

"Come stay with us. You can lie on rocks in freezing water anywhere. Roberto has cousins in town who will be happy to give you the lumpiest pallet in the house, if it pleases you."

Mondete shook her head.

"Wouldn't you like to know what *jongleurs* sing to each other when no one is paying?" Maruxa coaxed.

Mondete considered. "No one will sneak in while I'm sleeping and try to look under my hood?" she asked.

"The temptation is strong, but I'll see that no one does," Maruxa promised.

"Very well."

The *jongleurs* waited while she climbed back up to the path.

"Hmmph. You'd think the queen had just consented to dine with serfs," Roberto said.

"Don't you want to know what's under that cloak that frightened the Basques so?" his wife whispered.

Roberto was shocked. "But you just told her . . ."

"I know," Maruxa said. "No one will force her, of course. But she might just be cajoled into telling us the secret."

Maruxa was fortunately unaware that Mondete was thinking much the same thing about her.

They couldn't tell if Mondete were enjoying herself or not. Her hands appeared from the ends of her sleeves and took the food she was offered. Bites of it vanished under the hood. Roberto's cousin looked askance at this creature in his home.

"Why did you bring her?" he asked. "Did she threaten to curse you?"

"The poor thing is under a curse of her own," Roberto explained. "She can't harm anyone."

The cousin was doubtful.

But when the tables and benches had been cleared and the

dancing begun, Mondete sat up more alertly in her self-designated corner. The hood slipped farther back as she forgot herself in the music. The firelight touched her face. Roberto caught a glimpse of her ivory profile and missed a step in astonishment.

Lord, forgive me, he thought. *She's the image of the Blessed Virgin in the church at Jaca!*

Maruxa gave him a warning glance and he recovered his place in the dance.

When everyone else had gone to sleep, Mondete got up and left the house. She had a vague notion of settling among the roots of an olive tree in the court and waiting for Maruxa to appear. But she didn't need to wait. The *jongleuse* had heard her and followed her out.

"Don't you trust our hospitality?" she asked.

Mondete shrugged. "I prefer not to sleep inside. Things happen to you there."

"Yes, I know." Maruxa was shaken.

"You and your husband travel from one place to another," Mondete continued. "I don't think you realize how closely connected the communities you perform in are."

"We have often found that word of us has reached one castle from the last before we do," Maruxa said cautiously.

"In my . . . occupation, I often learned of things that had happened in the neighborhood," Mondete said. "Men seemed to feel they could tell me anything, no matter how despicable. I think sometimes the only difference between them and beasts is their clothes."

"And when they remove their clothing . . ." Maruxa was speaking more to herself than to Mondete.

"Exactly," Mondete agreed. "It was an open scandal that the wife of Hugh of Grignon took the wandering poets and minstrels to her bed."

"Whether they wanted to be there or not." Maruxa pressed her lips together until they turned white.

"Yes, it's not men or women; it's power," Mondete went on. "But most people don't know that sometimes Hugh had his revenge."

"Most people don't care," Maruxa forced out. "But it wasn't Hugh."

"I know. But he allowed it, encouraged his men to come find you when he knew your husband wouldn't be there to protect you."

"It's not Roberto's fault!" Maruxa said. "If he'd been there, what could he have done but get himself killed?"

"You never told him, did you?"

"Roberto was so ashamed of what she made him do. He thought that's why I didn't want him to touch me for the next few weeks. I suppose one of them told you, bragging?"

"Not even that," Mondete said. "Just for lack of anything else to say. He died of a fever the next winter. Perhaps he's in Hell now."

"That kind never go to Hell," Maruxa sighed. "I know a hundred stories about it. They repent and give everything to the Church with their last breath."

"Some don't have the chance," Mondete said.

Maruxa was startled by her tone. "Yes, that's true. If death comes unexpectedly, there may not be time to atone for a life of wickedness."

"Hugh of Grignon had his throat cut. It's hard to pray with no voice."

Maruxa didn't answer. The sky was becoming lighter now. It would soon be Saint John's Eve, the shortest night of the year. On the other side of town, Edgar and Catherine were busy examining the body of Rufus of Arcy. Finally, Maruxa spoke.

"I hated Hugh. He was weak and enjoyed hurting those who were weaker. I'm glad he died unshriven, but I didn't kill him."

"I know." Mondete got up from her place among the roots. "I should be going now. Please thank my host for the food and the music. They were beautiful. When I hear you sing, I almost forget what I am."

"Thank you," Maruxa said. "But don't you want to—"

Mondete was gone. Maruxa realized that the woman had told her nothing and that she had, for the first time, revealed the deepest secret of her heart.

Maruxa smiled. "Thank you, Mondete Ticarde," she whispered. Then the implication of Mondete's last statement hit her.

"If you did kill Hugh," she vowed, "may God forgive you, for you have more courage than I. I swear to spend the rest of my days lighting candles to the saints that they may intercede for you in heaven."

In the end, it was Hubert who arranged for the burial at San Martín and for Rufus's few possessions to be sent back to his family. Gaucher had sunk into a monologue of terror and self-pity.

"What are we going to do with him?" Edgar asked Hubert. "If we leave him here, he may not survive. But I don't know what he'd do if we tried to take him with us."

"It's a demon, I know," Gaucher told them. "The boy's spirit has cursed me. But how could I know? We should have killed him then. That would have been an honest mistake. It happened all the time in the war. They looked alike; they talked alike. There should have been some sort of sign."

Catherine was wearying of his whining. "Sir Gaucher," she said as politely as possible, "you have had a terrible ordeal, it is clear. But none of us were there in the war. We don't understand. Please, tell us what happened so that we can help you."

She had thought him rambling in shock or senility, but Gaucher suddenly fixed her with a perfectly sane pair of eyes.

"You weren't there," he said. "That's right. You can't know. We were fighting for the Faith, to free the Christians enslaved by the Saracens. But it wasn't that easy. It wasn't that clear when we stormed the cities who was what. Nobody warned us."

He stopped.

"Someone should have warned you," Edgar prompted.

But Gaucher was quickly regaining his composure. "Yes, but no one did, and now I'm the only one left alive who knows the truth."

"Except for the murderer," Catherine said.

Gaucher rubbed his fingers nervously against his palms. "That's right. But we're almost there. I can still atone. Norbert wanted to sell it back to the bishop, but I never meant to let him. One doesn't traffic in holy objects."

Hubert was tired, worn, and at the end of his patience. "What are you talking about, man?" he shouted.

Gaucher took a deep breath. "What I need is to explain all this to a priest," he told them. "Take me to Brother James."

Nineteen

Soon after. The church of San Martín, Estella.

Non amat Veritas angulos, non ei diversoria placent; in medio stat . . .

Truth has no love for corners; roadside inns do not please him.
Truth stands in the open. . . .
—Bernard of Clairvaux
Sermon on the Ascension, VI

*B*rother James was not pleased to see them.

"Another death? What will the abbot say?" he exclaimed. "But this one had no ties to Cluny, isn't that correct? If so, then you will have to deal with it yourselves. I was charged only with finding the one who killed Brother Rigaud. The rest has nothing to do with me."

Hubert tried to forget that this man was his older brother. It made it so much easier to loath him without feeling guilty about it.

"We've come to you in your capacity as a man of God," he forced the words out. "Sir Gaucher is deeply troubled by something from the past. We think this long-ago event is the key to why Brother Rigaud and the others were killed. But he will discuss it only if you are present."

James raised one eyebrow in an expression of scorn that was startlingly like Solomon's. "So now you expect me to forget how I was shamed in public and cheerfully help you?" he asked.

"It would be the Christian thing to do," Edgar said.

Though his voice held no trace of irony, James still looked at him in suspicion. "So it would be," he admitted, "but I have a condition of my own. If Sir Gaucher wants you to hear his story when I do, I won't object. But not her. The woman must leave."

He pointed at Catherine. She stared back at him in surprise. His hand shook. Hubert understood.

"Catherine, *ma douce*," he said to her, "don't be angry. Every time you look at him, he sees our mother reproaching him for his choice. We have enough to bear now. Your presence would only make it harder."

"It's not a tale you should hear anyway," Gaucher told her. "I would find it easier to tell it if you weren't here."

"I understand," Catherine said. "Is the Lady Griselle still at the church? Perhaps I could return with her to the guest house and wait for you there."

"Would you rather I went with you?" Edgar asked.

She kissed his cheek and whispered in his ear, "Not for anything. I want you to remember every word."

"I promise."

Griselle was almost ready to return anyway and was delighted to provide Catherine with an escort. "It's no trouble at all," she assured Hubert. "You've been so kind to me. And I'm very fond of Catherine. The poor child does seem exhausted. I'll see to it that she has a nice herb posset and goes directly to bed."

Hubert thanked her effusively. Edgar still worried.

"The Lady Griselle will take good care of me," Catherine told him. She lowered her voice. "It's only back to the guest house, and she has no reason to distrust me."

Edgar bent to kiss her again. "I want a report from you as well."

When they had gone, Gaucher leaned over to Edgar. "Not good to be so obviously fond of your wife, you know," he said. "People will talk. Look at what they say about King Louis and Eleanor."

"Yes, I know," Edgar said. "But I think I'll stay fond of her for a while yet, just the same."

Brother James wasn't interested in propriety within marriage. "The confession you wish to make, Sir Gaucher? Should we go into the church?"

"No!" Gaucher was horrified. "We should sit in the open where we can see if anyone comes close enough to overhear. But you misunderstood. This isn't a confession. I don't need absolution. I only wish to explain so that you can go to Abbot Peter when we reach Najera and tell him the story. He'll know how to advise me."

If James was annoyed by this demotion to messenger boy, he didn't show it. He motioned them all to stone benches outside the church.

"And this event was something that occurred when you and the others were at the siege of Saragossa?" he asked.

Gaucher nodded. "It was so long ago. Why should it come back to haunt us now? I don't understand. All these years, I tried to forget. And all the time, someone else must have been remembering."

He shuddered, pulled back his shoulders, composed himself and began.

"The siege of Saragossa was long, but in the end, with the help of God, we were victorious. Finally, we breached the walls of the city. We fought our way through the streets, cutting down any of the infidel who tried to stop us. The five of us became separated from the others. We wandered into one of those twisty alleyways where any turn could put you face-to-face with a dozen men with swords.

"But though we expected to be challenged at each turn, the street was empty. The natives had all run away. At the end, against the city wall, we found a small church. We thought it was empty, too. Then we heard something."

The three listeners leaned forward.

"Rufus found them, huddling behind the altar. A woman and a boy. They were clearly Saracens!"

He dared them to contradict him. No one else spoke.

"They were both dark, the woman more so. The boy had lighter skin and eyes, and red glints in his hair. But a lot of them do. How could we know?"

Edgar felt himself tense. He was glad Catherine wasn't here. He wished now that he had gone back with her. Gaucher went on relentlessly; they had wanted the story and he was telling it. Edgar knew that any word of reproach from him would cause the narration to end at once.

Gaucher continued. "We thought it was despicable that they had chosen to hide in a holy place, flaunting our beliefs, taking refuge in our charity. They were vile pagans. We were even more angry when Rufus unwrapped the parcel the woman was holding and found it was a statue in the image of the Virgin Mother. The woman spat at him. In a church!"

"Dreadful," Brother James said. Edgar gave him a sharp look. If he hadn't known better, he could have sworn that the monk was being sarcastic.

Gaucher didn't notice the tone. He didn't notice them at all. He was back in Saragossa, living the scene again.

"The woman tried to grab the statue back from Rufus. He had to beat her down with his mailed fist to keep her off him. The boy protested madly and tried to stop him. So Rigaud and I were forced to hold the child back. She cried out to him and beat on Rufus all the harder. Somehow, the woman's robes became torn. Rufus noticed that she wasn't bad underneath, for a Saracen. We all noticed."

Brother James froze. Hubert put his head in his hands. Edgar suddenly remembered that his father-in-law had been there when his mother and sisters were slaughtered by the knights on their way to free Jerusalem. He wondered if Hubert could bear being reminded so vividly.

Gaucher could tell that he was losing the sympathy of his audience. "It was a war, after all," he sputtered. "That's what one does. She was part of the booty. We didn't mean to kill her. She needn't have fought us so fiercely. She wasn't a virgin."

"In a church? How could you?" Brother James shook his head. "You at least told your confessor that, didn't you?"

"Yes, yes. I've done the penance he set," Gaucher said. "At the time, we forgot about the place being a church."

"And the boy, her son I presume, saw this?" Hubert's voice came from forty-five years away. Even James noticed.

The monk pressed his lips together tightly. "Then what happened?" he asked.

"The boy went mad," Gaucher said. "Cursed us most fluidly in good Burgundian. Norbert thought it was incredibly amusing. Then the child had the audacity to say that he was a Christian, the son of a famous French warrior. Well, they'd all like to be, wouldn't they?"

"You didn't believe him?" Edgar asked.

"Of course not. There he was, dressed like a Saracen. He had called out to his mother in their heathen tongue. And he was circumcised, just like them. Show me a Christian knight who'd let anyone do that to his son!"

"Yes, I can see your problem." Edgar controlled himself. He was surprised at his own strong reaction to this very common story. Perhaps it was because of the tales of atrocities committed by the Normans upon his family. The stories had been spoon-fed to him with his first solid food. Gaucher's tale was too similar. Edgar always had a certain sympathy for the conquered, even if, like the Saracens, they were so misguided as to their faith.

"How did you know the boy was circumcised?" Hubert asked.

"Ah, well." Gaucher coughed. "That was Rigaud, you know. The boy was well-dressed and groomed, about twelve or thirteen. Had a fine emerald ring, even. Rigaud thought he was probably someone's catamite. But from the way he squealed, I think we were probably wrong about that."

"How long before he died?" Edgar just wanted the story to be over.

"Oh, we didn't kill him!" Gaucher said. "We played with him for a while, just to let him know what happened to Saracens who blasphemed. We told him we'd come back when he was grown and finish him then. We left him tied up at a hitching ring."

"I see." Hubert spoke calmly. "As you say, it's not an unusual thing to happen when a city is taken. So why do you think this boy has returned after so long to claim vengeance? How would he know where to find you?"

Gaucher for the first time appeared uncomfortable. "Because a few days later we heard that a knight from Burgundy who had settled in Saragossa had gone out of the city to bring information to us. When he returned, he found his wife raped and murdered and his son tied up naked by a church wall, his senses having been taken from him by the experience."

"So the boy was telling the truth," Brother James said. "And you told no one?"

"Are you mad?" Gaucher replied. "The Burgundian must have had kin and friends in the town. We'd have been slaughtered." He took a deep breath. "Fortunately, we heard he was killed a few months later, in battle."

"That was lucky. And the boy?"

"We didn't worry about him at the time," Gaucher said. "What could he do to us? And what could we do for him? If the story was true, his mind was gone. We couldn't repair it. We thought the matter over and forgotten. But then, on this journey, things began to happen. The business with the pig parts."

"The what?"

Gaucher coughed again. "Nothing. Just a joke, we thought. Even Norbert's death didn't warn us. But then the ring appeared. Hugh hadn't been able to get it off the boy's finger, but he'd managed to pry out the stone. Later, he had it set in a new band. When he found the stoneless ring in his pack, we all knew at once whose it was. That's when I began to worry. He was taunting us, torturing us, letting us know that he was coming. When Hugh died, I wasn't surprised at all."

Brother James wanted to know about the other crime. Gaucher seemed to have ignored that. "What about the statue of the Virgin?" he asked the knight. "You stole it from the woman, didn't you?"

"We liberated it from the infidel!" Gaucher was indignant.

"And then, no doubt, gave it to your bishop," James said.

Edgar watched the monk with a growing sense of familiarity. Despite everything, the man was like Solomon. They had the same way of infusing a simple sentence with multifold layers of insinuation.

Gaucher was not as observant as Edgar. "Of course we intended to give it to a representative of the Church at once," he said. "But everything was in confusion and we didn't want it to fall into unworthy hands."

James nodded agreement. "This wasn't simply a crude carving, then. It was perhaps ornamented?"

"The crown was real gold, I'd swear," Gaucher said. "And studded with jewels, topped with a huge ruby. Well, who's to say how a venal priest might be tempted?"

"Actually, the blessed Pope Gregory listed quite a number of ways," James commented.

Edgar couldn't help himself. The tone of the remark was so familiar. He exploded with laughter. "That's just what Catherine would say!"

"Edgar!" Hubert was startled and angry. "This is not the time!"

"You're right. I apologize," Edgar said, quickly regaining his composure.

Brother James seemed disconcerted. "It's I who should apologize. I can't imagine what made me say that. Now, Sir Gaucher, you nobly kept the statue of Our Lady to protect it. That was twenty-five years ago. I presume in that time you were able to find a suitable guardian for it?"

"That's what I have to explain," Gaucher said. "It must be divine providence. It's waited all these years, so that Abbot Peter might receive it for Cluny."

"Waited? Where? Where did you hide it, then?" Brother James wasn't the only one bewildered.

Gaucher seemed to think he had been very clear. "Why, in Najera of course. We wrapped it in silk and leather and left it in the caves above the monastery. Norbert and the others made plans to come back and sell it for their own profit, but I knew Our Lord wouldn't let the image of His mother be used so. And now they've all been removed and there is no one left to keep me from rescuing it again."

The old knight looked around at them calmly. Edgar had the feeling that he ought to throw him a coin for such a fine performance. Hubert opened his mouth to protest at this unexpected ending. Brother James lifted his hand to stop him.

"Thank you," he told Gaucher. "I'm sure the abbot will be most pleased to accept your offering. Do you think you can find the hiding place again after so long?"

"Of course," Gaucher said. "I remember the spot exactly."

He stood. "And now you know why I have endured this long journey and borne the loss of my old comrades. When I see the statue once again receiving the veneration of the faithful, I will know that my last duty has been fulfilled. Afterwards

I plan to retire to my land and live simply, in prayer and contemplation, awaiting my call to heaven."

Gaucher wiped his mouth, and with the gesture, his posture altered so that he was no longer an exemplar of knightly virtue, but a mere mortal.

"Saint Ursin's vial of holy blood!" he said, "but all that talking's given me a horrible thirst. I could drink straight out of the river!"

Hubert collected himself enough to answer. "I believe our landlord told me he's been experimenting with a form of beer from the grain here. He has a cask you could sample from. Edgar and I will stay a moment to have a word with Brother James."

"Then I'll see you back at the inn," Gaucher said. "Beer, in this heat! Probably taste like donkey piss, but anything is better than water."

He set off for the guest house, sauntering as if he had just won a tournament. The other three gazed after him in wonder.

"How could he live under the weight of so many sins?" Edgar asked.

James shook his head to clear it. "The only thing he did penance for was rape inside a church! He probably wouldn't have mentioned it if it had happened anywhere else. How could his confessor let him go without instructing him?"

"Even the soldiers of William the Bastard did penance for the Saxons they killed," Edgar said.

"That's only because they were fellow Christians," Hubert reminded him.

"Not only," James spoke absently. He started to walk away from them, then stopped and turned around.

"Hubert—" he began. "Chaim. I have to know. It's haunted my sleep for too many years. Our mother, our sisters, were they . . . harmed as well?"

Hubert wanted to hurt his brother, this man who had disowned them all, but he couldn't lie. The truth was evil enough. "No, Jacob," he said. "Apart from being dragged from our home and having their throats slit, they were unmolested."

Brother James closed his eyes and exhaled.

Hubert took a step toward him. "How could you join with those who committed such an act?"

James sighed once more. "You won't understand. I have become a monk, not a soldier. Those men did a terrible thing, but that doesn't mean they followed the wrong faith—only that they were not good practitioners of it."

"Just because the hand of God didn't come down from the heavens and smite them, it doesn't mean that their faith was the true one," Hubert answered.

"I didn't convert out of fear," James told him.

"Why, then?"

"Because I was touched by grace. My eyes were opened and I believed," James said. "It's as simple as that."

"Not to me," Hubert answered shortly.

Edgar knew this was a debate without hope of resolution. "Brother James," he interrupted, "about this story of Gaucher's, how much do you think was true?"

Hubert and James had moved closer and closer to each other, until they were glaring barely a nose-length apart. At the sound of his name, James started and turned to consider the question.

"Almost all of it, I should say." He thought for a moment. "Certainly the parts he was most vague about. I think it would be worthwhile to go with him to search the caves at Najera, just in case he and his friends 'liberated' more than a statue from Saragossa."

The Lady Griselle fluttered about Catherine like a pigeon over a newly hatched chick. "I can send my guards for a litter if you're too tired to walk," she suggested.

"No, thank you. It's not far at all," Catherine said. "I'm quite well. I simply didn't feel like waiting while the men discussed their business."

"Odd, I always did," Griselle said. "But Bertran relied so on my counsel. He always wanted me with him at such times."

Catherine felt that there was a rebuke of Edgar in that. She started to defend him, then decided that she was taking offense too easily. She remembered from previous times that this was a problem that was magnified when she was expecting. So instead, she took this as a chance to find out more about Griselle.

"Your husband must have been a wonderful man," she commented. "It's rare to find a lord who prefers to stay home with his wife to joining other knights in tourneys and battles."

"We were devoted to each other," Griselle said, her face bleak. "He didn't believe in warfare for pleasure. But he trained for it all the same, and went when his lord commanded. He knew his duty. And he wasn't weak! His men both loved and feared him. Almost all of them chose to die with him rather than retreat."

"Including Hersent's husband," Catherine said.

"Yes, poor woman," Griselle said. "But at least she has the comfort of children and grandchildren. I have only the memory of love and my obligation to honor Bertran's memory."

"Your care of his soul is most commendable," Catherine said. "I've known other women in your situation who started their widowhood by searching for another husband."

"I've known them, too. Horrid women. But even if I desired such a thing, I couldn't think of it until my duty to Bertran is completed."

They had reached the guest house. Griselle called to the landlord to bring Catherine a hot infusion of herbs.

"It seems that we'll be delayed here for another day," she said. "I think I'll avail myself of the bathhouse. One never knows when one will have another chance."

Hersent went to their rooms to pack up the oils and toiletries for the baths.

"Would you care to come with us?" Griselle asked.

"No, Edgar and I bathed last night," Catherine told her.

Griselle smiled. "Ah yes, I used to so enjoy doing that. Bertran kept to the Saracen custom of shaving at the baths, you know, and taught me to appreciate it as well. Does that shock you?"

"I don't know what the custom is," Catherine admitted. She didn't really care to know. Now that she had her hot drink and was sitting down, the torpor was settling into her limbs. In a few minutes, she would be too tired to climb the stairs to her room.

Griselle didn't appear to notice. "I imagine that your father knows; he's very well-traveled. The fashion is for everyone, men and women, to shave the hair from under their arms and—" she raised her eyebrows coyly "—from their private parts as well."

Catherine stifled a yawn. "Really?" she said. "Whatever for? Is it part of their religion?"

"No," Griselle admitted. "Bertran said it kept the body from smelling too strongly and helped prevent lice."

"Oh." It really wasn't a topic Catherine wanted to pursue. The remedy sounded worse than the problem. She managed to excuse herself, stumble up the stairs and into bed.

It was just as her head touched the pillow that she realized she had been handed an important piece of information. Mondete wasn't the only woman among the pilgrims with a razor. But had Griselle told her intentionally, or simply to shock her? Did she realize how much Catherine and Edgar had guessed? Catherine thought that perhaps she was letting her sense of unease about the woman create ridiculous theories. Yet, hadn't Griselle been at the baths the night before? Who would go twice in the same week? Perhaps . . . but Catherine was too tired to speculate. In another moment, she was sound asleep.

Later, while Catherine slept, Edgar told Solomon about Gaucher's revelations.

"It's tempting to think that all these deaths are the work of one person set on revenge," Solomon agreed, "but even I find your conclusions hard to believe. Without a confession, I don't think you have a chance of convincing Abbot Peter. I don't even think you can convince Uncle Hubert."

"I'm not even sure I've convinced myself," Edgar said.

"So now what?"

"We go to Najera," Edgar said, "and let Gaucher search the caves for the statue. If we're right, that's why the murderer has let him live this long. It may be that the gold and jewels that ornament the piece are the only reason those men were killed."

"Not by those methods," Solomon said after a pause to think. "There was hatred in those murders, not just greed. There's a vicious malevolence behind all this. Someone wanted those men to be humiliated even in death."

Catherine thought it would be difficult to act normally now that she had decided who must be guilty of killing the knights. But she got up the next day, put her things into her pack for the journey, rubbed oil on her callused feet, and threw up out the window, just as usual.

The original group from Le Puy rejoined on the road. Along with them were the traders from Toulouse, among whom Eliazar was glad to hide. The translators, Robert, Mohammad and Hermann, going to meet with Abbot Peter, came too, riding among the monks. Gaucher rode with them, staying close to Brother James, as if his only possible source of protection now was divine.

Edgar had told Catherine, Solomon and Mondete about the old warrior's "confession." Mondete sniffed her disbelief.

"I'm surprised he even mentioned the woman," she said. "Gaucher has much more disgusting habits than that. But I suppose the citizens of Saragossa had locked up their livestock, so he settled for the woman and the boy. He wouldn't have been shocked by anything the others did."

She looked at Catherine half apologetically.

"Don't worry about her sensibilities," Edgar told Mondete. "Catherine has read extensively."

"I did see something in a penitential about bestiality once," Catherine said. "I still can't understand why the sheep has to do a harder penance than the man."

The other three looked at her.

"Do you think we could speculate on that later?" Solomon suggested.

Catherine looked at the ground. "Sorry."

Edgar put his arm around her. "Did you find anything out from Griselle?"

"Yes." Catherine was relieved to get back to the subject.

She repeated the conversation, concluding, "It was odd, really, how she told me about the razor, as if she wanted me to know."

"But that's ridiculous," Mondete said. "Even if she had wanted to, how could Griselle have killed all those men? She's half their size."

"And half their age," Solomon reminded them.

"But who else could have a reason for killing all of them?" Catherine asked.

"She has a reason only if her Bertran was the boy that Gaucher and the others tortured," Mondete said. "And even so, why would it take so long to exact revenge? Bertran was in possession of his land for fifteen years and more. Why didn't he challenge the knights?"

"I have no idea," Catherine said, "just as I can't imagine how Griselle could have managed to run a spear through Rigaud or pull Rufus up into the tree—unless her guards helped. How loyal do you think they are?"

"That's one of the many reasons no one will believe us if we accuse her," Edgar said. "All her servants will undoubtedly swear to her innocence."

"Brother James has to present Abbot Peter with the murderer when we reach Najera," Solomon reminded them. "If we don't give him the true one, he may well simply choose the person least able to defend himself."

"No, he won't," Edgar said.

"And why not?"

"Because, Solomon, your father is far too much like you."

Edgar wasn't entirely surprised by the blow Solomon landed on his chin. He flinched, but didn't fall. Catherine leaped upon her cousin.

"How dare you!" she shrieked.

Solomon was ashamed, but too angry to admit it. "How dare he say that? I am nothing like that man, and he is not my father! My father is dead, do you all understand?"

They nodded. Edgar rubbed his chin. "I understand," he said quietly, "but you are like him nevertheless."

Solomon poised himself to strike again. Edgar tensed. Instead, Solomon swung around abruptly and walked away.

Mondete watched him sadly. "I think he's beginning to understand God," she said. "The difficulty is that he doesn't like the revelation."

Then she, too, walked away.

Edgar turned to Catherine. "Why are we the only sane people left on this road?" he asked.

Catherine didn't smile. "Perhaps our madness is still to come."

She wanted to return to the subject of the murders, but the press of others' emotions and the heat of the day overwhelmed her. Without any warning, she began to throw up again, and then it was necessary to take up a much more personal topic.

The translators, Robert, Hermann and Mohammad, had no idea of the turmoil they had landed among. They were under the impression that the job they had been assigned—and for which they had been taken from their customary work—was the main concern of Brother James. Therefore they were not pleased to find that he had little interest in them and scant information regarding their duties.

"You don't even know where the abbot intends us to work?" Robert asked.

"He said nothing about it to me," James answered. "His secretary, Pierre, will tell you, I'm sure. I think the idea is dangerous, myself. Such books shouldn't be translated; they should be burned."

"Are you afraid that knowledge of the true words of the Prophet will lead to the conversion of the Franks?" Mohammad asked. "If so, I think you have good reason for your terror. Many of your people here have chosen to submit to Allah when they heard his Truth."

The Moslem was astonished when instead of responding with anger, Brother James began to laugh. "The conversion of the Franks?" he repeated. "From what? They can't read their own books, much less yours."

"Then why are you worried about a Koran in Latin?" Robert asked. "Do you fear for the souls of the monks?"

Robert was genuinely curious. He had come to Spain and

learned Arabic to study science, following the example of Adelard of Bath and others. He hadn't felt any contamination from the religion, only contempt from the Saracens he studied under for those they considered infidels. No one had thought him worth converting.

"I have no fears for my brothers," James told him quietly. "I simply feel that such heresy should not be honored by putting it into our language."

Robert shrugged. "The abbot doesn't agree with you. He believes that by understanding the infidels, we will be better able to refute their arguments and convert them to Christ."

James laughed again, shortly and without humor. "If this is what my lord abbot wishes, I will not gainsay him," he told the men. "But I think we would be better served if you translated the evangelists into the tongue of the Saracens to bring our Truth to them."

"An interesting idea. Have you suggested it to the abbot?"

"It's not my place to," Brother James said. "But it doesn't matter. Conversion comes from the heart, not the mind. We learn the words only later. If you will excuse me, I must keep a man from being murdered."

When he had left, Hermann turned to Robert and Mohammad. "My French is not as good as yours. Did he say murdered?"

"Perhaps he only meant it in a spiritual sense," Robert said. "Why would anyone want to murder a fellow pilgrim?"

Hubert had become accustomed to riding near Lady Griselle and Hersent by now. He didn't notice that Catherine and Edgar were far behind them, and he preferred to believe that Eliazar stayed with Aaron for the sake of discretion, not because he disapproved of Hubert's friendship with the woman.

It had been so long since a woman had seemed to want his company. Especially a woman like Griselle, with her refined gestures and golden hair. She reminded him a little of his wife, Madeleine, in the days when they were first married, before the uncertainty of his commitment to Christianity began to torment her.

Hubert shifted uneasily in his saddle. Why should he think of poor Madeleine now? She was far away, at the convent of Tart, and her mind was even more remote. It came to him with a shock that it wasn't only Griselle's manner that was familiar, but also her expression—so like Madeleine's had become in the end, as if only a lifetime of training kept her from self-destruction.

"Are you well today, my lady?" he asked cautiously.

She gave him a suspicious glance. "Have you been talking with your daughter recently?"

"About you? Of course not!" he said.

"Perhaps you should," she answered and lowered the veil she wore over her hat to protect her face from the sun, thus ending conversation.

Hubert was startled, then embarrassed, then angry. What had Catherine said to Griselle? It was bad enough when his brother lectured him on his friendship with the woman, but for his daughter to interfere was intolerable. He wheeled his horse about and went back to tell her so.

He found Catherine draped in front of Edgar on their horse. His anger died in his throat.

"She wouldn't wait," Edgar told him. "She needs a litter, but insists there are other pilgrims much more ill than she."

Catherine spoke without lifting her head from Edgar's chest. "I'm not ill," she insisted. "It's only the heat and the dust. Go away."

Hubert decided that this wasn't the time to rail at her for angering Griselle. But no matter what her condition, he wasn't going to allow his daughter to interfere in his life and he resolved to tell her so as soon as they reached Najera.

At the end of the file, Mondete and Solomon walked in silence. Of all the people in the party, they were the only ones who were in complete agreement.

Twenty

Najera, Monday, June 8, 1142; the day after Pentecost.

Set me as a seal upon thine heart, as a seal upon thine arm: for love
is strong as death; jealousy is cruel as the grave; the coals thereof
are coals of fire, which hath a most vehement flame.

Song of Solomon, 8:6

$\mathcal{T}$he red cliffs of Najera were rough and alien to Catherine's eyes, and the river was shaded with trees she couldn't name. But the water was cool and the breeze refreshing, and she began to revive almost at once. A night's sleep in a quiet room with no death nearby had made her feel almost normal again.

"Could you eat something?" Edgar asked when she awoke.

Catherine asked her stomach. It answered firmly. "No," she told Edgar, "but you should. Only not where I can see you."

"Very well. Rest a while longer. I'll return soon."

Catherine was happy enough to do that. But as Edgar turned to go, she grabbed his sleeve. "It's almost over, isn't it?" she asked, her voice that of a child needing comfort rather than truth. "We'll be at Compostela soon? No more mountains?"

Edgar didn't know. "Yes," he said. "A few more days, all gentle walks through valleys full of flowers and lush meadows of grass."

"Perhaps my dream meant nothing after all," she said.

"No, Master Abelard believed in it and so do I," Edgar answered. "But we may have interpreted it too literally. The crisis may be spiritual, not physical. We may have already survived it."

Catherine smiled at him. "Then we need only thank the good apostle for granting our wish and return home with our son."

"That's right. Nothing more to worry about."

Edgar went out whistling, but the tune stopped as soon as he shut the door. Catherine's smile faded at the same time. The closer they came to the shrine of Saint James, the more each feared that the worst was yet to come.

Peter of Montboissier, abbot of Cluny, was highly satisfied with his pilgrimage so far. His visits to the Cluniac daughter houses in Castille had been an excellent idea. He had been greeted with honor, almost adulation, and certain small irregularities in liturgical practice had been noted and rooted out before they blossomed into serious deviations. He had inspected the lands and collected some beautiful and fascinating gifts. One of his prize souvenirs was no more than a glittering white lump of salt that Peter himself had chipped from a shining mountain near one of the priories. Imagine! A whole mountain of salt miles from the sea! Thus did God remind man every day of His power.

But in his journeying, Peter had not forgotten Brother Rigaud. As soon as he learned of the arrival of James, the monk was summoned to his presence.

"I trust you have discovered the one who dared to invade our church at Moissac and murder our dear brother?" The abbot brushed aside the formal greetings that James had begun.

"Not yet, my Lord Abbot," James answered. "But I have discovered what I believe to be the motive for the death of poor Brother Rigaud. It lies in his secular life, I'm sure, and will leave no wisp of scandal upon our order."

He went on to tell the story as Gaucher had told it, adding his own interpretation of the knight's behavior.

The abbot interrupted halfway through the recital. "Do you think that the knights really believed that the woman and the boy were Saracens?"

"I think they did at first," James answered slowly. "Later they knew that the boy, at least, had been baptized. But, my lord, they were warriors conquering a city, and their blood was hot with rage. I don't think it would have mattered to them."

"No, I suppose not," Peter said sadly. "From what Rigaud told me, none of them were ever truly soldiers of Christ. Continue."

James hesitated for a moment before going on with the

story. He had felt a sudden rush of anger toward his honored abbot. The force of it horrified him. He had put all strong feeling aside with relief when he had entered the monastery. A passionless existence was all he asked for. Why must he endure this pain?

He steadied himself with a silent appeal to Saint James, his patron. It was seeing his brothers again, Eliazar and Chaim; they were doing this to him. Even more, it was Catherine. Since he had first glimpsed her, his nights had been tormented by visions of the gentle face of his mother covered in blood. He mustn't allow this to affect him. He was being tested. If he held firm, the Savior would soon have pity and remove this pain.

Brother James finished the story. At the first mention of the statue, the abbot sat up straighter.

"Where is it?" he asked.

"Presumably where the men left it so many years ago. Gaucher wishes to retrieve it himself and present it to you as part of his expiation."

"A laudable intent," Peter said. "He can bring it to me after Vespers."

"Ah, well, he would like to wait until the morning," James said. "He has asked to spend the night in prayer and purification. I have promised to accompany him to the hiding place as soon as we finish saying Prime tomorrow."

The abbot was not noticeably pleased at having to wait, but he acknowledged Gaucher's right to prepare himself.

"Facing the sins of one's past is a difficult task," he conceded. "They often smell more foul for being buried so long. But it is necessary to do so for true redemption, and that outweighs all other matters. I shall wait until morning."

James bowed and went out. In the corridor, he stopped and covered his face in shame. How could he have felt such anger toward the man who had taken him in and treated him equally with all the other men at Cluny despite his birth? It was Eliazar he should hate, who clung defiantly to the old ways . . . or Chaim even more, who prayed to Christ in public but denied Him in his heart.

James repeated over and over that he despised these men

who were no longer his brothers. He had found a new community of brothers. He said it over and over, just as he recited
his psalms. But the Great Deceiver continued to torment him,
placing images in his mind of the three of them as children,
Chaim barely walking, their sisters fussing over the baby and
laughing . . . until the laughter turned to screams in James's
ears.

With a low moan, Brother James turned his face to the
stone wall, cold even in summer. He knew he could not sleep
tonight. Better to keep watch with Gaucher. Prayer combined
with physical deprivation might finally rid him of these ghosts.

Also, he considered, it might be a good idea to attend Sir
Gaucher from a discreet distance. It wouldn't do to distract
him—unless, of course, Gaucher was moved in the course of
his vigil to retrieve the statue early.

James would have been even more furious if he had known
how exactly his plan paralleled those of Solomon and Catherine.

That evening Gaucher dined on beans without salt and water
without wine. He then dressed himself in full armor, taking up
his shield but leaving his scabbard empty.

"I shall not need my sword again," he announced. "I hope
you will all come with me tomorrow to witness my return of
the statue of Our Lady to her Church."

"Of course," Griselle spoke for them. "I confess that I am
eager to see this beautiful image of the Virgin. If it is to be hidden away within the cloister, I may have no other opportunity."

As the June twilight set in, Gaucher left.

Mondete rose from the corner where she had been waiting
and silently followed him.

"Where is she going?" Griselle asked.

"I imagine the inn is too comfortable for her," Catherine
answered. "She's probably seeking out a damp spot near the
river."

"With thorn bushes," Edgar added.

Griselle nodded sadly. "The poor thing. You'd think she'd
have punished herself enough by now."

She yawned. "Oh, I beg your pardon," she said. "The sun stays bright so much longer in Spain than in Burgundy. Isn't that strange? It must be later than I realized. I shall bid you all good night. Hersent?"

The maid followed her to their small room on the ground floor. The guards took up their positions in front of the door.

Catherine was fighting exhaustion as well. She didn't want to sleep. It seemed she had been doing nothing else for days. As the sky grew darker, Solomon and Eliazar stood to go.

"Our brothers have constructed an *erov* for the Sabbath," Eliazar told them, "as there is none in this town. We must be within its boundaries before the third star appears."

Solomon did not appear pleased. "I think I should stay behind, Uncle," he said. "There are enough to say the prayers together without me. I may be needed here."

Eliazar's jaw tightened. "Solomon, I would not have you drift into apostasy as your father did. I don't want you to come to make up the minyan, but to remind you of who you are. Your aunt and I didn't raise you to break the Sabbath."

Solomon put his hand on Eliazar's shoulder. "I know that. You taught me to fear the Almighty and to worship according to the Law. But I've strayed from it many times all the same, and for less reason."

"You wish to help save the life of this 'soldier of Christ'?" Eliazar didn't hide his scorn. "This man who is the same as those who have slaughtered your people? Let the Christians look to their own. They don't need you."

Catherine watched her cousin's face. There was something in his expression that she had never seen before. She had no name for it, and it frightened her.

Solomon looked directly at his uncle. "They may not need me, but I need to be here. Forgive me, Uncle, and include me in your prayers."

Eliazar did not go willingly or quietly, but he made no attempt to force Solomon to come with him. "A man who must be tied up and dragged to his prayers may as well not be there at all," he muttered.

"*Shabat Shalom*," Solomon told him as he left.

The only answer was the thump of the door as it closed.

Solomon sat down again. The others didn't look at him. Catherine hoped he wouldn't try to justify the hurt he had just inflicted on his uncle. He didn't. He poured himself another cup of wine instead.

"I told Mondete I would wait outside the church for her signal," he said. "If Gaucher intends to keep his word, we'll have lost a night's sleep for nothing. If he doesn't . . ."

"Then we'll have him," Edgar finished. "And probably the person who killed the others."

"Yes, all that they needed was for one of the knights to survive to lead the way to the hiding place," Hubert agreed.

Catherine wasn't so certain about this. It was possible for revenge and greed to be combined; they were a perfectly matched pair. It made sense that the original owners would want the statue returned to them. But there was something different here. The murders of the other men had been done too carefully. She suspected a more vengeful reason for allowing Gaucher to remain alive this long. She yawned again.

"Catherine needs her rest." Hubert nudged Edgar. "Take her up, will you? Don't scowl at me, daughter. I know you want to be a part of everything, but you have a duty to the child you carry that's greater than any other. You know that."

She did. She knew how worried they all were and how little it would take for them to make her remain here at Najera until after the baby was born. She mustn't let them do that. So for now, it was better to be compliant. And anyway, she could barely keep her eyes open.

"Don't worry, *leoffaest*," Edgar told her. "With so many people watching, it stands to reason that nothing at all will happen tonight."

Catherine awoke far into the night. Edgar lay beside her, making that odd snore of his that was half a whistle. From the other side of the room, Hubert's presence was much more pronounced.

She didn't know what had awakened her, but now that she was up, she might as well go down to the outhouse.

Edgar was used to being climbed over once a night and didn't stir. It was so warm that Catherine didn't bother to put on her shoes. She tiptoed down the stairs.

The snoring she had left behind was echoed by that of Griselle's guards, sound asleep in front of the lady's door. Fumbling in the dark, Catherine reached out for the bar over the door to the inn. She felt the slot, but the thick wooden plank was missing. Either the innkeeper had forgotten to put it in place or someone had gone out before her.

She pulled the door open and peered out.

Now she knew what sound had awakened her. In the dim light she could make out the shapes of two women hurrying away from the inn. They weren't following the path to the out-house.

I should go wake Edgar, she thought.

The two shapes turned the corner and vanished.

Solomon is out there watching, Catherine rationalized. *I should find him first and then come back and wake Edgar.*

She put a hand on her stomach. *What do you think?* she asked the baby. *Will Saint James protect us?*

Probably from harm, she concluded, if not from Edgar's wrath. Well, it wouldn't hurt if she just hurried after the two women to see which way they were going.

She used to have voices that warned her against such idiocy, but lately they were unaccountably silent.

Brother James knelt in a dark corner of the church, praying fervidly while keeping one eye on Gaucher, kneeling before the altar in the glow of the pilgrims' candles. The knight had not moved since he arrived. His back was straight and his head bent in an attitude of submission that was oddly flaunted by the glimmer of the golden streak in his hair. James was beginning to think that he had been mistaken in his suspicions. He had requested permission to be excused from the Night Office for a private vigil, but the bells told him when Vigils began and ended. He recited it to himself as he watched the knight.

When the last tolling ceased, Gaucher's head came up. He stretched his arms and slowly got to his feet, balancing on his empty scabbard until the stiffness in his legs wore off. James remained in his place, but tensed to move.

Gaucher bowed to the altar and crossed himself. He then went directly down the nave and out the door, as if he had no fear of being challenged.

James got up quickly, his knees aching from the rough stone floor. He followed Gaucher out and nearly tripped over the dark figure of Mondete as she, too, got up to go after the knight.

The monk grabbed her wrist. "I should have known it was you all along," he hissed. "Come with me. I'm putting you where you can't harm anyone, and in the morning, you're going before the abbot."

He started to drag her away, wishing he had brought someone else to take charge of her so that he could follow Gaucher.

"Father," a voice came out of the night, "let go of her. She's harmed no one."

Startled more by the form of address than the appearance of Solomon, James released Mondete.

"I'll stay with him," Solomon told her. "Will you go rouse Hubert and Edgar?"

Mondete hadn't made a sound, not even when James fell into her. She made none now, but lifted her cloak clear of her feet and ran for the inn. Solomon turned back to James.

"Do you want to take me to your prison?" he sneered, "or help me catch the one who is really responsible for all these murders?"

James reached out to touch Solomon's sleeve. Then he stopped. "I am not a priest," he said. "You don't call me 'Father.' "

The silence grew and solidified. "I won't," Solomon said. "Not ever again."

It was too dark for them to see each other's face.

There was a pause. James stepped back. "Do you think that the murderer is interested only in finding the statue?" he asked his son.

"No, but I think it's important to her that Gaucher not regain it."

"Her!"

"Yes," Solomon looked around. Gaucher had vanished. "Which way did he go?"

James pointed into the darkness. "That way," he said. "He told me that they had hidden the statue in one of the caves up there."

They hurried away from the church, down the road that hugged the cliffs. Most of the buildings clustered close to the abbey or the river. They were soon out of the village, and the pathway turned upward. Ahead of them was a narrow ridge along which there were a number of cave openings.

"I can't spot him," James said. "Did he take a lamp?"

"I don't think so." Solomon stopped again. "Neither did we. Are you sure he came this way at all?"

James looked up into the dark holes in the rock. "No," he said. "I just assumed this is the way he would go since he said this is where they hid it."

"And you believed him?" Solomon was aghast at his stupidity.

James slapped his palm against his forehead. "What's happened to me?" he muttered. "I was never so credulous, especially when an Edomite spoke."

"Then . . ." Solomon hesitated. "Then you don't believe that everything the Christians do in the name of their Savior is right?"

"I never said that." James's voice was low. "I can only answer for what I do in His name."

"Such as abandoning your wife and child?" Solomon bit his tongue. He hadn't wanted to say it. He hadn't wanted James to think it mattered to him at all.

"Yes," James said. "That was my sacrifice."

"No, you bastard," Solomon answered. "That was ours."

He raised his fist to strike, but they were both brought out of their personal acrimony by the clear, high sound of a scream.

"That's not Catherine," was Solomon's first response. "I know her scream."

"What difference does it make?" James said as they retraced their steps as quickly as possible in the darkness. "I think it came from somewhere near the church."

As they reached the space between the church and the rock, Solomon saw a growing crowd of people gathering around a still shape on the ground. From what he could see of the clothing, it was a woman.

"It's not Catherine. It wasn't her voice," he repeated to convince himself. Then another thought struck him. What if the scream had been from Mondete?

He pushed his way through the people until he could see the face lying on the stone. Her eyes were open and empty. Solomon felt a wave of relief and then guilt.

It was Hersent.

Catherine had followed the two women through the warm night with a sense of being in some ancient story where, at any moment, a talking bird would swoop by, or a friendly wolf would trot up and lead her to the secret treasure. This was not the world she lived in every day; it was a strange country where magic survived, where children became swans, and river spirits gave up immortality for earthly princes. The flicker of the tiny oil lamp the two women carried was a talisman, part of the enchantment.

So she wasn't surprised when Griselle and Hersent vanished through a narrow slit between the church and the rock. She followed them without fear, for how could stories harm you?

It was barely the space of a breath later when there was a scream and one of the women came stumbling out, falling all too solidly onto the hard earth.

Catherine ran to her and knelt at her side.

Hersent whimpered in pain, then made a noise in her throat horribly like the one Catherine had heard when Hugh was killed. The woman gripped Catherine's arm.

"Save her!" Hersent begged.

The grip released as Hersent's body went slack against Catherine. Gently, Catherine lowered her to the ground.

There was the sound of running feet. Catherine knew help was coming and so, reluctantly, she stood. Griselle was still in there. Someone had to go in and get her. Someone had to save her.

Catherine had intended to wait for someone with a torch and weapons. Then, above her head, a voice called to her from the dark. "Have no fear," it said enticingly. "I'm here to help you. To fulfill your dreams. It's what you've always wanted. Come up here. Follow me."

Catherine looked up. Way above her, the lamp was shining, the flame dancing in the night breeze. As she watched, it moved farther up the side of the rock face.

Help was coming. But the voice was calling her. There had been no voice in her dream that she remembered. But dreams were so uncertain. What if she were meant to follow? What if she failed the test and this child died as well? Catherine stood in torment. What should she do?

The light moved farther up. The voice was fainter. "Hurry!" it urged her. "There isn't much time."

Catherine decided. If one wasn't willing to take the leap, then faith had no worth.

But this was too much to ask of Saint James alone. Catherine clasped her hands quickly, then whispered as she entered the gaping crack in the cliff. "Holy Mother, I am trusting in you. please, don't let anything happen to my child."

There was no light inside, but Catherine didn't have time to fumble around. She hit her shin almost immediately on a sharp edge. A step. She bent over and felt with her hands. There was another. She placed one hand against the rough wall and started to climb.

Edgar woke to the echo of the scream from the churchyard. He didn't even need to reach out to know that Catherine was missing. He swung out of bed and grabbed his boots. Across the room, Hubert was doing the same.

"Where is she?" Hubert demanded.

Edgar's heart sank. He knew. "Somewhere high up," he answered. "I have to find her before she falls."

Hubert opened his mouth to upbraid Edgar for his lack of care of Catherine. With an effort, he stopped himself. She had got past him as well.

Neither of them concerned themselves with knowing where to search. If they followed the commotion to where the noise and confusion were thickest, Catherine wouldn't be far away.

They ran, almost literally, into Mondete, coming to find them. Her hood had fallen and her bald head shone in the torchlight, while her face was oddly shadowed, making her appearance that of a corpse, returned with evil tidings from beyond the grave.

"Gaucher has left the church," she panted. "Solomon and his father are following him. No—" she forestalled their questions "—I don't know where the scream came from. But Griselle and Hersent passed me as I was coming to get you, and Catherine followed soon after."

"Why didn't you stop her?" Edgar shouted.

"I promised Solomon that I would fetch you," she answered. "Catherine will meet up with the others when she gets to the church. She's in no danger."

Edgar didn't bother to answer her. He knew that Catherine was in danger, but he also knew that it was up to him to find her.

When they arrived at the church, they found a cluster of people circled about the body of a woman. Edgar's heart lurched until he saw Solomon standing apart from the group. If the body were Catherine, he would have been next to her.

"Where is she?" Edgar gasped as he and Hubert reached Solomon.

Solomon knew instantly whom they meant. "I haven't seen her," he said. "That *desfae* monk and I went off in the wrong direction after Gaucher. He'd slipped into that hole in the rock behind the church. The monks here say that it's an ancient stairway up to a ridge leading to any number of caves. But this is the only way out. He stabbed Lady Griselle's maid on his way in. He may have taken the Lady as hostage. The monks don't want to send their guards up in the dark for fear of getting her killed."

"Solomon!" Edgar stopped him. "Catherine's in there as well."

Solomon stared at him. "No one mentioned her. How do you know?"

"Mondete saw her going after Griselle," Hubert said. "She's in there with a murderer. I'm going after her."

Edgar looked at the darkness that he knew Catherine had vanished into. "No, I have to go," he said. "She's my wife and it's our child. I have the right, Hubert."

Hubert had already taken out his knife. He started to protest, then stopped himself again. Edgar did have the right.

"You go first, then," he said. "I'll come behind with a torch. She was my child long before you married her."

"I'm following as well," Solomon told them. "According to the monks, the passage is too narrow for more than one at a time."

They hurried over to the opening but were impeded by a pair of guards, townsmen under the authority of the abbey. "No one is to enter," the shorter one told them. "We're here to see to that."

Hubert sighed. "There's really no point in arguing, is there?"

"None at all," the guard answered firmly.

"Well, I suppose there's only one thing we can do then." Hubert sighed again and turned as if to move away. "Solomon?"

Solomon also turned, and then the both of them swung back, their fists connecting with the guards' jaws before the men realized what was happening. More men rushed up to join in the fray.

In the ensuing confusion, Edgar slipped into the darkness and started up the stairs.

As she climbed the stairs, the voice grew clearer and Catherine realized that it was Griselle. She couldn't understand how Griselle had managed to get ahead of Gaucher until she realized that Hersent had caught up to him at the entrance to delay him. Did Griselle know that the maid had given her life to obey her mistress's orders?

Griselle's melodic summoning led the knight up and up the staircase, in and out of the side of the cliff. Gaucher followed as if sleepwalking, his face turned perpetually to her light. Catherine wondered what they would do when they reached the top. From the darkness, Griselle answered for her.

"Come along, my dear," she crooned. "You've been pursuing me since Le Puys, almost as long as I've been pursuing you. I couldn't surrender to you with all the others around, could I now? Think of the scandal."

"I always knew you wanted me." Gaucher stumbled, then caught himself. "But why here?"

Griselle laughed. Catherine shrank into the darkness, even though she was sure she couldn't be seen. The light, frivolous sound terrified her.

"Oh, my Lord Gaucher," Griselle replied, "I know how you like it, at least with women. It's more exciting in a forbidden place, isn't it? A church, for instance, or a shrine, before a holy object. Wouldn't you like to have me on the floor of the cave with the Blessed Virgin staring down on us? Once more before you give her back?"

Catherine heard Gaucher stumble again. His chain mail rattled against the rock.

"You'd like to keep that on, too, wouldn't you?" Griselle's voice was as tempting as a serpent's. "You want to see the marks of the metal rings branded into my flesh."

"Oh, yes," he breathed. "How . . . how do you know that?"

She laughed again. Catherine shuddered and forced herself to continue after them. They had reached the top of the stairs and come out onto a narrow plateau. Catherine stayed on the final step and peered around the edge. Griselle had undone the brooch holding her cloak, then let the garment fall. She stood in the lamplight clad only in a short shift. It was untied at the neck and open so that her breasts were half uncovered. Her long blond hair fell loosely around her like Danae's shower. Catherine blinked. Griselle was really quite attractive.

"I know everything about you, my dear." Griselle set the oil lamp on the ground next to Gaucher and smiled at him invitingly. "I've heard it over and over. I know all your appetites, your pleasures—just as I learned those of your friends. But they were so ordinary, no imagination. You were the one who knew how to make things interesting, weren't you? I heard you were always the best."

He moved toward her, reaching out to pull the shift from her shoulders. "After tonight, you won't need to rely on the word of someone like Mondete," he murmured. "I knew you'd come to me one day. There's never been a widow as pious as you made out to be."

"Yes," she breathed, moving closer to him. "I was just preparing myself for you."

The shift fell to the ground as Gaucher pulled her against him, holding her tightly as he kissed her. When he let her go, Catherine saw the marks of the chain mail across her chest. What was the woman doing, letting him hurt her like that? Was she mad?

Gaucher reached around Griselle and began to lift her by her buttocks, but she pushed away. Catherine noticed that her right hand was closed as if she were holding something.

"At the shrine," she told him. "I want to do it just the way you like it best, with Our Lady watching. Which cave is she in?"

"I'll take you there," Gaucher said and lifted her so that her arms and legs were around him. He staggered a bit as he walked, but he didn't drop her as they entered the cave. A moment later he came back alone, wiped his brow, picked up the lamp and went back inside.

Catherine stood frozen in shock and embarrassed fascination. So this was how Griselle had lured the knights to their death. Rufus certainly; even Hugh might have found her too much to resist. She may have thought Norbert too old for her charms and so resorted to poison. But how could she have allowed herself to do anything so disgusting with those men?

But what about Rigaud? From what had been said, it didn't make sense that the monk would have followed her to an assignation. How had she convinced him to assume such a position for her?

The lamplight shone from the cave. Shadows reached out

as someone moved back and forth between the lamp and the door. There was a loud moan, but not of pain. Catherine did not want to go any farther. She did not want to see what was happening in there. She wasn't sure she'd have the courage to tell her confessor what she'd already observed.

But wasn't it her duty to prevent a murder, even if the would-be victim wasn't likely to thank her for intervening? Catherine moved toward the cave, wishing with all her heart that she had never believed in her dream, wishing even more that she could somehow get through this with her eyes closed.

Gaucher was a horrible person, but she couldn't allow him to be killed, especially in a moment of sacrilege. Catherine forced herself to the entrance to the cave. She swallowed hard, stepped into the light . . . and gasped.

Twenty-One

Inside a cave in Najera. The middle of the night.

Peccator, ama misericordiam, quia si non amas, non mereris.

Sinner, love mercy. For if you do not love it, you do not deserve it.
—Hugh of Saint-Victor
De Sacramentis Christianae Fidei
Libri II Pars XIV cap. V

*C*atherine paid no attention to the bodies writhing on the floor. They were mere movements in the dark. The lamp had been placed on a ledge before the statue, and the light shone steadily upon the dark face of the Virgin. She was about three feet tall. On her head was a golden crown, encrusted with jewels. Her cloak was covered with pearls, its edging of gold thread. Even though the statue had been hidden in the cave for many years, everything about it was as bright as if newly made.

But it wasn't the panoply that made Catherine gasp. It was the face of the Virgin. The carving was from a deep brown wood. Instead of being lost in the splendor of the robes, the contrast between the bright gold and the dark face only drew the eye to the tender simplicity of her expression. In her arms was the Child Jesus; a boy of three or four. The mother and son were looking directly at her, and Catherine had no answer to the question in their eyes.

Her thoughts were jerked back to earth as Griselle cried out and Gaucher laughed. There was a scuffle and then he gave a sudden yelp of pain.

"You *bordelere!*" he screamed. "That hurt! What was that? What did you stick me with?"

"Get off me, you pig!" Griselle shouted back, pushing against his weight. "Nothing half as painful as what you did to her, I promise. I know all about it. They held her down for you, didn't they? She had no way to protect herself. And before you were through, her body was a mass of cuts from the rings of your mail shirt. And when he tried to save her, you tied him up and made him watch. And when she was dead, you started on him."

Gaucher got up, rubbing his shoulder. "You're mad! What are you talking about?" His voice shook. He knew.

Griselle scrambled to her feet. "I'm talking about Bertran, my husband. The child you tortured and mutilated. You and your brave friends, all soldiers for Christ. My beloved didn't live long enough to avenge what you did to him and his mother, but thanks to God's mercy, I have fulfilled his oath."

"You?" Gaucher's voice was barely audible. "You did it? Norbert, Hugh, Rigaud, Rufus? You killed all of them?"

"No, my dear Lord Gaucher," Griselle purred. "I have killed all of *you*. You are the last, and the worst. And you will be dead by morning."

Catherine saw the shadow that was Gaucher stiffen.

"Poison," he said. "On the brooch."

"Much kinder than what you did to her," Griselle answered. "But I had no more time. And now I will take back the Lady you stole from Saragossa. My duty will then be finished."

She crossed in front of him to reach for the statue, but Gaucher grabbed her by her flowing hair and pulled her to the ground, beating at her with his free hand. Griselle twisted in his grasp, clawing at his face, both of them growling like wild beasts.

The statue gazed down on them with ethereal serenity.

Something inside Catherine snapped. "No!" she screamed, falling upon the struggling pair. She pounded on Gaucher's back, kicked with her bare feet at Griselle's flailing arms. "Not here! Not in front of her! Stop! Stop this now!"

Under Catherine's blows, Gaucher's grip on Griselle's hair slackened. She twisted in his grasp and bit his unprotected thigh. The knight threw back his head and roared, pulling harder. Neither gave any sign of noting Catherine's presence.

"Very well," she told them. "Kill each other. But not with Our Lady watching you. You can't shame her like that."

There was a stone jutting out of the wall that gave Catherine a step up to the ledge. She stood on it and took the statue from the niche, the wrappings clinging to its feet. It was heavier than she had expected. The gold must be solid rather than plate. She took a length of the wrapping cloth and tied it around her neck, making a sling to hold the statue. She nearly lost her balance coming down, but caught herself.

Cradling the statue in her arms, Catherine circled Gaucher and Griselle. As she passed, she brushed Griselle's foot. The woman looked up. Gaucher followed her gaze. They both saw what Catherine carried.

"Thief!" Gaucher shouted, dropping his hold on Griselle. "It's mine!"

"Never!" Griselle screamed. "Catherine, run!"

Catherine obeyed.

Outside the cave, the night was as black as the moment before Creation. Catherine paused, uncertain of which way the stairs lay. Behind her, Gaucher gave another roar and Griselle a scream. Then there was a brief silence, broken by the clink of mail as the knight rose to follow her.

Catherine turned the wrong way.

She kept her hand on the rock wall, afraid to trust her feet not to stumble in the darkness. But she couldn't find the opening leading down. Although her heart was drumming loudly in her ears and her frightened breathing all too clear, Gaucher seemed not to have discovered which way she had gone. He shouted again, ordering her to return.

The wall of stone turned a corner. Catherine reached out to feel how far the new wall went. Her fingers dislodged some pebbles that bounced to the ground with a rattle.

"There," Gaucher said quietly from not far away. "I've got you now. Give it back to me and I won't hurt you. That's my redemption you're holding. I must have it back."

"Catherine, don't." Griselle was standing behind him. "Would you let him buy his way into heaven? Bertran's mother bought that statue with her life's blood. I must have it to avenge her death. Give it to me."

The stones on the Virgin's crown were cold against Catherine's throat. "*Maria Mater*," she begged aloud, "what should I do?"

Climb.

The sandstone was pocked by the elements with hollows that could be used as hand- and footholds. Catherine didn't question, but felt around until she found something that she could hold onto, a hole to put her foot into. The statue hanging from her neck made it hard to get close enough to the rock. If she could only get a bit higher; there must be another ledge she could rest on until help came.

A hand grabbed at her foot. She shook it off in another torrent of pebbles. Gaucher swore furiously as he slid back down. Catherine continued to climb.

Finally, her hands felt a flat place above. Now all she needed to do was to hoist herself up onto it.

The wind was stronger up here. It whistled through the pores in the rock. The statue hanging across her chest and stomach made it impossible for her to pull herself all the way over the edge. She tried to adjust her burden with one hand so that it swung around behind her back. There. That was better. She put both hands on the ledge, braced her feet and knees in ridges in the wall and strained to lift herself.

She had just thrown one knee over the edge and was bringing the other leg up when the sling became unbalanced. Catherine felt the shifting and reached around to catch the statue as it fell out.

As it slipped through her grasp, she managed to take hold of the upraised hand of the child. The weight pulled her around so that she was now hanging over the side of the rock face, the statue dangling from her outstretched arm. Catherine could feel herself slipping back over the edge, the statue pulling her down. Below her, she could just make out the faces of Gaucher and Griselle turned up to her, arms reaching to catch the treasure.

"Catherine." The voice came not from below, but somewhere to the side. Catherine tried to turn to see who it was, but the statue began to swing alarmingly with the movement.

"Good. A little more and I can reach it," Brother James said. "I'm only a few feet from you, but the path narrows here. I can get hold of the statue, though, if you swing it harder to your left."

Catherine didn't think to ask how he had appeared, as if

by divine intervention, so near her. But despite her precarious position, she wasn't any more inclined to obey the monk than she was the two shouting at her from below.

"You only want her as a prize, just like they do," she panted, managing to grip the hand of the Child Jesus more firmly.

"No, not like they do," James insisted. "Not like Chaim and Eliazar either. Can't you understand? I gave up vengeance when I converted. I gave up everything. I only want to save you. Please, child, even if you despise me, you must trust me."

Still she hesitated. The sweat on her palm was causing the wood to slip. She slid forward in her attempt to hold on and had to scrabble back to avoid going over the edge.

"I'm afraid," Catherine said at last. "If I try to swing her and I can't reach you, she'll fall and break."

"Better a piece of wood and metal than you, child," James said softly. She could hear the tears he was forcing himself to swallow. "Catherine, I couldn't save my mother. Don't punish me more by preventing me from saving you, too. Please, if you can't move the statue to where I can reach it, then drop it to the jackals below. Our Lady wouldn't want you to die for her image. It's but a thing of this world, nothing more."

The darkness was not so thick now. Catherine could tell that others had arrived below. Someone had pulled Griselle away and wrapped a cloak around her, from which she struggled to break free. But Gaucher had found the toeholds in the rocks and had begun to climb, inching up toward her. In a moment he would be able to pull the image out of her grasp. Catherine closed her eyes and with an effort that wrenched all the muscles in her shoulder, swung the statue over to where Brother James waited, leaning with both arms stretched forward over the path on the other side. He caught the hem of the Virgin's cloak as Catherine let go.

She was left hanging halfway over the edge, her shoulder aching too much for her to pull herself all the way back up. But she was no longer in danger of falling.

Dawn was approaching. In the grey light, Catherine saw Gaucher's face as he realized that the treasure had been taken from him. Hatred flared from his eyes as he struggled to reach her anyway. Then a spasm shook his body and the hatred turned to terror. One hand went to his throat and he gave a se-ries of ever-shorter gasps as he fought to make his lungs work. He clawed the air with both hands, then fell back onto the ground, where he continued jerking as people gathered around in a futile attempt to help him.

The first light of the sun hit the red cliffs.

Catherine looked down. The town of Najera was far below her, the river still in predawn shadow. She hadn't realized how far up she had climbed. She hadn't known how small the shelf was that she lay upon . . . or that the only way down was either by the footholds she had used to climb up or a ridge no wider than the span of her hands.

On the other side of the ridge stood Brother James, hold-ing the Black Virgin. He put the statue down next to himself and reached out to her.

"It's not far, Catherine," he said. "Only a few steps and I'll have you."

She looked down. She saw the distance between herself and Brother James. She shook her head. Her stomach pitched and rolled. She closed her eyes and concentrated. This was no time for morning sickness.

"*Leoffaest.*" Catherine's eyes opened and she lifted her head. "*Leoflic Catherine, min lif.*" Edgar had come up behind Brother James. "Stay where you are, *carissima.* I'm coming for you."

"But you can't . . ." Catherine remembered the steps at Le Puys all too well. In her mind she saw his face again, drawn with terror at being up so high. She couldn't ask him to confront that again. She'd spent much of the trip trying to protect him from doing just that.

He didn't hesitate, though. He stepped firmly on the strip of crumbling rock and walked to her as steadily as if crossing a street in Paris. He knelt next to her and took her in his arms. Catherine began to cry.

"You know," he said, brushing damp strands of hair from her face, "there are those who might suggest that I should beat you for being here at all, for risking yourself so rashly. It isn't just your own life anymore, *deorling*."

"I know. It was stupid," Catherine admitted. "I felt as though I were meant to come. When I heard Griselle, I thought she was calling me, but it was Gaucher she wanted. She didn't even know I was there."

She pressed closer to him. "I was right, you know," she said. "Griselle killed all of them. I don't know how, but she did."

"Later," Edgar told her. "First we get you back to the hostel and to bed. Can you stand without getting sick?"

"I think so." She took a breath and got to her feet. "What's going on down there?"

Edgar didn't answer. Instead, he took her by the shoulders and led her confidently back to the pathway and down to the church.

Hubert never forgot the sight of the elegant Lady of Lugny, hair matted with dirt and blood, naked except for a cloak that one of the monks was desperately trying to keep her in, shrieking epithets over the body of Gaucher, knight of Mâcon.

"Has she gone mad?" he asked the world at large. Hubert was struck by the thought that it was somehow his doing, that this was what happened to every woman he fell in love with.

"She is possessed by evil, that is certain."

Hubert turned to find Brother James standing next to him, holding a statue of the Virgin Mary.

"Jacob!" he said. "That's nonsense! Look at her! Obviously that old man tried to ravish her and drove her senses from her."

The monk nodded slowly. "If that's what you wish to believe. Excuse me. I need to take this to the abbot. He will need to decide what's to be done about her."

Leaving Hubert not sure if he were referring to Griselle or the statue, James hurried to the abbey, where the rest of the monks had just finished saying Lauds. He was immediately granted an audience with Abbot Peter, but it took him some time to explain everything that had happened.

When Brother James had finished, Peter's face was grave. "And the maid, Hersent, was she killed because she knew what her mistress had done?" he asked.

"From what we can discover, Sir Gaucher stabbed her," Brother James told him. "because he thought she was trying to steal the statue from him."

"I see, but that doesn't justify the bizarre behavior of Lady Griselle or negate the fact that she had already prepared the poison. Her actions were planned." Peter leaned forward hopefully. "Do you think this was an act of insanity or possession?"

James shook his head and sighed. "No more so than any other deed of vengeance. Her husband made her swear to punish those who had murdered his mother and tortured him. Gaucher himself admitted the truth of it. Those five men committed heinous acts. They went beyond mindless cruelty or battle lust. Thinking that the boy was a Moslem, they even found a pig and made him perform sexual acts with it, to shame his Faith."

Peter looked at him sharply. "Does that offend you more than the knights' sacrilege concerning their own Faith?"

James returned the look with no hint of prevarication. "Everything these men did offends me," he said. "As it must all decent Christians."

Peter thought for a moment, pursing his lips. "There are many who will agree that her actions were justified," he said finally. "And yet, it was murder, pure and simple, whatever her reasons. I can't let her go unpunished. I take it she has admitted her guilt."

James nodded. "She glories in it."

The abbot winced. "Is she calm enough to be questioned?"

"The doctor is seeing to her, and one of the women among the pilgrims, the *jongleuse*, is taking care of her physical needs. Perhaps this afternoon she can be brought before you."

"Very well." Peter got up. "I must consult with Bishop Stephen and my advisers. This is a problem I would be rid of as soon as possible."

Brother James bowed. "And the statue?"

"You indicated that the knights wished it to be an offering

to the Church," Peter said. "It will look well in a chapel at Cluny and we shall venerate Our Lady whenever we gaze upon it."

At the hostel, clean and fed, Catherine was unraveling her own mystery.

"So the child in my dream wasn't ours," she concluded sadly. "I was so certain of it. It was the Child Christ of the statue instead. I suppose that means we can't be sure the baby I'm carrying will live."

Edgar disagreed. "It's not the nature of dreams to be unambiguous, even those sent as prophecy. You know that as well as I. In essence, what happened last night fits your dream. You were in danger of falling. The child was caught not by Saint James, but by his namesake, Brother James."

"And then when I believed I would die, you were there." Catherine snuggled closer to him. "And that was the deepest truth, the one wrapped around the first dream like a wall around a castle. I should have had more faith in you."

"No, you shouldn't have," he said. "I'm only human. The saints are a better repository for your faith."

"I'm not giving up on them," she laughed. "But you're the one I want to wake up next to every morning and lie down beside every night until I die."

"I love you, too, Catherine," Edgar sighed. "So will you please start taking more care that the day of your death is far in the future?"

"I promise," Catherine said and meant it.

The Griselle who appeared before the assembled witnesses and church prelates that afternoon was far removed from the wild woman of the night before. She stood quietly, guards on either side, dressed in her finest robes, her hair braided tightly and hidden under her widow's veil. It was difficult for those who hadn't seen her howling over Gaucher's body to believe the story. But as Brother James had told the abbot, she had no desire to deny it.

"For all the years of our marriage," she announced proudly,

"Bertran and I knelt each morning and evening and prayed for justice. At first he didn't know the names of the men; even their faces were blurred by time. Only the horror and hatred remained. Then one day he saw Hugh of Grignon wearing the emerald from the ring, the one Bertran's Saracen grandfather had given him. That he recognized at once, for he carried the empty setting with him always, on a chain around his neck. From that clue, we eventually learned the identity of the others."

"And why didn't your husband accuse these men openly and demand justice from the Duke of Burgundy?" Peter demanded.

Griselle looked at him. "A minor lord with a tainted heritage accusing five men, well-established in the area, of such things? Even if he could have brought himself to recount the indignities those monsters had visited upon him, how could he be sure he would be believed? His father was dead, his claim to his land through an uncle. He had no other family. No, we had to do this ourselves."

She was so reasonable. Peter could feel the mood alter in the room as people considered her arguments. The part of him that had been born a secular nobleman could sympathize with Bertran's dilemma. But he was not a layman now.

"Vengeance belongs to the Lord," he said firmly. "If your husband deemed it necessary, he could have challenged these men to trial by combat, although I personally find that an intolerable practice. But it would have been better to come to me or the local bishop for retribution. You did neither of these but preferred to murder these men by stealth, so that the blame might fall on others."

"No, that I did not intend," Griselle said decisively. "If my poor Bertran hadn't been killed in the service of King Louis, he would have managed it much better, I'm sure. But the duty was left to me, and I did the best I could. I never meant anyone to suffer for it but those men. That's why I killed each one differently, so that the deed might be attributed to bandits from the woods or a passing cutpurse. But there was no way I would leave their punishment to the Church. They all had to die, my Lord Abbot, and be damned."

Peter rose in his chair. "What are you saying, woman?"

Griselle seemed puzzled by his inability to understand. "What would have been the point of killing them if they had been shriven before?" she asked. "If they had repented, they would have been given the hope of heaven. This way, they will be punished for all eternity."

Many of those present crossed themselves hurriedly. Even the abbot appeared shaken. "You not only took their lives," he said in wonder, "but you intended to damn their souls as well?"

Griselle smiled. "Exactly. They deserved no less."

Peter sank back into his chair with a thump. Never before had he encountered anything like this. What was he to do with this woman? If he were a secular Lord and she a simple townswoman, it would be simple. He'd have her hanged and left to dangle at the crossroads. But Griselle was not only heir to her husband's property, she had powerful relations of her own. Even more, he could not in good conscience act as a secular Lord would.

He was a man of God, even if that sometimes got lost in the quotidian concerns of managing the abbey of Cluny and its dependents. And as such, it went against everything he honestly believed to allow Griselle to die in mortal sin, even though she had desired to send others to that fate. So he pushed aside the temptation to turn her over to the local ruler. Her soul would be fought for. That is what *he* meant by being a soldier of Christ.

Peter resolved to give Griselle one final chance.

"You have, by your own admission, brutally murdered five men, all of them knights of Burgundy and affiliated with Cluny," he intoned. "Even worse, you have done so in an attempt to deny them the opportunity for salvation. This is a deed so horrible that I know of no set punishment for it. There might, however, be a penance, if you can be brought to repentance."

Griselle smiled again, more wistfully. "I have fulfilled my oath to my husband, and gladly. If you must punish me for the fate of the knights, I would welcome death."

"Oh, no, Griselle of Lugny." Peter grew so stern that even Griselle was finally unnerved. She stopped smiling and stared at him with round, wary eyes.

"Even such murders as you have committed might be expunged with a life of honest penitence," Peter continued. "Your crime is far worse. Your sin is that of Lucifer, in thinking that you are greater than God."

In a corner of the room, unnoticed, Mondete Ticarde put her hands over her face.

Griselle was outraged. "I would never think anything so blasphemous," she sputtered. "I'm a good Christian. I go to Mass and pray daily. I've donated most of my property for the health of my soul and that of my husband. I give alms. How dare you compare me to the Great Deceiver?"

Peter was not impressed. "Those are only actions, and even Satan might perform them for his own ends. In your heart, you did not trust your god to tend to matters in his own way and time. Pride is the greatest sin of all, Griselle of Lugny. Our Lord may have intended something much worse or much finer for those men. And I believe that in the case of Brother Rigaud, at least, you failed. He confessed his sins to me when he entered our order. He suffered for them every day. By leaving him in such a position, you wanted us to think that Rigaud had returned to his old habits, but Brother James examined the body and realized that Rigaud was already dead when the spear was run through him."

"He would have bled more, and struggled as he died," James explained. "Your poison again, I presume. Therefore, Griselle, as he died innocent, you may have provided him with a direct path to paradise."

"No." But for the first time, Griselle was doubtful. "He was one of them. He treated Bertran as a catamite. All of them were evil and they all deserved to die."

Her eyes, unseeing, searched the room as she tried to make sense of what the abbot had said. Finally, she found a response.

"Would you have had me break my oath?" she asked. "When a man swears to avenge the death of a kinsman and does so, he is honored. I have done the same."

There was a murmur of agreement from those assembled. Everyone knew that an insult to one's family must be avenged. How could society exist otherwise?

Peter sighed. "Our Lord forgave His killers from the cross," he reminded her.

"But as you have told me, I am not Our Lord," Griselle snapped back.

Bishop Stephen tugged at Peter's robe. Peter bent to hear his advice. After a moment, he nodded and straightened.

"The good bishop is right," he said. "It's clear that you are not only arrogant, but also sadly in need of instruction if you are to be made aware of the enormity of your sins. Therefore I sentence you to finish the pilgrimage you set out on."

Griselle stared at him, waiting.

"But you are not to ride a fine horse or be attended by servants," he pronounced. "You are to go barefoot and in rough cloth. And you must carry upon your body five chains, each one the measure of the length of each man you deprived of life. I will set guards on you to be sure this is done."

Griselle showed no emotion. "May I be allowed to distribute my possessions before I leave?" she asked.

"There's more," the abbot told her. "After you reach the shrine of Saint James at Compostela, you shall be taken to our convent of Marcigny, where you will spend the remainder of your days in service to the sisters there, who will attempt to correct the many flaws in your theology and bring you to a true repentance of your acts."

"I would rather you hanged me," Griselle said flatly.

"Perhaps, but I hope that you will one day thank me for not doing so," Peter said.

He signaled the guards to take her away, and the party rose to leave. Hubert had been watching from the corner, not even sure why he had come to see this. Now he found himself stepping forward to address the abbot.

"My lord, I ask a favor," he said hesitantly.

Peter stopped and looked at him, trying to place him. He seemed familiar.

"My name is Hubert LeVendeur," Hubert said. "I'm a

merchant of Paris and, like Brother James, a convert to Christianity."

Peter smiled. "Welcome. What is it you request?"

Hubert couldn't believe he was doing this, but the words spilled out of him. "The Lady Griselle is not as strong as she would like you to believe, my lord," he said. "The lengths of iron that you have enjoined her to carry will weigh more than she does. She might not survive to reach Compostela under such a burden."

"That is her concern," Peter answered, but his tone left room for more debate.

Hubert took a deep breath. "I offer myself to go with her," he said. "I will walk beside her and carry the chains myself."

Griselle turned to him in horror. "No, Hubert!" she pleaded. "You mustn't!"

The abbot was about to agree with her, but something in the faces of the two before him made him stop to consider. "Why would you do this for her?" he asked Hubert. "Is she your mistress?"

"No, my Lord Abbot," Hubert said. "My reasons concern the state of my soul, alone."

"I must consult on this."

Peter and the other clerics held a brief discussion. At the end, Bishop Stephen nodded. Peter turned back to the assemblage.

"Very well, Hubert of Paris," he said. "I give you leave to take this task upon yourself. But once the chains are wound about you, they may not be removed until you stand before the shrine of the Apostle James."

"I understand," Hubert told him.

"No," Griselle wept. "Not for me, you mustn't, no, no, no!"

The guards took her out, still weeping. Hubert squared his shoulders. He had a much more difficult task before him. He had to tell Eliazar what he had just agreed to do.

"That whore has bewitched you!" Eliazar shouted. This was, so far, his mildest reaction. "To take on her punishment, you

must have been cursed. Why? She can't mean that much to you
. . . can she?"

Eliazar leaned across the table separating him from his
brother. Catherine sat next to her father, holding his hand. She
had no more idea than Eliazar what had caused Hubert to take
on Griselle's burden, but she felt somehow that it must be her
fault. Edgar sat on the other side of her, equally certain that the
whole matter had nothing to do with them. From across the
room, Solomon watched them all. He had no intention of taking either side; he had already chosen his own way.

Mondete sat on the floor by the cold hearth. She was holding a comb, one that had belonged to Hersent. She had found
it on the floor after the maid's things had been packed to send
to her children. Mondete had no idea of what she would do
with it.

Hubert had still not answered Eliazar's question. He could
feel all of them staring at him. Why had he done this? Was it
a misplaced passion for Griselle? He had been so close to lov-
ing her. Did he think this would win her? Could he want her
now, knowing what she had done? Did he have any answer to
give his horrified family?

"I think . . ." he started. "I'm not sure I can explain it, even
to myself. Eliazar, what would you do if you found the men
who murdered our mother and sisters?"

"I'd slit their throats," Eliazar said. "Starting from the
crotch. You don't think that Gaucher was one of them, do
you?"

"Of course not," Hubert said. "But he could have been; any
of them could have. And if he had been, would you be so
quick to condemn Griselle? We are also taught that vengeance
is in the hands of the Almighty, that we should forgive our enemies, but if you had found those who killed our family, would
you have been merciful, or would you have acted as she did?"

Eliazar was silent. "I don't know," he said at last.

"Neither do I," Hubert said. "And that is why I have decided to carry the chains for her. Perhaps by the time I reach
Compostela, I will have found the answer."

Epilogue

Santiago de Compostela, Saint John's Eve, Tuesday, June 23, 1142.

Libet iam et hunc claudere librum; sed in calce aliqua velim vel ante dicta quasi epilogando repetere, vel addere praetermissa.

We can bring this book to a close now, but here at the end, as an epilogue, I would like to repeat some things which have been said before, or to add some things which have been omitted.
—Bernard of Clairvaux
On Consideration, Book IV

$\mathcal{T}$here were more mountains between Najera and Santiago. There were dry winds and burning-hot days. There were storms with lightning splitting the sky and striking the earth, setting brush fires in the hills to the north. The pilgrims also walked through fields of heather that reminded Edgar of the countryside around the home in Scotland that he had abandoned for a clumsy, impetuous woman with untamable black hair and eyes of Norman-blue.

Catherine and Edgar accepted the discomforts as minor. They put aside their worries over the coming child, on whose behalf they had set out so many weeks before. Their quest seemed almost trivial beside those of the people who traveled with them. Catherine knew that her sorrow was as nothing compared to that of the other pilgrims, nothing to that of Hubert, who took each step bound in chains of iron.

"I can't bear to watch him," she wept one evening. "How can that woman endure it?"

Edgar had been watching Griselle. "I don't think she can. Abbot Peter was wiser than we realized. If she had carried the burden, she would have felt it a kind of martyrdom. Now it's her torture."

"And mine." Catherine took her cup and went over to give her father a drink of water.

Of them all, he was the one most at peace. "I heard a seagull calling today," he told her. "We should come to Santiago in another day's journey. This is the last of the mountains. How are you feeling, daughter?"

"Well," she assured him. "The nausea has passed and I'm stronger. I would help you bear these chains the rest of the way."

"You already do," he smiled.

He wasn't the only one in chains. Many had imposed the punishment upon themselves or at the request of their priests. There were many others now; the road was clogged with those limping, carried on litters, lepers with their wooden clappers of warning, the aged hoping to die at the feet of the saint, parents with children ill or born with deformities, and those who appeared whole but were bent under the weight of their sins. Among them were also those who came on a pilgrimage of thanksgiving, who had left their crutches and chains behind. Their joy gave the others hope.

Mondete could no longer walk apart from the others, for there was no end to the procession. She chose to stay near Hubert and Griselle. Solomon had planned on leaving the party at Astorga, when Maruxa and Roberto did, their pilgrimage complete when they saw their children running toward them. But something pulled at him to see the ending. Eliazar had turned south with the traders from Toulouse. Since his entreaties had had no effect upon Hubert's decision, he told them that he would see them again in Paris, when this madness, he prayed, would have passed.

Brother James did not complete the journey either. The emperor had been victorious in his siege, and the abbot and his party had gone to meet him and to discuss the matter of the payment of back tithes. James was not as relieved as he expected to be to part from his newly reunited family.

"Perhaps you are a Christian," he told Hubert when they parted. "If you should pass by Cluny sometime, remember that we have a hostel for travelers."

"And your son?" Hubert asked.

"That hasn't changed," James answered. "I have no son."

When the abbot's party departed, Solomon wasn't there

to see them or to be seen by the man who wasn't his father but whose eyes searched the crowd for him all the same.

It was customary, the night before arriving at Compostela, for all the male pilgrims to go down to the river and bathe them-selves, not just their faces and private parts, but totally. Solomon had no intention of joining in, but he wandered down that way just the same.

There by the water's edge, upstream from the celebrating bathers, he found Mondete. She had put her hood back and was holding Hersent's comb, rolling it from one hand to the other. Solomon noticed with surprise that her hair had begun to grow again, a brown stubble that was already beginning to curl at her ears.

"So you found what you were seeking?" he asked as he seated himself next to her.

"Yes, strangely enough," she answered. "It was Griselle who taught me. All these years, I hated God because He wouldn't help me. My parents sold me; Norbert raped me; all those other men hurt me over and over. And no matter how hard I prayed, God was silent."

"And He's spoken to you now?" Solomon wasn't sure what he wanted her to answer.

She laughed. "In a way. You see, Griselle didn't have any more faith than I. All her pious posturing was just that. Really, I think she hated God as much as I did. That's why she decided to deal out revenge herself."

"And?" Solomon prompted her. "A voice came to you out of the sky telling you not to follow her example?"

"My very dear cynic—" Mondete put her hand on his cheek "—you never really understood why I came all this way, did you? I didn't want revenge; I wanted peace. My hatred was destroying me, but I didn't have the strength to give it up. I still don't know why I was made to suffer so. I still don't think it was right, but in the past few days I have realized that my re-quest has been granted. Grace has descended upon me, and at last I have forgiven God."

Solomon held her hand against his lips. "That is a rare

gift," he said. "I shall have to continue my search, I fear, for nothing like that has happened to me."

"Where will you go?" she asked.

"Toledo, Granada, Alexandria, to the equatorial fire if I must," Solomon said. "Until I find the answer."

"I'm sorry I couldn't give it to you." She took her hand back.

Solomon grinned. "Don't be. Sometimes I find the search so interesting that I'm afraid I'll come to the end too soon."

"In that case, I wish you joy along the way," Mondete said. "And that is the most I've ever wished any man."

It may have been that the guards had not fettered Hubert very carefully. It may have been that he had grown thinner with the effort of carrying them, but as they approached the gate of the city, the iron chains slipped from his body and rattled to the ground.

Griselle stared at the heap of metal. "Thank you, Hubert LeVendeur," she said.

"I also needed to learn humility," he told her.

"But I have only learned despair," she answered. "I don't think that the nuns of Marcigny will be able to teach me otherwise."

She seemed to be waiting for him to go. The guards from the abbey were growing impatient. Hubert could think of nothing to say that would comfort her. He bowed.

"I have been glad to serve you, my lady," he said.

Griselle's lip trembled. "Hubert," she said. "I wish . . ."

He nodded. "So do I."

The guards took her away.

Catherine didn't know what she had expected Santiago to be like. If challenged, she would have admitted that her vision of ivory turrets and eternal spring were not likely, but she hadn't expected every street to be lined with souvenir sellers.

"Scallop shells! Sacred shells! Each one painted with the cross of Saint James!" an old woman shouted over and over.

"Solid silver chains!" someone else called. "To hang your

shell from! Crosses made from the cedars of Lebanon! Holy water from Jerusalem! Thorns from the crown worn by Our Lord at His passion!"

"Wine! Fresh in from Rioja!" This peddler was doing a brisk business.

At the shrine itself, the statue containing the body of the saint was surrounded by pilgrims, some pushing into the line ahead of the weak and the slow. Catherine and Edgar looked at each other in confusion.

"We're here," Edgar said. "Now what do we do?"

Catherine thought for a moment.

"I suppose we go home."

February in Paris was a world away from summer in Spain. A slushy rain beat at the shutters. The heat from the hearth reached only a few feet into the hall. Edgar sat alone, a blanket over his shoulders, half-asleep. Next to him was a wooden cradle with a rod above it to hang a curtain on. From the rod hung a silver scallop shell, embellished with a cross of Saint James, painted in red.

The door to the hallway creaked, and Edgar was alert at once. "What is it?" he asked, taut with fear.

"Only me," Catherine's maid, Samonie, said as she came in. "Well, not only me. I've also brought you your son."

The baby was wrapped in swaddling and wool so that it seemed to Edgar that Samonie was carrying a bundle of laundry. He didn't move at first. It wasn't possible; Catherine's pains had started only a few hours before.

"Catherine?" he asked.

"She's fine," Samonie said. "You can see her in a moment. She's dreadfully smug, seems to think she's finally learned the trick of it. Don't you want to hold him?"

Edgar held out his arms.

There wasn't much to see in all the wrapping, just a small red face, with mouth, eyes and nose in the proper places. The baby looked rather bored, considering he had already been to Compostela and back before he was born.

"He's whole and well?" Edgar asked.

"You can count the fingers and toes tomorrow," Samonie laughed, "but I assure you, they are all there."

Edgar stared at the crumpled red face in awe.

"Catherine wouldn't tell me," Samonie said. "What have you thought to name him? After your father or hers?"

"Neither," Edgar told her. "We've decided to call him James."

Afterword

Like Catherine and Edgar, I followed the pilgrimage route from Le Puy to Compostela. When I began, I viewed the journey as a research trip much like my earlier ones when I would visit archives and buildings and perhaps get a sense of the countryside that my characters would have passed through 850 years ago. What I didn't expect was to become involved in a tradition that has endured for over a thousand years and is still very much alive today. Perhaps a higher percentage of modern pilgrims now follow the route from a sense of adventure, rather than piety, but even today, it is impossible not to feel a kinship with all those who have made the journey before one. The road to Compostela is still crowded with pilgrims.

Many of the places mentioned in the book are not terribly changed from the twelfth century. That made it much easier to envision my characters' experiences. It was while climbing the volcanic cone to the chapel in Le Puy that I first realized Edgar was afraid of heights. In the village of Conques the tympanum is intact, although the paint has worn off. The torments of Hell are as fascinating today as they were then. All along the route, on both sides of the Pyrénées, there are still hostels for the pilgrims and churches that were old when Catherine and Edgar visited them. The scallop shell is still on signs pointing the way to St. James.

While I don't think I'll do the entire route on foot or even a bicycle, I would very much like to travel along it again, more slowly, in order to appreciate the magnitude of the journey that the pilgrims made. From the tenth century on, Compostela was the third most important pilgrimage site in Christendom, after

Rome and Jerusalem. Even though there were many people who took the trip more than once, it was considered dangerous. Before leaving, pilgrims made provisions for their families in case they did not survive. Often, a pilgrimage was made late in life, and the four knights in their sixties and seventies were not atypical.

Peter the Venerable did make the journey to Spain. He collected the back tithes from the emperor and commissioned the first Latin translation of the Koran. However, he returned to Cluny without ever visiting Compostela.

As always, I have done my best to make this book as accurate as possible, both as to historical data and the medieval worldview. But this is a work of fiction, designed to entertain. I hope that the reader enjoys the story. There will not be a quiz. As usual, most of my research never got into the book. So, for those of you who are curious about the period and especially the Pilgrim's Way, I have a bibliography which I will be happy to send if you send me a self-addressed, stamped envelope, care of the publisher.

Valete! Sharan